Shannon ♡

DEAR HEART, YOU SCREWED ME

ASHLEE ROSE

Ashlee Rose
Copyright 2022 Ashlee Rose
Second Edition

The author has asserted their moral right under the Copyright, Designs and Patents Act, 1988, to be identified as the author of this work.

All rights reserved. No part of this publication may be reproduced, copied, stored in a retrieval system, or transmitted, in any form by or by any means, without the prior written consent of the copyright holder, nor be otherwise circulated in any form of binding or cover other than that in which it is published and without a similar condition being imposed on the subsequent purchaser.

This is a work of fiction. Names, characters, businesses, places, events and incidents are either the products of the authors imagination or used in a fictitious manner.
Any resemblance to actual persons, living or dead, or actual events is purely coincidental.

OTHER BOOKS BY ASHLEE ROSE

STANDALONES

Unwanted

Promise Me

Savage Love

Tortured Hero

Something Worth Stealing

Dear Heart, You Screwed Me

Signed, Sealed, Baby

DUET

Way Back When Duet

NOVELLAS

Rekindle Us

Your Dirty Little Secret

A Savage Reunion

RISQUÉ READS

Seeking Hallow

Craving Hex

Seducing Willow

Wanting Knox

Pursuing Hartley

Tempting Klaus

Valentine Belle

ILLICIT LOVE SERIES

The Resentment

The Loathing

The Betrayal

LOVELOCK BAY SERIES

Wildest Love

Wildest Dreams

SINFUL READS

Sinful Brothers

Sinful Affair

All available on Amazon Kindle Unlimited
Only suitable for 18+ due to nature of the books.

DEAR DIARY,

*I've done something really bad.
I've slept with my best friend's dad.*

PROLOGUE

This wasn't supposed to happen.

This wasn't the life we planned.

We were meant to grow old together, watch our children make us proud daily.

But the life we planned was ripped away from me.

Life is cruel.

Vicious.

He was taken from me, and I have no control over it.

What is it they say? Your life is mapped out for you? Fate and all that shit… well, this isn't fate, this is God fucking me over in the worst way possible. I don't believe in fate anymore.

My motto is '*it is what it is*'.

My heart lurched in my chest before it shattered and obliterated into a thousand pieces. I was afraid it would never be whole again.

. . .

This wasn't supposed to happen.
　　This wasn't the life we planned.
　　But it is what it is.

~~Dear Diary~~
　　Dear Heart, You Screwed Me.

CHAPTER 1

TWO YEARS AGO

I pace up and down our small, boxy apartment. After five steps, I was at the other side of the apartment.

Elijah was due home any minute. He had a job interview this afternoon. He had been preparing for months. This was a big deal. It wasn't some small, two-bit job. He was hoping to climb the ladder in the stock market. He has had to kiss arse for two years to even get a little bite from the top guns.

And two weeks ago. He got it.

This would change our lives, financially. Home life would be harder, what with the late evenings and early mornings. He had to be dedicated to the job first, not me.

But that was okay.

I loved his drive and passion for his work, and I can't wait to have that drive. I just haven't been able to land anything yet. Sure, I went to university, I knew what I wanted to do, but I just haven't found my dream job.

I studied business and economics as well as English literature and public relations. Truthfully, I only chose English literature because I love reading. I enjoyed doing the PR side of things, so who knows. Maybe that's my calling.

Looking back over my shoulder I look at the small round table that sat between the small kitchen and lounge area, the candle flickering in the dimmed room. The table was set, a low hum from the oven filled the room as I tried to keep the dinner warm. I wanted to make a congratulations dinner, whether it was a good interview or not, I was still proud of him. I went back to pacing the floor, I was nervous, excited, apprehensive. I also felt sick to my stomach at the thought of him not getting this job. I stilled, turning my head to look at the long, skinny mirror at my reflection. I was wearing a low-cut black tee that was tucked into my high waisted skinny jeans. I would normally be in my pyjamas now, but not tonight. Everything had to be perfect.

The darkness began to draw in, it was the middle of October, and we were finally losing the lighter evenings which I hated. I loved the winter, just not the darkness that came with it.

My phone buzzed with a message from Elijah. My heart skipped a beat, my pulse quickened as I read it, the smile growing on my face.

He smashed it.

HALF AN HOUR HAD PAST; MY BROWS FURROWED AS I LOOKED AT my phone, opening the text from Elijah once more.

> Just leaving babe. It went well, love you x

My heart began to pump a little harder than normal, the blood rushing through my veins. I was an over thinker, I panic at every, little thing.

I rub my clammy palms down my jeans as I sat at the table. The candle beginning to dim before completely going out. My leg was shaking up and down, my fingers drumming on the table as I tried to calm the nerves. He had to get the train from the city, then drive the lanes from the station. It shouldn't be taking this long though.

An hour later and still nothing. Shit.

I text Elijah's friend, I wanted to know if he had heard from him, but he hadn't spoken to him either. I even messaged his mother, but again, she had heard nothing. I had debated whether to or not, but I had to ask. But of course, she was now in full panic mode with me.

It was dark outside, the rain and hail drumming down on the window pane, a sound I normally found comforting, but now it only filled me with dread and fear.

I picked my phone up and tried ringing him, I don't like to call him while he's driving, but needs must. And this was a must.

It rung and rung before I was hit with his voicemail.

Hey, it's Elijah. You missed me, leave a message and I'll call you back!

I cut it off before trying again.

Nothing.

I hold my phone in my clammy palms, standing from the table and pacing the floor back and forth once more.

I jumped when I heard a knock on the apartment door, throwing my phone down on the sofa I rubbed my clammy hands back down my thighs once more.

Please be Elijah. But then if it was Elijah… why was he knocking.

Stopping at the front door, I look through the peep hole and see two police officers. One male. One female. Hats under their arms.

Even though deep down inside I knew what was about to

come, nothing could have prepared me for what they were going to say.

My trembling fingers locked round the handle as I pushed it down slowly and opened the door. A solemn look on their faces. My heart sunk.

"Are you Ms Reese Hernández?" The male officer asked softly, his eyes not leaving mine.

I couldn't speak, I was rendered speechless. My heart skipping beats in my chest. I could hear the blood thrashing through my veins, before it pumped loudly in my ears. The air being snatched from my lungs. I could hear the humming of the male's voice, but it didn't make any sense. I couldn't hear anything. It all blended into one. My eyes lifted to see the female officer move towards me, her hand rubbing up and down the top of my arm in a comforting manner.

"Reese, are you okay?" her voice was soft and calming.

I nodded numbly. I edged back and let them step over the threshold of our apartment.

I stood for a moment, a million thoughts whizzing through my head.

"You should have a seat." The male officer extends his arm and ushers for me to sit on the sofa.

I nod again.

I do as they ask, sitting on the edge of the sofa, my fingers knotting in front of me.

"We're so sorry to tell you that your partner Elijah Moretti has been involved in a car accident. No other vehicles were involved."

The air was snatched from my lungs, my tears burning as they fill my eyes, my throat filled with an enormous lump that no matter how much I try to swallow, I just can't get rid of it.

Accident.

"Is Elijah, okay?" I ask, my voice a whisper as they left my lips. The hot tears rolling down my cheeks.

The female officer turned her head to look at her colleague, her poker face slipping before she turned to face me. She moved off the sofa, dropping to her knees and taking my hands in hers.

"Reese," her voice was low, "Elijah has been taken to hospital, we're here to take you to say goodbye." She repeated the words.

I nodded, the tears still flowing. "But is he okay..." as soon as I finished my sentence, her words hit me like a steam train.

To say goodbye. Those words float through my head once more.

Goodbye.
He isn't okay.
He isn't going to make it.
He was going to die.

That's when it really hit me. The pain that seared through me was as if someone had twisted a knife deep into my stomach before pushing it into my lungs so I couldn't breathe. My eyes widen as I fly from the sofa, my hand moving to my mouth as my fingers tremble against my lips. Then came the pain in my heart, it felt like my heart was being held, fingers gripping tightly before squeezing it and stopping the blood from pumping into it.

My legs were shaky, buckling beneath me before I fell to the ground and let out the most horrific scream that echoed and bounced off the walls of my tiny apartment.

I even scared myself.
My Elijah was gone.
Out of my life.
Forever.
And I was never getting him back.

· · ·

I sat on the sofa wrapped in a blanket, my parents and Elijah's mum, Vienna, were also here. My mum, Liz, handed me a hot cup of tea. My shaky hands took it from her, my opal eyes not lifting as I looked at the strong brew. The burn from the cup felt good on my numb skin, I just wanted to feel something.

Anything.

But I was dead inside. I didn't feel a thing.

"Drink up sweetie," my mum gave me a sympathetic smile. I turned my head slowly to look at Vienna who was a complete mess as she sobbed on the sofa. My mum wrapped her arm around Vienna as she tried to comfort her.

My pain is indescribable, her pain must be catastrophic.

To be stood there and watch as his mom had to make the decision to turn off his life support machine will live with me forever. The constant *what if* he wakes up, knowing you are robbing everyone of that moment. But she had to turn it off. He had no brain activity; he was never going to wake up.

I had lost him.

And there was nothing I could do.

I stood in the chapel of rest. My mum offered to walk me in, but I shook my head. I needed some time to be alone with Elijah.

To say goodbye.

He should still be here. We got his toxicology report a few weeks later, there was no alcohol or drugs in his system. He just lost control.

Just like that.

He was dead.

It didn't matter how much I tried to work out what happened, it was just one of those accidents.

It is what it is.

Silence consumed me; my eyes fixed on a peaceful Elijah's face. He looked like he was asleep. His lips were stained in a light pink, his cheeks looking just bitten as such. They put a little make up on them to make them not look as, well, dead? I shiver at the thought. I knew he wasn't here anymore. This was just his shell that protected his beautiful soul.

I let out a deep sigh, shuffling forward as I held his hand. A small gasp left my lips as the coldness of his skin vibrated through me. I just wanted to wrap him in a blanket to keep him warm. I hated that he was so cold.

"Elijah," I choked out, leaning my body over him, and sobbing into his outfit that he was due to be cremated in. How was this fair? Why was he taken away from me? We were meant to have forever, me and him, him and me. But now, it was just me.

Uncontrollable sobs leave me, I didn't want to leave him here all alone. He must be so cold, the same thought whirling around in my head repeatedly. I choke out as I lean up, my eyes wandering round the warmly lit room. They make it look so welcoming in here, but it's anything but. I palm my cheeks, trying to rid them of the tears that continue to fall.

My eyes move back to Elijah.

"I love you so much baby," I whisper, a couple of stray tears that I missed fall onto his white shirt that I chose for him. My fingers ran through his black hair, he used to love me doing that when he was tired from his day. What I would do to see his dark brown eyes once more, to hear his voice tell me he loves me. What I would do to feel his lips on mine for one last time. My heart obliterates.

I try to link my fingers through his, anything to just feel close to him again. But it was almost impossible.

I was living in my own hell, and I was scared I was never getting out of it.

I heard the door close softly behind me, my head

snapping round to see my mum walking towards me with a small smile on her face.

"It's time to go." Her voice was quiet as she wrapped her arms around my shoulders.

"Not yet mum, I'm not ready." My voice trembled; I shook my head from side to side.

"I know darling, but we have to go…" her grip tightened on the top of my arms as she tried to pull me away from Elijah.

"No!" I scream loudly, my throat stinging "No!"

THAT'S ALL I REMEMBER.

Everything after that I blocked out.

CHAPTER 2

PRESENT DAY

The sun streamed through the windows, the beams feeling good on my tanned skin. I loved the spring months, more so because it's my birthday month. Not that I have celebrated the last two, I just haven't been able too. I couldn't do it without Elijah. We always had our ritual. Presents, breakfast, macaroons, champagne, take away, *the notebook* and chocolate.

Every year.

But now, on my twenty-seventh birthday I am sitting here without him. Will this pain ever become bearable? Because honestly, I think I am broken for life. I haven't dated since; my mum has urged me so many times just to go for a coffee date here or there, but I am just not ready.

I wiped my brow with the back of my hand as I looked around my empty apartment. My mum stood behind me, hands on her hips slightly breathless.

"This is it," she sighed.

"It is…" I sighed with her, sadness consuming me. My eyes scanned the white walls, of our studio apartment. It wasn't much, but it was ours. We bought it after saving, always said we would keep it to rent out as a little injection of funds when we were ready to move into a bigger home and start a family.

I felt my throat bob as I tried to swallow down the large lump that was growing and swelling in my windpipe.

"You ready for your next adventure?" my mum's arm wrapped round my shoulders, squeezing me tight. My dad appearing to my other side.

"I think so…" I snorted a laugh, truth was, I was terrified.

"Don't think!" my mum let out a small laugh, "It's going to be everything and more, as much as me and your father don't want you to go…" her voice trails off as she looks at my father. His tanned, glowing skin radiates. My dad is Venezuelan, but he has always lived in England. He speaks basic Spanish, but always made sure when he was growing up that he answered his parents in his native language.

"No, we don't mi amor." My dad's voice was low as he pulled me into his embrace, squeezing me tightly.

"I'll only be a few thousand miles away," I choked back the tears. "I need this new start, for me…"

"We know," they say in unison.

I step away from them, as my eyes volley between theirs.

My dad's black hair sits away from his face, his green eyes glistening with unshed tears. My mum is fair with blonde hair and sparkling blue eyes.

I have my mum's hair colour of honey blonde and my eyes are a mix of the two, giving them an opal sea colour. I am lucky that I got his skin tone and not my mum's pasty colour.

"We're so proud of you." My mum's voice is tight as she swallows down the lump in her throat. "But you know you can always come home; your room will be here." My father nodded.

"I know," I whispered, "but I won't be home, only when I have a holiday." I nibble my trembling bottom lip. "You can always come to me? Once I am settled and in my new apartment, I will send you the details." I say cheerily, rushing towards my parents and wrapping both my arms round their necks, their arms linking behind my back as we stood embraced.

I was leaving for New York to be an assistant at Lordes PR. I gave them a quick internet search once I got a call from my head-hunter. I wanted to make sure I was well informed about the company I was going to. I would be working under an Adele Cliffe.

By the sounds of it, not many of her assistants last more than three months. Seemed a bit of a running joke. But I was determined to pass the three-month mark, I had to. I never really knew what I wanted to do, but after Elijah died I threw myself into anything and everything to keep my mind busy because as soon as I stopped, he filled my mind. I found myself working for a part-time PR firm, I started as a temp but once I found my feet I couldn't stop wanting to strive and make myself better. With each existing client helped and each new client signed, I had finally found my calling.

"Right honey, we've got to go." My mum broke my thoughts suddenly, her hand running down my back before it linked through my arm.

I nodded.

My dad walked out of my boxy apartment first, then my mum. I inhaled deeply, the hot tears pricking my eyes as I stayed anchored to the floor for a moment. Breathing in through my nose, trying everything to not forget the smell of our home. I swiped the angry tears away as they rolled down my cheeks. I was angry that he was taken from me, super fucking angry that I didn't get to say goodbye, and angry that we were robbed of our future. My future.

Lifting my shoulders up, I stood tall as I swallowed the large lump down.

"Goodbye Elijah," I whispered through choked sobs. I dipped my head down and walked towards the door, closing it behind me and not looking back.

That part of my life was over.

I had to move on.

Even if deep down, I didn't want to.

I had no choice.

Stepping away on trembling legs, I screwed my face up and cried.

My trembling fingers wrapped round the handle of my large suitcase as I walked it into Heathrow Airport. I was moving to New York for a year on a temporary work visa, if Lordes PR were happy with me and my work, my visa would be extended and then I could look at moving to New York permanently. I had no clue about America, I had never travelled outside of the UK, I hadn't even been to Scotland.

Boring, yes. But I was comfortable. Happy.

I still hadn't made my mind up if I would like to live in New York or return home to Ongar. I had to say a quick goodbye to my parents, I didn't want to linger any longer than I had too because if I held them, I wouldn't want to let them go.

You've got this. I muttered to myself.

Pushing through the crowds I stopped in front of the departure board, desk twelve. I nodded, swallowing hard as I headed towards the check in.

Sitting on the plane, I was upgraded to first class. Apparently, my new boss called forward to have me moved. I wasn't complaining but I felt so out of place. Letting out a shallow sigh, the air hostess appeared, smiling softly and handed me a glass of champagne. I smiled back at her, my trembling fingers wrapping round the stem before bringing it to my lips as she walked away to the next booth.

"Cheers to me," I muttered, holding it up and knocking it back.

Waking from my nap, I rubbed the sleep out of my eyes. It took me a moment to realise where I was. Sitting up, I looked round, but nothing had changed. Shuffling forward in my seat I looked out the window, a little smile creeping on my face as I stared into the fluffy clouds. I always thought heaven sat on top of the clouds, but that wasn't true. I didn't even know if heaven even existed. My heart clenched in my chest, constricted, and twisting as pain crashed through me. When Elijah passed, I begged every night while I cried myself to sleep for him to show me that he was still here. Just to give me a sign, to give me anything.

I would have been happy with the smallest thing.

The memories shatter me, my eyes stinging with unshed tears. I honestly didn't know how many more tears I had left to cry.

Elijah never came. He never gave me a sign. He never gave me anything.

That's when I stopped believing in something more. In any hope of another realm. There was nothing but darkness, sadness and emptiness.

Nothing more.

The words that I begged into the darkness when Elijah died, echo round in my head on a loop. *Show me you're still here. Send me something to make me feel again. To make me remember what it was like to love you.*

I swipe a lone tear away that runs down my cheek. I sniffle, leaning down and grab my battered, old diary.

I started this diary after Elijah died. My therapist thought it was a good idea for me to jot anything and everything down as it came to me. Fumbling around in my bag I grabbed a pen, turned the pages and started writing.

Dear Heart,
You screwed me.

My eyes fluttered closed for a moment before a tear fell from my lashes and splashed on the page, making the pen that I had just marked the pages with run.

Elijah,
Two years on and the pain hasn't eased. It's just become more bearable, which to be honest, makes me feel even worse.

I just don't know why. The guilt eats me alive.

I have a hole the size of my fist punched through my heart, it's just agape, a void filled with nothingness. Complete emptiness.

I'm empty and wrecked with grief.

New York. That's where I am going. New life, new start... starting all over again but this time, I am alone.

Without you.
Without us.
Just me.

I miss you.
More than you will ever know.

And I sob. Quiet, choking, heart-breaking sobs before my eyes fall back to the clouds.

"Where are you?" I whisper.

CHAPTER 3

Walking out of JFK, the hot air hit me as soon as I was out of the building. The air felt sticky, but the warm sun on my skin felt amazing. I stood for a moment, my eyes taking in my surroundings. I was here. I was finally here. I snapped my head round as I looked at the line of yellow taxis and I don't know why but it made me smile. I felt like I hadn't smiled in months, yet a simple yellow taxi could do that. You forget sometimes how the little things in life mean the most when you have lost something big in your life.

Slipping in, the taxi driver placed my suitcases in the boot.

"Where to lady?" he asked, his eyes pinned to me in the rear-view mirror. His tone was curt but not rude.

"Er, let me check. Sorry." I blushed as I grabbed my phone to search for my email. I heard the heavy sigh that left him before he tapped his finger on the meter that was running.

"The Plaza?" my voice was quiet as I fumbled to put my phone back in my bag.

"Got it," he said, looking over his shoulder and pulling out onto the busy roads. I sat back; eyes wide as I took the scenery in. I had always wanted to come to New York, but it was never part of our life plan. I sigh, my eyes dropping to my black painted nails as I linked my fingers together. I felt exhausted suddenly, I wanted to get out of my jeans and sticky tee. The air was humid. I wanted a cold shower, eat my weight in junk food and to sleep till tomorrow morning. I heard the best way to get over jet lag is to eat before bed, resetting your real time frame and body clock as such.

Pulling down a busy road, the taxi started to slow outside The Plaza. My eyes widened as I took the beautiful building in. This was my home for the next four nights while I got accustomed to the city and had my settling in sessions at my new job.

I was due to meet the head-hunter that hired me tomorrow morning for coffee. I was anxious but also excited.

"Hey, lady. Come on." The taxi driver's abruptness snapped me out of my inner thoughts.

"Oh god, I'm sorry." I panicked, fumbling around in my purse for my dollars. Passing him the notes, I pushed the door open and smiled at the impeccably dressed doorman. He helped me with my bags and suitcases as I watched the taxi pull back out into the road. I stood dazed for a moment; I was here.

Like, really here.

In New York.

Ready for my do over and new adventure.

I followed the concierge into the building, climbing the stairs slowly, white pillars sitting either side of the double doors. My jaw went lax as my eyes were close to popping out of my head. The gold and creams that wrapped round the large room were beautiful. The detail and décor were exquisite. I stood in the bright, airy arch that houses the gold revolving door. I was literally breathless. I don't think I would ever get over the beauty.

"Miss." The concierge's voice was low as I turned my head slowly to face him.

"Shall we go check you in?" he asked as his gloved hands

held onto the gold luggage trolley, his fingers wrapping round tightly.

I nodded, unable to speak.

I followed him, walking quickly so I stayed close to him. My eyes continued to scan the room as I took it all in, but I don't think I ever could. This place was phenomenal. I never wanted to leave.

Standing awkwardly at the check in desk, I waited patiently for the young man to finish up on his telephone call.

"Good afternoon, welcome to The Plaza may I take your name?"

I nodded, my voice escaping me for a moment. I swallowed the swollen lump in my throat back down as I drummed my fingers on the polished surface.

"Reese, Reese Hernández." I stammered.

The impeccably dressed man tapped his fingers on his keyboard.

"Aha, here we are. Reese, staying with us for four nights in a single room?" he chirped as he lifted his eyes from the computer screen.

"Yup," my voice barely audible. I felt out of sorts. Was it the jet lag? Or was it the fact that my heart was obliterated into a thousand pieces while being all alone and a million miles away? The sad realisation finally sinking in.

"Oh, it must be your lucky day." The young man's eyes fell back to his screen, pinning my eyes on his name tag. Michael. I like that name.

"You have been given a double with a view of the inner landscaped courtyard," his voice lifted, a hint of excitement lacing it.

"Oh," I blushed, more like he looked at me and felt sorry for me maybe?

"Derek will take your bags up, you'll be on floor eighteen." He says, pushing a card towards me. "That's your key, food is served throughout the day, breakfast starts at six-thirty and finishes at ten. Room service runs twenty-four hours. If you have any problems, just dial down to reception and we will be happy to help." He smiles at me as I take the card.

"Thank you," I just about manage.

"You're most welcome, we hope you enjoy your stay at The Plaza."

I nod curtly, turning on my heel and following the concierge.

Swiping my key through the lock, the concierge opened the door for me. My mouth fell open as my eyes bulged in my head.

Woah.

The beautifully panelled walls hugged the room in an ivory white, the carpeted floors felt soft under my feet even though I had my shoes on. The large double bed sat in the middle of the room with a huge gold ornate headboard.

If Derek the concierge wasn't here watching me, I would have dived onto the bed.

"I assume everything is okay for you, Ms Hernández?" Derek's voice was warm as I snapped my head to face him.

"Everything is perfect." I gush, a small smile dancing across my lips as I turn to face the room again.

The door closed softly behind me causing my head to turn. The smile still evident on my face.

"I'm here Elijah." I whispered to the empty room, a burn in my throat, the tears stinging behind my eyes.

I wasn't going to unpack right now; I needed a long soak in the tub and then I was going to eat my weight in food before crashing for the evening.

I felt exhausted.

Mentally.

Emotionally.

Physically.

I woke up feeling groggy as hell. I didn't sleep as well as I would have liked. The jet lag, the noise of the busy New York streets and the unfamiliar surroundings had me feeling uneasy. Looking at my phone it was six am, which means it was around lunch time back home. I sighed, rolling on my back, and letting my phone fall into the plush duvet. I felt so out of depth, as if I was drowning slowly and struggling for air.

I could do this, I knew I could.

Everything just felt like a battle. I hadn't been in therapy for over a year now, I could finally talk about what happened with Elijah without crying which was apparently a good sign when it came to the grieving process. Even though I still cried at times when I thought about him, I am only human. The pain is still so raw, and even though it had been two years, I was scared that the pain that seared through my heart would never leave. I mean, how could it? How do you get over the one person that was made for you? I truly believe he was my soulmate, but maybe this was a sign from the universe that we just weren't meant to be.

Or was it that he was my first love.

The one to help me grow and find out who I was. The one to give me a hard life lesson to see what I truly wanted.

But what if it was him that I wanted? I just wanted him. Me and him.

We were planning for babies, lots of babies. But we never got lucky. We stopped trying after he wanted to further his career and work his way up the stock market ladder, but we weren't being careful if you get my drift. We tried for two years, and once Elijah got his break in his job, we were going

DEAR HEART, YOU SCREWED ME   25

to book an appointment with a fertility doctor to see if we could find what the issue was, if there even was an issue.

But alas, we never got there.

I knew I wanted children; I knew I didn't want to find anyone else to start a family with, so I made the choice to do the parenting gig on my own. I wanted to start my job, find my feet, and then look at being artificially inseminated.

But that was my three-year plan, I was nowhere near ready at the moment.

I had to focus on my life here for a moment, find my feet and get my foot firmly in the door at my new job.

"Right," I called out to the room as if someone was here. Throwing the heavy duvet back I padded into the bathroom, turning the shower on. The room quickly filled with steam; rubbing the condensation off the mirror I smiled to myself.

"Here is to day one of our new adventure." I said to myself, my voice chirpy as I tried my best to sound upbeat and happy.

Inhaling and exhaling deeply, I dropped my pyjamas and stepped under the hot shower, letting the water sting my skin. It was welcomed. To feel anything other than grief-stricken pain.

Once showered I towelled myself off and made my way back into the room. I had no clue what to wear. The sun was beginning to break behind the clouds, but on checking my weather last night on my phone it said the sun was going to be hot. I needed something to keep me cool, but also so I didn't burn.

Opting for a cute, cap-sleeved oversized tee and high waisted denim shorts, I slipped my feet into my sandals. I ran my fingers through my golden blonde hair, I loosened the waves that had formed from not drying my hair last night.

I wasn't a girly girl; I didn't really care much for my appearance as such.

Flicking my lashes with a light coating of mascara, I

dabbed some concealer under my dark bags and smudged some clear gloss onto my plump lips.

Nodding at myself in the mirror and happy with the way I looked, I grabbed my phone and my rucksack and decided to go for breakfast. It was still early but that suited me. I could do with some quiet time to calm my nerves before I had to meet Julianne this morning.

Opening the door, I turned quickly and grabbed my key card. I would be pretty useless without that. Shaking my head, I closed the door behind me and turned the sign for the house keeping. I had made my bed and tidied, but I guess they would still want to come in and freshen it up.

Walking slowly down the long halls, I took my time. I didn't want to rush, I had no need. If one thing Elijah's death has taught me, it's that I need to make the most out of my life. Appreciate the little things. The birds singing, the sun shining, the sound of rain belting down and hitting the windows. All the stuff you take for granted, that's what people miss the most.

It's not the grand gestures, the thousands of pounds in the bank.

It's the memories and experiences.

If you died tomorrow, your boss would replace you easily. Your money would go to whoever and you would still be buried in the ground with nothing.

You come to the world with nothing. You leave the world with nothing.

Everything is materialistic.

But not your memories. They go with you beyond the grave... to well, wherever you end up. I was pulled from my deep and morbid thoughts when I was greeted by a young girl, smiling at me as she showed me to a table.

"Are you expecting anyone else?" she asked, her eyes glistening, her perfect smile still sitting on her beautiful face.

"No, just me." I shrugged, a sad smile on my face.

"Oh, okay. That's not a problem," she nodded curtly. "I'm Connie, by the way."

"Reese," I smiled.

"Nice to meet you, Reese. If you ever need anything, toiletries, room service, a friend… just give me a shout."

"That would be lovely, I could use a friend," I laughed.

"Then I'm your girl. I get off at six, how about I show you the town?" she pulled the chair out and sat opposite me, lifting the jug of water off the table and pouring me a glass.

I hesitated for a moment trying to think of an excuse to why I couldn't go. But then, I heard Elijah's voice in my head.

Go.

I swallowed the large, burning fire lump down deep in my throat before I could let the sting in my eyes get worse and nodded.

"Why not?" a nervous laugh escaped me as I grabbed the cup of water and swallowed a few mouthfuls to try and wet my throat that had somehow gone from a burning ball of fire to the Sahara Desert.

"Perfect, I'll meet you down in the lobby at six-thirty," she winked, pushing off the table and walking back to her hostess desk. My head turned as my eyes followed her. She had long brown hair that was tied in a low ponytail, beautifully tanned skin that made her green eyes pop.

She was the definition of perfect in my eyes.

She had curves in all the right places, an hourglass figure. I would kill for a body like that. I was straight with hardly any curves. I hoped as I hit puberty that I would fill out a bit, but no. I am like a surfboard. Flat.

But we always want what others have right?

Blowing the breath through my nose, I turned back around and sat for a moment taking in the large restaurant. My stomach groaned; I was starving. Pushing out of the chair I walked quietly over to the buffet. My eyes widened, my mouth watering at all the different options that were in front of me.

Sitting back to my table with my eggs, bacon and pancakes I filled my teacup up with English tea. Taking a mouthful, I groaned in appreciation. I loved a cuppa. I didn't mind coffee, but I much prefer a cup of tea. It just hits different. Especially out of a china cup.

Placing it back on its saucer, I tucked into my food. I wolfed it down, I hadn't realised how hungry I was. Maybe it was the jetlag? I always had a big appetite, but I just felt famished this morning.

Once I ate a second plate of food, I sat back with a fresh pot of tea and people watched. You had all walks of life here. Businessmen and women, families, couples, older couples, and people who were alone. Like me.

I always wondered what people's stories are, I always become so fascinated with people's backgrounds and I don't know why. I always want to know everything about someone, what makes them tick, what makes them happy, sad, and everything in between. But I hardly ever ask because I get shy. I mean, why would a stranger tell me about their selves inside and out.

I pulled my phone out and saw a message from my mum. Smiling, a small pang of pain shot through my heart. I missed them both.

I had never been this far away from them, but I knew I had done the right thing by coming here to try and get a fresh start.

> Sweetie, how was your first night? Mum xo

I tapped back

> Hi mum, dad. First night was okay, slept okay and just having breakfast. I am also going out tonight with my new friend Connie. She works here. Very friendly. I like her... :)

I watched as the dots appeared on my screen

> I am glad you made a friend, but please be careful. You don't know this place. Or this girl. What if she is one of them girls that lure you in and sell you onto a sex trafficking gang?

Oh my god. Only my mum would come up with something like that. I snorted a laugh as I began to tap back.

> Mum, seriously. I'll be fine. I'll message you my location, keep an eye on my locator app if it makes you sleep easier.

Before she could message back, I sent another one.

> If I am in danger or need help, I'll send a poo emoji. ;)

I knew that would wind her up, but I couldn't help but have a little tease with her. She would be spitting feathers to my dad right about now.

> Reese, this is your dad. Please don't do that to your mother. But yes, we will watch your app. Be safe, have fun and good luck meeting your head-hunter this morning. Call us when you're back, we love you xo.

I let out a small snort of a laugh before tapping a response back and dropping my phone into my bag. I was going to finish my tea, head back to my room to freshen up and use the loo then head to meet Julianne.

CHAPTER 4

Walking down the unfamiliar streets, Julianne messaged me to tell me where to meet. It was about a ten-minute walk. I thought about waiting for a cab, but the street was so busy I didn't stand a chance. Not a little newbie like me who didn't even know how to hail a cab.

Back home in England we called for a taxi and the taxi office sent a car to your address, or you had Uber.

Did they have Uber in New York?

I needed one of those books; 'New York Tourist Guide for Dummies'.

I was clueless.

I followed my map app on my phone, following the blue line that lighted up my route. I wasn't too far now. I was so anxious, but also excited. I couldn't wait to start my new job and get stuck in. It would stop my lonely mind from wandering and making up fake scenarios in my head like it always did.

I stopped outside the small café, 'Stop the World' and smiled.

Placing my phone inside my bag I took a deep breath and pushed the door, a small bell chiming above my head. My eyes scoured the room, I had no clue what this Julianne looked like, but I'm sure she would see me… right?

Knotting my fingers together I smiled awkwardly at the hostess that walked towards me.

"Can I help you?"

"Erm, I'm looking for someone called Julianne?" my voice was low, I could feel it trembling. The hostess looked at me as if I had spoken in another language.

"Reese!" I heard a female voice call. Turning my head to the left I saw a petite woman waving her arm in the air. I blushed, pointing to Julianne muttering nonsense to myself as I walked towards her.

"It's so nice to finally meet you!" her French accent thick as she wrapped her arms around me.

I felt awkward. I wasn't really a hugger.

"You too," I smiled as I pulled from her embrace and sat down at the small table. She joined me but not before getting one of the waitress' attention and spinning her finger over the table.

"Coffee, okay?" she asked.

I nodded. I didn't want to tell her I preferred tea, I thought it would come across rude.

"Perfect."

We sat silently for a moment until the coffees were in front of us.

"So firstly, welcome to the big apple! I have lived here for about five years, originally from Paris, hence the accent. We have an office over there, but I got offered a promotion and I couldn't turn down the money," I saw a small smile play on her lips. Her honey eyes glistened, her black ringlet hair sat neatly at her jaw and her cheek bones were chiselled and a prominent feature on her flawless face.

"Have you ever been to Paris?" she asked as she bought her cup to her lips and took a mouthful of her coffee.

I shook my head, wrapping my own fingers around my

cup and mirroring her move. Wetting my lips as I placed the cup back on the table. *Wow, it was bitter.*

"Never left England until now." I admit shyly.

I saw her eyes widen, "You'll have to come to Paris with me someday, it truly is beautiful." She chimed. "I'm not very well travelled either… My mother is from Paris, my father Jamaica. They split when I was younger, I used to go to Jamaica every school holiday," she shrugs, "but now it's once a year if I am lucky…" her smile slipped for a moment, her eyes falling to her cup as her fingertips drummed against the china cup.

"Have you been there this year?" I couldn't stop myself from asking.

"Not yet, I am hoping to get over there before Christmas."

"I bet you can't wait." I smiled at her now.

"I can't."

Silence fell over us for a moment. She took another mouthful of her coffee before reaching down into her bag and pulling out a pile of paperwork.

"Okay, now to the boring bit… updated contracts." She smirked, "And I just want to say, I have got to say that Lordes Public Relations have had their eye on you for a while. We are all really excited to have you join the team."

"I am excited to be here."

It was the truth, but I was also terrified.

After the longest coffee date in the world, everything was signed and finalised. I was to meet her here on Monday and then she will take me to the offices to meet my team.

I felt out of depth, but I knew I could do this.

I had worked hard to get here, and I wasn't going to give up now. Was I ready to work with brats and people who don't like listening to you? Not really.

But I had to start somewhere.

Not all clients were bad, just the selected few so it wasn't very fair of me to tar them all with the same brush.

I was back in the hotel room and after a cool shower to wash the sweaty city off me, I flopped down onto my bed. I could really do without going out tonight, but I felt rude on Connie. She had been kind enough to invite me out so I couldn't turn her down.

I had no clue what to wear, I didn't even know where we were going.

All I wanted to do was call Elijah. I missed him so much.

Reaching across for my phone I unlocked it and called his number, the pain in my heart never eases when I do this. And for a moment, I think he is going to answer. I debate cancelling the call because the pain is unbearable. But then I hear his voice.

Hey, it's Elijah. You missed me, leave a message and I'll call you back!

My eyes well as my throat tightened. Cutting the phone off I dropped it into the duvet as I felt the familiar sting behind my eyes.

Don't cry.

Palming my eyes before the tears could escape, I sat up on the edge of the bed and closed my eyes to try and calm my breathing.

Deep breaths Reese. Deep breaths.

I didn't lay moping for long, I had to get up and get dressed. I needed to be ready for six-thirty when Connie finished her shift. I felt like I could literally climb into bed and sleep until tomorrow morning. That's how exhausted I was feeling. I didn't even go down to the restaurant for dinner, I ordered junk food from room service and ate the entire thing within minutes. I binged a few episodes of *Friends* before pulling myself from the bed to shower. Padding towards my wardrobe, I scanned the clothes hanging up. Did I go smart casual with a pair of skinny jeans and a nice top? Or did I wear a dress and heels and go overboard? I much preferred wearing jeans and boots, or jeans and trainers. I have always been more of a tomboy, but I did own two dresses. I felt myself getting worked up over the night and it hadn't even started yet. I couldn't even remember the last time I went out; I was a bit of a hermit and a loner and much preferred staying home and curling up with a film or one of my smutty romance novels. But I have been so much worse since Elijah died.

I like my own company and I am okay with that.

Stepping back from the wardrobe, I looked from left to right, from right to left. Closing my eyes for a moment, I held my hand out, curled my fingers and pointed my index finger straight. Moving it side to side, I counted to five and stopped. My eyes pinged open and I saw it had landed on a black mini dress.

Shoot.

Sighing and rolling my eyes, I let the doubt and anxious thoughts slip out of my mind as I hastily grabbed the dress before I could talk myself out of it. Dropping the hotel dressing gown to the floor, I slipped the dress up my smooth legs and pulled the thin straps over my shoulders. One good thing about having a small frame was I had small boobs too. I never had to wear a bra if I didn't want too.

Running my fingers through the end of my knotty blonde hair, I loosened the waves that were set from this morning. Applying a small amount of concealer to hide the dark circles under my eyes that I had become accustomed too. I struggle with sleep, and when I do sleep I feel like the same scenario plays over and over in my head.

Giving myself a curt nod, I stepped back and slipped my feet into my high top all white converse. I wasn't feeling the heels. I stepped back over to the wardrobe and grabbed my tatty cropped leather jacket and pulled it over my shoulders. Not that I needed a coat, the air would still be sticky and humid, but it was more to cover myself up. To keep me hidden and out of anyone's sight. Skipping over to the bed, I grabbed my phone and looked at the time. It had just gone six-twenty-five. Time to go.

Spritzing myself with a light spray of my Miss Dior Blooming Bouquet, I grabbed my clutch before throwing my debit card, a few stray dollars, my room card and my phone inside of it.

I don't even know why I take my phone. I don't hear from anyone. I just sit quietly scrolling through people's perfect lives on social media.

But anyone can hide behind a screen and show the world just how happy they are, right? This world is full of pretence. Full of people putting on a show for the outside world to see. People saw these fake lives and craved it. But it wasn't real. It was just pretend.

Like the fairy tales and the happily ever after you were promised as a child.

They weren't true. Prince Charming wasn't coming to save you.

Snapping myself out of my thoughts, I headed for the door and slammed it behind me. I walked cautiously down the long corridor as I stepped towards the lift. The hotel was quiet for a Friday night, or was it because it was early? I had no clue.

The doors pinged open; smiling I walked forward into the lift and spun round. My heart was beating erratically, my blood thumping through my veins. My mum's words echoed in my mind, I didn't know Connie. Could she really be that nice that she wanted to invite me out and be my friend?

Oh my god. Reese.

I internally cursed myself.

Of course, she could have. Get your mother's words out of your mind. The lift came to a halt, the light indicating that we were on the ground floor. Inhaling deeply, I stepped out onto the hard floor and walked towards the lobby, my eyes searching for Connie. I looked around the beautiful, large space but couldn't see her.

Have I been stood up? Was it a joke? Take pity on the poor English girl. I felt the heat rising in my cheeks as my blush crept across my face. It's fine. I could style it out, act as if I had forgotten something and go back to my room. Unzipping my bag, I began to fumble around as if I was looking for something, turning on my heel as I did and started making my way back towards the lift lobby.

"Reese!" I heard Connie call out. My head snapped up as I looked over my shoulder to see her bouncing towards me. She was wearing a tight, mini red bandeau dress with black and white converse. I scoffed. I liked her style.

"Hey!" I called out, pulling my hand from my bag, and doing the zip up quickly.

"You look beautiful." She smiled as she wrapped her arm around my shoulders.

"As do you," I smiled back at her even though inside I felt awkward as fuck.

"You ready?" she chirped as her fingers laced through mine, dragging me through the lobby.

"Ready as I'll ever be." A nervous laugh bubbled out of me.

"Come on, it'll be fun. Let me show you the hot spots of upstate New York. Prepare to be dazzled Reese!" The smile on her face was so big and infectious that I felt my own smile grow as bubbles of excitement popped in my belly. I needed a good night out and I had a feeling that Connie was the right girl for it.

My brows furrowed in confusion when we walked into one of the hotels bars, The Palm Court.

"Don't worry, just the start of the night – plus the guys in here all come down from Wall Street." She smiles sweetly looking over her shoulder at me as my steps falter.

Elijah.

"Big money. I aim for us not having to spend a cent tonight," she winks.

My heart races, my palms sweaty as I hear the air whoosh out of my lungs.

"Reese?" I hear the concern on Connie's voice when she stops and turns to face me.

"I'm fine," I gasp, trying to shake the grief away for a moment.

I see the look of worry on her face, her eyes volleying between mine as she waits for me to explain.

But I can't.

How do you explain the explosion of grief that consumes you every hour of every day?

Pulling my hand from hers, I shake my head softly and walk towards the bar. I needed a drink, anything to numb the pain if even for a moment.

We sat by the window and watched as the bar continued to fill with people.

"Wow it does get busy in here doesn't it!" I shout over the loud chatter from a table of men behind us.

She nods, smiling as she takes a sip of her red coloured cocktail.

I chose a wine, easy and simple.

"Do you come out every weekend?" I ask as I take my own mouthful.

"Most," sitting back into the booth she swirls her straw round, "but it's hard with shift work and my friends work at the hotel too so it's rare we all get off at the same time. Alex might meet us after his shift, but who knows. He can be flaky," she beams.

"That sounds good. Be nice to make some more friends if he does come." I shrug my shoulders up as if it isn't a big deal, but in reality, it's a really big deal.

"So, Reese, tell me about you." She leans forward, her elbows resting on the table.

Just as I was about to open my mouth a couple of the guys behind us wrapped their arms over the top of the booth and turned to face us.

"Ladies," the twang of his American accent made my tummy flip.

"Hi," Connie said in a high voice, turning the top half of her body to face the guys. I stayed where I was. My head dipped but lifting my eyes to look at the men.

One had copper hair, emerald, green eyes, and a jaw that was sharp and chiselled. He looked like he had walked straight out of a magazine. The other guy had blonde hair, blue eyes and glorious tanned skin.

"What are you beautiful ladies up to tonight?" The copper haired man asked Connie.

"Oh you know, having a few drinks, we may go dancing... get some food... see how we feel." Her head snapped round to smile at me. A small smile danced across my lips. I couldn't work out if it was forced or real. I found it really heard to decipher between the two lately.

"What about you handsome?" I watched as Connie flirted effortlessly. I felt the skin under my cheeks begin to glow as the blonde-haired God's eyes were pinned to me.

"Not sure yet, having a few drinks, we may go dancing... get some food... suppose we will just see how we feel." He winked, his teeth sinking into his bottom lip as he pulled at it softly.

"Sounds like a sturdy plan," Connie laughed, "maybe we will see you later?" I couldn't work out if she was asking or telling this guy.

"I'll bet on it." He winked again, pulling his business card out and passing it to Connie.

The air crackled between the both of them for a moment before the copper haired guys friend swooped in.

"Would you ladies like another drink?" he asked, but his eyes and attention were pinned on me.

"We would *love* another drink." Connie beamed, pulling her straw out of her glass and knocking her drink back.

"Woohoo for me, a glass of sauvignon for Reese."

"Reese," the blonde-haired God tested my name out on his tongue, his accent and how velvety his voice sounded covered my skin in goosebumps.

I blushed again.

Get a grip woman.

"Do you still want wine? Or would you like something else?" he asked softly as he slid out of the booth behind us and stood at the end of the table.

"Wine is fine, please," I mutter, managing to find my voice.

His eyes widened slightly, a small smile creeping onto his face.

"You're English?" he seemed surprised.

I nodded.

"Oh, Colt here loves an English girl, don't you buddy?" The copper haired guy bellowed as he stood behind Colt and squeezed his shoulders over his suit jacket.

I watched as Colt rolled his eyes and shrugged his friend's hands off him.

"Excuse us, I'll be back with your drink." He turns and walks toward the bar, his friend following him.

Connie looks at his card before flipping it between her fingers.

"Kieran." She smiles before turning it over again. "Always good to have a backup for us to find if the night dries up." She winks before putting it in her bag.

"Do you do this all the time? Pick guys up?" my tone came across abrupt, I didn't mean for it too.

"Most of the time yeah, I'm single. I'm young. I am *always* careful, no harm in a bit of fun is there. I don't want to settle down anytime soon," she shrugs her shoulders up, her eyes burning into mine.

"I get it." I smile at her.

"What about you? Is this the norm for you?" she leant across the table. Her fingers linked together as her hands rested on the surface.

"No," a scoff of a laugh left me, "do I look like I do this often?"

"No," she laughed with me, "are you with someone back home?"

My heart crushed inside my rib cage.

I shook my head, my eyes falling to the table. I couldn't look at her, because if I did then she would see the pathetic mess I was. Swallowing the burning lump down in my throat and blinking away the tears, I willed myself not to cry.

"Reese?" Her hand slipped over and covered mine.

"I'm fine," I sniffed, pulling my hand from hers. Wrapping my fingers round the stem of my wine glass I knocked the remainder back.

I felt Connie's eyes on me as she watched. Slamming the glass base on the table with force, I shook my hands out and cracked my neck from side to side.

"I'm okay." I smiled at her.

I wasn't okay.

Far from okay.

But I didn't want to get into this tonight.

Colt and Kieran stalked back over to the table with our drinks and a tray of shots. I heard their table cheer as they stopped and placed the drinks down.

Colt handed me a shot glass, then handed one to Connie.

"To new friends," he called out.

"To new friends," we chimed, clinking our glasses together and swallowing the sambuca. I winced, gritting my teeth as the burn coated my throat. But it was welcomed.

Anything to get rid of the sickly feeling that was deep in my gut.

Connie slammed her glass on the table and done a little dance in her seat.

"They were good!" she shouted as she shuffled up to let Kieran sit down next to her. I done the same letting Colt slide in next to me. I stilled as his cologne filled my nostrils, my skin burning at the closeness of him. Turning my head to the side slightly to look up at him, I could see he was uncomfortable.

Was it time to go home yet?

"So, Reese, what brings you to New York?" Kieran asked as his arm slipped behind Connie.

"New job opportunity." I smiled, but my smile soon faltered as Kieran started whispering sweet nothings into Connie's ears making her giggle and blush.

"Where is your new job?" Colt asked, his voice low and soft.

"I'll be working for a PR company, a little out of my depth but I got head-hunted so I must be doing something right." I giggled awkwardly.

"You must be." He smiled.

"You work in stocks I'm assuming?" Even saying the words made my heart drum, the blood thumping in my ears.

He just nodded, sipping his beer from the bottle. "I never wanted to go into stocks, I'm not about this lifestyle." Now it was his turn to laugh awkwardly. "I wanted to be a teacher, but my father wouldn't allow it. Told me I had to go out and get a real job." He sighed, shaking his head and picking the label off of his bottle.

"Oh wow." I said surprised, my eyes widening as I took a big mouthful of my wine.

"Yup," he laughed, "but it's not all bad. I got to meet these jerks." He nodded his head towards Kieran whose tongue was currently down Connie's throat. "You must be very brave to come to a new city alone."

"Or stupid." I laughed, "I would have been an idiot to turn this job down, so I had to pull up my big girl knickers and get on a plane."

"Knickers?" he scoffed.

"Yeah?" I furrowed my brow, "oh, you call them panties I think?" I blushed.

"We do." He laughed "You're cute when you blush."

His words only making me blush even more.

CHAPTER 5

I stood in the toilets waiting for Connie. My head was fuzzy, the alcohol was swimming in my veins.

"Come onnnnn," I drawled out, "I need a wee!" stamping my trainer on the floor.

"Okay! Calm down!" her already thick accent seeming to get thicker the more intoxicated she got.

The cubicle door swung open; a one-eyed and squinting Connie walked towards the sink.

"I can hardly see." She giggled as she washed her hands.

"Then that means you have had enough." I nodded over enthusiastically before shutting the door shut.

We hadn't made it anywhere else; we were still in The Palm Court at the hotel, which to be honest, I was sort of glad about. It meant I was no more than five minutes from my bed.

Stumbling out of the loo, I walked to the sink to see Connie topping her lipstick up.

"I'm surprised you have any lips left after your make out sessions with Kieran," I raised my eyebrows as I tousled my hair root with my fingers.

"He is a good kisser," she puckers up and blows me a kiss

in the reflection of the mirror. "I am totally going to jump his bones tonight."

I giggled. I don't know why but I checked my phone, a subtle ache in my heart reminding me of my life back home.

"You going to take Colt back to your room?" Connie's words pulled me from my thoughts.

"I don't think so." I laughed, all of a sudden, I felt sober.

"Why not? He is hot!" she shouted.

"He is hot, but I don't know…" I twisted my fingers together.

"Reese?" Now it was her turn to raise her eyebrows at me.

"What?" I stammered as I done anything to avoid eye contact.

"What aren't you telling me?" her voice was soft now, her head turning so she was looking at me. Her arm reached out, her fingers wrapping round my wrist as she pulled me towards her.

"It's nothing," my voice trembled.

The silence was deafening. I could see how concerned she was, her brows furrowed in her forehead, her eyes glassed over as they moved between each of mine.

I inhaled deeply before closing my eyes.

"I haven't been with anyone in over two years…"

I wasn't ready to tell her about Elijah yet. That wound was too painful and I didn't want to get into it while drunk as I have no control over drunk words and a truthful heart. A drunk mind speaks a sober one, telling everyone your deepest and darkest secrets that you would never tell a soul.

"Two years?!" she dropped my wrist and held her hands on her cheeks as she processed my news. "How have you not closed up?" she sniggered, stepping towards me, and pulling me into a tight embrace.

"It's okay, Connie will help you out." She whispered in my ear before laughing.

If only it was that simple.

Holding onto Connie for dear life as we walked back into the bar, I was suddenly feeling exhausted. Jet lag plus alcohol was kicking my arse.

She dropped my hand as we reached the table, leaning up on her toes and whispering in Kieran's ear, his lips curling into a beautiful smile.

Colt's beautiful blues trailed up and down my body as I stood, fingers knotted in front of me.

I could do this.

It was just sex.

And to be honest, my vagina needed some action.

This was no strings attached sex.

It was just sex.

I WAS LAYING ON MY BACK IN MY HOTEL ROOM, MY DRESS PULLED up round my waist as Colt thrust in and out of me.

This was doing nothing.

Was I dead down there? Was this the karma I get for leaving it so long?

"Oh babe, does that feel good for you?"

"Mmhmm," my eyes widening as he continued.

This did not feel good.

"So tight," he groaned, his voice strained.

Probably just extra dry.

"Fuck, I am going to come so fucking hard." He shouted out, his head tipping back, his eyes clenched shut.

This was so awkward. I wanted to face palm myself. I needed this over. I had never had to fake an orgasm before, but here goes nothing.

"Yes, yes yes!" I cried out, then putting my hands over my mouth trying to muffle my laugh.

I am going to hell.

A puffed out and sweaty, but satisfied Colt rolled onto his back, a shit eating grin spread across his face.

"Was that good for you baby?" he asked as he leant up on his elbow and kissed the tip of my nose.

"So good." I whispered.

I was mortified and now completely sober. Swinging my legs over the edge of the bed, I stood and pulled my dress down and walked towards the bathroom.

I stopped at the door to see Colt tie the used condom up and throw it in the bin. I shuddered. I felt gross.

When I walked back into the room, Colt was laying there waiting for me.

Oh no, I needed him gone.

"Would you mind if we called it a night? Jet lag is killing me, and I need to sleep. I have a big meeting with my headhunter tomorrow."

"It's Saturday," he frowned.

"I don't pick the days kiddo." I said sarcastically as I helped pick his clothes up off the floor.

I heard him huff as he started getting dressed.

"Can I see you again?"

"Let's leave that up to fate shall we." I smiled as I pushed him towards the door.

"Can I call you?"

"No problem." I beamed, opening the door and shoving him out into the hallway. "Thanks for tonight it was..." I paused for a moment trying to find the right word. "Memorable." I nodded curtly.

"How can I call you if I don't have your number?" he asked just as I was about to close the door.

"Fate!" I rushed out, closing the door and pulling the chain across.

I shuddered as the ick crawled over my skin.

I needed a shower.

. . .

After I showered, I slipped into a pair of cotton sweatpants and an oversized tee. I felt too wired. I was overtired, the alcohol that was once pumping through my veins now left me with a pounding headache. Sitting on the edge of the bed I leant across and grabbed a bottle of water out of the mini fridge. Sure, they were probably going to charge me about twenty dollars for a bottle of water, but I was gasping.

Lying in bed I was restless. I wanted to sleep but I couldn't. The guilt consumed me over what I had done tonight. I was disgusting. How could I have done that to Elijah? I felt my stomach churn and twist as nausea swept over me. I shouldn't have slept with him. It was too soon... wasn't it? How do you know when it's time?

The back of my eyes stung, my throat scratchy and burning. How did I have more tears? I cried so much in the shower, I thought I cried myself out. Obviously not. Palming away a stray tear that rolled down my cheek, invasive thoughts bombarded me; I couldn't help but see and feel the betrayal that Elijah must be feeling.

He was the love of my life and I had been with someone else.

Throwing the duvet back I bolted from the bed, grabbing my key card and my purse and ran for the door, slamming it behind me.

It had just gone two am, I wasn't sure if time moved more slowly here of if it was just the jet lag.

Pacing slowly down the quiet hallways, I headed for the lift. I don't know where I was going, but I needed a drink. Something to calm my guilty conscious and my erratic heart. Walking into the dimly lit lobby, I was amazed to still see it somewhat busy this late in the evening, or this early in the morning should I say.

I contemplated going back to The Palm Court, but I didn't want to risk bumping into any of Colt's friends. I would die of embarrassment. My eyes scanned the large space and spotted the Champagne Bar. It seemed fairly quiet. Perfect.

Dipping my head down, I headed over to the bar.

I wasn't dressed for it, but I didn't care at this point. I was past caring.

I found a row of empty bar stools and headed towards them. Perching myself on the edge, I grabbed the menu and quickly scanned it. I didn't fancy champagne, but it made sense to have it. I was annoying myself.

The friendly bar lady came over to me. She had pulled back blonde hair, stunning emerald eyes and red lipstick that made her pale skin pop.

"Welcome to the champagne bar, what can I get you?" she smiled, her hands pressing against the high gloss worktop.

"Just a glass of Champagne please."

"Any one in particular?" One of her brows raised.

"I'm not fussy." I smiled back, but saying that, my credit card might be.

She gave me a curt nod as she turned on her heel and headed to the other side of the bar. I pulled my eyes from her and let them fall to my lap. I felt so out of my depth here, but I was hoping that once I started my job that things would fall into place. They had to right?

A beautiful crystal champagne glass was slid towards me.

"Oh, thank you." I smiled, unzipping my tatty purse and pulling out my credit card.

"No need, the gentleman across the bar paid for it." Her smile widened as her eyes moved to the handsome man that was sitting at the end of the bar. Holding up a crystal tumbler with an amber liquid in, his brown eyes penetrating through mine. My heart skipped a beat, my tummy flipping nervously.

I nodded shyly, then quickly turned my head, so I was facing forward again. I had already fucked up once tonight, I wasn't going to do it again.

Bringing my glass to my lips I took a large mouthful, the bubbles fizzing on my tongue before popping.

It was delicious. After pulling the glass away, I licked my lips wanting to make sure I got every bit of it.

I could feel his eyes burning into the side of my head, but I didn't want to give in and look at him, because I was afraid if I did, I wouldn't be able to pull my eyes from him.

Finishing the rest of the glass, I held it up to the bar lady who came tottering back over to me.

"He bought the bottle." She beamed as she reached and grabbed the open bottle out of the fridge and poured me another glass.

My jaw fell laxed for a moment as I turned to face him, but as I did a blonde-haired woman ran her fingers over the top of his shoulders, gaining his attention. I couldn't see her face, just her short, wavy blonde hair and her back. No doubt she was beautiful. He stood slowly, but not before his eyes found mine again. He smiled and winked at me before turning on his heel and walking out of the bar with his lady.

Of course, someone as handsome as him would have an even more beautiful woman on his arm.

I sighed, shaking my head from side to side before looking back at the bar lady.

"He left you this." She handed me a small piece of headed note paper.

You looked like you needed a drink.
Enjoy it on me.
K x

I looked like I needed a drink?! To be honest, he wasn't wrong. I looked like trash.

I gave the bar lady a weak smile.

"Thank you," I muttered as I folded the note paper up and slipped it inside my pocket.

Cheers to me.

Knocking back the rest of my drink, I waited for my new bar lady friend to re-fill my glass.

This is exactly what I needed.

To get intoxicated to the point where I pass out.

CHAPTER 6

Oh.
My.
God.

Slapping my hand around for my phone, I couldn't bear to open my eyes.

Now I get why they call them Champagne headaches. I have never had a headache like this.

After I finished my stranger's bottle, I ordered another one. I was in good company. Me, my credit card and my champagne.

Ugh.

Rolling on my back, I clutched my phone in my fingers. I lifted my arm slowly, one of my eyes just about open as I looked at the screen. It was eleven am. I don't think I came to bed until at least four. Who keeps a cocktail bar open all night? This hotel. That's who.

I had no plans today, and to be honest, that's the way I wanted to keep it. If I can get my hungover arse out of bed, I may go for a walk through Central Park, get a coffee and just sit for a while. Sometimes it's nice to disconnect yourself from the world for a while and listen to the birds singing, the children laughing, the trees softly dancing in the light breeze as the leaves rustle together. Sighing I dropped my phone into the duvet. I lay for a moment, my eyes pinned to the ceiling as I replayed the evening over and over in my head.

First off, Colt. What was I thinking?

Alcohol. That's what I was thinking.

First one night stand and it was awful. Maybe it's because I didn't have a connection with him? Because isn't sex meant to be between two people that love each other?

I was disgusted with myself.

Even thinking about last night was making my stomach roll with nausea.

Those thoughts were soon replaced with the mysterious K.

He was so beautifully and tragically handsome. His sharp and chiselled jaw line. The light brushing of dark stubble that surrounded his plump, bow lips. His hazel brown eyes that seemed so deep I wanted to dive into them and lose myself. The sun kissed glow of his skin that looked flawless. The thought of running my fingers across his skin, just to see if it felt as good as it looked.

My lips parted as my mind wandered away. I didn't even know who he was. Just knew that his name began with a K, or did it?

But it didn't matter how he looked or how I got the tingles all over my skin at just the thought of him. He was clearly with someone.

And I was no home wrecker.

He was just being kind. He no doubt took one look at me and thought what a poor unfortunate girl. Clearly out of her depth in a stunning hotel that was being loaded onto an already heavy credit card.

He was just being nice.

That's all.

Nice and friendly.

Throwing the duvet back I walked into the stunning, large and light bathroom and turned the tap on for the tub.

I needed a nice bath. Sinking deep into the bubbles and laying there with a clear mind while blasting Taylor Swift from my phone.

It sounded just like heaven.

A pang of pain shot through my heart.

Heaven.

If it was heaven at least I would see my beautiful Elijah again, even if it was just one last time. If I knew the last time, I saw him would be the day he passed, I would have never let him go. I would have made him stay in bed, kissing me, me kissing him. Loving him for as long as I could. My fingers would have traced over his pale skin, drawing a map that only my fingers knew, that only my heart could remember the way to.

The thought of never getting him back again was a heavy weight in my heart, an ache that would never leave. It may ease, but it would never leave. He was imprinted in my heart. I may fall in love again, but his heart would always belong to mine. And mine would always be tied to his.

At least we both got to say I love you one last time.

He died knowing how much I loved him, our love had no limits, it was infinite.

Shutting the tap off, I pulled my clothes from last night away from my body and dropped them to the floor. Dipping my toe in, my skin spreading in approving goosebumps as the heat warmed me.

Slipping into the bath and submerging myself, I reached for my phone and pressed play on *All Too Well – Taylor Swift.*

And then I cried.

It had just gone two pm. I needed to eat, my stomach growling reminding me that I hadn't eaten since yesterday afternoon.

I walked through the hotel lobby, wearing a lemon summer dressed and tanned wedges, my cross-body bag hugging my body.

I saw Connie come bounding towards me like an excited puppy dog.

"Hey girl," she called out, wrapping her arms around my shoulders. "On a scale of one to ten, how rough are you?"

"A solid eight." I said, the alcohol still lingering on her breath making my stomach roll.

"Damn! I'm about a six. I had the munchies once I kicked Kieran out. He was a rocket in bed." She nudged into me, dropping her arm from me and slipping it through my arm instead.

"Lucky you." I groaned as we stopped before the revolving doors, her arm pulling out of mine.

"Oh no…" her eyes widened, her fingers tucking her hair behind her ears.

"Was it a crap lay?"

"Proper crap." I flushed with embarrassment. It could have been me? Maybe I was the shit lay.

"Oh girl, I'm sorry." She winced before pulling me into a tight embrace. "I'll make it up to you, we will go out on the town and actually make it past the hotel doors tonight." She winked before laughing.

"To be honest, I feel dead on my feet. Can we take a rain check?" I gave her my best puppy dog eyes, my hands pressed together as I pleaded with her.

I watched as she rolled her eyes so far back into her head, I was worried they would get stuck.

"Fine!" she crossed her arms across her chest, "I suppose I can let you chill." She shook her head side to side, "but, next weekend… we're out."

I smiled at her, "I pinkie promise." Holding my little finger out and waiting for her to wrap her little finger round mine.

"And you never break a pinkie."

"Absolutely not." I nodded before we broke away. "Enjoy the rest of your shift, I'm going for a walk." I sighed a blissful sigh.

"Lucky bitch," she groaned, "I still have five hours left."

"I hope it goes quick!" I beamed, holding my hand up to say bye before disappearing through the revolving doors, the sun beating down on my skin.

Sitting at a small table with a cup of soda and a shake shack burger and crinkly chips drizzled in a cheese sauce. This was just what the doctor ordered for my hangover.

It was delicious.

Central Park was heaving and buzzing, and I loved the energy I felt from the park. I had always dreamt of coming here and now here I was.

Sitting here and soaking up every single moment of it.

Once I was finished, I cleared my mess and started walking. I had no clue where I was going, but I didn't care. I just needed to walk and clear my mind. It felt too heavy with everything that had happened over the last few hours, plus it was always filled of what ifs and grief with Elijah. I never wanted to lose him from my thoughts, his memories and the heaviness I felt at his loss were in a safe vault. He was never being cleared, even if I met someone new, he would never be replaced. His memories were too far etched into me to ever be erased.

Eating an ice-cream as I wandered through the winding paths, I approached a large lake. Smiling at the kids standing and feeding the ducks. *The little things that make you smile.*

I used to love feeding the ducks. Something so small, but so enjoyable. Perching myself on the edge of a bench I just sat and watched while I finished my ice cream. I wish I had some bread myself so I could feed them, but now I know, next time I come I can be more prepared.

I was lost in thought when someone sat next to me. My head slowly turned before my heart hammered in my chest.

It was him.

"I hope you didn't have too much of a headache this morning." He smirked as he turned to face me. I felt my heart skip a beat, the breath catching in the back of my throat. Dripping from head to toe in an Armani suit and Louboutin Oxford shoes.

He looked delicious. He smelt even better. A weird combination of bitter and sweet... I just couldn't put my finger on it.

My tongue darted out as I licked my lips.

"No," I shook my head, snapping my head back around and focusing on the ducks, wagging their little tails as they lapped up the bread, their quacks echoing round the park.

"Do you like ducks?" he asked, his leg crossing over the other one, his hands resting on his knee.

"Erm," I blinked for a moment, "they're okay I guess?" what a strange fucking question.

Do I like ducks?!

"You're British?" I saw a small smile cross his lips.

"Yup." I breathed out.

Why was this so awkward?

"Where in England?"

"Near London," I smiled softly, my mind flashing to back home in Ongar.

"I have offices in London, I normally head over there two to three times a year." His eyes were still fixed ahead, he was also now watching the ducks.

"Oh" I mustered; I felt the crackle in the air.

"I'm Killian," he turned to face me, holding his hand out for me to take.

Killian. The K.

It made sense now.

"Reese." I smiled, wrapping my fingers round his hands as we firmly shook, I felt my skin smother in goosebumps before it tingled from my fingertips right through to my toes, my heart humming before a strong spark coursed through me.

Pulling my hand out of his quickly as if his touch hurt, I patted it on my dress.

"Well, it's nice to meet you Reese." He stood slowly as he pushed the button through his navy suit.

"You too and thank you for the Champagne." I swallowed, my mouth dry. Could he see my vein in my neck throbbing, my chest heaving as my heart thumped beneath my skin?

"You're most welcome, hopefully I'll see you again soon." He winked before turning and walking away into the distance.

I watched until he was gone. My eyes fell to my hands, studying the small blue ring that sat on my middle finger. I had it made from Elijah's ashes, so he was always with me. The rest of his ashes were given to his parents who scattered them at his favourite cove in Cornwall.

I didn't agree, I thought they should have kept some of them but who was I to decide? He was their son. I didn't have any rights in their choices.

Losing my Elijah benefited four people, so he was a superhero.

Someone got his heart, his kidneys, his liver and his lungs. It makes my heart swell momentarily thinking four people got to live because of him, but it took me a while to get to this point. First came grief, then anger... unbelievable anger. I mean how dare those four people get to live, and my Elijah didn't. It didn't seem fair.

His heart was so strong, but not strong enough to keep him with me.

The burn in my throat apparent, the sting behind my eyes almost unbearable. Swallowing the lump that was lodged in my throat back down, I stood quickly and walked back towards the hotel. That was enough sight-seeing for today.

I dragged my heavy legs along with my heavy heart to the hotel, my head down the whole way. I had fallen back into my black hole and that's where I wanted to stay for the evening.

I needed a sad film, chocolate, and wine.

Then I would cry and cry some more.

It's a process.

A coping mechanism.

Even two years on.

Climbing into the bed, sitting in my comfy pyjamas, I flicked through the pay to rent movie channel.

Smiling softly, I saw *The Notebook* on there.

This was perfect.

Heartbreakingly perfect.

I reached across for the chocolate and the cheap bottle of wine I bought on my way home. This was my evening sorted.

CHAPTER 7

Eyes stinging, red and swollen, my nose streaming as I stepped out of bed and walked towards the hotel door. Rubbing my nose with a tissue, I looked through the peep hole to see Connie standing on the other side with a bucket of Champagne and two glasses. Rolling my eyes but smiling, I unchained the door and opened it.

Sniffling, I held my hand up to wave.

"Oh my god, Reese, what's happened?" her voice was panicked as she placed the champagne on the side table just inside the door before her arms wrapped around me and held me.

"I'm okay, I've just finished watching a film." I muttered, my voice thick with sadness as the tears sprung to my eyes again.

"Are you psycho?" she pushed back out of the embrace; her fingers still firmly curled round the top of my arms, "You *chose* to put yourself through this absolute misery?!" her voice getting higher as her eyes bounce between mine. "There is enough shit and upset in the world but yet, here you are, sitting in a dark room bawling to a film that you chose to watch!"

"It helps." I shrug not wanting to elaborate anymore on it. Turning on my heel and walking back to my bed, I flick the tele over and let old *friends* re-runs play in the background as I clear my bed picnic for Connie.

"Looks like you have had a right good time." Her voice was laced with sarcasm.

I scoffed.

"Don't judge." My eyes narrowed on her, before I broke into a smile.

"No judging here baby girl, just observing." She nodded firmly before winking. A small laugh bubbled out of me as I felt the bed dip slightly when she knelt on it.

"Champagne?" she asked, her eyes widening with happiness as she held the bottle up.

I nodded.

Why the fuck not.

I had just broken my heart all over again and Champagne always seemed like a good idea after heartbreak.

"That's my girl." Connie sung as she popped the cork which caused a small, excited scream to leave her.

I giggled, grabbing a glass and putting it under the foam that bubbled out of the top.

Licking my fingers from the excess spillage, I bought the glass to my lips and took a large mouthful, humming in appreciation at the taste.

It was delicious.

I watched as Connie placed the ice bucket on the floor and plopped the bottle back inside. She grabbed her phone, smiling like a lovesick teen as her fingers danced across the screen. The annoying tapping filling the air.

"Who you texting?" I asked, leaning across and nosing at her phone screen.

She didn't hide her messages; I could see it was Kieran.

"Going well then?"

"At the moment." She shrugged her shoulders up nonchalantly before throwing the phone on the duvet.

"Have you messaged Colt? You know, a second test drive…"

"No." I shook my head "Just no. Not for me." I turned my nose up in disgust.

"Okay, we will find you a new guy to hump."

I choked on my mouthful of champagne, spitting it back into my glass.

"Oh Reese," Connie spat. "this is expensive champagne that I stole from downstairs, don't waste it." She tsked.

I rolled my eyes are her, "Twat." I muttered under my breath.

"A what?" she furrowed her perfectly smooth forehead.

"A twat."

"What language is that?" she sounded so confused, her brows digging in, her lips curling in distaste.

"It's English," I laughed hard, "it means a stupid or obnoxious person…" I muffled my laugh as I took a mouthful of my backwashed champagne. Disgusting.

"Rude." She snorted before drinking her own champagne.

The silence crackled between us for a moment as we both watched the tele.

"So, tell me about this film, why was it so sad?" she asked, her eyes still glued to *Friends*.

"Young lovers, they have a lot going against them in the beginning," I sniff, my voice thick as I try to ignore the ever-growing lump in my throat. I continue telling Connie all about it, skimming over certain details. Connie just stares at me wide-eyed as she listens. I sniffle, my breath shuddering as I tell her about the ending, my lip trembles as the ending of the film replayed over and over in my head.

"That sucks." Connie spits, her hand slapping into the duvet.

I nod, finishing the mouthful of Champagne that is left in the bottom of the glass.

"It's tragic, but also beautifully comforting." I continue nodding.

"What happened to girl meets man, they fall in love, the end!" she rambles, her hand flying in the air as she does. "That's what you want right? You want to meet the man of your dreams, fall in love, get married and have loads of kiddies before growing old together." Her voice speeding up.

"Life doesn't work like that," I muttered, a small sigh escaping me, twirling my empty glass on my thigh as I sit for a moment.

"It does, that's what all of them romance novels I read say… and what about Cinderella and Snow White?"

"They're just fairy tales, fairy tales aren't real." Inhaling a deep, sharp breath. My tone was harsh, but I didn't want Connie thinking life was as simple as that.

"How do you know?" Her brows furrowed, pulling away from me slightly.

"Because they're not, they're just that. Fairy tales." I snap.

"Hello, my name is Reese, killer of dreams." She snarls, jabbing her finger to me.

"Not a killer of dreams, just letting you know that life is a bitch and not a fucking fairy tale."

She rolls her eyes and falls into the pillows, huffing as her body sinks into the feather down pillows.

"Sorry sweetie, but it's the truth. Ain't no prince on a white horse coming to save you."

"What happened to you to make you think like that?"

I stilled for a moment, swallowing as I tried to make some saliva in my mouth to coat the dryness.

"Something that I hope you never have to go through." I whispered as I laid next to her, praying she didn't ask what happened.

"What happened?" her head turned to the side as she

looked at me, but I couldn't look at her. My eyes were pinned to the ceiling of the hotel room as I took in all the detail. I felt a single tear run down my cheek and dissolve into the pillow underneath my head.

"I lost the love of my life," I just about managed to speak out, my voice cracking.

I heard the gasp that left her, her hand reaching across and resting over the top of mine on my stomach. I knew she wanted to say something, but she didn't have the words, she didn't know what to say.

"It's okay," I smile softly, another tear rolling past my lashes.

We didn't speak for what felt like forever, we just lay side by side, hand in hand as I cried silent tears. A heavy weight lifting from my chest after telling Connie that I had lost Elijah, even if it was a small bit of information. It was still something new that I had been able to do.

I know we hadn't known each other long, but I never wanted to know what it was like to not have her in my life.

She came into my life for a reason, my guardian angel.

Hopefully my Elijah sent her to me.

I needed a best friend, and Connie was just that.

My best friend.

CHAPTER 8

Monday soon rolled round. I was anxious and excited. This was the first day of my fresh start, the one I so desperately needed. A new chapter in my life, and the chapter of my new adventure.

Tucking my white silk blouse into my high waisted cigarette trousers, I slipped my feet into my new Louboutins that Connie hounded me on. Apparently, I *needed* them. And I hated to admit it.

She was right. Damn that girl was good.

My blonde hair was pulled into a high ponytail and makeup barely visible. I had a light flick of mascara and a dusting of bronzer across my pronounced cheek bones. My lips had a smudge of lip balm over, given them just a small sheen.

My phone rung on the bed; turning quickly I smiled when I saw my mum's name light up the screen. Answering face time, my smile only grew.

"Oh, look at you." My mum beamed as she cocked her head to the side, my dad's head popping up behind her.

"Mi amor." He sung, his eyes full or pride and admiration.

"Are you all ready for your big day?" she asked, the excitement in her voice evident.

"Yup!" I sighed blissfully, running my fingers through my hair.

"Okay darling, have the best day. Message us when you're home."

"It'll be late."

"It doesn't matter."

I smiled wide, "Love you both."

"Te amo, mi amor," my dad replied before the phone went dead.

My heart ached a little more today than it normally did after our phone call. This was a big step for not just me, but them too. I always worked with my parents, even when I went into PR I would work with them on evenings or weekends. They had a small patisserie and bistro they ran, serving the best Venezuelan food and cakes you would ever taste.

Reaching down and grabbing my large work bag, I dropped my phone, purse, and key card into it. It was pretty empty, but I wanted to be prepared in case I had work stuff to bring home.

Closing my eyes, I inhaled deeply through my nose before letting the breath out past my lips.

"Let's smash this." I said to the empty room, nodding at myself in the mirror reflection and walking out the door.

Walking out onto fifth avenue, I stood at the kerbside as the doorman hailed me a cab. I was grateful to him. I needed to figure out using the subway, but not today.

"Where to?" the doorman asked as he held the door open for me to climb in.

"Park Avenue, 1156." I smiled at him, a small blush heating across my cheeks.

"You heard the lady, Park Avenue, 1156." He repeated to the driver.

"Thank you," I said softly, smiling at him.

He stepped back from the kerb, smiling and tipping his hat towards me.

Why couldn't everyone be as kind as him?

The taxi driver indicated and pulled into the busy road. Here we go.

Pulling up outside the large, glass skyscraper I was taken aback.

"Wow." I mouthed.

The beeping of the meter caught my attention as I fumbled through my purse and threw him some notes.

"Thank you," I chimed as I climbed out the car and looked back up.

Lordes Public Relations.

I was amazed, it was a lot bigger than I thought it would be. Pulling my eyes from the impressive building I locked eyes with the security guard that stood outside. Earpiece in, hands locked in front of him. He intimidated me.

Shaking off the nerves that crashed through me, I stepped forward and headed for the door.

"Ma'am," he nodded curtly as I pushed through the glass revolving doors. The air left my lungs as I took in the work of art in front of me. The floors were high shine marble throughout, the desk in a matching marble worktop, the base solid oak that wrapped around in a half moon. The walls were panelled with beautiful art hanging from the walls. All abstract and all stunning.

Rushing towards the desk, I placed my hands on the marble and instantly removed them.

"Welcome to Lordes Public Relations," the impeccably dressed girl at reception said.

"Hi, it's my first day here."

"Welcome, you must be Reese Hernández? Is that correct?"

I nodded.

"Fabulous." She tapped her long nails into the keyboard. How she typed with her fingernails like that amazed me. She stood up, handing me a visitor pass. "Here, take this. They'll do your ID today, then at the end of the day just hand the visitor pass back to me," she smiled. "If you go through the turnstiles, second lift, floor eight." She held her hand out, showing me the way.

"Thank you very much," I smiled before stepping back and following her instruction.

Pushing through the turnstiles I walked towards the lift, pressed the button and waited anxiously. I played with the lanyard of the visitor card, I needed to keep my hands busy as my stomach was a ball of nerves.

The doors pinged, inhaling deeply I walked into the lift, turning as the doors closed. The lift moved quickly to the eighth floor, and I was grateful.

Stepping out, my high heels clicked along the marble floor. I wasn't really a heel wearer, wedges yes, heels, no. I had to keep repeating what Connie had told me, heel to toe. Heel to toe. I thought the heel was going to give out and I would slip and fall on the high gloss tile. That's all I needed on my first day.

I stilled for a moment as I walked through a large open planned office, my eyes scanning and scoping the space in front of me. Heads popped up from their desk dividers at the new girl standing out like a sore thumb.

Some were dressed smartly like me, others were more casual.

Now I knew, I would go for the latter. I was a tomboy, not a girly girl at all. I didn't mind the odd dress, but I was mostly a baggy shirt and jeans kind of girl.

Swallowing the lump in my throat, I headed towards the

receptionist that sat behind a small desk in the corner. Smiling as I stood in front of her, her doe eyes pinged up from the computer.

"Can I help?" she asked sweetly.

"I hope so," I laughed as nerves got the best of me. "My name is Reese, I am starting here today." My smile growing now.

"Ah, yes. The British girl." She smiled back at me. She pushed off her desk and walked round to stand next to me, holding her hand out for me to take. "I'm Taylor, I'll take you through to Adele." I shook her hand before following her down to the back of the office where panels of glass faced me.

I sort of felt like I was thrown in at the deep end, but I'll get there. As I walked behind Taylor, I kept my head high and my eyes forward when I heard Julianne call out, "Reese," her tone warm as she wrapped her hand round my shoulders, walking beside me.

"Hey," my voice was quiet as we approached the office.

"Go in, Adele is expecting you." Taylor smiled, knocking on the glass door then turning on her heel and walking away.

"You seem nervous." Julianne whispered as we waited to be called in.

"I am," a nervous laugh escaped me.

"Don't be, you've got this," she nudged into me as she stepped forward to open the door and greet Adele.

"Julianne, Reese," the woman smiled as she welcomed us into her office. She had shoulder length blonde, wavy hair. Her green eyes glistening under the bright office lights. She sat behind her desk, elbows on top with her chin resting on her hands.

"First off, Welcome to Lordes and to New York. How is the jetlag?" Adele asked, her eyes pinned to mine.

"Thank you," I said loudly, "I am pleased and excited to be here." Rubbing my sweaty palms on my trousers, I could feel Julianne looking at me which made me even more anxious. "The jetlag is good, a lot better than it was. I am settling in nicely here."

"That's good, I am glad to hear that." She dropped her hands and pulled out some paperwork, shuffling it round her desk. "So, as you know, we are Lordes Public Relations, we work closely with influencers, singers, low key actors and many more. We have been running for nearly twenty years and continue to grow every month. I loved your work ethic and commitment when Julianne showed me your résumé, have you always worked in PR?" her eyes were back on mine. I felt the sweat trickle down my back from my hair line.

I nodded.

"Part time as an assistant for Rocke PR." I nodded again, "I worked for my mum and dad's bistro as well, so could only really do part time," I nibbled on the inside of my bottom lip.

"But, in that short time *you* landed one of the biggest influencers, Coby Swift. I mean, that is huge!" she dropped the paper, leaning back in her chair and crossing her legs.

"I mean, it was a joint effort," I blushed feeling incredibly uncomfortable with her praise.

"Well, your manager seemed to blow the smoke up your ass, so that's all on you baby." She winked, "but honestly, when Julianne here found your name and what you had achieved in such a short time, we knew that we needed you working with us. I mean if you can land Coby Swift, I'm sure you can land us some big named guys over here!" the excitement in her voice was bursting out of her.

"Let's hope so," I scoffed a laugh, widening my eyes in horror at my comment.

"No doubt here. We wanted you, we got you. I am ready for us to take Lordes PR to the next level, and I am so excited to have you here doing it with us." Adele sat back in her office chair and clapped her hands together quickly.

"I want you as my assistant for the time being, I have to

have a lot of meetings with investors and the board, so it'll be nice to be able to pass a few of my jobs over to you if that's okay?" she asked, but I knew she wasn't actually asking me. She was just being polite.

"Of course." I nodded and smiled sweetly. Something about her made me uneasy, a familiarity coursing through my blood but I couldn't for the life of me place her, but then again, maybe she just had one of those faces.

"Brilliant. I will get you a small desk set up outside my office, it'll all be ready for tomorrow morning, so in the meantime, Julianne," Adele's eyes now moved from mine to my little HR friend, "why don't you show our new colleague around the offices and then take her for some lunch. I have one of the investors in this afternoon so will be otherwise occupied." I felt the tension in the air for a moment, my eyes moving from Adele to Julianne before they fell back to Adele.

"Of course." Julianne smiled sweetly, pushing off her chair and waiting for me to stand.

"It was lovely meeting you Adele and thank you again for this amazing opportunity."

"You're most welcome," she tilted her head to the side before turning to face her computer, silently dismissing us both.

I nodded to myself, picking my bag up from the floor and following Julianne into the hallway.

"And breathe," she whispered, linking her arm through mine as we headed towards what I assumed was her office.

A small laugh escaped me, "That felt intense."

"But that's the hard bit done; Adele is wonderful to work with if you're on her side. You cross her, she will make your life a living hell." Julianne whispered before looking over her shoulder.

"I can survive that; I have lived through hell... well... I still am." I shrugged my shoulders up softly. Before Julianne could ask me anything about my little outburst, she ushered me into her office and closed the door behind me.

She gestured for me to sit down before she sat behind her computer.

"Just give me ten, got a quick couple of emails to send and then I'll be your tour guide..." she smirked before rolling her eyes.

I suppose she was busy and the last thing she wanted to do was to show the new girl around.

"If you're busy, I can just wander round the office... I don't want to be a burden." I blush, the heat on my cheeks evident.

"Don't be silly, I would love nothing more than to show you around, then I'll take you for lunch and a glass of wine or two..." she looked at me for a moment, letting her jaw drop open as she over exaggerated her wink to me.

I giggled before I let my eyes fall to my lap as I knotted my fingers. I heard my phone beep, reaching down quickly I pulled it out of my bag and saw Connie's name.

Hey bitch tits, I hope you have a fabulous first day and there is some hot CEO that will fuck your brains out. If not, I'll buy you a BOB.

Love your face. Dinner tonight?
Your new best friend.
Connie x

I couldn't help but laugh. I tapped a quick response telling her to piss off with her battery-operated buddy, that I wasn't going to fuck the CEO and yes, I wanted dinner tonight. Sliding my phone back in my bag, I sat back in the chair.

"Is it just you in HR?" I asked.

"No," she smiled, her eyes on her screen as she tapped away, "I am director of the human resource department, my team are just outside the door, on the table of eight. They are the best group I could ask for." Her eyes met my gaze before they moved back to the screen.

I didn't respond, just turned and looked over my shoulder and out of the glass panelled office as I saw her team sitting there.

I hope I made friendships like that here, I know I had Julianne, but I craved friends. I was always a loner. It was me and Elijah. He was all I knew. All I had.

My throat burned, but I switched the emotions off.

Not now.

Not here.

"Okay, let's get the tour sorted. No doubt Adele will want to show you off to the investors, a big shot like you means more money for this department." She winked.

I fumbled picking my bag up and standing from my chair as I fidgeted with my shirt buttons. "I'm honestly no big shot." I shook my head from side to side.

"To her you are," she smiled, opening her office door for me to leave. I did.

"You'll have a laptop and a company phone by the end of the day, all ready for tomorrow." Julianne beamed as she walked me across to her team, introducing me one by one.

I felt so out of depth.

But it was fine.

I had this.

CHAPTER 9

Walking back into the office with a full belly and a head of bubbles from the one-to-many glasses we had at lunch, true to her word, there was a mac laptop and blackberry sitting on Julianne's desk for me.

I felt a little overwhelmed suddenly.

Okay, so I was going to be Adele's bitch for a while, but once I showed her what I am capable of, I will hopefully be moved up to working with a client and alongside them. But it was early doors. I needed to just keep my head down and do my work.

I sat opposite Julianne as she opened my laptop and began tapping away. My thoughts went back to lunch when she explained that Adele liked to play with the investors a little, giving up the goods to seal the deal as such.

I couldn't understand how women, and men for that matter could act like that. I felt cheap and dirty after my one-night stand with Colt. I internally shudder. Never again.

Even thinking it gives me the ick.

"Okay, you are all set up." Julianne smiles as she spins my brand, spanking new laptop round to face me.

I felt so grateful.

"Thank you," my voice is barely a whisper.

The silence falls around us as I skim my finger across the sensitive track pad. I couldn't wait to get stuck in. I jumped at the sound of the high piercing ring of Julianne's phone.

"Yup." She sighed, rolling her eyes once she heard the voice on the other end of the phone. Placing the phone back in the cradle, she stood from the desk.

"Come, come." She chimes as she walks past me. I close the lid down on my new laptop, standing quickly and rushing out of the room following her.

I knew where we were going, we were going to Adele.

Maybe it was for me to meet the investors?

Julianne rolled her eyes, sighing deeply then plastering a smile on her face as she knocked on the glass door, Adele called out for us to come in.

We walked into the room, Julianne closing the door behind us as I stepped aside. I saw a dark-haired man sitting in the seat opposite her, her eyes leaving him as they met mine.

"Reese," her tone was more of a purr, "meet our top investor, Killian Hayes."

I stood still, my eyes raking up and down the back of the fine specimen of a man that was sitting in front of me. He turned slowly, standing, his dark eyes trailing up and down my body. A smirk curling on his lips. I felt the air leave my lungs; my eyes widened. *It was him.*

"Reese," his tone was low, his eyes dragging up and down my body again. He pushed off his chair and stepped towards me, closing the gap between us. His hand darted out for me to shake; wrapping my fingers round his I tried ignoring the rush of current that swarmed through the tips and down to my toes. "It's nice to meet you."

I blushed and quickly pulled my hand from his. *I wonder if he felt it too?*

"Likewise."

He smiled before sitting back down opposite Adele, her eyes pinned to him. Then it clicked, the air catching at the back of my throat and making me cough. That's why I recognised her. My mind flashed back to Friday night when he sent me the bottle of champagne, the blonde lady whose fingers skimmed over his broad, muscular shoulders that rippled under his shirt. My heart pulsed under my skin.

"Reese is my new assistant, for the time being…" she laughed, but it was over exaggerated.

I raised my brows, my own laugh softly chuckling out of me.

"Well, I look forward to working a lot more closely with you." Killian said as he looked over his shoulder at me.

I just nod, dropping my head and rubbing my lips together.

Killian and Adele fell into light chatter between themselves. Me and Julianne just stood there eyeing each other.

"Was there anything else you needed?" I couldn't help but notice the clipped tone that Julianne had with Adele when she asked.

"No, that'll be all." She smirked; her eyes pinned on Killian. I mean, who could blame her. He was a work of art.

Julianne nodded, turning, and walking out of her office.

"Oh, and Reese." I heard Adele call out just as I stepped over the door threshold.

"Yup." I spun round and smiled wide as our eyes connected.

"Just so you know, it's company policy that no staff members are romantically involved with anyone else in the business, or investors for that matter." She nodded curtly.

"Noted." I sniped before turning round.

"Close the door behind you please."

I didn't respond, just done as she said.

"So that's how you want to play it..." I muttered under my breath as I caught up with Julianne.

Sitting in a little Italian restaurant just a few blocks down from the hotel, I sipped on my red wine.

"She is obviously just trying to warn you off, she must see you as a threat." Connie smirked as she twisted some spaghetti onto her fork.

"I don't think she sees me as a threat per se, I think it's more she wants to make it clear that I am not to touch what is clearly hers." I shook my head from side to side softly. "Not that I would be interested in him at all, he is too old for me." I crinkle my nose up in disgust.

"How old is too old?" wiggling her eyebrows, "asking of a friend of course," she rolls her eyes, looking up at the ceiling.

"I would say easy mid-forties?"

"Not too bad, that's around my dad's age and let me tell you, my dad used to have some fit friends," she winks.

"Connie!" I lean over the table and swat her.

"What?! I'm not close to my dad, I see him once, maybe twice a year *if* I am lucky." She sits back in her chair, "but his friends... well, more like business friends," she curls her fingers over and admires her perfect coffin shaped nails.

"Disgusting." I stick my finger down my throat and pretend to heave.

"Don't knock it until you've tried it," she smirks, her eyes finding mine again.

"I have never, ever looked at my dad's friends and thought, 'do you know what Mr Smith, I want to fuck your brains out', just no!" I burst into laughter.

"Your dad obviously doesn't have hot as sin friends, and let me tell you, they know how to treat a woman." She winks before picking up her wine glass and taking a large mouthful.

"They know just how to work your body and what buttons to press," her tongue darts out as she licks her top lip.

"I actually feel a little grossed out." I curl my lips in disgust.

"Your loss." She shrugs, the glass covering her nose as drains her wine.

"What does your dad do?" I ask trying to change the subject.

"Erm, marketing? Money?" she looks around for a waiter, "I don't pay much attention to be honest, he's just a sperm donor that pays into my savings for when I am twenty-five. That's all there is too it really," she said as if it didn't bother her, shrugging her slim shoulders up.

"Sperm donor?!" I nearly choke on my wine.

"Yeah, my mum used a sperm bank to have me and contacted the donor to let him know that his sample had been used. My mum is gay, her and her wife wanted a kid and hey presto, egg plus donor sperm equals me!" she beams as she clicks her fingers and points to her glass.

The waiter silently nods at her before scarpering away.

"Wow," I blow my cheeks out.

"Yeah, it's pretty cool I suppose."

"How do you feel being a sperm donor baby?" I ask, hoping I am not overstepping the line.

"It doesn't bother me. My mums were pretty honest from the get-go, my mums are my parents. Not my sperm donor."

"That's good that they were honest with you."

"Why do you ask?" one of her perfectly shaped brows sat higher.

"I am thinking of doing it myself." I admit, internally hoping the waiter hurries up with the wine.

"What turkey basting yourself?" she looked confused as she sat back in her chair studying me, a hint of a smile on her lips.

"For fuck's sake," I breath out, shaking my head.

"Joking…" she giggles, "but I'm curious, why?"

"Well, I wanted children with Elijah," I swallowed the burning lump, "but that didn't happen, and I can't bear the thought of ever falling in love with someone else. I have always wanted children, it's a big dream of mine. So, I thought that once I was settled with work and the dust has settled, I would do the parenting thing by myself." A small smile creeps onto my lips, but it doesn't get very far as I am reminded of the pain.

"Oh," was all she managed, her eyes glued to me as she watched. "Well, that's a very brave thing to do and I admire that." Nodding gently, she reached for her glass and bought it to her lips. "What happened to Elijah?"

I had to tell her sometime, but deep down, I knew she knew. She just wanted the confirmation from me. I took a deep breath, swallowing the lump that was bobbing in my throat back down.

"He died."

CHAPTER 10

The last couple of months had flown, summer was well and truly over here in New York. The sun still shone but the evenings were drawing darker, the air nipping that little cooler at your skin.

Work was going well. I was busy. I liked being kept busy, it stopped my mind wandering back to Elijah.

Adele on the other hand was like working with Satan. She was horrendous. Everything that was laid out in my job role was non-existent. I was literally her dogsbody, doing all the shit work she didn't want to.

But I mustn't complain. It's a foot in the door, one step closer to being where I need to be. Plus, they paid for my apartment for the first year. Perks and all that. Then after I pass my probation and get my visa they will contribute half of my rent.

She had been even more like Satan today, maybe she hadn't been fucked in a few days or she had her period.

No investors had been to see her, maybe she had upset them.

I snapped out of my thoughts when Adele walked past me, stopping at my desk and looking me up and down. I was dressed up as I was meeting Connie at the hotel ready for drinks and a concert. I couldn't wait.

"Hi," I smile at her, my fingers still tapping on my keyboard.

"Do you have the numbers I asked you for this morning?" her tone was clipped and bitter.

"Yup," the smile still plastered across my face. I turned and grabbed the A3 spreadsheets and handed them to her. "I also sent two copies to your email; I always like to have a backup."

"Thanks." She sighed, turning and stomping into her office, slamming the door behind her.

I heard a ping on my email.

Julianne: *wow, she's even more a bitch today then she normally is.*

I scoff a laugh before replying.

Me: *I know, God knows what has happened. You're safe down there... I feel like I am in the firing line.*

Closing my email, I turn back to the task I was working on when I saw Adele's office door swing open with force.

"These numbers are wrong, did you even check them?!" she snapped at me, throwing the spreadsheet on my desk.

"I'm sorry... but the numbers are right. Do you want to show me where you think they are wrong?" my brows furrowed as I asked her, my eyes scanning over the document. The numbers weren't wrong.

The answers were there in black and white. This department was losing money like there was no tomorrow. It was a bottomless pit.

"This says we're losing money," she rolled her eyes.

"That's because we are..." I winced as she snatched the spreadsheet out of my hands.

"How can I give this to Killian? He will pull the plug on the department and then we will all be out of a job by Christmas."

"It's the events… you're putting on these grand events hoping to get big clientele through the door. You need to wine and dine them, show them why *they* are the special ones. Not invite them to a massive event with their competitors." I muttered.

She stilled; I could see the cogs turning in her head.

"You want to represent the handsome and dark Harlen Laufer from Blood Lust, so what can you do to get him through the door?" It was me questioning her… not the other way round. "When I got Coby, I researched him for weeks, maybe even months. I found out everything about him, his likes, his dislikes, his hobbies, his coffee order… you name it, I knew it." I sat a little taller. "You need to make them feel like they're the only person you're interested in, as if they were the only person in the world." I smile at her, my eyes volleying back and forth from hers.

"Then get on it," she snapped, "is that not what I am paying you for?!" she huffed, flicking her blonde hair over her shoulder, and walked into her office slamming the door behind her again.

"No, you're paying me to do your shit." I grumble, placing my elbows on the edge of my desk and putting my head into my hands.

Breathe.

"Well, aren't you a smart little cookie?" I heard his voice before I saw him. Flicking my head up I saw Killian saunter over to me, hands fisted deep into his fitted suit pocket.

I didn't respond. I didn't want to anger the dragon any more than I already had by talking to one of her fucks.

I sat up tall, straightening my back as I googled Harlen, and clicking straight onto his social media profile.

He sat on the edge of my desk, his toned and peachy arse

fitting perfectly. He crossed his leg over the other then held his knee with his hands. My mind flashed back to when I saw him in the park. He sat exactly the same.

"Can you move?" I grunted at him, looking up through my lashes at him. He didn't. His lips twitched as he tried to fight the smile that was desperately trying to dance across his mouth. He shook his head.

"I'm not sure how much you heard, but I am already on her shit list, I don't need you making it worse." I hissed as I pushed him slightly, causing him to have to steady himself.

"Oh, Buttercup. Don't worry about her," he cocked his head towards her office. "She is like a bear with a sore head, I'll sort her out." He licked his bottom lip before he stood from the desk. *Eurgh.*

I tsked, shaking my head as I focused on the screen for a moment. I heard his shoes hit the marble, my eyes quickly raking up and down his back before his arse held my gaze. He had a perfectly, peach bum. It looked amazing in his tight suit trousers. When he stilled and turned. I averted my eyes quickly.

"Were you just checking out my ass?"

"No!" I scoffed a laugh, it coming out a lot louder than I intended, the blush on my cheeks giving me away.

His eyes darkened, his lip curling at one side. He stalked back over to me.

"Meet me for drinks tonight?" his hands pressed onto the desk as he leant down so our eyes were level and I swear I felt the ground move beneath me. I heard the air whoosh out of my lungs as I tried to catch my breath.

"I have plans," my voice managed to stay calm and collected.

"Cancel them." His voice a little sharper now.

"No," I whispered as I felt my heart race in my chest under my capped sleeved dress.

"Then meet me after, it's a work thing…" he licked his top lip, his eyes falling quickly to my heaving chest.

"Maybe…" I breathed.

"You have my number, text me and I'll meet you." And with that he was gone.

Holy fuck.

Walking into the hotel with a huge smile on my face, I saw Connie standing there looking as beautiful as ever. She was wearing a gold sequin mini dress with high top Nikes.

"You look amazing!" she called out as she started walking towards me. She always made me feel good about myself, even if I was looking like crap.

I wore a black capped sleeve mid-thigh dress and had my doc martens on.

"You look hot," I winked at her, our arms locking around each other as we embrace.

"Let's go and see some hot rocker dudes." She says wrapping her arms around my shoulders. We were off to see an upcoming indie band called *Chord*. I had heard of some of their songs, but Connie was low key obsessed with them. We were heading to Brooklyn; it was my first time on a subway. I still hadn't braved it by myself.

"Brooklyn is going to be a lot different for you, you're used to the upper east side baby," she nudged her shoulder into me before locking her arm through mine.

"So are you." I laughed, the cold air making my breath smoke in front of me.

"I know, but I am used to it there too. You are not."

Okay so it was true.

I have wanted to go Brooklyn as soon as I was here, I don't know why. I liked the difference in worlds. The spoilt rich girls and boys in the upper east side, and then the rest of us.

We hopped on the train and sat in light chatter until we approached our destination.

Walking towards this small warehouse, anxiety sliced through me.

Connie sensed this, lacing her hand through mine and giving it a gentle squeeze. We showed the doormen our ID before being let through into the dimly lit space.

"Drink?" she asked.

I nodded. I needed alcohol to rid me of the nerves. But to be honest, the alcohol would probably make it worse.

Connie was back quickly, handing me a beer in a plastic cup.

"Cheers." I called out, pushing our cups together.

"Cheers," she smiled, bringing the cup to her lips, and taking a big mouthful.

The concert was amazing, Connie was fully submersed in their music and a little smitten by the lead singer who kept winking at her while he sang. She was giddy.

Walking back to the hotel I heard her huff.

"What's up?" I asked.

"I'm horny so I am just debating whether to use BOB or whether to call Kieran. I mean, he wasn't the best, but he certainly wasn't the worse…"

"Stick with BOB. At least you know you'll finish," I laughed which caused her to laugh too.

"I mean, can you imagine what it would be like sleeping with Tryst from Chord? I bet he is a machine in the bedroom." I muttered. I heard another sigh leaves her.

"He prob fucks like a pro." She said a little sheepish.

I nod in agreement.

"Talking of fucking…" she stops in front of me just before we reach the entrance of the hotel. "Have you fucked anyone else yet?" her hands on her hips as she waited.

"Nope." I shrugged.

"Okay, I'm getting you a vibrator tomorrow."

I couldn't help the smirk. That's that then.

BACK IN THE HOTEL BAR, THE DRINKS WERE FLOWING, AND Connie had spent the last half an hour on her phone no doubt texting Kieran.

I was getting bored and frustrated.

"Babe, if you want to go see Kieran, don't let me stop you." I said sweetly, hoping she got the hint, put the phone away and stayed with me.

Her big doe eyes looked up at me, "Would you be okay if I left though?"

Backfired.

"Yes, of course. Go and see your fuck buddy." I smile at her, even though my insides are begging her not to go.

"I love you." She leapt off her stool and threw herself at me.

"Love you too." I held her tight before I let her go. She didn't look back as she walked out The Palm Court and disappeared into the night.

Sighing, I swung round on the bar stool and ordered myself a vodka and lemonade. Holding the notes out to pay, the bar man shook his head from side to side. I looked at him confused, then it clicked.

Turning slowly on my stool, there was the God himself, sat a few spaces down. Killian Hayes.

And damn, him and them suits done something to me... making me all weak at the knees and shit.

I nodded, giving him a half smile before wrapping my fingers around my glass. I watched as he stood slowly, heading towards me.

"You're welcome." His low, gruff and sultry voice causing goosebumps to erupt over my skin. "May I?" he asked as he stood next to me, asking if he could sit down.

"Be my guest."

He sat, ordering himself a vodka and lemonade too.

"You didn't call," he said as he paid the barman.

"I didn't need too, you were here."

"Bullshit, you were never going to call," he tipped his head back and let out a throaty laugh, it was a lovely sound.

"I guess you'll never know," I winked at him.

We ordered drink after drink, we chatted like old childhood friends, and we laughed at the stupidest things.

But my god, it felt good to laugh.

We walked out of the hotel, or should I say stumbled. I was hungry, famished. I felt like I was wasting away.

"I need food." I mumbled.

I knew this was bad. I was out with one of the investors of the firm I worked for.

"I know a great lobster restaurant." Killian hummed as he laced his fingers through mine. I didn't remove them. I liked the unfamiliar tingle that spread up my arm, smothering my skin. It was nice to feel something other than pain.

"I don't want bloody lobster." I groaned, pulling on his hand as I walked ahead of him, turning and laughing.

"Oh, I am sorry." He pulled a stupid face while attempting the worst British accent I have ever heard. My stomach hurt from laughing so much.

"That is the worst accent ever… please don't ever do that again," I choked out, laughing through happy tears. He smiled, his eyes glistening as he laughed with me.

"I want a kebab or something stodgy, like a big, fat juicy burger." I licked my lips, stopping in front of this run-down burger van.

"No way. Nah-uh," he shook his head from side to side, "You'll get sick from there," he screwed his nose up, pulling me back. I resisted and tugged him back towards me.

"What's that?" I asked, furrowing my brows as I stepped towards him, running my thumb over his bottom lip and pulling it down.

"What?" he pulled back, his eyes dropping as if he was trying to look at his lips and wiping his thumb across his bottom lip.

"Oh, sorry, for a minute, I thought I saw a silver spoon in your mouth." I swatted him, dropping my hand from his and joining the queue for the greasy burger van. I heard a scoff from behind me but ignored him.

"What do you want posh boy?" I called out.

"I'll wait."

"Oh, stop it, I'll get you a cheeseburger." I rolled my eyes. I stilled when I felt his warm breath on the back of my neck, his large hands running around my waist as he held me into him. I wanted to pull away, take his hands off me and ask him what in the hell he was doing, but I forgot how nice it was to be held. To be touched.

His nose buried into my hair as he inhaled deeply, his lips moving to the lobe of my ear, "How about we go back to mine and we eat there…" his voice was barely audible. My skin erupted in goosebumps, my stomach knotting.

"I… I…" I stammered, turning round to face him. I buckled and froze. Lacing my fingers back through his, I ditched the idea of food and ducked into the first bar I saw, I needed tequila. And a lot of it.

I wasn't brave enough for this shit yet.

Adele's warning rung in my ears, I needed to step cautiously. I couldn't sleep with him.

We could be friends, but that's all we could be.

Even if his touch brought me back to life in that small moment.

I couldn't fall for him.

I wouldn't allow myself.

CHAPTER 11

Holy shit.

My head.
My throat.
My ribs.
Everything hurt.

What in the ever-loving fuck had happened last night? I tried to open my eyes, but nope. It was too bright. I was laying on my front, my face covered in my hair. I swatted my hand around the bed for my phone, maybe Killian knew what happened because I have no memory from the first tequila shot that I inhaled.

My hand continued hitting the duvet when I felt a body. I froze, my eyes pinging open as I turned my head slowly. I was in my bed, that was one positive.

Secondly, Killian was next to me, face down. His dark, chocolate brown hair all over the place.

For some reason, relief washed over me.

Okay it could have been worse.

I turned over slowly, not wanting to wake him. Panic rose up my throat as I lifted the duvet to see I was completely naked.

No, no, no.

Sneaking a peek at Killian, I saw he was also naked. My eyes gazing a little too long at his peachy bum. Man, it was even better in the flesh.

Pulling the cover tight over me, I internally groaned and put my hand on my forehead. It's fine.

We were intoxicated.

There is no way we would have slept together.

Closing my eyes, I inhaled deeply.

My brows pinched together as I felt cool metal on my head. Opening my left eye and squinting I could see a band.

"You have got to be fucking kidding!" I sat bolt upright in bed, holding my hand out as my eyes widened and focused. I saw the wedding band sitting snug on my ring finger.

"Oh my fuck," my voice was louder now, stirring Killian next to me.

"Keep the noise down, Jesus, my head is pounding." He rubbed the sleep out of his eyes, pushing himself up and taking a moment to take in the room that he was laying in.

I counted down in my head.

Three, two, one...

"What the fuck!"

There we are.

His beautiful dark brown eyes found mine. "Reese?!" he stammered, turning over and sitting with a puzzled expression on his face.

"Morning," I chirped, holding my left hand up.

His eyes darted from mine to my hand, from my hand to my eyes.

Slowly dropping his head, he holds his left hand out to see a matching gold band wrapped round his ring finger.

"Well, fuck," he rubbed his face, reacting when the cool metal touches his flushed skin.

"This can't be happening..." I whispered. "What happened?" I groaned, falling back into my bed.

I was married.

To him.

"I have no clue, and I am no detective…" he wiggled his eyebrows in a playful manner "but I think… I *think* we got married last night…" I heard a deep, heavy sigh leave him as he flopped down next to me. The silence was deafening between us.

"We're both naked." I blushed, holding the duvet tight to my body. He lifted his side of the duvet and looked under, his lips pouting, his brows sitting high on his forehead.

"So we are."

Silence fell between us, once more.

We didn't have sex.

We couldn't have.

Our eyes were pinned to the ceiling, my fingers drumming on my bare chest.

"You don't think we... you know..." I winced.

"No, no… we were far too drunk." He shook his head from side to side.

"But not too drunk to fly to Vegas, how did we even get to Vegas?!" I shrieked when it all started settling in.

"I own a jet."

Of course, he does.

"So we were that intoxicated that we managed to get to an airport, get air traffic control to give us the green light to fly, fly to Vegas, get married then get back on said plane and come home…" my head hurt just thinking about it. The remanence of alcohol making my head pound alongside my confusion.

"Seems so." His tone was flat, unbothered. It unnerved me.

Why wasn't he panicking?

I was full blown having a mini panic attack.

"How are you so calm?!" I turned my head to look at him, my eyes searching for some sort of facial expression but there was nothing. His eyes stayed pinned to the ceiling. He said nothing.

"What are we going to do?" I whispered, fear pricking my skin, tears burning behind my eyes. "I was supposed to marry Elijah." My tears were falling now and there was no stopping them. I felt Killian's eyes on me.

"You're with someone?" I could hear the shock in his voice, but he wasn't angry or disappointed... maybe it was disbelief. But his voice was laced with something.

"Was," I sniffed, rubbing my eyes.

"Was?" he repeated.

"Yeah..." I trailed off. I couldn't get into this now. I wasn't ready to tell Killian my past. I don't think I would ever be ready to open up to him like that.

I need an annulment.

I couldn't stay married to him.

Killian Hayes.

My husband.

"We need to annul our marriage."

"But if we slept together..." Killian began, but I leant over pressing my finger to his lips.

"No one knows if we did, no one was in the room, we were too drunk to remember if we had sex. So, let's just say we didn't."

Killian nodded quietly, his eyes not leaving mine.

"No one needs to know. Not my friends, my parents or Adele. Fuck!" my eyes widened. "Definitely not Adele. She'll fire my arse." I panic, dropping my finger from his plump, delicious lips and roll out of bed, pulling the duvet with me.

Killian froze, reaching across and grabbing the pillow from behind his head and covering himself up.

I spun, my jaw lax as I saw him lying there with just a pillow covering his cock.

He had a dusting of dark hair over his chest, his

shoulders, arms, and chest toned. I couldn't help but notice a scar that ran from just under his collar bone, down to his ribs.

I didn't spend too much longer looking, I turned and ran into the bathroom, slamming the door and locking it behind me.

This was not happening.

Adele was going to kill me.

I was going to be fired.

I would have to go back home with my tail between my legs because I got drunk on tequila and married one of the investors.

I am never drinking tequila again.

Once I was showered, I slipped the lock across and sneaked out of the bathroom. I could hear him on the phone. Tiptoeing out, I didn't want to eavesdrop.

"Can you come and pick me up from Park Avenue in half an hour please?" his voice was hushed.

Good.

He is going.

It should make me happy... but instead, for some reason it stung.

Pacing into the open planned kitchen, I flicked the coffee machine on.

Killian was standing by the window watching the hustle and bustle of the city.

"Coffee?" I asked.

He turned slowly, his eyes dragging up and down my body as he took in my appearance. I was wearing leggings and a cropped vest. I was going to use the apartment block gym to try and sweat out the hangover.

"No, thank you," his smile was tight, he had one hand fisted in his pocket as he just watched.

I smiled back at him, turning on my heel quickly and grabbing a mug and opting for a cup of tea instead.

Wrapping my fingers around my hot cup, I stood with my back against the worktop as I stood silently watching him. He was tapping the screen of his phone.

It was like the night after drunken sex. Tension. Awkward. And I still have to see him through work from time to time.

"Are you okay to sort out the annulment?" I mutter as the rim of the mug sits on my bottom lip.

"Lawyer is already drawing up the papers." He mutters back, not lifting his eyes from the phone screen.

The silence falls again for a moment before his phone beeps.

"I've got to go," he presses his lips into a tight line before walking towards me, his Louboutins clicking along the hard wood floor as he does.

"See you around, *wife*," he smirks, slipping his phone in the inside of his suit pocket before walking out of my door, making me jump in my skin as it slammed shut.

Damn it.

AFTER A GOOD WORK OUT IN THE GYM, I HAD DROPLETS OF SWEAT beading on my forehead, my skin covered in a sheen of sweat. Patting my head with my towel I started heading back to my apartment. I needed to call Connie, but there was no way I was telling her what happened last night. I needed to keep it quiet. As soon as it was over, I would fill her in on everything. But I couldn't risk losing my job, I couldn't risk fucking up this quickie break up. Peeling my clothes off, I fell on the bed and called Connie.

She answered after the first ring.

After telling me all about her night with Kieran we said we would meet for lunch tomorrow. My hangover was

DEAR HEART, YOU SCREWED ME

beginning to creep back over me. I needed junk food and a binge-worthy tv series.

That sounded like the perfect Saturday.

AFTER TWO HOURS OF *FRIENDS* I STOOD TO GRAB A GLASS OF water. Filling my cup I padded back to the room, my eyes moving to my bedside unit.

Pulling the drawer open I saw my diary staring back at me. I felt like I hadn't written in it for so long, I was overdue an entry.

> Dear Diary,
>
> It's been a while and I'm sorry.
>
> Life has been hectic, work, social life, accidental marriage.
>
> Yup.
>
> Dickhead here got so drunk that she woke up this morning with a ring on her finger. And it gets worse.
>
> It's with one of the big investors of the company I work with.
>
> I was told no dating co-workers or investors.
>
> Well, I went one up and married him.
>
> Adele is going to kill me.
>
> And Elijah? He is going to be frowning from heaven. I am sure I am going to hell. Because that's what I deserve. He has been gone two years, and here I am married.

Of course, I am going to get it annulled. I can't be with him.

We can never go there.

I have majorly fucked up.
Over and out.
R X

Slamming the diary shut, I felt the rage coursing through me. How could I have been so stupid. Pressing my palm to my head I closed my eyes.

I had to calm down.

It was going to be fine.

'Deep breaths Reese' I repeated over and over in my head.

My phone buzzed on the bedside unit, I reached across and grabbed it. An unknown number flashed up on my screen.

> UNKNOWN:
> Reese, We are sitting in front of a judge in three weeks, Friday. Earliest I could get us in. I'll pick you up and we will go together.
> Killian.

I let out a sigh of relief. Three weeks.
That's all I had to get through.

CHAPTER 12

Sunday whizzed by in a blink of an eye. I hated that the weekends passed too quickly. Stepping into the office Monday morning, I dumped my bag on my desk to see a pile of paperwork.

Brilliant.

This is not what I signed up for and I was still no closer to getting where I wanted to be. Hanging my trench coat up on the coat hook behind me, I pulled my chair out when the phone rang. It was Adele's line. I quickly glanced down to my bare finger, relief washing over me that I remembered to take the tacky gold ring off as I walked into the office. I shoved it into my pocket.

"Yup." My tone was curt and to the point.

"Office." So was hers.

Happy Monday.

Pressing the phone back into its cradle, I stood straight and held my head high as I walked into her office, knocking before I did.

"You wanted to see me," I smiled as I stood in the doorway, Adele was sitting scrolling on the mouse of her computer.

She called me in using her free hand. Closing the door behind me I sat down.

A few moments passed before she looked at me, her hands crossing over on her desk.

"So, over the weekend I have been thinking about what you said. How we need to appeal more to the clientele that we want." I nodded. "And one of our investors also agreed with you. He overheard the conversation on Friday."

Killian.

I felt my skin prickle in goosebumps. I run my hands up and down my forearm trying to get rid of them.

"Oh." I managed, breathlessly.

"I would like for you to organise something to suit Harlen. I want you to wow him, and if, and I know… it's a big if, but if you sign him… you'll be promoted." She forced a sickly smile across her face.

Wow, gee… thanks.

"That would be amazing." I beamed, a genuine smile on my face.

"You have one week," her tone was clipped as she turned slightly to face her desk.

Fuck.

"One week?" I stammered as I repeated her last words.

"Mmhm," she hummed as she nodded, "what's wrong? Are you not up for the challenge?"

"Oh, I am. I just wanted to make sure I heard you right." I fiddled with my fingers on my lap.

"Good, and that paperwork on your desk. I need it back by midday." Her eyes left mine as she shooed me away with her hand.

Double fuck.

Pushing off the chair, I quickly exited her office and closed the door behind me. How in the hell was I going to land Harlen Laufer in a week! Sitting back at my desk I dropped my head into my hands. *What to do, what to do.*

I pulled my phone out of my bag and tapped Connie's name into it.

ME
Bitch face, you up yet?

My eyes glued to the screen, I waited for the ticks to appear.

CONNIE
Just. What's up?

ME
I need help. I need to land Harlen Laufer in a week.

Even typing the words made me panic.

CONNIE
Holy fuck. Yeah, you're screwed.

I rolled my eyes.

ME
Thanks dickhead, how am I going to get him?

CONNIE
You're not.

Jeez, thanks for the vote of confidence.

I dropped the phone back in my bag and opened the internet. I could do this. I done this in my sleep back in England.

Pulling up his social media profile I clicked through his pictures. It was either him with his vamp teeth and blood, or his body. And man, did he have a body.

"Busy, are we?" Killian's voice floated over me like silk. Panicked, I slammed my laptop screen down.

"I am actually, aren't you?" I argued back.

"Not particularly," he pulled his hand out of his pocket and looked at his nails. I noticed he still had his ring on.

"I'll be honest, that's not something I want to be seeing my wife look at," his voice was low, gruff and totally hot.

My eyes widened.

"Quiet." I pressed my finger to my lips shhing him. "And why have you still got your ring on?"

"More importantly, why *haven't* you got your ring on?" his brows sat high in his forehead.

"Because I don't need to have it on."

"Are you, or are you not married to me?" he stepped forward, both palms pressed down on my desk.

"Unfortunately." My voice is steady.

"Then, while we are married, you wear your ring." He cocks his head, a delicious smile creeping onto his face.

"I don't want to."

"I didn't ask if you wanted to… I am telling you," his tone grew more serious, his eyes ablaze with fury.

"I can't lose my job." I sounded pathetic.

"You won't," he stood tall, "put the ring back on."

I grunted as I fisted the ring from my pocket and slipped it back on.

"There, happy?!"

"Very."

"I hate you."

"I love you too, sunshine." He pouted, before a stupid smirk crossed his lips, slipping into Adele's office and closing the door.

What a prick.

Sitting at lunch with Julianne, I twisted my fork into my pesto spaghetti.

"What's biting you?" Julianne muttered through a mouthful of her meatball sub. "You've hardly eaten."

"Just this Harlen Laufer stuff, I feel like Adele is trying to throw me under the bus."

"She is," she wiped the corners of her mouth with a napkin.

I sighed as I continued pushing my spaghetti round the plate.

"You know I would help you if I could, but I am useless with things like this." She shrugged her shoulders up apologetically.

"I know you would," I reached across and placed my hand over hers, giving her a weak smile.

"Now eat up, let's brainstorm."

And brainstorm we did.

Walking back into the office with a few ideas bouncing around my head I sat down to get stuck in.

I sent a lengthy email to his email address. I had no clue if it was just a spam account or his actual one. The next stage would be stalking him. That made me anxious. I didn't want to seem like an obsessed fan, I hadn't even watched his show. Maybe I should, at least that way we would have something in common. I hoped. Nothing on his social media profile really jumped out at me, I knew where he went for his morning coffee because he always tagged the location so at least I had that to fall back on. But that was last resort. I needed to do this for Adele, but mostly for myself. I wanted to prove myself so bad; prove that I was so much more than her dogsbody who done her dirty work. I had jotted down a list of things I wanted to check out on Harlen so that would be my task tonight. I didn't have any plans anyway. Connie said she may come over, but she has been seeing Kieran quite a lot. I don't believe her. She is being too secretive; she is normally so open but for some reason she is acting a lot shadier. Maybe it's just me. Maybe it's because I have a secret that I can't tell her. You know, the secret where I am married to one of the investors of the company.

I mean, seriously. How. How could I have been so reckless. So bloody stupid. I managed to push the thoughts out of my head as I locked my computer and waved to Adele through the floor to ceiling glass panel. Wrapping my scarf around my neck and shrugging my trench coat on, I began to walk towards the main lobby. Julianne was deep in conversation; I would have waited but I just wanted to get home. I couldn't waste any time. I didn't want to deliver this on Friday, I wanted to deliver it tomorrow, if possible, but I mean... it was impossible.

Did we have it as a company to push Harlen out into the big, wide world more than he already was? I doubted it, but this was my job. I needed to get him over to Lordes PR whether it was the last thing I done.

My heels clicked across the high gloss marbled tiles as I pushed through the turnstiles and waved bye to the security guards. My small smile dropped from my face as I saw the hustle and bustle of the city. I didn't like it when it was busy.

Escaping out of the rotating glass doors, the cold air caught in the back of my throat. Autumn was here, in full swing. Pulling my coat around my tiny frame, I dropped my head and began walking towards the subway. I was in my own world when I heard a toot of a horn. Turning my head to see a black Mercedes SUV slow down kerbside. I didn't even have to guess who was behind the dark tinted windows. The back passenger window slipped down to reveal a beaming Killian. His brown hair pushed off his face, his dark, brown eyes bright as they pinned to me.

"Get in the car," he called as the car halted.

"I'm fine, I can walk." I huffed, tightening my scarf before beginning to walk again. I heard the engine start again.

"I didn't ask if you were okay, I told you to get in the car," his tone was clipped and short.

"I don't want to get in the car." I snapped "I'm not some

damsel in distress that needs saving. Take your pissy Chelsea tractor and go away."

"Chelsea tractor?" I could hear the confusion that laced his voice. I smiled smugly to myself as I continued to walk. There was no way I was getting in his car. I picked up the pace and began walking quicker. I needed to get somewhere he couldn't. I needed to stay away from him. Us being close, together… it wasn't good for either of us. It would only be a matter of time before the tension grew too thick, before the air between us began to crackle that little bit louder, his fingers making my skin burn, his mouth making my lips bruised in the best possible way…

Shaking my head side to side softly, I turned the corner and began to slow slightly. This was a one way, no chance of him getting down here. I played over my to do list in my head as I walked, I was so desperate to make Adele happy. But then again, even if I did make her happy let's be honest… if she finds out I am married to Killian, I would be fired on the spot. It's clear as day that they have some sort of relationship… whether it is strictly business or… more.

I shuddered, he wouldn't be with her now he was married to me, would he?

Damn it Reese, why would you care?!

My subconscious snapped at me. She was right. I shouldn't care. Big deal we were married by an Elvis impersonator in Vegas, it means shit. It was nothing but a stupid, drunken mistake.

Like Ross and Rachel in Friends, except we were getting it annulled, we were not getting a divorce.

"Hey, wifey, wait up!" his voice was loud behind me. I stopped, looking over my shoulder before rolling my eyes.

"Why can't you get the hint? I don't like you; I don't want to walk with you. I was just fine before you came along and ruined everything," I snarled at him, slapping my hand down on my thigh.

His jaw dropped open, his brows meeting in the middle as he stood tall. He was really tall. Huh, I didn't notice before. Weird.

"Sorry, did I force you to marry me?" Killian's voice was raised as he stepped towards me.

"For all I know, yes!"

"Don't be so fucking ridiculous," he shook his head as I continued to walk away from him.

"Keep walking Reese, I will keep following. I have nowhere else to be," I heard the amusement lace his voice.

"I will. You have fun trying to keep up," I bit back, refusing to look at him again.

This is how we walked the whole way to the subway. Him two steps behind me. I was grateful to see the train pull in just as I got onto the platform. I was so over today, I just wanted to go back to my apartment.

I sat down between two handsome men on the busy subway, smirking at the fact that Killian hadn't managed to get a seat. He fisted the red tag rope above his head as the train began to move. I was satisfied. I was scrolling through my phone when the guy beside me accidentally nudged me as the train moved off the rail slightly, my head snapped up to look at him as he apologised. I smiled and told him it was fine before dropping my head again. That's when I saw Killian's shoes by my feet.

I slowly looked up through my lashes at him, blinking. He was stood over me, fists balled by his side like a raging bull. What the fuck was his problem?

"I suggest you move," he spat through gritted teeth to the guy next to me who had just apologised.

"Killian," I gasped.

"I was here first," the guy retorted back.

"Bully for you. Now get up so I can sit next to my wife," his voice was like venom, his tongue sharp.

"Sorry man, I don't want any problems. Here, have your seat," the young man got up and scuttled away.

Killian smiled, proud as punch as he sat next to me. He let out a relieved sigh before he leant forward and caught the attention of the guy who was sitting on the other side of me.

"I suggest you fuck off too," he nodded, "run along." Killian shooed him away and the guy scarpered up the other end of the carriage.

I wanted the ground to swallow me up. I was so embarrassed.

I didn't talk to Killian for the rest of the train ride. I was so angry with him. How dare he feel like he can speak to people like that. As we pulled up at my stop, I rush to my feet and bolt for the door. As soon as I was on the platform I ran for the stairs, hoping and praying that Killian didn't manage to get up quick enough.

Good, he didn't follow. Hopefully he got the message. Douche bag.

Standing on the pavement, I held my hand up and hailed a taxi before slipping in and giving the driver my address.

I pulled my work phone out and ran through the list one more time when I saw an email from Harlen Laufer.

My heart drummed and raced in my chest as my fingers hovered over the keyboard.

"What's the worst that's going to happen?" I muttered to myself.

My heart fluttered; I was nervous. Opening his email, my eyes scanned for the important words.

He was in.

HE WAS IN!

I dropped my phone in my lap and let out a sigh of relief before I looked at the screen again and read his email slowly:

Reese,
  I must say this sounds like an exciting and tempting invitation.

But first, before we sign on any dotted lines, may I suggest we meet in person? I always like to get a feel for the people I agree to work with.

I wasn't really looking for a new PR company, but my current PR team and agent are a bit ancient in their ways and I want to continue to grow, ready for when Blood Lust comes to an end. Because let's face it, all good things must come to an end.

How about we meet tomorrow for lunch? I have a proposition for you. I'll meet you at Sarabeth's at noon and we can go from there.

Look forward to seeing you,
Harlen.

Holy shit.

This could be it. I tapped my calendar and added our business lunch in. This was good. This was exciting. That finish line of tomorrow was looking very promising. I played out the moment I rocked into Adele's office with the paperwork from Harlen two days into my task. Then I would watch that smug smirk on her face disappear as quick as her fake arse attitude.

Nothing could wipe the smile off my face. Paying for the taxi, I jumped out and headed towards my block, greeting the doorman as I did.

"Evening, Miss Reese," he tipped his top hat at me. I loved it here, I really did.

Walking through the lobby of the apartment block, I headed for the lift. I wanted a nice bubble bath, a glass of wine and then I wanted to write a list of questions to ask Harlen tomorrow.

Pushing the lift button, I pulled my phone out and tapped a quick message to Connie. I just wanted to check in and see how she was. It was strange that I hadn't heard from her today. My brows pulled and knitted together for a moment before I felt my phone vibrate.

CONNIE
Will call soon, Love you bitch tits. X

Smiling, I dropped my phone into my bag and watched the lever on the lift drop to the ground floor. Stepping into the empty lift, I blew a breath of relief. I hated small, crowded places. Spinning round so I was facing the door, watching it close but just before they closed, a familiar black shoe stopped it.

"Hope you don't mind me riding with you." The goosebumps from his silky voice smothered across my skin.

Killian.

"I do actually." I rolled my eyes hard and tsked as he pressed the button for my floor.

"You're an irritant." I snapped, refusing to look at him and watching the lift buttons light up as we reached each floor.

"I've come to the conclusion that you're quite nasty," he turned to face me; he sounded somewhat wounded. His eyes softened as they fell, rubbing his lips together before licking them.

The breath caught in the back of my throat as I gave in to the pull to face him. The tension was thick, the air felt thin as I gasped for air.

"I'm not nasty." I muttered; I don't know why, but it hurt more than it should.

"Don't be sad Buttercup, I like it," he wiggled his brows up and down, his eyes roaming over my body. "You're feisty…" He stepped forward, smashing the emergency stop button. The lift came to an abrupt halt, making me unsteady on my feet as I grabbed the handrail to halt myself.

"Killian!" I shouted, throwing myself towards him as I tried to pull his hand from the button.

"Not happening, petal." His lips played into a devilish smirk. It was panty melting, but it wasn't going to work.

"Please, Killian. I am claustrophobic. I can't do this." My

breathing fastened, my eyes scanning round the elevator walls as I tried to catch my breath. With each gasp, I felt more and more light-headed.

"Let me come up to your apartment and eat dinner with you." His hand was still over the button.

"Killian," I cried out, I felt the clamminess of my skin, the sweat pricking and beading on the surface, the walls closing in slowly around us as black dots invaded my vision.

"Agree to it," his voice was low, but possessive. He liked being in control.

"No," I breathed, my whole body trembling as I tried to calm myself.

"Say yes," he smirked, his hand still firmly on the button.

"Fine, fine!" I shouted, you could hear the panic that ripped through me, the fear apparent in my voice.

"Good girl." He licked his lips, pushing the emergency button. The lift continued its climb.

I closed my eyes, trying to control my breathing. I was a trembling mess.

The lift pinged when it was on my floor, I pushed off the wall that was holding me up and barged past Killian.

"You're an arsehole." I spat at him as I walked towards my front door.

He was hot on my heels, his scent surrounding me like a bubble. I hated to admit it, but he smelt delicious.

Pulling my keys out of my bag in my trembling hands I opened the door quickly, before turning to close it in his face. But him and his poxy shoe were there stopping it. I saw his large hand curl round the door.

"Wife. That's not fair, you agreed to it."

I threw my bag on the floor, storming towards my bedroom and slamming it shut.

"I only agreed to it to get you to push the button you fucking lunatic!" I shouted back, my voice hoarse.

He could stay out there.

He made my blood boil. I don't know what it was about him. He got under my skin and I hated it. He never got to me before but now I despised him.

Maybe it was because he was the collateral damage that could destroy my career in a heartbeat. He could destroy everything I had sacrificed and worked so hard for. I was the bomb and he was the detonator. One, small, slip of the finger and it was over.

I slid down the wall, my knees pulling into my chest as I wrapped my arms round myself. Closing my eyes, I focused on my breathing. Inhale for five, hold it for three, slowly exhale. After a few attempts, my heart started to slow. I tilted my head back so it was on the wall, my eyes pinned to the high ceilings. I heard a gentle knock on the door.

"Reese," his voice was low, soft, calm.

"Go away Killian," I snapped. I was ready to burst into tears at any minute, but I wouldn't let him see me cry.

I saw the doorknob twist. Why couldn't this man listen to one simple instruction?

He popped his head round the door, scanning the room before he saw me huddled in the corner and cuddling myself against the wall. His eyes softened; his sharp jaw unclenched as he saw me. Stepping into my bedroom, he closed the door behind him before dropping to his knees in front of me. His large hands cupped my face before lifting it to look at him.

"I'm sorry," his voice was so low, it was barely audible. I could see the remorse in his eyes as they volleyed back and forth from mine. "So sorry," he leant in and pressed his lips to my forehead, lingering for a moment. My stomach flipped at the feel of his lips on my skin, our first bit of intimate contact and it was after he was a complete, arrogant prick.

I nodded, sniffling and my intake of breath sharp. He pulled away, standing slowly in his expensive and tailored suit.

Pushing off the floor, I sulked into the open plan living

and kitchen area. I slumped on the sofa. Killian followed but headed to the kitchen. I didn't let my eyes follow, I focused on the blank, white wall in front of me. I needed to spend some money on the apartment and make it a bit more homely. It came already furnished but I bought all new bedding and mattress. The thought of someone sleeping in that bed gave me the ick. I didn't have long to be lost in my thoughts as Killian was back with a large glass of wine, holding it out towards me. I took it gladly and sighed.

"Thank you."

He rubbed his lips into a tight line, stepped back and headed for the door.

"I'll be back soon," the sound of the door closing behind him echoing around in the deathly silence.

"Don't rush," I snarled out to the empty room. Bringing the glass to my lips I took a large mouthful. I hummed in appreciation at the taste of the wine. It tasted even better because I was so desperate for it.

I heard my phone ringing in my bag, hopping up I ran and rummaged in my bag that Killian had hung up on the coat hook. Smiling when I saw it was Connie, I clicked answer.

"Why have you been so MIA?" I laughed.

"Oh, you know, boy stuff," she laughed back.

"Mmhmm, wish I had that problem," even though I did have that problem, all of six-foot-six of a problem, wrapped in the perfect suit with a killer jaw line and deep brown eyes.

"I am sorry for being a crappy friend, dinner tonight?" I could hear the desperation in her voice.

"As tempting as that is, I have so much to do ready for my lunch with Harlen Laufer tomorrow, I really can't be going for dinner, but how about tomorrow?" I said with hopefulness in my voice.

"Boo, you whore," she cackled.

"Okay Regina George," I rolled my eyes in humour.

"But seriously, tomorrow is good. I'm on a late shift tomorrow, start at eight so can we go straight after you finish work?"

"Of course, how about we eat in the hotel, that way we don't have to rush as much."

"Perfect. I'll meet you at five-thirty?"

"Five-thirty is perfect."

"See you tomorrow bitch tits."

"Love you," I felt the smile on my face growing.

"Mwah, love you more," she kissed before the phone went dead. Slipping it back into my bag I padded to the bathroom and began running the water. I couldn't give a shit if Killian turned up as I let myself wrinkle in the bath and was locked out in the hall, banging on the door. He deserved it.

Turning the tap off, I stripped off and let myself submerge into the bath. The hot water felt good on my tense skin. It was tense because of my accidental husband. And what a beautiful, persistent twat of a husband he was.

I felt the tingles spread through me at the thought of his plump lips pressing against my skin. For a small moment, I wondered what they would feel like on my lips, his tongue pressing and invading my mouth. Was he dominant? Or did he like the girl to be dominant... who am I kidding? He is fucking dominant. I thought about how his fingers would circle and trail over my skin before they slipped between my legs, grazing over the most sensitive part of my body and showing me what it is like to feel and be loved again. But my thoughts were soon plagued with him doing that to Adele and me somehow watching and not being able to shout out.

I slipped under the bubbles and screamed, I needed them out of my head. It was wrong. My head should just be filled with Elijah. Always Elijah.

The guilt crushed me in an instant; pushing out of the water, I let the tears fall. It didn't help with the guilt that it was Elijah's anniversary of his death a few weeks ago and that date lays heavy on my shoulders. The pain didn't ease like I thought it was going to.

No, it was still prominent, and the ache was a constant reminder of what I had lost.

I reached for my wine and downed it. I wanted to feel anything other than the betrayal I felt. Would I ever be able to move on? Or more to the point, did I even want to move on?

CHAPTER 13
KILLIAN

I felt like a complete dick. I don't know what it is about her, but I want to push her, I want to see how much she can take from me. I want her to fall for me. I want that the most.

I am a possessive ass, I know I am.

But I don't care. She is mine.

Legally bound to me. Until death do us part.

Or at least until the annulment; the thing is, I don't think I am quite ready to give her up yet.

Sure, she is eighteen years younger than me, but do I care? Do I fuck.

Walking along the sidewalk, I stopped at the small Chinese restaurant. I didn't even know if she liked Chinese, but she needed to eat. Plus, I needed to get out of her apartment for a bit, I needed to let her cool off. I had crossed a line tonight.

Pushing on the door, the warmth hit me as soon as I was in the restaurant.

"Welcome to Wok 'N' Roll, table for one?" The young male waiter asked me.

Pushing my hand through my hair, I shook my head.

"I ordered take out, called about fifteen minutes ago."

"Ah okay, name?" he asked, stuffing the menu back under the host station.

"Hayes."

"I'll go and check if your order is ready," he smiled at me before disappearing into the back. I stepped aside and out of the way for eager diners who were hoping to get a table and out of the cold New York air. The temperature had dropped, it was freezing.

I pulled out my work phone, my finger hovering over her name. I don't know why I felt the need to want to message her, but I fought the urge. Leave her be. *You have done enough.* My subconscious reminded me. Slipping my phone back in my pocket, I held my hand out and looked at the tacky, yellow gold ring on my finger. How in the fuck did we both manage this? I know we were intoxicated, but to fly to Vegas and actually get married. I mean, it could be worse... Reese was beautiful, feisty and smart. She ticked all my boxes. It's just a shame it was an accident, and she didn't like me the way I seemed to like her.

"Mr Hayes," the waiter returned with a bag of food.

"Thank you," I muttered, taking it from him and heading back into the cold. I wish I had my coat. I left it in the car when I hopped out and followed her home. Even that confused me, I have never chased a woman before, but I think it is because she is so adamant she hates me, it just makes me want her even more. The more she pushes against me, the stronger the pull towards her.

When you know you can't have something, you always want it more.

Fisting my hand in my pocket I pulled out two sets of keys. Smirking to myself at the shiny new key that I stole from front desk. I wasn't going to leave her alone. I hate the fact that she is in that apartment by herself, this way I can just pop in when I am in the area... or the building.

Little does she know I own that building, and guess who lives on the top floor in the penthouse?

Bingo.

You got it in one.

I was bound to her, her bound to me.

Whether she liked it or not.

Shivering, I approached the apartment block.

"Mr Hayes," Frank the doorman tipped his head.

"Frank," I smiled, stopping for a moment on the carpet that was laid out front of the building. "Go and get your coat and scarf, you'll freeze out here. Temperatures are plummeting tonight. I'll stand guard," I winked, a soft chuckle leaving me.

He nodded, rushing through the small side door and into the concierge office. Frank had worked here for as long as I could remember. He was in his late sixties and didn't want to retire. He lost his wife a few years ago so I suppose he likes to be busy. I don't see him as staff, I see him as family. He comes round for thanksgiving as well as Christmas. We both are loners together, but not this year. No, I had Reese.

It was the beginning of November; I didn't like the thought of her sitting in that apartment by herself at Christmas. But who am I kidding, she will probably have bigger plans than wanting to spend it with me.

Yes, I am a powerful man, I own a lot of businesses and buildings but in this line of work, I don't have friends. I have business associates and acquaintances, but not friends.

Well, apart from Frank.

Friends make you weak. Friends are envious of what you have spent years building from the ground up. That's the case in my experience. I am better off alone. That way, no one can screw me over.

Frank re-appeared with a scarf wrapped round his neck and his coat on.

"Keep warm Frank," I nodded to him before pushing into

the apartment lobby. The warmth danced over my skin which caused a shiver to run up my spine.

Heading down the hallway towards her door, I paused for a moment thinking I should knock. I decided against it, I knew her already. She wouldn't open it. Slipping the key into the door lock, I twisted it and let myself in. Placing the bag on the work surface, I unloaded the cartons and chopsticks onto the side. I had no clue what she liked so I got my favourites in hope that she would like them too.

I banged around in her cupboards to find two plates and cutlery. I filled two glasses with chilled wine and left it on the counter. She didn't have a table so standing and eating it was. Maybe I could buy her a small table, put it by the large window. That way she can look out while she eats. Shaking my head side to side I walked quietly to her bedroom, the door was ajar. I pushed it but she wasn't in there. Turning on my heel, my brows furrowed. Had she gone out? Her coat and bag were still hanging where I left them. I walked towards a closed door, waiting for a moment before I pressed my ear to the door. I could hear muffled whines. Twisting the brass doorknob I burst into the room.

There she was sitting in the tub with bubbles surrounding her and black tears rolling down her cheeks.

Her eyes widened as she tried to cover herself up, even though she didn't need to. I wasn't looking. She reached for her bath sheet and covered her wet body. Not really a wise move seeing as her sheet is now wet.

"Are you okay?" I asked, my eyes glued to her red rimmed ones.

"What do you think!?" She hissed at me as she stood from the water abruptly, the water whooshing and spilling over the top. She pulled the bath sheet tight round her petite frame and stormed past me and into her room.

Well fuck, I really did get to her.

I walked over, my shoes getting covered in the spilt bath

water and reached into the tub to let the water out. Drying my hands on the small hand towel that was hanging up, I then put it on the floor and tried to dry up as much of the water as I could. Turning, I walked back out into the lounge. I was sick of her trying to run from me.

Barging through her bedroom door, I saw her sitting on the edge of her bed wrapped up.

"Reese, I am really sorry for doing what I did to you," I whispered.

"It's not that Killian, sure it was a dick move but that's not what's got me upset." She shook her head side to side. Her blonde hair sat clung to her face as it dripped onto her lap, her green eyes looking up through her long lashes as she looked at me.

"What is it?" I asked, stepping towards her cautiously.

"I don't want to talk about it," her tongue darted out and licked one of her tears that had run onto her lip.

I wanted to taste her tears, taste her lips, her mouth on mine.

I crouched down in front of her, brushing my thumb pad across her cheek and catching a stray tear.

"I know you don't like me, but I am always here if you need me. Don't suffer alone," my voice was low, my breath shaky. Just that small bit of intimacy was enough to send a shockwave of current through to my heart. I loved the buzz I got off her. It was addicting.

She sniffed, her beautiful eyes looking deeply into mine, baring her soul for me to see. I could see the pain and grief as clear as day now. I felt like I could feel everything she was, and it was excruciating.

She was so pure.

She was once in a lifetime. My once in a lifetime.

Standing I stepped back to give her some space.

"Dinner is out in the kitchen when you're ready, take however long you need," I turned and walked out of her room before closing the door behind me. I inhaled deeply, walking towards the apartment door and closing it behind me. I had to leave her alone for the evening.

But tomorrow, tomorrow I would be back and every fucking day after that.

She was mine.

And that's the way I wanted it to stay. She needed me more than she knew. I was going to be everything she could want and more.

I was adamant to make it my mission.

Whether she wanted me or not, she wasn't going to get rid of me that easily. I was like a dog with a bone. I wouldn't give up. Never will I give up on her.

But she must stay my little secret for a while longer.

CHAPTER 14
REESE

Wearing an oversized tee and fluffy rainbow pyjama trousers, I padded out into the kitchen. My eyes scanned the room, but Killian wasn't here. I felt the surge of disappointment course through me. But then what did I expect? I have been nothing but a bitch to him, I'm surprised he came back earlier.

My stomach groaned as I smelt the food that was sitting on the counter in front of me. Walking over, I saw the two plates and the two glasses of wine.

"I'm such a brat," I sighed, leaning over the worktop and opening the cartons.

Noodles, rice, spring rolls and steamed dumplings. Picking the chopsticks up I looked at them strangely, I had never used these before. I thought going for the spring roll would be easiest, but I was fooled. Stabbing my chopstick through the spring roll and dipping it in the sauce they came with before taking a massive bite. My taste buds exploded; I hadn't realised how hungry I was.

Once I was finished, I boxed the leftovers and put them in the fridge. Pouring Killian's wine back into the open bottle, I grabbed my own wine and sat on the sofa in the deadly silence again.

Just me.

Sighing, I reached over for my phone, my finger hovering over his name, but I just couldn't bring myself to do it.

I was disgusted with myself and my behaviour tonight. Sure, I don't like him, but I don't have to be a nasty bitch to him.

Letting my phone drop down beside me, I finished my glass of wine.

Putting my empty glass in the sink and double locking the door, I took myself to bed.

The morning came too quickly. My sleep was shocking. I had so much going on in my mind that was overwhelmingly consuming that I spent most of the night with my eyes pinned to the ceiling. No amount of concealer was going to cover these puffy eyes of mine today.

Showering quickly, I pulled my blonde hair into a high ponytail and dressed in high waisted grey suit trousers and a fitted shirt.

I walked towards the door before stilling and looking at my hand, I didn't have my ring on. I contemplated walking out the door without it, but something inside was niggling at me to put it on. So, I did. Slipping the cheap gold ring onto my finger and stepping out the door before I had the chance to take it off again.

I was glad to get into the lobby of the offices, it was so cold outside. The temperature had fallen significantly over the last couple of days and today I was really feeling it. I wasn't sure if it was the lack of sleep that didn't help, but it was noticeable. Nodding a curt hello to the security guard, I whizzed through the turnstiles and straight into the lift. I shivered as I felt a chill dance up my spine. I saw the lift doors re-open, and for a moment I wished it was Killian that stepped inside, but it wasn't. It was an older woman who was dressed impeccably. She made me feel underdressed suddenly. I fidgeted nervously as I watched the lights hop to each floor. I was relieved when we stopped at my floor; strutting out I headed straight to my desk. I had some last bits to sort out before my lunch meeting with Harlen.

The morning slipped by quickly, no one interrupted me, not even Adele which was strange. But it seemed like she had other things on her mind instead of bugging me. My phone alarm rang, it was show time. Locking my computer and pushing away from the desk, I grabbed my bag and ran for the elevator. I didn't want to be late.

Throwing my dollars at the taxi driver, we pulled up outside *Sarabeth's*. I was nervous, my stomach was flipping, my heart was racing. I wanted this deal so bad.

My eyes widened as they took in the beautiful room around me. I didn't expect this. It was so decadent and had a beautiful rustic feel to it. The server approached me and took my name. He nodded and showed me to a quiet booth by the window. A sea of relief washed over me when I saw that Harlen wasn't here yet.

Okay cool, I had time to go over my notes.

Sitting down and putting my bag next to me, the server hovered.

"Can I get you anything ma'am?" she asked politely.

"I'll just have a glass of water while I am waiting, thank you," I smiled up at her. "Certainly."

She walked away.

I skimmed through my notes, I knew the questions I wanted to ask him. I just needed to do something that would wow him. Show him that we were the right company to take him and his name forward. That he needed us more than we needed him.

The waitress returned with a cup of water and placed it down on the table.

"Thank you," I muttered as I reached for the glass and bought it to my lips. I felt parched suddenly.

I drank half the glass before placing it back on the table. Checking my phone I had five minutes until our scheduled meeting. My brows pulled together for a moment, I hadn't heard from Killian, but then again why would I after the way I treated him last night.

I didn't have a moment more to think about it when I felt his presence, my eyes lifting I saw Killian strolling towards me. How in the ever-loving fuck did he know I was here?

"Wife," he greeted me, leaning down and kissing me on the cheek as he lingers for a moment.

"What are you doing here?" I whisper-shouted with a slight hiss in my tone.

"Can't a husband come to see his wife and wish her good luck?" he stood, hands fisted in his pockets. A pang of guilt shot through me.

"Thank you," I muttered, turning my attention back to my notes in front of me.

"You're welcome. Dinner tonight?" He asked as he rocked on the balls of his feet, his gaze burning into mine. I gave into the pull and turned to look up at him. He really was something else. Brown eyes that just invited you in, visible dark stubble coating his chin and strong jaw line. His dark hair tousled and messy, short enough to look smart, just long enough for me to run my fingers through. I wonder if it felt as soft as it looked.

"Reese," his delicious voice pulled me back round.

"Errr, I can't. I'm sorry. I have plans already." I said with a grimace, giving him a small shrug.

"Well, when can I see you? After?"

"Can I let you know?" I asked, my tone rushed. My eyes looking past him to see Harlen Laufer talking to the waitress. She turned and pointed in my direction with a smile on her face.

"What is there to let me know? It's either yes or no," his tone was short; I could hear the frustration.

"Yes, fine." I snapped as my eyes looked back up to him. "My meeting is here, can you go?" I shooed him away like he was an annoyance.

He smirked, his lips twitching.

"Please," I whispered.

He nodded and stepped back respectfully before turning and walking away.

My heart was drumming in my chest as I watched him look at Harlen before they brushed shoulders. I could see Killian clenching his jaw, his fists balled as he continued walking.

Exhaling deeply, I stood up to greet Harlen.

"Reese?" he questioned as he closed the gap between us.

"Yes," I smiled, "Hi Harlen, it's so nice to meet you." I held my hand out for him to shake.

"Nahhh, I don't do handshakes. I'm a hugger," he beamed, wrapping his arms around me and pulling me in. His accent surprised me. He wasn't American. He was Australian.

I felt awkward. I didn't like over affectionate strangers.

A nervous laugh bubbled out of me, as I stepped back to tuck myself back in the booth.

I took in his appearance, jet black hair, crystal blue eyes. He was clean cut, handsome and casual. He wore a leather jacket that covered a plunge v neck tee, black ripped skinny jeans and leather biker boots.

Not what I had in mind at all. Sitting down opposite me, I heard my phone vibrate. I gave it a glance.

Killian.

"Excuse me one moment," I muttered, unlocking my phone to see his message.

> KILLIAN
>
> Tell your friend to keep his fucking hands off what is mine, wife.

I rolled my eyes, locking my phone and dropping it into my bag where it couldn't distract me.

"Sorry about that."

"Ah kiddo, it's fine. Don't worry about it." He held his hand up and gave me a small smile. The waitress re-appeared handing us some menus.

"Thank you," my eyes scanned the menu.

"Have you eaten here before?" he asked, lifting his eyes from the menu for a moment. I shook my head from side to side.

"Mind if I order for you?" one of his brows lifted as he held my gaze.

"Nope," my voice was timid.

"We will have two of the lobster rolls and two margheritas."

I licked my lips. The lobster roll sounded delicious; my stomach groaned in agreement.

"How long have you been over in the US?" he asked as he sipped on his glass of water that the waitress brought him automatically.

"A few months," I nodded, my fingers slowly running up and down the glass of my own drink.

"How you finding it?"

"I like it," I smiled at him. "How about you?"

"Couple of years now, I came over when I started the show." He sat back, crossing his arms across his chest. "I'll never go back home."

"No?" I furrowed my brow at his statement. I could never rule out going back home, I would miss it too much, and I would miss my parents so much more. There is only so much video calling you can do. Even if I moved here, I would make a point of going back home. I would have too.

"I have nothing at home for me," his bright and wide small faltered for a moment as if he was remembering something, but he didn't let the façade slip for long before he was all toothy grin again.

"I see." I nodded; my head turned as I saw the waitress walk over to us with food. It smelt divine and looked like heaven.

"Can I get you kids anything else?" the older waitress asked, she was different to the one that seated us.

"Our drinks?" Harlen asked her, his tone was playful and not rude in the slightest.

"Oh shoot, I am sorry. Let me go and sort that out for you right now," she tsked, rolling her eyes before walking away and muttering to herself, her hands waving around on the air.

I stifled a laugh.

I reached for a chip and popped it into my mouth. "So Harlen, what is this proposition you have?"

"Wow, straight into the business talk," he laughed, "I like it, eager and ready for blood." He clenched his hand and banged it on the table making me jump. He was excitable. Like a big ball of energy.

"Well, I have this really boring event to go to on Saturday and I would love for you to be my date," he said while grabbing a handful of chips and shoving them into his mouth.

"Saturday is going to be a little too late," I admitted, the blush pinching my cheeks.

We were interrupted when the waitress came with a tray and put four margheritas down in front of us.

"There we go sweetness, on the house," she winked at Harlen before turning and walking back towards the bar.

"Result," he nibbled on his bottom lip and nodded his

head like one of those nodding dogs you see in the back of cars.

"Mm result indeed," my eyes widened for a moment, as I grabbed the glass and took a mouthful. Oh man it was delicious and could go down far too easily.

When I meet Connie tonight, I am ordering myself these.

"You were saying?" Harlen asked as he took a bite out of his roll.

"Saturday is going to be too late…" I felt so awkward.

"Late for what?" he looked a little confused.

"I have a deadline to sign you by Friday, if not then… well…" I winced at my words.

"Well, that's not going to work is it…" he sighed, pushing his plate away as he reached for his phone and started tapping.

He put the phone to his ear before holding his finger up and telling me he would be one moment. Stepping out of the booth he walked out the front door.

And I've blown it.

Shit.

CHAPTER 15

I WAS ANXIOUSLY DRUMMING MY FINGERS ON THE TABLE, MY appetite suddenly gone but my thirst growing. Downing both margheritas, my eyes stayed glued to where Harlen disappeared to. I couldn't lose my job. I had to win him back.

Pulling my phone out of my bag I had two messages from Killian. I ignored them. I didn't have time to read his stupid messages. I didn't know what to do, did I call Adele and tell her I fucked up? Do I call Connie and get her to try and calm me down or do I call my mum and beg her to book me a plane ticket home.

I could feel the cold sweat starting to prickle over my skin. My heart drummed in my chest, I couldn't calm it.

Reaching for Harlen's drink I knocked it back.

I stilled when I saw him walking back towards me, a sly smirk on his face as he sat opposite.

"Thirsty, were we?"

"Very." I nodded, blushing. Slightly embarrassed I had been caught. I could feel the alcohol warming the blood in my veins.

"It's sorted. You're coming with me on Saturday, and you have a three-day extension. So, depending how it goes on

Saturday, you could have a new signed actor on your books by the following Wednesday. Game face ready, baby?" he winked.

I swallowed hard.

"Born ready." I said with as much confidence as I could, but my trembling voice let me down and showed him how weak I was.

"Let's discuss, shall we?" he clicked his fingers and ordered another round of drinks. This time I went for a virgin margherita. I don't think Adele would be happy with a drunk Reese back in her office.

Sitting in the restaurant of the hotel, Connie was eyeing me.

"What?" I laughed as I took a mouthful of my cocktail.

"You seem different?" she huffed as she grabbed a breadstick from the middle of the table.

"I'm fine, just a little stressed out about this ball on Saturday. I have never been to something like this."

"I'll help you." She boasted a beautiful smile.

"You've been to a ball?" I asked, the look on my face showing her that I was shocked.

"I have, well only a couple when I was younger. My dad goes to things like this all the time. They're not too bad, bit boring but it's all normally for a good cause."

"You called him dad?" I smirked.

"I meant sperm donor…" she blushed. Seems to me she cares for her *sperm donor* a little more than she says.

"Yeah, this is for charity. A children's charity I believe." I shrugged.

"That's going to be heart-wrenching," she sighed, "But an amazing cause."

I nodded.

"How are things with you? It feels like it has been forever…" I pretended to think, putting my finger to my chin and pulling a confused face, "oh wait… it has." I poked my tongue out before laughing out loud.

"I have been busy," she said, flustered. Pulling her long brown hair off her neck as she fanned her slowly growing red face.

"With Kieran?" I asked.

She stared at me, it took her a moment before she dropped her hand and shook her head.

"Who?" I leant forward. She didn't say anything. "Connie, who have you been seeing?" I don't know why but I could feel my stomach knotting at the thought of something bad going on behind the scenes.

"Is something going on?" I lowered my voice now as I leant closer to her.

"No, no…" she replied, "nothing like that." Her head shook from side to side. "I have been seeing someone, but it's so new and it's going so well I just don't want to jinx it. Just trust me that I am okay though yea?" she reached across and squeezed my hand with hers.

I sighed, taking a moment before agreeing reluctantly.

"Thank you," she whispered before looking at her watch. "I'm sorry, but I've got to go. Want me to call you a cab?" she asked.

I shook my head, "I'm going to stay here for a bit, I'll speak to you tomorrow?" I smiled at her.

"Always," she smiled back before blowing me a kiss.

I settled the bill and moved to the bar. Ordering a bottle of water, I needed to knock the alcohol on the head. I had work tomorrow and I didn't want to be working with a hangover.

I sat and listened to the light chatter around me, a splinter of pain shattered through my heart. I missed just sitting and talking to Elijah. We would talk about the most random things. I never got those couples that just sit opposite each other during dinner and not say a word to each other. How can you not have anything to talk about? Something always happens, there is always something to talk about. Breathing out heavily, I turned slowly and looked around the room. It was busy for a Monday night. I agreed with myself that I would finish this drink, then I would head home. I needed an earlyish night and it had just gone eight.

Spinning back round to face the barman, I played with the edge of the beer mat he had given me. The hairs on the back of my neck stood, as I felt a shiver blanketing my skin.

"Mind if I join you?" Killian's voice ripped through me.

I shook my head.

I heard the bar stool drag along the floor before he sat down next to me.

His hand rested on my bare leg as he lent across and placed his lips at the shell of my ear. "You look beautiful as always," my skin burned, my stomach flipped.

A small smile crept onto my face.

"Can we go back to mine? Or to yours? I just feel like things have been a bit hasty between us... we haven't really had a chance to get to know each other since last weekend." He rubbed his lips together.

"Mine?" I breathed out. I didn't want to go back to his. I liked being home, and if I had enough, I could kick him out.

He nodded, a small hint of a glisten in his beautiful brown eyes.

Man was I a sucker for those eyes.

He threw a handful of dollars on the bar, laced his fingers through mine and pulled me off the stool. I couldn't help the butterflies that swarmed my stomach, the heat that burned down low in a place that hadn't felt this kind of heat in a long while.

The goosebumps erupted over my skin as his thumb brushed against the back of my hand as I followed him to my apartment.

I felt like we had a love hate relationship, but there is a thin line between love and hate isn't there?

The lift doors closed, and as soon as they were I felt his body against me, pinning me to the wall. His hands gripping my chin, lifting my head up to look at him.

"I didn't like you sitting on your little date today," his whispered, his breath on my face. He was so close, all I needed to do was edge forward slightly and our lips would meet.

"It wasn't a date," my voice was strong even though I was trembling on the inside.

"It looked like a date," he said through gritted teeth, his jaw clenching and ticking as his lips hovered over mine. Maybe I should just *fall* forward, just so I could kiss him. I imagined what his kiss would be like, but now I wanted to feel what it was like.

"You acting all possessive is a bit much don't you think? We have been married all of five minutes. We don't know each other…" I whispered.

"I am possessive over what is mine. And you, Reese, are mine," his voice was low.

I rolled my eyes.

"Roll your fucking eyes again Buttercup and see how I punish you," his voice was low and made between my legs pulse.

I swallowed hard, my eyes burning into his. The tension was thick, my heart was racing at a thousand miles per hour.

"You like the sound of that don't you, petal?" he smirked, letting go of my chin and stepping back away from me as the ping of the lift echoed. Turning on his heel he stalked out into the hallway, holding his hand out for me to take.

I didn't take it.

I walked past him and headed towards my door.

I wasn't going to be an easy accomplishment, and I wasn't going to sleep with him. Unlocking the door, I dropped my bag and kicked my shoes off as I fell onto my sofa. I felt wrecked. The high of today finally taking its toll.

Killian sauntered over to me, his dark eyes trailing up and down my body as I lay on the sofa. He sat on the edge, lifting my feet onto his lap as he began rubbing my tired feet.

I moaned. Oh, wow that felt good.

"Nice?" he smirked; his eyes pinned to mine.

I nodded. "Very."

"Anything for you, wife."

I blushed slightly; I don't know what it was about him that got me flustered.

Placing my feet back down beside him on the sofa, he stood and shrugged his suit jacket off his shoulders and laid it over the arm of where I was laying.

Pushing up I walked towards the kitchen and flicked the kettle on.

"Tea?" I asked, looking over my shoulder, but he was there, behind me, his hands pushing around to my stomach.

I ignored the feelings he made me feel. I couldn't do this.

Turning round, I shook my head softly from side to side. Pressing my hands on his hard chest, I didn't want to acknowledge the burn that I felt from touching him, or the way my blood rushed through my veins. Sparks coursed through me, re-igniting feelings that I had pushed far away. Feelings that I hadn't felt for a very long time.

I pushed him back with a little more force now.

"I can't," I whispered, dropping my head. I felt his hand on my chin, tilting my head back so I looked up at him.

"Why not?" his voice was low, "You can't deny that you feel this too."

I felt the breath in the back of my throat catch.

I shook my head again, rendered speechless all of a sudden.

Shoving him harder now so he had to step back, I turned to ignore the burning that was pumping through me.

Was I denying how I felt? And did he really feel it or was he just saying it because he was desperate for sex?

Grabbing two mugs out and throwing a tea bag in each one, I added the boiling water from the tea pot that whistled on the hob and filled the cups. I needed to get a plug-in kettle, it was so much easier. Pouring a dash of milk in both, I spun to see Killian still standing there. Eyes hooded, devouring me.

Pushing a cup into his hand I walked past him and sat up one end of the sofa. I needed to put some distance between us. Killian took the hint and sat at the other end.

The silence fell between us, my eyes were staring ahead but I could feel his eyes on me.

"How did your meeting go?" he asked as he brought the cup rim to his lip and took a mouthful, his brows lifting in surprise.

"Have you never had tea before?"

"No, it's…" he stopped for a moment before taking another mouthful. "It's nice but I feel like it's missing something," he admitted. Placing my tea on the coffee table in front of us I walked towards the kitchen and picked up the sugar pot. I have gotten so used to making tea for myself I forget to ask people how they want theirs.

"Here, try this," I say with a smile as I drop a teaspoon of sugar into his tea before giving it a stir. He eyed me suspiciously before taking another mouthful.

A delectable groan left his mouth that warmed the inside of my legs. Fuck if he groaned like that with a bit of sugar, imagine what he would sound like if I was pleasuring him. How would he react if I fell to my knees now and tasted him, pleasuring him until he hit his climax and pumped into my mouth.

"Perfect," he purred as he smiled up at me.

"Good," I quipped, rushing into the kitchen, and placing the sugar back down on the worktop before I joined him again.

"Why are you fighting what is inevitable?" His question threw me, hitting me out of the blue

"Inevitable?" I scrunched my nose up.

"Yes." His tone was short and snappy.

"I'm not. This," I moved my index finger between the both of us, "this is not inevitable. This is a drunken fucking nightmare."

He whistled through his teeth before letting out a low laugh.

"Oh Buttercup, you really don't get it do you...?" he placed his cup down on the table and edged closer to me.

"Get what?" I whispered, my fingers tightening their grip around my cup as I edged towards the arm of the sofa. His eyes dropped to my legs as his hand touched my thigh, gripping a little harder now.

"I'm not letting you go..." his eyes flicked up to meet mine which volleyed back and forth between his.

"We're getting this farce of a marriage annulled."

"And what if I don't want too?" I could hear the frustration that was lacing his voice.

"You don't have a choice." I spat through gritted teeth, pushing him off me and standing away from him.

He didn't move from his slightly hunched over position on the sofa. How could it be possible to find this guy drop dead gorgeous but also detest him at the same time?

"I think you should go," I turned my head so I was staring out the window. I didn't want to look at him.

He didn't say anything, but I heard him walk towards me. He towered over me, his hand moving to the base of my throat as he wrapped his fingers round it.

"I won't give up easily petal," his lips pressed to the shell of my ear as he whispered, causing goosebumps to smother over my skin.

"Let me take you out Saturday."

My hand shot up and wrapped around his wrist as I yanked it away from my skin.

"I already have plans," I licked my lips, smirking at him.

"With who?" his jaw ticked, clenching and unclenching as he waited for my response.

"Harlen," I said a little louder than I should have.

"What?" He growled, his dark eyes narrowing on me. He didn't like that answer.

"You heard me." Pushing him away from me I walked towards the front door, unchaining it and opening it wide for him.

He stormed over to me; I could see the rage etched over his face.

"You aren't going."

"Sorry? Who do you think you are?" I shouted at him; I didn't care that the door was open.

"Your husband."

"Might as well be fake husband." I rolled my eyes, "I'm going." Crossing my arms across my chest and holding my own.

"Like fuck you are," he said through clenched teeth.

I felt my own rage brewing. Who did he think he was? The arrogant, narcissistic piece of shit. I dropped my arms before slapping him hard around the face. My eyes widened as he stood tall and steady. He didn't falter. Just stood there like fucking goliath.

His eyes darkened as they hooded, he grabbed my cheeks, shoving me against the wall before his lips crashed into mine. I could have pushed him off, I could have refused to open my mouth… but I didn't. I let him in, let his tongue invade my mouth as it danced with my own. This was so much more than I imagined. His lips were rough and hard on mine, his kiss was raw. It was as if my kiss was the only thing that was going to save him, as if kissing me was the only way for him to get the last of the oxygen. As much as the kiss was amazing, sense finally crept over me as I shoved him away.

"How dare you?" I snapped, stepping towards him and shoving him again. But I didn't stop. It felt good to let some of that rage seep through. I shoved him again, this time he stepped back. I smirked up at him. Compared to him, I was tiny. He was tall, broad, and heavy. I was no match for him, but it didn't stop me from going at him.

"Finished?" he taunted me, stepping closer to me as he pinned me back to the wall.

I panted; my eyes glued to his as I saw the humour in them. Slapping his chest hard over and over, he grabbed my face hard and smirked at me.

I don't know what happened, but something inside me snapped. My hungry eyes burned into his, words stayed unspoken between us and all I felt was desire. Burning, raging desire. My hands flew to his hair, entwining my fingers through his brown locks. His mouth covered mine before his hands moved from my cheeks, skimming down my body and ran under my bum, lifting me up effortlessly. My legs wrapped around his waist as I clung to him. Pinning me against the wall, his pelvis pressed into me. I could feel how hard he was, fuck. I felt my insides melting, the apex between my thighs burning. His fingers wrapped round the buttons of my shirt before ripping them open. Holy shit.

His lips crashed into mine, his large hands roaming over my bare flesh. Pulling his lips from mine, they moved to my jaw, my neck, my collar bone, nipping as he continued. His fingers pulled on my bra strap, slipping them down my arms so he could get to what he wanted. Pursing his lips round my small, pert breasts, licking and sucking as he did. My stomach knotted and twisted as the pleasure coursed through me. My hands tugging onto his hair, my small moans escaping my lips as he continued. I forgot what this felt like. To be worshipped and pleasured in this way again. His skilful mouth concentrated on every part of my bare skin before the primal animal returned.

"I need to fuck you, Buttercup," he growled against my skin.

"Then fuck me," I panted, lifting his head to kiss me. I needed his lips on mine.

Holding me tightly he walked towards my bedroom, kicking the door closed behind him as he dropped me onto the bed.

Unbuttoning his belt, he pushed his trousers and boxers down in one swift move. I perched myself up on my elbows. My torn shirt still on, my eyes trailed down his body to see what he was packing. And he was fucking packing.

Hard, thick and fucking beautiful.

His fingers worked quickly as he undone his shirt and let it fall to the floor before leaning down. His arm moving forward, his hand cupping my covered pussy as he shoved me up the bed towards the headboard.

"You are wearing too much," he growled as he crawled over me, his fingers unbuttoning my trousers and tugging them down my legs.

I had small black cotton shorts on. No fancy lacy knickers. I was a comfort kind of girl. Hooking his fingers in the side of them, they were down and off in one swift movement.

I covered my face, the blush creeping over my skin. His fingers trailed and skimmed up from my hip bone, dancing across my stomach before he rolled my hard nipple between his fingers, his other hand gripped onto my thigh.

"I am going to own you; you will never want for another man again," he growled, his lips lowering round my nipple as he bit and nipped, then sucked hard. A pang shot through my lower stomach. His hand moved from my thigh before slipping between my legs, two fingers pushing into me harshly. My back arched slightly, my breast pushing into his mouth. I heard him groan, my eyes watching him. Slowly pumping his fingers in and out of me, stretching me and getting me ready. I was ready to combust. Every sensation was alive and ready to explode. I felt myself tightening around his thick fingers, but he pulled them out just before I could. Pushing them between his lips, he licked them clean as he knelt back and sat between my parted legs.

"So fucking beautiful." Growling, he leant over me, grabbing one of my knees and pushing my leg up and wide as he slipped straight into me. My breath catching at the back of my throat at the feel of the size of him. My pussy stretching round him in the most delicious way.

I didn't care about anything from that moment on. All I wanted was to feel wanted by this beautiful man.

Pulling his cock out to the tip, he stilled for a moment before pushing back into me hard and fast.

I cried out.

He done it again.

His eyes fell between our connected bodies, watching as he teased me. Teased us both.

His fingers gripped and tightened around my knee, his other hand held me down as he gripped my hip before he rode me hard. His cock filling me to the hilt, stroking and hitting my g-spot. "Yes, oh fuck yes," I cried out, leaning up on my elbows to watch him fuck me. Gliding his hand up my body, he wrapped his fingers round my throat and ploughed into me. My whole body smothered in goosebumps as my pussy clenched around him.

"There's my good girl, taking my cock like it was made just for you. Come for me Buttercup, come for your husband. I want to feel you come over my cock," he growled as his hips thrust faster into me, the sound of our flesh smacking against each other was turning me on even more than I already was. "Good luck getting that fucking annulment now," I heard the taunt but ignored it.

"You're mine, do you understand?" he grunted.

"Yes," I breathed. "Killian," I cried his name out, my whole body trembling as a shiver danced over me before I came hard. My orgasm splintering through me, my head tipping back as I saw stars.

"My good fucking girl," he spat through gritted teeth, his fingers tightening slightly round my throat as he orgasmed, emptying himself inside of me. I fell back, collapsing as I panted, Killian laying over me.

"Well wife, you are everything I thought you would be and more," he whispered, pressing his lips to my head before rolling on his side and behind me. His arm draped over me, pulling me into him before I fell into darkness.

CHAPTER 16
KILLIAN

Rolling over in a bed that don't belong to me, my arm hit an empty spot next to me. My eyes pinged open as I saw that Reese had gone. I could still smell her scent, vanilla with a hint of peach. Pinching my brows together, I slowly sat up and looked around the room. Clothes discarded everywhere, a smirk pulling one side of my lip up.

Sign of a good night.

I knew she was going to be a good fuck, but last night surpassed all my expectations. Her tight pussy, how she stretched and took my cock like it was made for her. Last night was just a taste of what I had to come. She was mine.

Throwing back the covers, I padded over to where my clothes were and grabbed my boxer briefs. Pulling them up, I reached for my shirt and pulled it over my shoulders. Opening the bedroom door I saw Reese standing at the coffee machine on her phone.

I walked slowly towards her, clearing my throat as I did so she didn't think I was eavesdropping.

"I gotta go," she says hushed, "I'll speak to you later." She smiles into the phone and cuts it off before placing it face down on her worktop.

"Morning," she chirped, turning and handing me a cup of coffee. My eyes roamed freely up and down her body. She was slender and petite. She was wearing a satin long sleeved pyjama shirt and matching booty shorts. She was perfect. The thought of her long, toned legs wrapped round my waist again made my cock twitch.

"Morning," I smiled at her, taking a mouthful of the black coffee she had given me. "No cream?" I asked.

"There is milk in the fridge if you want it," she gave a small shrug of the shoulders as she walked towards the sitting room. I loved her British accent, she sounded sexy as hell.

I didn't bother with the milk. Just sauntered after her like a fucking love-sick puppy.

I sat on the armchair, my long fingers drumming on the arm as I pinned my eyes on her.

"Has anyone ever told you that you look like Daniel Gillies?" Her question threw me out.

"Who?" I looked at her confused, I had no idea who this Daniel Gillies was.

"That's a no then," she laughed, "He plays a character in a tv show called *The Originals*. You just kind of look like him, that's all," she smiled, but it slipped quickly as she lost herself in thought.

"Is he as good looking as me?"

"He is so much better," she winked before knocking her coffee back, she stood from the sofa and walked back to the kitchen.

"Where you going?" I asked her, turning and watching her like a hawk.

"Work." She smiled as she placed her cup into the sink.

"Stay home?"

"No," she winked again, as she headed towards the bedroom. I shot up and followed her, she rolled her eyes when she saw me appear.

"Saturday?"

"What about it?" she said as she jumped up and down, pulling her work trousers up.

"Go out with me."

She laughed, shaking her head side to side as she looked to do her button up.

"Nope."

I felt the aggravation begin to bubble inside of me. My jaw clenched.

"What do you mean, no?"

"I mean, no," she laughed as she grabbed a white blouse and slipped it on.

"Don't tell me you're still going out with fucking Harlen."

"Got it in one baby," she taunted me as she brushed her long, golden hair.

"You aren't fucking going," I growled, "did you not hear what I said last night? You belong to me. You are mine." I stepped towards her, my arms snaking round her waist as I pulled her against my body.

"I did hear you, but Killian, I am going. You aren't going to stop me, nor am I going to listen to you or be manipulated by you in any way." She gave me this sickly-sweet smile, her green eyes glistening as she looked up at me, before shoving me away.

As she spun away from me, I grabbed her wrist, pulling her back into me.

"Tell me you're not going." My lips pressed to the shell of her ear as I whispered. I heard her breath hitch, my hand skimming up her side before wrapping my fingers round her throat and tipping her head back as I nipped at the bare flesh of her neck.

"Tell me," I asked again as I continued.

"I'm going," she snapped, pulling my hand from her throat and stepping away from me.

"What didn't you understand last night? I told you that you're mine. Mine."

"Yes Killian, so you have said. Many times." She rolled her fucking eyes at me. Pushing her in the back, she fell on her front on the bed, I knelt behind her, pinning her so she couldn't move. Unbuttoning her pants, I slipped them down along with her cute panties and revealed her bare ass.

Perfect. Rubbing the palm of my hand over her cheek, I leant over her back before whispering in her ear.

"Remember when I said to you that if you roll your eyes at me again, I'll punish you?"

She didn't respond, but she nodded. Gliding my fingers across her cheek, I slipped them between her legs, swirling my fingertips at her wet opening. Her pussy so ready for me.

I heard a small moan escape her.

"Tell me…" my voice was low as I continued teasing her, "are you still going out on Saturday?" slipping my two fingers into her a little more now, stretching her.

She whimpered.

I continued.

"Buttercup, I can't hear you."

"No," she breathed.

"There's my good girl, all it took was a little persuading…" I trailed off, biting my bottom lip as I slipped my fingers out of her. Kneeling back on my knees, I pulled her up. She spun round, flustered and clearly a little pissed off that I didn't finish. Standing slowly, my head craned down as I looked at her.

"You're a dick," she spat as she yanked her pants back up.

I smirked.

I know.

She bent down and picked my suit trousers up along with my jacket that was laid on her bed and stormed past me.

"Reese…" I said low and slow as I followed her out of the room.

She unlocked her apartment door and threw my clothes out into the lobby, then turned and picked up my shoes from the floor and launched them one by one down the corridor.

She stood proud, dusting her hands off together as they clapped.

"I am still going on Saturday; your little show didn't work. Now get out of my fucking home," she snarled at me.

I was seething. The rage oozed out of my pours, the red mist slowly covering my eyes.

I stepped towards her, pushing her against the wall.

"I will see you Saturday," I said through gritted teeth. I could feel the heat radiating off her, her eyes volleyed back and forth from mine. She didn't give a shit.

"You won't," she smirked, shoving me away then sticking her middle finger up. "I fucking hate you," she pushed me again towards the open door. "I can't wait for our annulment."

I laughed a deep, throaty laugh as I stepped out of the door. Turning to face her, the smirk was dancing across my lips.

"We fucked baby, there is no more annulment." I continued laughing before she slammed the door behind me.

CHAPTER 17
REESE

Who did he think he was? My good mood had been ruined by him. The last words he said to me circled round and round in my mind. *We fucked baby, there is no more annulment.* He wouldn't do that to me… would he? I shook my head from side to side quickly. I am not giving him another moment of mind time. Pulling my hair into a ponytail, I slipped my shoes on and grabbed my bag before running for the door. I didn't want to get a taxi, I wanted to walk to clear my head of a certain individual. Again, he who shall not be named.

I must admit though, the sex last night was phenomenal, who knew sex could feel that good. But that was a momentary slip. It won't happen again.

A pain seared through my heart at what I had done. I knew I couldn't stay celibate for the rest of my life after Elijah, but it still didn't make it easier. Each time I slept with someone new, I felt like I lost a little bit more of him. Bit by bit, little by little, piece by piece.

The cold air nipped at my skin, my eyes watering in the blistering cold. I couldn't believe how quick the temperature had changed. We didn't get weather like this back home in

England. My phone buzzed in my pocket, grabbing it I saw Connie's name. I smiled.

Slipping my earphones in and waiting for them to connect, I answered.

"Good morning," my breath was short as the cold air filled my lungs, my legs moving faster so I warmed up.

"Morning, my little sugar plum fairy. How was your evening?" she asked, I could hear people talking behind her. She was obviously on reception duty. Her favourite.

"Evening was…" I stopped for a moment before nibbling my lip, I couldn't tell her. Not yet. "Quiet," I scoffed. "Yours?"

"Eh…" she stilled; I could hear the smile in her voice.

The phone line fell silent for a moment. "Any idea on thanksgiving yet?" she asked.

She had been asking if I wanted to spend thanksgiving with her to save me being alone, but I thought I would have gotten home. But what with everything going on with Harlen and Killian, going home doesn't seem the right thing to do right now.

"Well, if it's not too late, I would love to spend it with you," I smiled.

"Yay! This is so exciting! I can't remember the last time I had a friend over, I'll let my dad know."

I swallowed hard.

"Your dad?" I stammered slightly, "I thought we would just be together."

"Who do you think is cooking the turkey?" she scoffed, "it isn't going to be me, duh."

"Oh man, your dad isn't going to want me there, it's fine, I'll sort out a microwave dinner meal," I waved my hand through the air, my eyes traveling up as I looked at the tall building that I worked in.

"You will not!" Connie shrieked.

I rolled my eyes, my cheeks burning as I thought back to this morning before the lust turned to rage.

"Only if you're sure," I said quietly.

"Positive."

"Why aren't you with your mums?"

"They're away for their anniversary or some shit," I heard her snicker, "so daddy dearest it is."

"Ah okay! I've got to go Con, I'm at work. Dinner tomorrow?" I asked softly.

"Dinner sounds perfect."

"Bye Con," I said, cutting the phone off and slipping it into my bag. Inhaling deeply, I pushed through the rotating glass doors and headed straight for my desk.

I HAD JUST COME BACK FROM LUNCH WITH JULIANNE, WAVING BYE to her as I continued to where I sat when I stilled. Sitting in my chair with his feet on my desk was the devil himself. My husband.

"What do I owe the pleasure?" I rolled my eyes, stopping in front of my desk.

"Eyes," he winked, his eyes trailing up and down my body.

I stood waiting for him to answer my earlier question. He just sat there fucking smirking.

"What do you want, Killian?" I snapped now; my arms crossed in front of me.

"Just wanted to see my wife, is that okay?" his fingers pressed into the bottom of his chin.

"Don't bullshit me," my voice was low as I leant across the desk, pressing my hands flat to the surface.

Now he rolled his eyes at me, kicking his feet off my desk he sat up straight in my chair.

"Do I have to have a reason?" he asked, his eyes glued to mine.

I didn't answer. I suppose he didn't.

"Can I have my chair back, I am busy." My tone was

clipped, dropping my arms as I walked around the side of my desk.

"Yup, the lady I want to see is just walking in..." his eyes moved from mine as he watched Adele walk towards us. Killian pushed up, done his suit jacket up and began walking towards where Adele was and I just stood there, like a fucking moron watching. Adele didn't even look at me as she walked past, just held her head high, smirking. Killian fell into step behind her, stopping before her office and winking at me before the door closed.

Ugh.

I couldn't help but feel tense the whole time Killian was in there. I couldn't see anything because of the stupid frosted glass. The bitter taste coated my tongue at my thoughts. What if he was fucking her in there? And more importantly, why the fuck did I care? I wasn't the jealous type, but what didn't help was the fact that he had his beautiful dick inside me last night and now there was a small chance he was balls deep in her. I shuddered at the thought.

I wasn't a jealous person, and green definitely wasn't my colour but I was wearing a pretty shade of it right about now. I shouldn't even be jealous. Our marriage and relationship are a farce. It was nothing, we were nothing. I am being silly, I knew that we couldn't even stand each other if I was being honest, there was just a sexual attraction. That's all.

Scrolling up and down on my work document, I couldn't seem to get going. I knew what I needed to do; I had a check list of work piling up around me. Yet my fucking mind was in that office with them.

Chances were that Killian wasn't getting his glorious cock sucked off by the dragon behind that door, they were no doubt in a boring meeting. Yes, that was it. A boring meeting.

Slipping my earphones in, I blasted *Blondie* through them. I needed a distraction. And she was the perfect choice.

An hour later and halfway through *Sunday Girl* I saw

Adele's office door open. Killian walked out before turning and shaking her hand. I dropped my eyes quickly and focused on the task in front of me. I didn't want to show him for one second that he had invaded my thoughts.

My stomach rolled as she gave him a sickly smile, her eyes flicking over to me before she stepped back and closed her door.

The sound of Killian's shoes clicked along the floor as he stopped in front of my desk. Leaning over, he grabbed my earphone out and put it into his ear. His brows pinging up as he heard the chorus of *Sunday Girl*.

Pushing off my chair, I snatched it from his ears.

"Don't touch what's not yours," I snarled at him, sitting back in my chair and shoving the earphone back in my ear.

He removed it again.

"But you are mine, so technically I can touch them," he let out a soft chuckle.

"I'm not yours," I shook my head, "Do you just come here to annoy me? Because, unlike you, I am busy. I actually have to do work here to get paid." My tone was sharp as I averted my eyes back to my screen.

"Oh, I am *very* busy with work," he glanced over at Adele's office and licked his lips slowly.

"You're disgusting, get away from me," I shooed him away like the annoyance he was. He walked round to the side of me, lowering his lips against my ear.

"You didn't think I was disgusting when you took my dick last night, Buttercup."

I stilled, my stomach flipping, the familiar burn warming my belly before moving between my legs.

"Last night didn't happen. It was a mistake." I swallowed hard before clearing my throat.

"Oh baby, it happened. Your moans are still replaying over in my head."

I inhaled deeply. I could feel the tension between us, the

pull that was gravitating us towards each other, but I couldn't give in again. Last night was a moment of weakness.

"Keep going Killian, I dare you," I grit out.

He straightened up, a cocky smirk on his face.

"I want you to spend thanksgiving with me next week," his voice was low, his hands fisted into his pockets.

"Sorry, I'm busy," I didn't even give him the satisfaction of looking at him.

"With who?" I could hear how thick his voice was, his jaw must ache from how much he clenches it.

"Harlen," I smirked. I wasn't, but he didn't know that.

"You better be joking Reese," he snarled as he pushed his hand through his luscious locks in frustration.

"Or what?" I taunted, turning in my chair to look up at him, "You going to stop me?" I shook my head from side to side before returning to my work.

He didn't say anything, just turned on his heel and stormed out of the office like a raging bull. Good riddance.

My phone rang, flashing Adele's name. Clicking it onto speaker I answered.

"Yup," the frustration clear in my voice.

"A minute." She snapped then the phone went dead.

Here we go.

Walking into her room with a spring in my step I knocked before waiting to be called in. Opening the door, I plastered a shit eating grin on my face.

"You wanted to see me?" I smiled as I stood, closing the door behind me.

"Why did I see Killian Hayes storm away from your desk just a moment ago?" she pressed her fingers into her chin as she waited for me to answer.

"I'm not sure. He was asking me what my plans were for thanksgiving, then his phone rang, something about his STD results being back and that he needed to see them urgently," I shrugged, clicking my tongue on the roof of my mouth.

I watched as her eyes widened. My head dropped slightly, my jaw becoming lax.

"Oh…" I breathed, thumbing behind me, "Oh…" I feigned realisation kicking in. "Are you and him a thing? Shit, sorry…" I winced. "I would give him a call if I were you."

She didn't say anything, but then why would she? I had just got my validation that they were… are… or at least had slept together at some point.

"Will that be all?" I locked my index fingers as I asked her quietly.

She shooed me away; giving her a polite, curt nod, I turned on my heel before that shit eating grin I told you about spread so much further on my face. Before I was even out the door, her phone was in her hand.

Game on Killian.

CHAPTER 18
REESE

Twenty missed calls.

Twenty.

I still continued to ignore Killian. I was angry. Real fucking angry.

Turning my phone off, I threw it into my bag while I sat quietly in the back of the taxi. I just wanted to get home. I was frozen. A nice soak in the tub is just what the doctor ordered.

Passing the driver his money, I grabbed my bag and walked into my apartment block before heading straight for the lift. I needed to get mentally prepared for my date with Harlen and I was looking forward to it so much more now.

After my bath, I slipped my ring off and dropped it into my underwear drawer. That can stay in there for the foreseeable.

Wrapping a towel around my body I padded out to the kitchen and poured myself a large glass of wine. Heading back to my room, I heard a bang on the door.

I ignored it, knowing full well who it was.

Bang bang bang.

"Go away!" I shouted, slamming my bedroom door shut.

Standing on the other side of the door, I took a sip of my wine, smiling to myself that he listened to my request.

Oh, how wrong was I to underestimate Killian Hayes.

"Reese!" His voice bellowed through my apartment. The shock was evident on my face when I opened my bedroom door to see a raging Killian in my apartment.

"How did you get in?!" I screamed, pulling my towel tight to my body.

"A fucking STD, really!?" His voice was low as he growled at me.

I snorted a laugh before rubbing my lips together.

"Well, you should be more careful," I tried so hard to hold it together, sipping my wine.

"I'm not fucking laughing Reese."

"How's Adele? I hope she hasn't caught anything." He was pissed. His eyes were almost black, the hot air breathing through his nose filled the silent room.

"Stop talking," he growled as he stepped towards me, his hands cupping my face as his mouth covered mine. His hungry tongue darting past my lips and caressing mine. My wine glass fell from my hand and landed on the rug. But I didn't care at this moment.

My arms hooked around his neck as he dropped one of his hands from my face and pulled the towel away from me. I automatically wrapped my legs round his waist before he sat me on the edge of the worktop in the kitchen.

"I am so fucking mad at you," his voice was low, shaky as he tried to restrain his rage.

"And I am so fucking angry with you," I retorted back, "I knew you were fucking Adele," I spat, I couldn't stop the vile taste that crept into my mouth.

"The only one I am fucking is you." A calmness replaced the rage in a second.

"I don't believe you." My fingers were laced around the back of his neck as my eyes burned into his. The air was thick around us, this hate and pushing and pulling was unbearable, but it worked somehow. The smell of him filled my senses, an oaky musk coated in aloe vera with a hint of cotton. A weird combination but it smelt good on him.

"I don't lie," he whispered as his rough hands grabbed the small mounds that were my breasts, squeezing hard before his tongue flicked and licked my pert nipple. His hot mouth sucking expertly, his teeth grazing over my exposed skin. My head fell back as the pleasure ripped through me.

"Have I fucked Adele… yes," he muttered against my skin. I ignored the feelings of betrayal and the roll of nausea that crashed through me. "But not since I married you." His lips trailed down, his hands skimming down my small curves before they landed on my thighs, gripping my skin tighter. "It's only been you since then," he breathed, falling to his knees and pushing my legs wide.

"You're such a brat, do you know that?" he asked as he looked up at me through his lashes, his brown eyes glistening.

Pulling my bottom lip between my teeth I bit down hard.

"But you're my brat," he growled as he parted my pussy lips with his tongue, licking and sucking over my clit. My fingers wrapped round the edge of the worktop as I tightened my grip. His tongue glided up and down my folds, swirling at my opening before sucking my clit hard.

My head fell forward, lust taking over as I watched him. He was still in his suit, on his knees in front of me. His tongue buried deep inside of me, while I sat on my worktop completely naked as he showed me new realms of pleasure.

Pushing the tip of his finger at my opening, he plunged deep into me as his tongue flicked over my nub. I felt my walls clamp and tighten.

"Killian," I cried out. He didn't let up, his tongue moved quicker now, circling as his finger pumped in and out of me, curling to stroke my g-spot over and over.

My legs began to tremble, a shiver dancing over my skin as I came, my orgasm crashing through me like a freight train.

I was breathless, but my eyes stayed on him as he pulled his finger out and sucked it dry, the whole time he had his eyes on me. Standing slowly, he grabbed my cheeks with his hand, squeezing them before dipping his tongue into my open mouth and kissing me. The air snatched from my lungs, causing them to burn at the loss. But he didn't stop, I didn't want him to stop. His kiss was fierce and rough. His spare hand skimmed up my bare thigh, gliding his fingertips across my hip bone, continuing up my side. Rolling my still hard nipple in his finger and thumb before his fingers carried on over my shoulder and down my arm. They stopped at my hand that was still curled round the worktop. Pulling away, his eyes fell to my fingers before they burned back towards me.

"Where is your ring?" his jaw clenched before he nibbled on the inside of his lip.

"I took it off," I shrugged.

He stormed away from me and into my room. I rolled my eyes, slipping off the worktop. Moment over. Rushing behind him I grabbed the towel off the floor and wrapped it around my frame.

He was rooting through my drawers when he smirked, his eyes focused on something in my underwear drawer.

Oh shit.

He pulled out the silver vibrator Connie bought me a few months back.

"And who is this?" he asked, one of his brows shooting up.

"His name is Harlen," I chewed on the inside of my cheek. His head snapped round so quickly, his eyes darkening again as he stalked towards me. Vibrator in one hand, ring in the other. He stopped in front of me, sliding the ring back on to my finger.

"I mean it Reese, take it off again, I will fucking super glue it to your finger," he growled. I snorted.

"Now get on the fucking bed, legs wide for me..." he smirked, pulling my towel from me.

And I did as he asked.

"Such a good girl, this is the only other cock that is allowed inside of you," he leaned down and kissed me on the forehead. He ran the cold, silver vibrator through my folds, causing a gasp to leave me at how cold it was on my sensitive skin. "You're going to take this like the fucking brat you are, and you're not to come until I tell you to..." he licked his lips, his eyes watching as he slipped the vibrator into me. "Do you understand me, wife?"

CHAPTER 19
REESE

The nerves in my belly were unsettling. I had no idea what I was going into this evening, and I didn't like it. I felt unprepared. Connie sorted me out a dress; work was so hectic that I didn't have a chance to slip out and choose one for myself. Killian had kept a bay, and it made me feel a little uneasy. Maybe he was starting to get fed up with me. He had hardly been at work, and when he was at work, he was locked in Adele's office which annoyed me. Then once he was done, he walked past me as if he never knew me. And that really got to me.

I sat on the edge of my bed in my short set waiting for Connie. She wanted to come and play dress up for the afternoon. I was grateful because I was useless at things like that. I was tomboy, I didn't do the girlie things that I should. I can't even follow a simple YouTube video. I sat tapping my thumbs on my screen. I wanted to message Killian, but the stubborn streak in me wouldn't allow it. He was obviously still sulking about me calling my vibrator Harlen, or he was annoyed that I wasn't going to spend thanksgiving with him. Either way, he had to man the fuck up. He must have been late thirties, that was just a guess though, but he needed to start acting his age and not a fucking teenager. The buzzer went, and I dropped my phone before dashing to the door. Peeping through the small hole in the door, I saw Connie with a suitcase, a dress bag and champagne. A slither of excitement shot through me as I opened the door.

"You ready to be Cinderella-ed."

"That's not even a word," I giggled as I stepped aside, letting her in.

"It is," she rolled her eyes. "Okay, you don't seem too bad. I can work with this," her hand lifted up and down my body.

"Gee, thanks," I rolled my eyes, my cheeks heating at the thought of what Killian done to me earlier in the week for rolling my eyes.

"Now, chop, chop," she sung as she shoved the chilled bottle of champagne into my hand. "Pop the bottle, I'll meet you in the bedroom," she smirked, wiggling her eyebrows.

"In your dreams," I laughed out loud, shaking my head as I walked towards the kitchen. Grabbing two glasses, I popped the cork and watched it fizz slightly before pouring out some of the golden liquid. I took a quick sip, the bubbles popping on my tongue. It wasn't the best I had tasted, but it also wasn't the worse.

Slipping back into the bedroom, my dress bag was hanging up on the wardrobe and Connie had spread all her make-up out on my dressing table.

"Right, my beautiful, come come…" she smiled at me, patting the stool with one hand, the other reaching for her glass. I smirked, putting the glass into her hand. She took a big mouthful, wincing slightly.

"Oh wow, that is shocking." She laughed, placing it on the dressing table. She spun quickly, clapping her hands together. "Let's do this."

I swallowed hard.

"Yes, let's."

An hour later and she was finishing up my make-up. I

begged for her to keep it natural. I didn't want to have a cake face. I hated when make-up looked so thick on skin that it went all lumpy and cakey.

She tousled my golden, honey blonde hair into beach waves. Harlen assured me I didn't have to be over the top, and the fact that Connie had been to one or two of these things, she could back him up.

"Perfecto," she clapped her hands together, beaming at her work.

I sat and stared back at the girl in front of me, wow, Connie really did work her magic. My eyes had a light dusting of gold and a more natural colour, making the hint of green in my eyes pop. My long, black lashes framed them perfectly. My cheeks had a hint of rosy blush, then finished them off with bronzer. My lips were coated in a pillar box red. I would have never chosen this myself, but it worked. Like, really worked.

"Wow," I mouthed again.

"Now get your dress on," her feet moved quickly as she jigged on the spot.

Moving to where my dress was hanging, I unzipped it to reveal a short, mini white spaghetti strap dress.

It was stunning. It really was.

My hands were still on the bag as I turned to face her, "I am going to freeze my little nips off in this," I choked out a laugh before my eyes roamed over the material in front of me.

"Yes, yes you are," she nodded, "but never fear, you have a coat, right?"

"Of course, I have a coat." I rolled my eyes.

"Then you'll be fine," she smirked, her tongue darting out. "Now get the dress on, and make sure you're wearing some cute little panties. Not your big girl panties." She shook her head in a disapproving manner.

"I'm not getting my leg over, jeez, it's just a business deal."

"Hmm, we will see," she winked.

I discarded my clothes and let them fall to the floor as I took the dress from the hanger, stepping into it and pulling it over my little curves. I settled for a seamless, nude thong. The dress clung to every bit of me, I didn't want a knicker line and I certainly didn't want to go commando.

No.

I didn't need a bra on which was amazing, one perk of having small boobs. There was small, embroidered silver stars scattered over the thin material.

"Shoes?" I asked, looking down at my bare feet.

"The only shoes that you can pull off," she hummed, reaching into the bag that sat down the side of my bed. She handed me a white box, with *Louboutin* on the front.

Please don't be heels. Please don't be heels.

Opening them I saw the most beautiful pair of high-top leather trainers, with the painted red signature sole.

"How did you…" I stopped, looking up at her with the burn of my tears threatening.

"Thank my sperm donor," she shrugged. "The man has more money than sense."

"Please tell me you got yourself some?"

"Of course, I did. We're matching boo," she chimed.

"I love you."

"Not as much as I love you, now, get your shoes on. It's time to go."

I STOOD ON THE PAVEMENT, CHECKING MY PHONE EVERY FEW seconds. Harlen had messaged to tell me he was on his way, but I couldn't mask the disappointment I felt that Killian had ghosted me for most of the week. I haven't been easy, I know that… but I thought we sort of understood how each one of us worked; I obviously read that wrong. I mean, we don't know anything about each other. We have one thing in common. We're married.

That's it.

I have two weeks to go, then I'll be free. I am slightly hopeful that he will keep his mouth zipped and we can have an easy annulment, I really don't want to be divorced.

I clicked on his name, seeing one unread message.

> KILLIAN
>
> Remember… tell your friend to keep his fucking hands to himself and off what is mine, wife.

I scoffed a laugh. Possessive, demanding, beautiful, fuckable Killian. Lifting my eyes I saw a blacked out limousine pull up to the kerb. The window slipped down.

"Get in! You'll freeze your tits off," Harlen laughed before doing the window back up. I scuttled forward, opening the door and launching myself in.

He was wearing a black dinner suit jacket that was fitted to perfection, a high neck ruffled satin shirt that hung over his cropped cigarette trousers. He finished his look off with black, high-top trainers.

He looked amazing.

His black hair was styled and his crystal blue eyes sought out mine.

"You look very hot," he wiggled his brows before they dived down.

"You don't look too bad yourself," I flicked my long blonde hair over my shoulder in a dramatic fashion.

"We won't have to be there long, just a few things we have to do, then, I'll sign on the dotted line."

I widened my eyes.

"For real?" I shrieked.

"For real," he smiled at me, handing me a glass of bubbles and clinking our glasses together.

I couldn't wait to go to the office on Monday and shove that down Adele's throat.

We fell into light chatter before we pulled up at our destination. We stopped outside the Rockefeller Plaza. I was half expecting to see the tree up, but maybe November was a little too early.

The driver stepped out and opened Harlen's door, he climbed out but stopped and reached in for my hand. I was anxious. I hated being the centre of attention and I was about to live my worst fear.

My trembling hand reached and clasped his. His head dipped down as he gave me a wonderful smile. My nerves subsiding for a moment until my foot touched the red-carpet underneath me and I heard the loud chatter and the sound of clicking cameras.

Holy hell.

He clung to my hand, pulling me close to him as his arm wrapped around my waist.

"Harlen! Harlen!" one reporter shouted as we posed for photos.

I didn't sign up for this.

"Who is the mystery girl? Is she your girlfriend?"

Harlen chuckled softly, dropping his head before meeting the reporter's eyes. "You'll never know."

He held his hand up silencing the onslaught of questions that were being fired his way, ushering me inside.

"I'm sorry about that," he whispered as we checked in our coats.

"It's fine," I wave it off, even though inside I didn't feel fine. I felt horrible knowing that Killian was going to see those photos and assume something was going on. But then, I shouldn't really care. He screws around with Adele so why should I be worried about him seeing me with Harlen.

Taking the ticket for my coat, I dropped it into my purse

and followed Harlen into a packed-out room. I smiled at the function room name, *Rainbow Room.*

I loved Rainbows, it was our thing, but ever since Elijah passed, I fell out of love with them a little. It was ours. Not mine.

I rubbed my thumb over the blue ring that sat on my finger, an uneasy ache filled my chest all of a sudden making everything feel heavy.

A small sigh left me.

"You okay?" Harlen stopped, stroking the back of my hand with his thumb as his eyes searched my face.

I nodded. I couldn't bear to open up and tell him what was hurting.

"Okay," he smiled, "let's get a drink."

I STOOD WITH A GLASS OF CHAMPAGNE IN MY HAND, MY EYES scanning the room as I watched people flock Harlen. He was a well sought-after actor and very talented by the sounds of it. All we had to do was to get over this event and then he will be on our books for the next five years. And if he wanted to leave, he would have to pay a heavy escape fee. But here is hoping he doesn't want to leave, unless Adele is a raging bitch and tries to jump his bones.

I wasn't quite sure why I was here or what Harlen wanted me to do, but he assured me that he would let me know soon. He kept gazing over at me, small smiles pulling at his lips before turning his attention back to whoever was trying to lick his arse. There was something about him. He didn't openly flirt with me, I didn't feel like a piece of meat in front of him. I didn't feel any sort of sexual desires from him, and somehow that made me feel a lot more comfortable around him. I wanted him on my side, I could see him as a friend of mine. A lifelong friend hopefully.

I was pulled from my thoughts when an older woman stood on the stage, mic in hand as she scanned the room.

"Good evening, my beautiful guests," she said loudly; the room cheered. I just stood, eyes pinned to her before I felt an arm snake round my waist.

"You ready?" Harlen asked.

"Ready for what?" I said, distracted as I listened to the woman natter on.

"For betting on me."

I snapped my head to the side, "Betting!?"

"Yup, I am being auctioned off... and you need to beat these horny women or no signature," he smiled; his eyes full of mischief.

"How am I paying? Monopoly money?" I stammered, pressing my hand to my now clammy forehead. I began to panic. "You didn't think of telling me this before?! I could have sorted something out."

"Shhh, it's fine. Just bid, I'll sort out the rest," he winked, stepping forward, "and Reese..." he stilled and looked over his shoulder, "good luck, these ladies are ruthless..." he snickered before walking into the crowd.

"So, ladies, get your check books, credit cards and your husband's wallets..." the room erupted into cackles, "because here is the first of the line-up, the one and only Harlen Laufer. The Charity *Chasing Rainbows* ambassador and founder. The charity supports the dreams of terminally ill children, making their dreams a reality. Please, make as much noise as you can." The blonde bombshell clapped her hands together, the room echoing in chants and noise.

I felt my tears prick at the back of my eyes, the burn in my throat evident as I swallowed hard.

Sneaky little one he was.

Harlen took the mic, his eyes moving round the crowded room.

"I just want to thank you all for coming out to another one

of my fundraisers, you know this is a cause very close to my heart, after losing my nephew to neuroblastoma cancer two years ago, he will forever be four, forever be my rainbow loving angel. He showed me a strength I didn't even know was possible, and every day that I am blessed with another morning, I thank him. He was my hero, always was, and always will be. So, get ready to dig deep, don't be shy..." his eyes found mine before he winked.

I palmed a stray tear away from my cheek. I felt broken.

He dropped the mic, kissing his fingers and holding them up to the sky as he did.

The backdrop of the stage changed to neutral pastel colours with a picture of the most beautiful little boy I had ever seen. I choked, my eyes filling like a tsunami. I couldn't stop them even if I wanted too. I was distracted when a suited man handed me a paddle with the number one on it. My brows dug deep, then I realised what it was for.

"Okay ladies... let's start the bid. You get Harlen Laufer to yourself for forty-eight hours... opening bids start at ten thousand dollars!" the woman was back, her excited voice echoed round the room.

Ten Thousand!?

Wow.

I watched as two women fought back and forth with their paddles.

Harlen's eyes locked with me, widening slightly as they continued.

Twenty thousand, thirty thousand, forty, fifty, sixty.

I knew what I was doing.

"One hundred thousand," one lady screamed at the top of her lungs.

I felt a spike of adrenaline course though me.

"Two hundred thousand!" I screamed.

Eyes found me, my skin blushing as I felt the attention of the room.

I wanted the ground to swallow me.

"Two hundred thousand! Going once..." the blonde bombshell shouted out.

"Three hundred!" a skinny woman looked down her nose at me.

"Five hundred thousand!" waving my paddle in the air, I saw Harlen smirk at me.

"Hungry ladies in the room tonight," the host laughed as she stroked Harlen's arm seductively.

"Five hundred going once... going twice..."

My heart thumped; I could hear the blood rushing in my ears. I was eyeing the woman, her husband stepping towards her and whispering something in her ear before he shook his head.

Too bad, told off by your husband.

"Sold! To the cute little thing in the white dress," she cheered, the room cheering with her.

I blushed again, the crowd parting as Harlen walked over and grabbed me round the waist, squeezing me tight.

"Thank you," he whispered in my ear, kissing my cheek.

"I hope you know I have no way of paying it," I whispered back.

"I've got it covered. Give me half an hour and we will get the contract signed yeah?"

I nodded.

"See you in a bit, go and get a drink," he winked before disappearing into the sea of people again.

I let out a happy sigh, happy to have helped in a way and elated that he was going to sign with Lordes PR.

To say I was buzzing was an understatement.

Ducking out, I headed towards the bar and ordered myself another glass. The bubbles were going to my head, but I didn't care. I needed to let my hair down a bit and enjoy myself.

Thanking the waiter, I turned and watched the hustle and

bustle of the room. People were dancing and enjoying themselves. It was nice to see.

Bringing the glass to my lips, I let the bubbles dance over my tongue when I felt someone next to me, his arm slid around my waist, his lips by the shell of my ear.

"Careful not to drink too much, wife."

The goosebumps erupted over my skin, a cold sweat forming on the back of my neck.

I stepped to the side, trying to ignore the deep hunger he made me feel, the raging fire in my belly and the apex of my thighs just being close to him.

"Nice little bid on another man..." he clenched his jaw; I could hear the tightness in his voice.

"Jealous, are we?" I raised my eyebrows, facing him before knocking back the rest of my glass then turning to face the bar staff to order another.

"I think you've had enough, don't you?" he snarled.

I shook my head. "Not nearly enough to have to deal with you," I rolled my eyes, the corner of my mouth twitching as I thanked the barman and took the glass from him.

"Do not piss me off, wife," he growled.

"Or what?" I knitted my brows together, holding my head high as I challenged him.

I heard the low rumble in his throat.

"Where have you been?" I snapped, "you think you can come to my apartment, all burly and shit, eat me out and then ghost me?" The elastic band that had stretched had finally given in. I didn't want to care, but I did. I did care. I wanted to know why he had acted as if I didn't even exist anymore.

"Baby, I'm right here," he goaded, a beautiful smile on his face.

"Fuck off, Killian," I waved him off, turning my back on him as I began to walk away, but his hand wrapped around my wrist, pulling me into him.

I try to pull away, but all he does is tighten his grip. His nostrils flare, his jaw tight and ticking as he clenches it.

"Get. Off. Of. Me." I seethe at him through gritted teeth.

Tugging me behind him, he walks to the exit of the function room. I fight against him, trying to pull my arm out of his vice like grip but it was no use.

"Two things…" his voice is low as he opens what seems to be store cupboard, pushing me inside then locking it behind him.

"One, I am a very, *very* jealous man. And when something is mine, it is only mine…" he tugs at his bowtie and it unravels. "Two, if I tell you to do something, you do it," his eyes fall to my left hand, eyeing my ringless finger. "I wasn't joking when I said I was going to superglue it to your finger," he snarled, pushing forward and wrapping his long fingers round my neck as my back hit the wall. His lips hovered over mine, his teeth sinking into my bottom lip as he tugged on it, a moan escaping me. His free hand skimmed down my body as his fingers played with the hem of my dress.

This was wrong.

I shouldn't be giving into him, again. But, here I am. Letting him do what he wants to me because I am too weak to say no.

My breath hitched, the sparks coursing through me. His fingers tightened around the base of my throat, his fingers skimming under the bottom of my dress as his fingertips drew small circles on my skin.

"Killian," I breathed, my voice barely audible.

"I want you crying my name out so loud that every person in here knows you belong to me."

I whimpered. His hungry hand pushed my dress up round my waist, holding it there as his hand that was giving me the perfect necklace roamed down my body, hooking inside my thong and slipping it down my legs. He slowly crouched down, helping me step out before he stood, bringing my thong to his nose and inhaling before shoving it in the front pocket of his tux.

His finger fumbled with the button on his trousers, shoving them down just past his bum. His hand was wrapped back round my throat, pinning me harder against the wall, gently squeezing and putting pressure on my skin.

Grabbing my thigh, he wrapped one of my legs round his waist, the head of his cock cresting and crowning at my soaked opening.

"So ready, so wet," he smirked as his voice trembled. Pushing his hand up my throat slightly, making my head lift higher, thrusting his cock into my pussy, hard and fast.

"Good girl," he groaned, his eyes burning into mine as he fucked me hard against the wall. His pumps were slow and punishing. He was showing me just who I belonged to. It was him. It would always be him.

"You see how your tight little pussy takes my cock deep? It's mine, we fit perfectly Reese, when will you realise that?" he pants, his grip on my thigh tightening as I begin to tingle all over. "You. Belong. To. Me." he growls, pounding into me harder now, his cock pulling out to the tip, stretching me before slamming back into me. My back hitting the wall, but it felt good. I didn't want him to stop.

"Killian," I breathe.

"Say it louder," he orders.

"Killian," I cry out.

"What is it brat? Tell me," he goads, his fingers loosening around my neck as he grins down at me.

"I'm close," I cry, "so close."

"I can feel your tight little cunt contracting around me, you love being fucked by me, don't you? You like me using you, showing you who is in control. You act like a brat because you want this…" he buries his head into my neck, sucking and nipping on my bare skin. The pleasure rips through me as he continues to suck, his hand dropping from my throat and running under my bare bum, pulling my cheeks apart as he teases his finger in a place no man has been before.

"Killian," the panic is apparent in my voice.

His fingertip pushes into my arse, I feel myself tighten around him.

"Act like a brat, I'll treat you like one," he growls, both of his hands under me now as he rocks his hips into me, hard and punishing thrusts.

"Now fucking come for me, wife," he orders, his finger now filling my arse completely as I come hard, my whole-body trembling and shattering around him.

"Such a good girl," he praises as he finds his own high, his orgasm causing him to shudder.

We both still, his finger slipping out of me, but his hard cock still buried deep inside of me. Grabbing my throat, his lips reach my ear.

"Now, I want you to go out there, like the brat that you are and get him to sign that fucking contract, so he belongs to my company while my cum runs down your legs." His voice is low, pulling out of me and tucking himself back into his trousers. I stand on shaky legs, trying to catch my breath before he plants a kiss on my forehead and walks for the door.

His company?

CHAPTER 20

I had my hair scraped onto my head; my messy bun had strands of golden blonde falling out of it. I didn't have a clue what I was doing, my kitchen was a tip. Grabbing the canned yams out of my cupboard, I turned my nose up. I googled yams, and they were sweet potatoes. I didn't even know you could get them canned. Preheating the oven, I scanned through my check list. Patting my hands on my apron, as I sang along to *Enchanted – Taylor Swift.*

I drained the canned yams, placing them into a baking dish with a few chunks of butter evenly over the potatoes. Sprinkling brown sugar lightly before layering with miniature marshmallows.

Placing my hands on my hips I looked at the mush in front of me. I didn't know if this was a main, a side or a dessert? I would never put potatoes with marshmallows. I scrunched my nose up before slipping it into the oven.

Perfect.

Reaching for the already opened bottle of wine, I topped my glass up feeling pretty pleased with myself.

I looked around my kitchen, I decided to give the green bean casserole a go, but looking at it, I don't think I'll bother taking it. Something, somewhere along the line, well, something went wrong.

I heard a bang on the door, rushing for it, I swung it open to see Connie.

"Hey!" I called out.

"Hey you, you not getting dressed?" she eyed me, her eyes looking at my apron of the body of a busty woman wearing next to nothing.

I looked down at myself.

"I've just got to clean myself up," I chimed, a little tipsy.

"What is that smell?" she asked, turning her nose up and sniffing as she followed the scent into the kitchen.

"Oh my fuck, is that green bean casserole?!" she called out as I followed.

"Well… it is meant to be," I shrugged.

"Bin it. Do not offend the food of our ancestors with that shit," she cackled. She picked the container up and dumped it straight in the bin. I went to object, but she was right. I couldn't show up at her dad's place with that.

"Are you cooking candied yams?!" her eyes widened as she looked at the darkening dish in the oven.

I nodded happily, now them; them I am proud of.

"Oh, we don't eat yams," she winced, I could see the sorriness on her face, but it didn't take long before she stifled her laugh.

"So all of my hard work has gone to shit," I slapped my hand down on my thigh.

"I'm sorry," she laughed, swigging from the bottle and slamming it down with force. "My dad makes lovely baked sweet potatoes, so we can just load up on them."

"Screw that, I'm bringing the yams!" I call out, "Now give me five, let me get myself presentable." I start to walk towards my bedroom, "and Connie," I call out, "don't let my yams burn."

"Wouldn't dream of it," I could hear the sarcasm dripping from her tone. I chose to ignore it.

Half an hour later, we headed out the door. Connie sabotaged my yams. One job, all she had to do was keep an eye on my marshmallows, but instead of being a beautiful golden goo, they were black and crispy. Not at all like the photo on the website. I was pissed. I didn't get changed, just brushed out my hair and added a little make up. I was wearing a scoop neck red, puffed sleeve jumper and black high waisted jeans, finishing off my look with patent Dr Martens. Tucking my hair behind my ears, I held my hand out for my ruined yams, and began heading for the main lift. Connie stood, just shaking her head from left to right.

"This way," she called me back with her index finger. I looked at her confused, my brows pinching as I turned to follow her. We headed to the opposite end of the corridor and stood by a wall.

"Erm, what are you doing?" I leaned in and whispered in her ear.

"Just watch," she smiled.

"Is this some platform 9 ¾ magic?" I giggled as I watched her pull a key card out and insert it into a little slot in the panelling.

Huh, I would never have noticed that.

The door slid into a false wall and presented a private lift.

"Connie…" my voice trailing off as I followed her into the lift.

"Yup?" she asked, leaning over and pushing the button that said PH.

"Your dad lives in my building?"

She nodded.

"Huh," I raised my eyebrows, watching the doors close before we moved quickly to the top floor.

I don't know why but I felt nervous, what if her dad was horrid? She didn't exactly speak highly of her dad, just referred to him as her sperm donor most of the time, even if sometimes I could tell she thought more of him than that. I inhaled deeply as the doors pinged open into a lavish, brightly lit lobby.

"Dad?" she called out as she walked inside, I followed closely behind her. This apartment was amazing. The views of the New York skyline were to die for. She was right, her dad did have more money than sense.

"Hey Princess, in here!" he called out, and I froze. My skin smothered in goosebumps as the voice splintered through me. I watched as Connie picked up the pace and disappeared round the corner.

"Hey Daddy," I heard the sickly sweetness in her voice.

"Happy Thanksgiving Pumpkin," he cooed back at her, "where is your friend?"

"Oh," I heard Connie sigh, "she was right behind me."

I couldn't move. My legs felt like they were cemented to the floor.

Connie re-appears, a beaming smile on her face, then following behind her was Killian.

My breath caught in the back of my throat, my eyes widening before I dropped the china dish I was carrying, everything happening in slow motion. Connie's eyes moved from me to her dad then to the dish that was free falling out of my hand, my eyes were focussed on Killian. Our gazes burning into each other, tension growing constantly between us when all of a sudden, the loud smash of my dish on the tiles made me jump, pulling me out of my trance.

My candied yams.

"Shit," I whispered, my hands moving to my hair as I stepped back. I couldn't believe what was happening.

"You okay?" Connie asked as she went to step towards me.

"Pumpkin, don't, stay there." Killian held his arm out in front of Connie, stopping her. "Let's get this cleaned up, we don't want either of you getting hurt now do we…" his eyes flicked to his daughter before moving to me. I could feel the burning desire inside of them; my heart lurched in my chest. My eyes fell to his hand, his ring was still on. Mine wasn't. Damn it.

An older maid ran out with a dustpan and brush, Killian ushered Connie back to where they came from. I finally let out the breath I had been holding.

I followed them sheepishly. I had never felt so out of my comfort zone. As I turned the corner, I saw the lavish dining room table that was filled with decorative pumpkins, candles sitting either end of the table. I saw Connie questioning Killian. Locking my fingers together, I stumbled forward.

"I am so sorry about the yams," my voice was low and quiet.

Killian's head turned to face me, his eyes soft, "Don't worry about the yams."

I nodded, swallowing hard. I wanted Connie to look at me, but she wouldn't.

Had he told her? Or was she just trying to piece the parts of this fucked up jigsaw together.

"Excuse me, I need the bathroom," I muttered, stepping back but waiting for someone to tell me where to go.

"It's the third door on the left, just past the kitchen," Connie smiled, her eyes softening for the moment.

I gave a small, weak smile, turning on my heel and walking towards the toilet. As soon as the door was closed, I let out a deep breath.

I need to get out of here. Standing opposite the mirror, my fingers wrapped around the porcelain sink.

"It's just dinner," I muttered. "He works with you, or you work for him?" I shook my head in confusion. I didn't know what was going on. What a cluster fuck.

I closed my eyes. I just needed a minute. That's all. Then I was going to sit out there, eat the food, drink the wine and be thankful.

My eyes flicked open when I heard the door click open, then close again. I felt my heart skip a beat, my breathing fastening. I knew it was him. My body reacts to him, even if I don't want it to.

"Buttercup," his voice was raspy, my skin pebbled.

I stood straight and tall as I faced him. Crossing my arms across my chest, my eyes scanned up and down his body. Wearing slim fitted jeans and a fitted V neck tee showing off the light dusting of his chest hair, the top of his scar on show.

"Didn't think to tell me you had a daughter?" I snapped, my tone was sharp, but I was angry.

"Ree-" I cut him off.

"Don't Reese me! You didn't tell me you had a daughter; you didn't even tell me you live in the same apartment block as me!" I shouted.

"You never asked," he snapped back, stepping towards me.

"I never had a chance to!"

I heard him exhale slowly, his breath shallow.

"I don't just live in this apartment block, I own it…" I saw him wince slightly.

"Of course, you do, same as the company I work for." I rolled my eyes.

"Technically yes, but also no…" he smirked.

"Don't fucking smirk," I snap, "I am pissed at you! And what am I meant to say to Connie?" I stood, waiting for him to answer, but just as he opened his mouth, I stopped him and continued, "Oh sorry bestie, not only am I screwing your hot as fuck dad, I am also married to him. SURPRISE! I'M YOUR NEW STEP MUM!"

"Will you keep your voice down," he looked over his

shoulder, warning me, that delicious pull at the corner of his mouth lifting, "you think I'm hot as fuck?"

"Fuck off Killian," I shake my head, crossing my arms again.

"Don't swear under my roof... little girl." He glared down at me, stepping towards me, cornering me against the wall.

"Sorry... Daddy," I taunted him. I was raging. I could feel how hot my blood was thrashing through my body.

His jaw clenched, his eyes on my lips. The tension was thick, the walls closing in around me. I couldn't breathe.

"I'm going back to my *friend*," I sighed. Pushing off him, I opened the bathroom door and stormed out, not looking back.

I was on a thin line.

I found Connie swigging champagne from the bottle. Stepping over cautiously, I linked my fingers together as I held them in front of me.

"Hey," I said sheepishly.

"Hey," her tone was more clipped.

"Look, I can explain..." I just about managed, I'm sure my throat was about to close. I stammered over my words, shit this was harder than I thought it would be.

"I work with Reese, I'm her boss, sort of... I'm her boss', boss." Killian said from behind me. "I didn't tell her I had a daughter, that's why she was so shocked," he continued, standing next to Connie and hanging his arm over her shoulders.

"So that's all it is?" Connie said a little unconvinced.

"Yup," me and Killian said in unison.

"Fine." She rolled her eyes.

Connie walked towards the fridge and grabbed a new bottle of Champagne. Killian watched her for a moment before he turned towards me. A devilish look on his face as his eyes devoured me. He rubbed his fingers through his stubble, licking his bottom lip as he stepped towards me, his lips moving closer to my ear.

"I'm not finished with you yet, wife."

My heart drummed, rendered speechless before he recoiled back and disappeared into the kitchen as I heard him talk to a guy.

Connie reappeared with a glass, handing it to me.

"Thank you, and I'm sorry for not telling you."

"Don't apologise, you weren't to know…" Connie rolled her eyes, looking over her shoulder to see her dad and Frank the fucking doorman appearing.

Was it time to go home yet?

CHAPTER 21

WE SAT AT THE LAVISH DINING ROOM TABLE, THE CREAM tablecloth hanging over the edges and finished off with a red trim. Pretty, understated. My mouth watered at the delicious food that was in front of us. Turkey, mash, baked sweet potatoes, green bean casserole and bread rolls. It would have been perfect if my candied yams were still in the picture, but they weren't. They were now in the bin after being smashed all over Killian's floor.

Connie was chatting away, but I wasn't listening. I was too busy watching Killian who was sitting next to me, chatting to Frank. The way his dark eyes were roaming over me, seductive and sultry. The way his cheeks hollow slightly under his high cheek bones before his jaw scoops into the perfect rounded point. His jaw is sharp and defined, dusted in a dark stubble that I loved. I loved feeling the friction of the roughness on my smooth, soft skin.

"Reese," Connie threw a roll at me, "did you hear me?"

I tore my eyes from Killian, nodding, "Yeah, yeah," I muttered back.

"Perfect, I'll set the blind date up," Connie squealed,

clapping her hands. My eyes widened, my pulse racing under my skin. I'm sure you could see it throbbing.

"Cool." I rushed out, reaching for my wine and gulping it down. I didn't dare look at Killian.

"Frank, would you like to give thanks?" he asked coolly as he took his own mouthful of wine. *Too coolly.*

Frank nodded, clearly delighted being asked to do so.

The smile on my face from listening to Frank say his piece soon slipped as I felt Killian's hand grip onto my thigh tightly, dancing his fingers over the material of my jeans.

I tried to steady my breathing, my breath trembling as it passed my lips. Connie was digging into the food, piling it onto her plate.

"Sort yourself out some food, please," Killian said low, his fingers still working their way to the apex of my thighs.

My breath caught, his fingers trailing along the seam that was sitting right where he wanted to get to.

Leaning across, I grabbed the spoon and started filling my plate.

"Good girl," he whispered.

The burn in my belly was distracting, the sweat beginning to bead on my forehead presenting itself for the table to see. I exhaled deeply as his hand left my body to plate his own food up.

Taking a small mouthful of turkey, my eyes moved to Connie who was deep in conversation with Frank. My heart warmed, it made me realise how much I missed my parents. I rubbed the ache in my chest, I'll call them as soon as we're finished.

"How's work going Connie?" Killian asked as his hand found it's place back on my thigh, slowly trailing back to where it was.

"Ugh," she rolled her eyes hard, "it's going okay, I can't moan." She shrugged, shovelling a mouthful of mac 'n' cheese into her mouth.

"When are you going to come and work for me?" he asked, his words slow as his finger ran up and down my core, the seam of my jeans hitting me in the right spot every time.

I tried to disguise my shaky breath.

"When hell freezes over," she jabs at her dad with her fork before throwing him a wink.

"Oh, come on Princess, it's not that bad... just ask Reese here," his head turns slightly, his eyes falling to me as his fingers continue to stroke me in slow, teasing strokes.

"Not bad at all," I say on a whisper, my grip tightening round the fork.

"Apart from Adele right?" Connie snickers.

"Yeah... apart from her," I roll my eyes back, but was it in pleasure or from the frustration of her name? "The raging bitch."

His fingers move in small, slow circular movements now, my orgasm at tipping point.

Connie really giggled now as she forked more food into her mouth.

"She's not *that* bad," he leaned in, speaking low in my ear, his finger pressing harder now and causing my clit to throb. I couldn't hold off. The tingles swarmed me, a shiver dancing over my skin like a cool breeze as I came, my head falling forward. As soon as he got what he wanted, he pulled his fingers away before bringing them to his lips and running them across his bottom one.

The sadistic fuck.

"Pumpkin Pie?" he asked, throwing his napkin on the table and pushing back off his chair.

CHAPTER 22

Walking arm in arm with a slightly tipsy Connie we headed towards my apartment. Unlocking the door, she tumbled through it.

"Thank you for inviting me to thanksgiving," I smiled, "I had a real good time."

It wasn't a lie. I did have a good time.

"You're welcome, you're always welcome. Sorry my dad is a bit stuffy and uptight, just old and stuck in his ways," she said, flopping down on the sofa.

"He isn't old," I choked out a laugh, sitting next to her.

"He is," she side-eyes me, "he is forty-five."

Oh okay, so he is older than I thought. But, he still isn't *that* old.

"Old man," I laughed, reaching for my phone. "Just going to call my parents."

"Dude, time difference." She sighed; my eyes focused on the time.

Crap.

It was already gone nine here, so my mum and dad would be soundo by now. I'll call them tomorrow as soon as I wake.

It's been a couple of days since I heard their voices or saw their faces. I missed them.

The pain crept into my chest.

Connie was smiling into her phone, I took a moment just to replay today.

I am sleeping with my best friend's dad.

The realisation hit me like a steam train.

My thumbs hovered over his name, before clicking it and smirking at the message that presented me. My mind was still back at the table where he made me orgasm during dinner. He knew what he was doing.

> ME
>
> Guess who just found out how old you are…
> Old man.
>
> Old men are not really my kink.

Before I could think about it, I sent it, nibbling on the inside of my lip as I felt the heat flush to my cheeks. Dropping my phone into my lap, I turned to face Connie.

"Right, I want to know details. Who has you smiling into your phone like a loon?" I asked, my elbow resting on the back of the sofa, my head in my hand.

Connie was laying straight on the sofa, her head resting on the back of it. She turned her head slightly to face me, holding her phone to her chest.

"I don't wanna say yet, it's going so well…" her eyes fell from mine for a moment before meeting them again, "I'm worried I'll jinx it."

"I get it," I smiled at her, "but please just tell me… is it Kieran?"

She shook her head from side to side. "Nope, that cock has long sailed." Giggling, she twisted her body now, her eyes searching my face.

"Good, he didn't deserve you."

"How about you? Anything I need to know?"

The answer was on the tip of my tongue, I hated that I hadn't told her, but I couldn't... even more so now.

"Nope, went out with Harlen. That was unexpected," a laugh bubbled out of me.

"Unexpected, good? Or..."

"No, it was good. I had a real good time," I smiled.

"Will you see him again?"

"I'm not sure, the ball was kind of left in his court." I shrugged trying to throw her off. "Wine?" I asked as I stood from the sofa and rushed into the kitchen before she had even answered.

"Am I okay to crash here tonight? I can't be bothered to taxi it back."

"Yeah," I shouted from the kitchen, uncorking the wine and pouring us two big glasses of red.

Waltzing back into the lounge I handed her the glass.

"Thanks boo," she yawned, snuggling into my sofa and pulling the fur throw over her.

We clinked glasses before we got comfortable on the sofa with *Jane The Virgin*.

Patting around under the throws for my phone, I found it sitting down the middle of the cushions. Pulling it out, I nearly choked on my wine to see three messages from Killian.

KILLIAN

Old man? Who you calling old man?

KILLIAN

I'll show you old man when I am throat fucking that name out of your mouth.

KILLIAN

Answer me Reese, or is the brat back? If you don't answer in the next five minutes, I will be over there and showing you just what this 'old man' can do to you.

My eyes widened as I saw the time. Fuck.

I looked over at Connie who was softly snoring, the hood of my hoodie pulled over her face.

Bang bang bang.

Throwing the covers back, I rushed up and ran for the door. Looking through the peep hole, I saw a pissed off Killian standing there.

I had two choices…

Open the door and let him bolt through.

Ignore him until he kicks the door in.

Slipping the chain across, I opened the door slightly.

"Sorry, this isn't the care home. I think you're lost and slightly senile," I choke.

"I swear to fucking God, open the door," he growled.

"No," I shook my head, looking over my shoulder, "Connie is asleep."

"And?"

"And nothing. Go away." Pushing the door closed, his shoe slipped into the gap quickly. His fingers wrapped around the edge of the door as he pushed it open.

"Killian!" I whisper-shouted, stepping back as he stepped over the threshold and closed the door gently behind him. His eyes moved from mine as he looked over at his daughter asleep on the sofa.

His head dropped to look at me, his hand wrapping round my wrist as he dragged me into the bedroom and shut the door. I didn't even have a chance to stop him.

His eyes darkened, that beautiful, strong jaw clenching as he stepped towards me. Wrapping his fingers around my throat, he pushed me onto the bed. The smirk played on my face, *what was wrong with me?*

He fell to his knees, his large hands pushing my loose pyjama t-shirt up round my neck, his fingers trailing down the side of my body, his lips following where his fingers have been. He squeezed my waist, feeling the smirk from his mouth on my skin and his teeth nipping gently.

"Killian," I whine, sitting on my elbows as I watch him. His fingers wrapped in the waistband of my shorts before he ripped them down my legs, throwing them across the room. I gasped, my teeth sinking into my bottom lip.

"Quiet," he ordered, his lips pressing across my pubic bone. I wiggled under his mouth, my fingers scrunching into my sheets.

"You want to act like a brat, I'll treat you like a brat," he growled, his tongue pushing through my folds, swirling his tip over my clit. My hips bucked up, his hand pushing and grabbing my waist, holding me in place. His eyes lifted, piercing into mine.

"You better be quiet, little girl. We don't want to wake my daughter now do we... I'm not sure she would appreciate seeing her dad tongue fucking her best friend."

Oh fuck.

Plunging two fingers deep inside of me, he was rough. But I needed this. I needed the release.

"I'm addicted to your pussy," he whispered, kneeling up and looking down as he watched himself finger fuck me. The hand that was pinning me down slid up my body, grabbing my boob hard, his fingers rolling and pulling on my nipple before he groped me again. His rough hands were all over me, marking me, owning me and putting me in my place like a naughty child.

"I'm close," I cried, my head tipping back as the waves of pleasure rippled through me, his finger plunging in deep before pulling to the tip and swirling his fingers in my arousal.

His head lowered, kissing across my hip bone before he bit me, hard. He stilled, his fingers slipping out of me as he crawled over me and pushed them through my lips.

"Now taste yourself," he groaned.

I licked and sucked his fingers clean.

"But that is as close as you'll get to coming, only good girls get to come, and you, brat… are not a good girl."

He stood, shaking his head from side to side before turning and walking out of my apartment.

What the f… that mother fucker.

Or more like, daughter's best friend fucker…

Once he was gone, I lay frustrated and horny as hell. I lay there, my fingers gliding down my stomach before dipping into my shorts. Rubbing my sensitive clit, I felt the pleasure course through me. Pushing a finger into my wet, hot pussy I felt myself tightening as I came hard.

It was a release, but it wasn't as good as when Killian done it.

CHAPTER 23

It had been a week since thanksgiving, Connie was none the wiser that her father popped over that evening. And she was never to know. I felt like all these secrets were building up around me, each one a heavy weight on my shoulders.

I felt like shit, I didn't want to see Killian. I had blocked his number after the numerous messages from him.

He wanted me to act like a brat? Well, here she comes.

Walking into the office, I held my head high. He had been here every day. Seeing Adele and then hanging around my desk. I didn't have anything to say to him. I needed to shut this down, I could feel myself falling for a man I don't even want.

I had my plan and I needed to stick to it.

Find my feet at work, continue to save and when I deem the time is right, find a sperm donor. Oh, and get my marriage annulled.

I wanted to approach Connie and talk to her about it, and maybe if she doesn't mind, sit down with her both her mums to ask what clinic they used. I knew this is what I wanted; I just didn't want a six-foot-six hunk of a man in tow.

I had to cut ties. Our annulment is this week, and seeing

Killian is only going to burn the bridges and put us at a risk of a divorce. Here is hoping he will keep his lips sealed. For both of our sakes.

Sitting at my desk, I lost myself in my work. Harlen was moving over at the end of November to work with us here at Lordes PR and I was so excited. There was a certain buzz in the air around him. It was good. It was going to be amazing for Lordes. Blowing out my cheeks, I waited for my email to load up. The only way I was prepared to talk to Killian was through my emails.

Petty? Absolutely.

I saw Killian's name at the top, my heart falling from my chest for a moment. I swallowed hard, hovering my mouse over his name.

Reese,

Just wanted to confirm our appointment for Friday, I will collect you and we will ride together.

Regards,
 Killian Hayes

No way was we riding together.
Clicking my fingers out, I began typing a reply.

Killian,

I don't think it is wise for us to ride together, do you?
 Let's just meet at the courthouse.
 My papers are signed, make sure yours are too Killian.

Regards,
 Reese

Closing my emails down, I lost myself in my work. I needed a clear head, and Killian certainly didn't help with that.

I decided to take an extended lunch with Julianne, I wanted to be out of the office when Killian arrived for his weekly two-hour meeting with Adele. No doubt probably getting his dick sucked.

I shuddered at the thought. I hated the thought of him being with her, but I needed to get used to it. Because as of Friday, he was nothing more to me than my best friend's dad.

By the time I got home, it was dark outside. I worked a little later as there were a few things that needed tying up that Adele just couldn't wait till the morning for. I felt exhausted.

I skipped dinner, got undressed and climbed under the covers before reaching for my diary. It had been too long.

Dear Diary,

Today was another hellish day. What with avoiding Killian and having to deal with Adele... it's got to be worth it right?

I feel like as each day is passing, I'm losing a little more of Elijah and it hurts me. I know I have to move on, it's part of life. And yes, being with Killian helped me feel again, but it also made me feel like dirt. How could I do this to Elijah? Does this make me a terrible person?

Inhaling, I rub my chest with my palm, the ache in my heart presenting itself.

I don't know what I am doing. I don't know the direction I am meant to be heading. I have wanted this job for so long, and yet now I have it, I don't feel content like I thought I would.

I'm sorry for the heavy offload, it's just I have no one else to talk to. Sure, I have Connie and Julianne, but Connie is Killian's daughter, and Julianne works with me so knows Killian. I can't go spilling the tea on him to either of them. Then what with being married to him as well, it's a hefty weight to carry around with me.

But Diary, there is a silver lining.

Come Friday it'll be over. I will be free to go back to my life plan without him being in the way.

Little steps.

One step closer.

Everything will be okay.

I smile to myself as I close my brown leather diary and stash it in my bedside unit.

My eyes were pinned to the ceiling, I was exhausted, but I couldn't seem to sleep. Was there a small part of me that wanted to be with Killian? Absolutely.

But we couldn't. We would never work. We were too volatile.

My phone pinged, sighing I reached across and picked it up. Smiling, I saw it was Connie.

> **CONNIE**
>
> Bitch tits, my dad said he has been trying to get hold of you for days. Here is his number in case you need it. Knowing him, he probably took a digit down wrong.
>
> Contact: Sperm Donor

Rolling my eyes, I shook my head to myself.

> **ME**
>
> I'll sort it.

I wasn't going to unblock him; I had no need to. He can email me, and I'll pick it up at work tomorrow.

CHAPTER 24
KILLIAN

MESSAGE FAILED TO SEND.

Damn it! Clenching my fists before running them through my hair and tugging at the root, I dropped the phone on the side.

I hated having to ask Connie to get involved, but I didn't know what else to do. Sure, I could go down there, bang on her door or just let myself in with the key and start a riot but where would that get me?

I knew I had pissed her off, she wouldn't give me the time of day. But this whole freezing me out shit was a bit immature, even for her.

Stalking up and down my apartment, my head was screaming at me to go down to her apartment and demand she speaks to me.

Sighing, I stopped in the archway of my kitchen, my eyes falling to the paperwork that needed to be signed ready for Friday.

I wasn't ready.

I didn't want to get our marriage annulled.

Drumming my fingers over the paperwork, my eyes scanned the document. I wasn't doing this.

Snatching my phone up, I called the number on the phone and left a voicemail.

I wasn't doing this now. I said I needed a push back on the annulment. Reese was going to be annoyed at me, but it had to be done.

Opening my emails, I tapped out a quick one to her. She wouldn't read it now; she never checks her work emails of an evening… I know that, or, if she does, she never responds.

Reese,

I have just picked up a voicemail from the courthouse, our annulment has been pushed back a month due to a schedule clash. We now won't be seen until the first week of January.

Looks like you're stuck with me for another month…

Killian

Puffing out my cheeks, I slip my phone into my back pocket and head for my whiskey. I needed something to take my mind off of it all, and whiskey done the trick.

Padding over to my leather sofa, I sat down, tapping my long index finger on the rim of my crystal tumbler.

Trust it to be me to fall for my daughter's best friend. Obviously, I didn't know that before we got boozed up and married, but still. She was twenty-seven, I was nearly twenty years older than her. But I didn't care. I didn't even know if we would work out, but I wanted to try. I couldn't deny the chemistry and energy that I felt between the two of us, it was so much more than just a sexual attraction. Bringing the rim of my glass to my lips, I took a big mouthful. The welcoming burn coating my tongue before caressing my throat. Wincing as I felt my belly warm with the amber liquid, I jolted when I heard banging on my front door. My brows dived down, pinching as I put the tumbler down on the coffee table.

Bang bang bang

"Hold up, I'm coming." I shouted out, storming for the door.

"Open the fucking door, Killian!" I heard her strong, British accent through the door. My mouth pulling at the corners, my cock twitching.

What was wrong with me? I am even attracted to her accent.

Swinging the door open, I plastered a smile on my face as my eyes raked up and down her body. I've never gone for the slender, slimmer type before. But Reese? Well, there was something about her. Her petite frame, her small breasts that sat pert and perky all the time. She had a slight curve on her hips, her bum peachy but her legs were slim and toned. She was the complete opposite to what I was used to. And sometimes opposites attracted the hardest right?

"Take that fucking smile off your face, Killian." She moaned, her pouty bottom lip sticking out, her opal eyes dark and hooded as she glared right through me.

"Oh, Buttercup… don't be like that," I teased, stepping back and letting her in.

She was wearing a cropped white tee that showed her smooth, flat stomach and high waisted black pants. She didn't even have shoes on, just her socks. She must've darted out in a rush. Her breaths were heavy, as she stood tapping her foot on the floor, her arms covering her chest.

"What do I owe the pleasure, wife?" I taunted. I loved getting a rise out of her, and that is exactly what I got by sending that email.

"Your email was a joke, right?" she spat, slapping her hand down on her thigh.

"Does it look like a joke?" I lifted my brows, fighting the urge to break into a smile at her pouty, angry face.

"What is this schedule clash bullshit?" she growls, her eyes not leaving mine.

"How do I know? Just doing the right thing as a husband and keeping you updated." I shrug, trying to act nonchalant.

She began pacing, her hand held over her mouth as she walked the length of the hallway of my apartment.

"What's wrong?" I ask softly, stepping a little closer to her.

"Nothing," she sighs, stopping before turning to look at me. "I just want this over, I want my life back." Her voice trembled a little, this was a side to Reese I hadn't seen before. Vulnerable. My brows knitted as I took another step closer to her.

"Am I really that bad?" I teased, but you could hear the slight sting in my voice.

"No," she breathed out, her answer coming out in a whisper. Taking another step towards her, I had to fight the urge to not wrap my arms around her and embrace her. Her lips twisted into a shy smile.

"Then what's a few more weeks?"

"This wasn't part of the plan," her voice quiet as she looked up at me.

Taking one last step forward to close the gap between us, the breath caught in the back of her throat.

"Plans are boring," I whisper, my eyes volleying back and forth between hers. I could see the vulnerability in them, the look of pain, guilt, anguish all rolled into those beautiful green eyes.

"Mine wasn't," she shook her head, dropping her head down, her fingers linking together.

"Tell me about it…" I nudged a little, I wanted to know all of her… truth was we didn't know each other that well.

We worked together.

She was my daughter's best friend.

And we were married. Accidentally married.

"Reese?" I tried to coax her out of her mind. "You know we could make this work; we could give it a go... I can give you everything you want." Fuck, what was I saying?

She inhaled deeply before stepping back away from me, shaking her head.

"I want a baby, Killian. I want a family." Her eyes lifted as she looked at me dead in the eyes, not faltering at all, and fuck I swear I saw tears pooling.

I choked, stepping away from her and putting considerable distance between us. Her eyes burned into me; I could see her chewing on her bottom lip. Shaking her head softly. Her arms dropping by her side.

Say something you idiot.

But words failed me.

"And that's why we won't work Killian," a scoff of a laugh passed her lips before she reached into her pocket and pulled the ring out. Walking towards me, she grabbed my wrist, turning my hand up and dropping it into my palm.

My head and heart were screaming at me, but it was useless. I was too stunned to talk.

The door slamming behind me made me jump, finally catching up with everything. My eyes dropped to look at my hand. The cheap, gold ring sitting there. Clenching my hand into a fist, I squeezed tightly.

"A kid?" I mutter to the open emptiness and silence that surrounds my flat. "Fuck no, I'm too old for that."

CHAPTER 25
REESE

Why am I crying?

Frustration filled me; my eyes raw from the tears that have been shed. I have no right to cry, it's not like we promised each other forever and always. We got drunk, got married and hooked up a few times. I knew we were wrong for each other; this was never going to be more than what it was.

An accidental marriage.

Of course, he wouldn't want kids, he was forty-five. He had a twenty-one-year-old kid, why the fuck would he want to become a dad again now?

I was angry with myself. Why did I tell him? I could have just kept my stupid mouth shut and lied, but no, I had to tell him I wanted kids. There was a part of me deep down that thought we could give it a go, but then who was I kidding? We were never going to work.

We were completely different ends of the spectrum.

Did it matter that whenever I was with him, my world was like looking into a kaleidoscope? The burst of colours that I had never seen before, everything was so black and white until him.

Until him.

Guilt and grief crushed me. I shouldn't even be feeling like this. I had Elijah. I loved Elijah.

Loved.

Elijah wasn't here anymore. Elijah hadn't been here for two years and yet my heart still stung every time I done anything remotely close to moving on.

Maybe I wasn't meant to move on.

That wasn't in the plan.

The plan was to do this by myself, for me, for Elijah. Become the best mum I could to a baby that he couldn't give me.

To a baby I couldn't give him.

The burn in my throat was too much, the lump felt like it was choking me.

I had fallen into self-wallowing, and when I had no tears left to cry, I fell asleep.

The week at work passed in a blur, every time I heard the office door go my heart jumped and fluttered at the hope of it being Killian. But it wasn't. Of course, it wouldn't be Killian.

I told him what I wanted.

He didn't want it.

He never did.

He saw me as a hot piece of fluff that he could tap and own when he wanted too. He didn't want anything more than a fling.

Flings seem fun, but not when you start catching feelings for a man you shouldn't. He was out of bounds. We needed to end the relationship that we had going on anyway. It wasn't fair on any of us, especially not Connie.

Walking to the subway, I caught my train and headed home. Me and Connie were having a wine and Chinese night tonight. I had a deadline due by Monday and Adele had been even worse in the absence of Killian. She had been hard to work under, putting unrealistic pressure and deadlines on me. I was still no closer to getting my new job title that she had promised if I signed Harlen.

Harlen was due to start in a couple of weeks, but little old me was still being Adele's dogsbody and truthfully, I was fucking sick of it. I just didn't know how much more I could stick it out.

Moving thousands of miles away from my family and Elijah for what? An empty promise of a job that was never coming.

Tapping out of the subway, I walked home in the arctic weather. We were meant to be getting snow here over night and I was excited. I couldn't remember the last time we had snow in December back home in England.

Nodding my head to a near frozen Frank, I stepped into the warm apartment lobby and headed for the lift. I always get nervous walking into the building now knowing that I could cross paths with Killian at any moment. He had kept his distance, and as much as I may be hurting a little, it was needed.

The distance will only shut down the feelings that I feel for him. It was just a crush, but then again, I don't even think it was a crush. Just a sexual connection.

Like petrol and fire.

Burn well together but only to cause cataclysmic damage.

Unwrapping my scarf and letting it hang, I dropped my long, puffy black jacket from my shoulders and hung it up over the top of my scarf. I felt frozen to my bones. Checking the time on my phone, I still had an hour before Connie came over. I wanted a hot bath and I needed to video call my parents. It felt like it had been forever. Sitting on the edge of the bed, I held my phone up waiting for it to connect.

"Reese, mi amor!" My dad beams into the phone.

"Hey papa," I smile, but it doesn't quite meet my eyes like it normally would.

"Qué equivocado, mi el amor?" his brows furrowed, the look of worry etching his face.

"I'm fine pap, honestly dad. Just work, it's kicking my arse."

"Well don't get too stressed out, work is meant to be enjoyable, you should work to live, not live to work." A small smile pressed into his lips.

He was right.

"I know," I puffed out, "it's just my boss promised a promotion if I got Harlen on the books. I got Harlen on the books and still no promotion. Every day I go in to ten tonnes of shit-"

"Language!" my mum scolded. I might be twenty-seven, but I still didn't like cursing in front of my parents.

"Sorry," I winced, "ten tonnes of work on my desk. I am basically her personal filing cabinet."

"I'm sorry Princess," my dad's words pull at my heart, the sting pricks behind my eyes as I try to blink away the unwanted tears.

"It's okay," I laugh, palming my eyes, "it's just not what I thought it was going to be, part of me just thinks I should pack up and come home. There is nothing here for me, well, apart from Connie." I smile, but how long would I have her once she found out about me and her dad?

"You are not coming home Reese!" my mum shouted in the background, banging and clattering round. I saw my dad look to the side before the phone was ripped from his hand. "You listen to me Reese Gloria Hernández, you are not getting on a plane and coming back home. We miss you; we do. But you have so much more to aspire to out there. Don't come back to settle for working with me and your dad. You deserve so much more." Her voice softened considerably now, "Don't give up because of some bitch. Go in there and show her what you're capable of, and if she doesn't pull though, fuck her off."

I snorted a laugh, wiping the stray tear that had escaped and rolled down my cheek. My mum hardly swore unless something really got to her, and I guess Adele got to her. I mean, she got to me. She was like thrush; a fucking irritant.

"Don't stop following your dream because of one person," she smiled, her own eyes glistening.

Truth was, it wasn't just one person. It was two.

"I won't," I sighed. She was nattering away when I heard the buzzer go, making me jump.

"Who's that?" mum asked.

"Connie…" I looked at the time on my phone, my brows digging in, "I think…" she was early. Connie was never early.

"Go on love, I'll speak to you tomorrow."

"Okay Mum, bye, love to you and Dad." I blew a kiss into the phone at my parents before cutting it off and throwing it on the bed.

Skipping to the door, I swung it open to see Killian.

Not today Satan.

Shoving the door shut, I slipped the chain across.

"Go away, Killian!" I shout through the door.

"Reese, please," he begged, I felt my heart clench for a second before my walls were back up.

"Nope," I replied, turning my back and walking towards my bedroom, slamming the door.

Take that Killian Hayes.

I wasn't giving in. He was the one that acted like a complete dick when I told him I wanted a baby.

He could have let me down gently; fuck I don't think I would have cared if he ended it right there with me. But the fact he said nothing, he kept his mouth shut, that's what hurt the most.

He banged on the door loud, over and over but I didn't care. He could bang to his little heart's content. His daughter would be here soon, and he would have to explain why he was like a possessed angry caveman trying to smash my door down.

Awkward.

Padding back to the lounge area, I connected my phone to my Bluetooth and played *abcdefu – GAYLE.* I turned it up so loud, just in case he didn't get the message. I danced in front of the door, flipping it off as I sung the song at the top of my lungs.

Shaking my hips, I walked to the fridge and grabbed the bottle of white wine. Biting the rubber cork out the top with my teeth, I took a big mouthful. I wasn't going to cry over him anymore.

We were done.

Finito.

Over.

Maybe I would cry over his beautiful dick. But that's the only tears that would be shed.

After a while, the banging stopped completely. I had to show him that I wasn't a pushover. I knew what I had to do, and he wasn't going to steer me in any other direction other than where my dreams were.

The buzzer went again, smiling I ran for the door, peeping through the peephole and getting excited when I saw Connie with the Chinese and more wine. Sliding the chain across I opened the door, throwing myself at her.

"Woah, hello to you too," Connie laughed as she stood her ground.

"Hey," I beamed, taking the Chinese from her and walking into my apartment.

"Having a little party for one, are we?" she winked, placing the wine bottles down on the side.

"Yeah, why not?" I shrugged as I fisted the bag and pulled out the cartons. "You okay?" I asked as I lifted my eyes from the bag to look at her.

"Yeah, I am," she blushed; I knew that blush… that was a very good blush.

"Good," handing her some chopsticks, we sat in light conversation while we ate. Mainly about me and how much I disliked Adele.

"Just leave her ass, she doesn't deserve you," Connie sighed, shaking her head side to side. "I don't like her either, she is always sniffing round my dad. It's weird." I stiffened at her admission. So she knows that they're close.

"Were they together or something?" I asked, trying not to seem too desperate to know.

"No, well, I don't think so," she shrugged, "I wouldn't know, to be honest. I just know she is a like a fly round shit." I snorted. "He helped her start the company you work for, it didn't even click with me when you mentioned Adele before," she looked at me slightly apologetic. "She just doesn't let up. I honestly think she is one of the reasons my dad has never settled down. She is so prominent in his life that no woman can stand it," she shoved an egg roll into her mouth, her eyes watching me. I didn't want to let on that I was involved with her dad. *Was* being the appropriate word.

"Seems that way," I agreed, suddenly losing my appetite. "So, what is the reason for the beautiful smile that has been plastered on your face from the moment you walked in the door?" I poked her, "Or should I say, who is the reason…"

She blushed, helping me tidy up before we collapsed onto the sofa with a bottle of wine.

"Spill all, I don't want any detail missed out…" I winked at her, sipping my wine.

I heard the blissful sigh leave her before she started giggling.

"Well, first off… don't be mad, okay?" the slight twang of her accent warmed my heart, I loved her voice.

"Why would I be mad?" pinching my brows, I pushed my shoulders back, my back going up slightly.

She rolled her eyes, "For not telling you sooner."

"You've been too coy and secretive, it's kept me intrigued. It *is* unlike you to bite your tongue…" I let out a small laugh.

It seemed like she let out a sigh of relief, she looked at the ceiling, smiling before her eyes met mine again.

"Tryst," was all she said.

"Tryst!? From Chord?" I shrieked.

A laugh bubbled out of her before she shuffled forward and hugged me.

"Do you know how good it feels to get that out?" she said relieved as she hugged me tightly, "I really thought you were going to be angry with me."

I shook my head, my own arms squeezing her tightly now, "I could never be angry with you. Ever." I whispered, all of a sudden, a guilt ripping through me. I needed to tell her; we both did. I swallowed hard, my throat dry.

"Connie," I whispered.

"Yeah?" she asked as she let me go and sat back into the sofa.

"I…" I clammed up, my throat going tight, I couldn't do it. I felt like I was suffocating. She sat there, waiting for me to spit out whatever it was I was trying to say, but the words never came.

"I love you," I smiled, my cheeks pinching with red before I pulled her back into me. I was a fucking coward.

"Ah, boo, I love you too."

CHAPTER 26

I SAT AND LISTENED AS CONNIE TOLD ME ALL ABOUT TRYST AND what they had been up to. It sounded like a whirlwind romance, but she was happy.

"Oh Con, I am so happy for you," I beamed as I tugged her towards me, cuddling her once more. I felt all warm and fuzzy inside for her.

"Thank you," she squeezed me before pulling back, "just don't tell my dad. Not yet… he isn't the biggest fan of Tryst," she winced.

"I wouldn't tell your dad. We work together, we're hardly friends." *Liar, liar, pants on fire.* My subconscious sung over and over. I ignored her. "How does your dad know Tryst? I didn't think you saw your dad that much?" I furrowed my brow.

"I didn't, I still don't. The odd holiday here and there, but he always told my mums he wanted me to know who he was and vice versa. He didn't want to be an anonymous donor. After my mums picked him, he pulled his sample out of the fertility clinic that it was stored in. He was happy he could help one couple and decided that was enough." She shrugged, "Don't get me wrong, he hasn't been a shitty father per se, just never really made much of an effort until I was manageable and potty trained. He used to drop in when I was a new-born apparently, but that soon dwindled to nothing once his work picked up," she sighed, "but anyway, yeah Tryst. We went elementary together, then into middle school… blah blah," she rolled her wrist to indicate they went through school together. "We always dated on and off, but he was the geeky loner that kept himself to himself, and I was in with the popular crowd. We ended up clashing and I was too busy having fun with the girls." She winked, "then he reached out, asking if we could meet up, have coffee, ya know?" taking a mouthful of wine, her tongue darted out to wet her lips, "so after a lot of uuming and ahhing I gave in and met him, and yeah, the rest is history."

"Oh Connie, that is amazing. Childhood sweethearts," I placed my hand over my heart, feeling the thump against my chest. Suddenly, sadness ripped through me. My smile that was once there had now faded.

"Reese?" The concern in Connie's voice choked me.

"I'm sorry, I'm fine," I nodded, blinking the sting away that was threatening behind my eyes.

"You're not fine."

I sniffed, wiping my nose with the sleeve of my jumper.

"Talk to me," she coaxed, her voice soft as she moved closer to me, her hand on my thigh.

Nibbling on the inside of my lip, my eyes fell to my lap. My fingers locked together, my heart raced under my skin.

"Reese," she whispered.

Looking up at the ceiling, I tried to blink away my tears. I tried to ignore the poignant burn that was in my throat. But I couldn't.

"It's just, um…" I sniffed, my head slowly dropping forward as I looked at her.

"You're scaring me."

"I lost my first love, Elijah." I whispered, the tears rolling down my cheeks before slipping off my chin. She knew he died, but she didn't know what happened. "Two years ago, Elijah died while on his way home from a job interview." I could barely talk, the crushing weight in my chest was overpowering. "He crashed, lost control we think; I was told there would have been no pain because of the impact." I sniffed. My eyesight blurry as the tears cascaded down my face. "It took a while for it to sink in, I just couldn't believe he was gone. We were childhood sweethearts, engaged to be married, planning our future, our family..." I choked, inhaling deeply as I tried to calm myself down. I had done so well without the tears, but now it was as if the flood gates had opened and I couldn't stop.

"Oh," I heard Connie sob, launching herself at me, wrapping her arms tightly around my shoulders as she held me while I sobbed. No words were exchanged, they weren't needed.

She just comforted me. And that's all I needed and wanted.

I needed my friend.

THE DAYS WERE ROLLING INTO ONE; MY WORKDAYS WERE HECTIC, my evenings were quiet which is what I needed.

"What are you doing for Christmas?" Connie asked as we walked aimlessly round the busy shops.

"My mum and dad are flying over, what about you?" I asked, picking up a peter pan collared red jumper, holding it up.

"Just with my mums, seeing as I was with dad on thanksgiving, I'll be with them." She nodded towards the top, "I like it, it's cute," she smiled.

I held onto the jumper as we continued walking.

"What are your traditions?" Connie asked.

"Christmas Eve?"

"Yeah."

"Erm," I stalled for a moment, blinking. "Well, back home we spend the day baking with Christmas music playing, then we cosy down with *The Santa Clause* and drink hot chocolate before getting tucked up in bed." A laugh bubbled out of me.

"That's cute," she smiles as she picks up a gold, sequin number.

"What about you?"

"We all share one present each, then we go for a walk round times square and take in the ambience. Then it's back home for wine, Chinese and bed ready for the big, fat man." She winks, holding the dress up against her slender, lean body.

"I like it. And I love the dress, buy it," I nod at her.

"Why don't you and your parents spend Christmas eve with us? It'll be lovely," Connie asks as she lays the dress over her forearm and continues browsing.

"Let me see what they say, if that's okay? They get in on the twenty-third and I know my mum is going to be drama with the jet lag," I laugh.

"Okay, that's cool. But I hope you can make it," she shrugs, and for some reason it pulls on my heart. "How was work this week?" she asks as we continue our walk around.

"Eugh, hell," I sigh, "I honestly think I'll quit; I can't stand her. She treats me like dirt, your dad gives in to her every demand…" I stick my finger down the back of my throat and pretend to gag.

"That's Adele."

"Well Adele can get fucked." Pulling my finger out and flipping the shop around me off, I heard a deep rumble of a laugh come from behind me.

Killian.

I felt my skin erupt in goosebumps, my heart thumping in my chest, the air sucking out of my lungs. Connie spun round, her long, brown ponytail swishing against my arm as she did.

"Dad! What are you doing here?" Connie's surprised voice echoed.

"Just thought I would pop in; I saw your location on my phone app," I can hear the smile in his voice even though I haven't turned round.

I inhaled deeply.

"Of course, you did, weirdo." Connie smirked.

"Reese?" Killian asked, letting out my breath I spun around.

"Oh, hey," I smiled, waving awkwardly.

His delicious smile spread across his face.

"Can I have a word?" he asked, his voice lower now. "It's a work thing, I know it's the weekend but it's really important…" I could see the hope in his eyes.

I felt Connie's eyes on me, before they moved back to her dad.

"I mean, I would have called you, but you blocked my number."

Rolling my eyes, I stepped forward.

"Oh, Mr Hayes!" I gasped, holding my hands over my mouth, "I am so sorry… I'll unblock your number. I must have done it by mistake! I didn't recognise the number, I didn't want just any old perv keep messaging me," I smirk, walking past him before lowering my voice so only he could hear, "you have five minutes." I snapped, walking towards the front of the shop. I heard the mutter of their voices as I walked away.

Crossing my arms across my chest, I looked out on the busy pathway, it was heaving with Christmas shoppers. I ordered most of mine online, I didn't like being in busy places. I made an exception for Connie because I feel like I have been so busy with her dad and work that I haven't made much time for her. Swallowing, I tried to coat my dry mouth and throat but it didn't work.

My body reacted to him before I heard him. I hated that it betrayed me like that.

"Brat," his voice was low, it was like a growl as he stepped behind me. I stilled.

"Connie," I whispered.

"Connie has gone to pay for yours and her clothes, so we're alone… apart from the hundreds of people walking past this shop."

"What do you want?" my voice was shaky, but I stood tall. I didn't want him to see just how much he affected me.

"I want to see you; you're freezing me out and I don't like it," his fingertips brushed down my arm. I snapped, turning to face him.

"I'm freezing *you* out?" my voice was a little louder now, rage brewing inside of me. "You froze yourself out when you acted like a pillock," I snorted.

His brows pinched, he was taken aback by what I said.

"Pillock?" his brows dug in now, his eyes narrowing on me.

"A simpleton, a fool, an *annoyance*," I growled, shaking my head, "I don't have time for this." Stepping aside, I tried to rush past him to get to Connie.

His hand stuck out, spreading across my stomach, and stopping me. The sparks that coursed through me from that one touch, amplifying my nerve endings. My breath caught in the back of my throat, stumbling back in front of him where he wanted me.

"Don't run from me," one of his brows arched.

"Not running, just don't want to be here anymore," I said with annoyance, arms crossing across my chest again.

"Oh, Buttercup. You're such a brat," his hand grasped my chin, holding it tightly.

"I've heard you're not happy at Lordes, is that true?" he asked, his voice softer now as if he was actually concerned.

I hesitated for a moment, my mind whizzing with how he knew. *Connie.*

"Yes," I sighed.

His brows furrowed, his head lowering as he craned his neck.

"Why didn't you say anything?"

"Because it's nothing to do with you," my eyes bored through his, his beautiful brown eyes had hints of caramel running through them.

"It has a lot to do with me," he breathed, his minty breath on my face.

Rubbing my lips together, I pulled his hand away from me and he let me.

"I've got to go," I whispered, I couldn't be this close to him. He was killing me. Stepping around him, his fingers grasped my wrist and pulled me to face him.

"Reese," his eyes volleyed back and forth between mine, "come to my office on Monday, unblock my number and I'll send you the address."

"I'll ask Connie, there is no need for me to unblock your number."

"You're so fucking petty," he growls.

"Yup," I flicked my long blonde hair over my shoulder and walked towards Connie, ignoring the low hum of a growl that came from behind me.

We headed for a small restaurant on the corner of 5th avenue. The snow that had settled last week had begun to melt but we were in for another storm over night. Unwrapping our scarfs and coats we piled them on our shopping bags. The warm air from the restaurant nipped at our frost-bitten skin causing our cheeks to redden.

We ordered ultimate hot chocolates, finished with whipped cream, marshmallows and mini peppermint candy canes.

"What did my dad want?" Connie asked as she swiped her finger through the whipped cream and sucked it off.

My shoulders slumped forward slightly.

"He knows I want to leave," I pinned her with my eyes, I knew it must have come from her.

She bared her teeth to me, a big smile, "You're not mad, are you? Please don't be mad," her voice coming out as a beg.

I wrapped my fingers round my cup, bringing it to my lips as I shook my head, "I'm not."

"Good, I done it for you."

"I know you did."

"What are you going to do?" she asked, swiping more cream.

"Go to his office," shrugging my shoulders up.

"Maybe he will offer you a job," she smirked.

"I doubt that, not sure if I want to work with him anyway," I said honestly, taking a mouthful of the thick, velvety hot chocolate. It was delicious.

"Why?" her brows pinched.

"I don't know." That was the truth, I didn't know. Maybe it was because we were married, we've fucked, and that little slither of hope that we did have of taking our relationship to the next level was crushed when he didn't answer when I told him I wanted a baby in future. "Wouldn't it be weird me working directly under your dad?" It's already kind of weird that I work for his company and have Satan as a boss.

"Well, don't rule it out, okay?"

"I won't. As long as I am away from Adele, I'll be happy."

"Hey! I could get you a job at the hotel if you need a little float between."

"Thank you hun, I might take you up on that."

It would help if I couldn't find anything, and I really

didn't want to rely on Killian to get me a job just because we were married.

"Anything for you my little sugar plum," she smiled, stabbing a fork into her chips and shoving them into her mouth.

I snorted a laugh as I ate with her.

Walking arm in arm back to my apartment block, I couldn't feel my hands. It was so bitter out.

"How are things going with Tryst? Any idea when you're going to tell your dad?" I nudged Connie. I heard her sigh.

"I will, soon," she nodded, "he probably won't even remember him, he didn't like the fact I was dating. He is a little over the top," she air quoted 'little.'

"No shit," I laugh, I knew how Killian could be.

"But he may be okay now, I am older, more mature and sophisticated," she nudged me back.

"That you are," I winked, stopping as we waited outside the apartment block.

"I'll set a date up soon, me, you, Tryst and I'll sort the blind date out for you," she winked.

I felt myself tense at the thought of going on a blind date, but I needed to get over Killian, and a date would help that. Hopefully.

"Yeah," I muttered, looking into the building, "You wanna come up or?"

"I would love too but I have a date with Tryst tonight so need to get dressed."

"Okay hun," I pulled her in for a cuddle. "Thanks for today, I suppose I better thank your dad for these too!" I blushed, holding the shopping bags up.

"Don't worry about it, he offered." She stepped back and began walking away.

"Have fun tonight and be safe!" I called out after her.

"I will!" she called back before turning and disappearing into the distance.

I waited till she was out of sight before walking into my block.

"Afternoon Reese," Frank tipped his head as I approached.

"Hi Frank," I smiled, walking towards the lift, and heading to my floor. I was grateful to be inside the warmth. I had big plans tonight, me, wine and a good film.

The doors pinged when the lift stopped; grabbing my bags I began walking towards my apartment. Once inside I dropped the bags to my feet and shook my coat and scarf off. Ramping up the heating, I froze when I saw a huge bouquet of red roses sitting in the centre of my worktop. It took me a moment to move. Stepping slowly over, I reached for the card sitting in the beautiful flowers. Clasping it between my thumb and index finger, I couldn't help the smile that crept onto my face.

Reese,

Let's start again.
I'm taking you on a date.
See you at seven.
K x

The swarm of butterflies that fluttered in my stomach made me feel slightly giddy, or was that the nausea setting me off? Popping the card back into the little holder, I grabbed my bags from the front door before heading to my bedroom to get dressed.

I couldn't help the niggle that was distracting me, part of me thought this was a disaster, that we should just leave it.

But I couldn't. Something was telling me that I needed to go, I owed it to him and myself.

Putting my new red, peter pan collar jumper on I paired it with high waisted skinny black jeans and doc martens.

I wanted comfort. I had no idea where we were going, I just hope it wasn't anywhere uptight and stuffy. Hopefully Killian knew that too. But who was I kidding, we didn't know one another at all.

Pulling my hair into a low ponytail, I applied some lip balm and pulled my beige trench coat on. Checking the time, it had just gone seven. I headed to the front door, walking out and locking up when I saw Killian standing in the hallway waiting for me.

"You look pretty," he smiled at me, stepping towards me and kissing my cheek.

"Thanks," I blushed at his words, "thank you for the flowers."

I took a moment to appreciate the fine specimen of a man in front of me. He was handsome as hell, so beautiful. His dark brown hair was styled to perfection and pushing away from his face. Brown eyes that glistened as they raked up and down my body. A dark grey turtleneck sweater that was covered by a black puffer coat, with black jeans and boots.

He looked delicious.

"Ready?" he asked, holding his hand out for me while looking at my finger that was missing the ring.

"Where are we going?" I asked, lacing my fingers through his.

"It's a surprise," he winked, pulling me into him and kissing the side of my head.

I didn't say anything, tightening my grip on his hand, he led me out to the street. I felt excited, anxious and apprehensive. I was hoping we could have a fresh start; we needed to start over. Even if we were just friends, got our annulment and then continued our friendship. He would always be in my life now because of Connie, and I was never not going to be friends with her.

We walked out into the lobby of the apartment block and past Frank. Killian gave him a curt nod and pulled me into a waiting car at the kerb.

"Fancy car," I teased as he closed the door behind us.

"Eh, it's okay," he smirked, leaning across and strapping me in before seeing to his own seatbelt.

"Going to tell me where we are going yet?" I asked, slightly hopeful.

"Nope," he tapped the side of his nose as the car pulled off into the busy, evening traffic.

"Spoil sport."

The silence fell through the car for a moment, it didn't feel awkward, just a little unnerving. Was he feeling as nervous as I was? The butterflies swarmed my tummy, feeling like it was constantly somersaulting.

"I want us to get to know each other a little better…" he turned to face me, a glint of something showing in his dark pools. "I know you work for me; you know my daughter and you're British… That's all I know." His shoulders shaking softly as a light chuckle vibrates through him.

I nodded in agreement.

"And I know that you're possessive, a father and my boss…" I knocked my shoulder into him which caused another laugh to leave him. His large hand found its place on my thigh, a soft squeeze letting me know he also agreed.

"So, let's get to know each other," his voice was gentle as he looked out the windscreen at the tail of red lights.

"What do you want to know?" my voice was barely audible through the thick tension and the low rumble of the car engine.

My eyes focused on his fingers as they drummed on the steering wheel of his Porsche.

"You like my car?" he wiggled his brows.

"I do," I laughed, "it's nice." I nodded. I knew nothing about cars.

"Yeah? Do you know what it is?"

"Duh… it's a Porsche," I rolled my eyes.

"Rolling your eyes again, wife?"

I nibbled my bottom lip trying to stifle my laugh. Was it wrong that I liked rolling my eyes at him?

"And yes, it's a Porsche… do you know the model?" his grip tightened on my thigh.

"Erm…" I blushed under his assault, "What is this, twenty-one questions?" I quipped.

He tipped his head back and let out a low grumble of a laugh.

"I'm sorry, just trying to lighten the very solemn mood I feel like is surrounding us."

I sighed. He was right… the mood was off.

"It's a 911 GT3, I thought you might have commented on my rose gold wheels," he winked at me, "Connie thinks they're girlie."

"I didn't really pay attention," I admitted, rubbing my hands together for something to do.

"Well, when we stop, you can tell me," he smirks, "now, tell me something about yourself, anything…"

I inhaled deeply. I didn't want to mention Elijah just yet, it was too soon. My fingers rubbed and twisted at the ring on my finger.

"I am half Venezuelan," I shrugged my shoulders up.

"Mother or father's side?"

"Father." I smiled.

"Did you always want to work in public relations?" he asked as the traffic began to move.

"No, I never really knew what I wanted to do. I sort of fell into PR work and just followed it. I used to help my mum and dad with their little bistro too." I nodded, pouting my lips as I thought back to my parents. I couldn't wait to see them.

"I see."

"I'm petty and act like a brat…" the corner of my mouth turned up slightly.

"Well, I know that already," he winked before turning down a side road.

Blushing, I turned to face out the window, taking in the sights of pretty New York. We pulled into an underground car park, Killian's car engine roaring round the space.

"Where are we?" I asked, sad that we had lost the Christmas lights.

"A parking lot," he smiled as he pulled into a car parking space that had reserved under it.

"This space is reserved," I pointed out as I shuffled to the edge of my car seat.

"I know, it's my space."

"Of course, it is."

"Problem?"

"Nope." I held my hands up, a smile creeping across my lips.

"Good." He turned the engine off, leaning towards me and kissing me on the tip of my nose. "Wrap up baby, it's cold outside," he whispered, opening his door and rushing round my side. Opening my door, he held his hand out for me to take which I did gladly.

"You ready for our date?" he pulled me into him. His arms snaking around my waist as he held me close, his lips inches from mine. I wanted nothing more than for him to kiss me, to hold me and tell me he wanted to give this a go.

But he wouldn't.

"I am," whispering, my hands moved to his chest as I pushed him away. I couldn't be this close to him. It was if water was filling my lungs, slowly drowning in him.

I began to walk towards the exit of the car park, Killian's fingers wrapping round my wrist as he tugged me back towards him.

"Hey, why are you running off?" his brows pinched.

"I'm not, I am just excited." I couldn't even smile fully, my heart hurt, and I had no idea why.

"Walk with me," I didn't know if he was asking me or telling me. I nodded; his fingers laced through mine as we walked together. And for the first time ever, it felt right.

"Any idea where we are going yet?" Killian asked as he watched me.

"No idea," I breathed, it was a struggle to talk when I was this close to him. He suffocated me.

He tugged me into the busy streets, my hands instantly clammy at the hustle and bustle.

"You okay?" he asked.

I nodded. I didn't want to tell him this was my worst nightmare; he didn't need to know. He continued leading me to our destination, I stilled, my eyes widening as we stopped at the Rockefella Ice Rink.

"Ice skating?" I asked, turning to face him, the cold nipping at my cheeks making me blush.

He nodded. "You can ice skate, right?"

"Of course, the question is Mr Hayes, can you?"

"I am a pro," he said confidently as we went to get our boots on.

We sat down, Killian handing me my boots as I slipped them on. I waited for Killian who was acting like a princess as he struggled to get his feet into the boots.

"Do you need a bigger size?" I asked, biting the inside of my cheek to stop myself from laughing.

"I got my size, I'm a twelve," he huffed, pushing his hand through his hair as he tried to squeeze his foot in the boot once more.

"You remind me of the ugly sister in Cinderella when she is trying to fit into the slipper that is *clearly* too small for her…" I rolled my eyes, shuffling towards him and pulling his boot off his big foot. "I'll go get you a bigger size, old man," I teased, walking on the blade of the skate boot. I probably shouldn't be doing this but if I wait for princess, we won't ever skate.

Shoving the next size up in his face, he took them from me and placed them on his feet.

"There we go Princess, they fit, okay?" I snorted as he grabbed me to stand up and steady himself.

"Fuck off, Reese."

I cackled as we both made our way over to the ice rink.

I stepped over the small step to get onto the ice, Killian followed and held onto the side the whole time.

I glided onto the ice, stopping, and waiting for Killian.

He stood there, his hands gripping to the edge. I thought he said he could skate, what in the ever-loving fuck was he doing?

"What are you doing?" I shouted across.

"Just getting used to it!" he shouted back, clearly flustered and frustrated.

"Do you need me to hold your hand?"

"No thank you!" he stamped across the ice. My brows sat high as I watched him in front of me, he was like Bambi on ice for the first time. A pro? He wasn't a pro.

Rolling my eyes, I skated over to him and took his hand.

"Trust me?" I asked.

He grunted in response.

Holding onto his hand tightly, I led him into the ice-skating stream. He couldn't skate for shit, he was walking, not gliding.

"I swear to God Reese, if I fall…"

"You'll hit the ground pretty damn hard," I laughed, "just remember big boy, this was your idea…" I taunted as I let go of him and glided elegantly before skidding my skate to turn and face him.

"Just push your feet forward, as if you're skating across your beautifully, polished marble floors back home."

He rolled his eyes at me.

"What have I said about you rolling your eyes at me," placing my hands on my hips as I teased him.

"Reese," he growled at me in a warning tone.

"What you going to do? Stamp your way over to me," I let out a belly laugh.

"Don't push me."

"Come on old man, come and get me." I licked my top lip slowly, taunting him.

And he did. He stamped his way over to me, grabbing me and holding on for dear life before I lost balance and fell, taking the brunt of the fall.

I burst into laughter, Killian laughing with me as he lay on top of me.

"Shit, Reese, are you okay?!" his voice was panicked, his eyes volleying over my face. I nodded, laughing still.

"Well, I didn't think we would be doing this on our date," he said breathless.

My laugh died out; our eyes connected as we both locked our gaze.

"We better get up," I whispered.

"I don't want to…"

"I don't think the other skaters will want to keep skating round us."

"Screw the other skaters," he growled, his hands cupping my face as his lips pressed into mine.

My heart swelled in my chest, my hands entwining in his hair as I tugged, his groan vibrating through me as our tongues danced with each other's.

"Killian," I breathed, breaking away, "we need to get up." Trying with all my might to shove him off me.

He gave in, pushing himself up onto his knees. He held his hand out for me to take, pulling me up, I managed to push myself to my feet, but Killian was still on his knees.

"I need help," I saw his cheeks blush.

"Do you now?"

"Reese don't start…" he sighed, but I could see the amusement dancing in his eyes. I held my hands out for him to take, he weighed triple of me, I don't know how I was going to help him.

With a lot of failed attempts, I finally got him up.

"Jesus," he panted, undoing his coat, "who's idea was it to come ice skating?!" he said, wrapping his arm round my shoulder and pulling me towards him and kissing the side of my head. "Let's get these death traps off our feet."

Once we were back in our own shoes, I began walking back towards the car when Killian stopped me, shaking his head from side to side.

"We're not done yet," he winked, pulling me next to him. We headed back towards the ice-skating rink, but this time we walked alongside it.

"See how elegantly they're all skating?"

"What's your point Reese?"

"You didn't look like that… I thought you said you were a pro."

"I'm a pro spectator," he snorted which caused a laugh to bubble out of me. Killian stopped me, turning me to look at the Rockefeller tree, I was stunned. My eyes slowly moved up the tree, taking in every inch of it. It was truly breath-taking. I have seen it on television and in films so many times, but actually standing in front of it, seeing it in person was something else.

"Wow, it's beautiful," I whispered, that's all I could manage. Words failed me.

"I know right," I felt his stare on me. After a moment, Killian's hand wrapped around my waist as he moved behind me, his face nuzzling into my neck as I felt him inhale my scent. "But it's not as beautiful as you."

My skin erupted, a shiver dancing up my spine causing the hairs on my arms and neck to stand tall. I couldn't explain how he made me feel. I knew it was wrong to feel anything towards him, but I couldn't stop myself.

We were so wrong for each other.

But the pull towards him was too much for me to ignore. Turning around to face him, I had to catch my breath. I don't think I would ever get over just how beautiful he was. My fingers brushed against his stubble that was dusted over his jaw line, the friction making the tips of my fingers burn. My hands clasped his face, pulling his lips down to meet mine. I wanted to be strong and fight the urge, but I couldn't. Even if this was our last kiss, our last date, our last moment of just us. I wanted it to be here. In this picture-perfect moment where nothing else in the world mattered apart from us two.

"I never want to stop kissing you," he whispered against my lips before covering them again.

My heart skipped a beat. I felt constricted.

"The feeling is mutual." Pulling away from him, I sucked my bottom lip in, "but this will never work, Killian." The prick of tears formed behind my eyes, but I blinked them away. I didn't want to cry.

His callous thumb rubbed against my cheek, brushing a lone tear that ran down.

"We can make it work," he whispered.

I shook my head from side to side.

"I can't do it to Connie, *we* can't do it to Connie; and that's without going into any of the other reasons." The familiar burn coursed down my throat; my lungs tight as I gasped for air. It felt as if a steel pipe had been thrust into my windpipe.

Killian just nodded, his hand still cupping my cheek before he stepped towards me, his lips pursing before placing them onto my forehead. He lingered for a moment; my eyes closed as I felt the tears begin to fall. And this time, I didn't stop them.

"Come," he said softly, taking my hand and leading us away from the Christmas tree.

I didn't know where we were going, I just hoped it wasn't home yet.

We sat in a cosy, tucked away coffee shop. The smell of the coffee beans drifted through my nose. Behind the counter there was fresh cakes and pastries as well as an assortment of little chocolates.

Killian walked back to the table with two fully loaded hot chocolates. I smiled and took mine from him as it warmed my hands.

He shrugged his coat off and laid it next to him on the free seat next to him in our booth.

"Let's talk," he reached across, taking my hand and rubbing his thumb across the back.

"What do you want to talk about?" my smart mouth working quicker than my brain.

"Everything. I said earlier, I want to know everything about you," he smiled.

I nodded, inhaling deeply as my eyes fell to the melting whipped cream on my drink.

"Okay," breathing out my held breath, trying to calm the firework of nerves that were exploding inside, my heart jack hammering in my chest. "So, you remember when I said I was supposed to marry someone else?" I still didn't lift my eyes, I couldn't look at him, so instead I focused on my drink, watching the cream slowly melt into the thick, brown liquid.

"Yeah," his voice was low.

"Well, I was engaged to my childhood sweetheart, Elijah." I felt the needles prick behind my eyes, but I was determined not to cry. I could do this.

"What happened?" he asked before I could continue.

"He passed away two years ago; he was on his way home from a job interview. He had worked so hard to get to that point, to take the next step he needed for his career. He text me to tell me he was leaving, but he never showed up. Next thing I knew, I had the police on my doorstep telling me that he had been in an accident and that I had to say goodbye..." I felt the wobble of my bottom lip, but I ignored it. I needed to get through this story without crying. "I didn't believe it, I kept asking if he was okay even after the police officer told me they were taking me to say goodbye. No one else was harmed, but my Elijah, he just didn't make it." I sniffed, blinking away the pool of tears that were beginning to fill my eyes. "We had planned our lives, we were trying for a baby but because of his job plans, we put it on hold for a few months... we never got the chance to become a family." I swallowed the apple sized lump down, my eyes still cast down. "He was the love of my life, I never thought I would move on..." but now I lifted them, my watery gaze catching his stare and holding it.

His own eyes were glistening with unshed tears.

"Until..." he swallowed.

"Until..." I nodded.

The silence crashed over us, the tension thick in the air. My eyes fell back to my hot chocolate, the cream completely melted into my drink now as the marshmallows bobbed up and down.

"I'm sorry Reese." Killian's arm stretched across the table, his fingers wrapping around my wrist.

"It is what it is," my eyes flick back up to him, I am sure I can feel my heart cracking all over again, the guilt eating me up.

"Don't say that." Killian shook his head.

"What?" my brows dug in as I furrowed them.

"Don't say 'it is what it is'."

"Why?"

"Because you're accepting that what happened is okay."

I yanked my arm away from him.

"That's not what I am doing," I snapped. "I have accepted

what happened, I haven't accepted anything more than that. Anything anyone does to me now doesn't bother me as much as losing Elijah. People may hurt me, Killian, people might make me cry, but I won't beg anyone to stay, I won't beg for anyone to love me. Don't love me? Fine. If they want to leave? Leave. I am broken, Killian. There is nothing that can hurt me as much as Elijah dying did. I have accepted that this is my path, this was my fate, *it is what it is.*" I steadied my gaze, not blinking or breaking contact with him for a second.

"That was not your fate Reese, *this* right here is your fate. The moment you're living in now is your fate. I believe you make your own fate; I don't believe your life is mapped out for you. It's bullshit. You either want to grab life by the balls or you let life royally fuck you over. I chose the first option. You don't think I haven't had my fair share of *'it is what it is'* moments? I've had a handful. But I chose to go against the grain and changed my mindset." I saw the clench in his jaw, his eyes narrowing on mine.

"Bully for you." I threw myself back into the booth sofa, crossing my arms.

"Reese..."

"What?" I quipped.

"Don't act like this... I was just trying to make you see things how I see them." His voice was soft as he continued, "What happened to..." he stalled for a moment, his eyes searching mine as he waited for my acceptance to say his name. I nodded softly. "What happened to Elijah was devastating. No one should have to go through losing the love of their life... but it has made me understand you that little better. Selfish of me, I know." He sighed, rubbing his stubble, licking his lips, "Can I take you home?"

I could feel he wanted to say more, but maybe he was scared of crossing the line.

"Yeah," I whispered, grabbing my coat from the side of me and slipping out of the booth. I shrugged my coat on and waited for Killian. He threw some dollars down, took my hand and we walked to the car.

The snow was falling around us, the air was bitter.

"You didn't tell me anything about you."

I felt his grip tighten on my hand.

"Let's save getting to know me for another night…" he turned his head, looking down at me as he smiled.

I nodded. I had overloaded him tonight.

But we both knew this was the end.

We both knew we were a losing game.

There wasn't going to be another night.

We only had tonight.

And I wanted to remember it all.

CHAPTER 27
KILLIAN

How could I have not known about what happened to her?

But then again, how was I to know? We didn't know each other. We still didn't know each other.

It was the end of the road for us.

I knew she was right about Connie. I had to put my daughter above anyone I loved, because she was my world.

I was a shitty father, but I was trying to make it right.

Sure, I was her 'sperm donor' as she liked to refer to me, but I wanted to be so much more than that to her. I didn't want anything to fuck it up.

Pulling the car into the underground parking lot of our apartment block, I cut the engine. Turning in my chair, I faced her.

"Spend the night with me…?" I asked her, my eyes connecting with hers. She was flawless. Pure. Everything I would want in a woman.

But she is right. We wouldn't work. She wants what I can't give her, and it is selfish of me to ask her to not have kids because I don't want them.

"I would love to," she smiled, the familiar blush creeping onto her golden skin.

Thank fuck she said yes.

Opening the door, I walked round to her side and helped her out. We walked hand in hand to the back entrance of the apartment block. No words were exchanged as we waited for the elevator. If this was our final goodbye, I wanted to remember every part of her. I wanted my fingers to trace her outline and every curve of her slender body. I wanted this evening imprinted on my brain, so I always had it.

There was something about her that had me addicted. The thought that after tonight she was going to be just a *friend* made my chest heavy, an unbearable pain searing through me.

I had never been in love.

I had never wanted to be in love.

And the one girl that could make me want it was out of bounds.

She was my daughter's best friend.

We were never meant to be together.

Opening the door, I let her walk through into my penthouse first then I closed the door. I stepped behind her, taking her coat off her shoulders and hanging it up before I took my own off.

She was still standing with her back to me. I closed the gap between us, my hands wrapping around her waist as I held her, my hands splayed across her stomach. I buried my nose into her hair and inhaled as I smelt the familiar vanilla and peach undertones. I loved her smell. I wanted to bottle it up, so I always had it.

I heard her sharp intake of breath as my lips pressed to the pulsing vein in her neck. Her heart was racing. Slow, soft kisses I planted over her bare skin as my lips made their way to her ear lobe, stopping when I got to the shell of her ear.

"I want to make love to you," I whispered, which caused a shudder to rip through her.

Her hands moved over mine as she pulled them off me. She turned slowly to face me, her eyes locking with mine and I swear I felt the ground move beneath us. She was bearing the window to her soul, she wanted me to see all of her, and I finally did. I saw it all. Every imperfect, beautiful, soul destroying and heart-breaking piece of her.

And now I wanted to spend the entire evening trying my hardest to put her back together again. To make her feel complete.

Her small hands moved to my face, holding me in place as she pushed onto her tiptoes and kissed me. Her sweet moans humming through her, she was delectable. I wanted to take her breath away, I wanted to hear her sweet moans fill the room.

My hands roamed over her body before our fingers entwined, "Come."

A simple word, but so powerful.

I led her through to my bedroom, her eyes widening as they roamed around the room.

The walls were a greige, my queen-sized bed sat central against the wall dressed with a black, solid wood headboard. The room was pretty plain, but it worked for me.

I didn't want her to get too in her head, I padded over to her, my arm snaking around her back as I pulled her body close to mine.

My finger on my other hand hooked under the shoulder of her red sweater top. Slowly pulling it down to reveal her glowing, tanned skin. Pressing my lips to her neck, I glided them across to her collar bone and over her shoulder. Her small hands wrapped around the fabric of my sweater, clinging onto me.

Pulling my lips from her was harder than I imagined, it took so much strength to pull away. My fingers clutched the hem of her sweater top as I pulled it over her head and discarded it on the floor. Moving down to her jeans, I fumbled with the button and watched her push them down her slender, long legs. My cock was throbbing in my jeans. She was beautiful. She stood in front of me, in her little black panties and matching bra. She reached up and pulled her long, honey blonde hair out of her hair tie, running her fingers through the root to loosen it up. I watched as it cascaded down past her breasts, sitting at her ribs.

She stalked towards me, her hands on my sweater as she pulled it over my head. Who would have thought something as simple as undressing each other could be so sensual? I made quick work on taking my pants off, kicking them off my feet. Our bodies pressed together, my hands in her hair as I tipped her head back, my lips slanting as they covered hers. Our tongues caressing and moulding together. I walked her towards the bed, our lips still locked. The back of her knees hit the edge of the bed as I gently nudged her, so she fell on her back into my comforter. Her golden hair fanned around her, her legs parting for me.

"Buttercup, this is going to be slow, hard and fucking amazing," I whispered, kneeling on the bed between her legs.

She bit her bottom lip.

"Don't bite your lip." I warned, gripping her chin tightly as I kissed her fiercely before I bit her bottom lip, causing a moan to escape her. I stilled, clicking the music on in the bedroom, *Chris Brown – Take You Down* filled the room.

"Aren't you a bit old to be listening to music like this... *old man*," Reese teased as she bit her bottom lip again.

I groaned, my cock thickening.

"Old man," I scoffed. I wanted to own her and mark her and that's exactly what I was about to do.

My calloused fingers popped her breasts from her cotton bra, rolling her hardened nipple between my two fingers as my tongue caressed hers.

"Killian," she whimpered.

I smirked against her lips.

I continued, my hand dropping from her chin as it skimmed down the side of her body and slipped into the side of her panties. She was already soaked for me. Swirling the tip of my fingers at her opening, coating them in her arousal before they circled over her sensitive clit. She moaned, my cock straining against my jockey shorts. I wanted to be in her so bad. But I couldn't, not yet. Because if I slipped into her soaked cunt now, I would come. I didn't want it over yet. I slipped my fingers through her wet folds and pushed two of them inside of her, curling them as I stroked her g-spot. Her back arched, pressing her pert little tit into my mouth. I groped her, squeezing her breast as I sucked hard, my tongue swirling over her nipple.

"Fuck," I heard her curse.

"Don't come yet, brat," I said against her hot skin.

I trailed my wet mouth down over her sensitive skin, stopping at the top of her panties. Darting my tongue out, I licked across her lower stomach before pulling her panties off and discarding them to the floor.

Her bare pussy on show, glistening as she took my fingers like the good girl she was. Gliding my hand up over her stomach, I kept it there as my mouth covered her mound, licking and sucking over her clit. She writhed over my comforter, her legs trembling as I brought her close to her impending orgasm.

Her fingers wrapped themselves in my hair as she tugged at the root, pushing me deeper into her greedy little cunt. I licked and sucked, dragging my tongue between her folds as I continued to pump my fingers deep into her pussy.

Without warning, her whole body shook as she came. I slipped my fingers out and moved my mouth down as I drank her honey. I didn't want to waste a single drop.

"Killian, fuck," she cried out, her back arching, her legs

trembling as her orgasm ripped through her. I pressed her back down with my hand, so her back fell into the bed. I didn't want her to move, I wanted to drink her, I wanted her still while I enjoyed every drop of her.

After her body stopped convulsing, she grabbed my hand and moved it off her body. She sat on the edge of the bed, her fingers dipping into my shorts as she rolled them down my thick thighs, my hard, thick cock springing out.

Her eyes widened, licking her lips as she looked up at me.

Her lips pursed as she edged closer to me, her lips locking round the tip of my cock. My cum beading on the tip. She licked it off, then took me deep in her mouth as she sucked me hard. I didn't want to come in her mouth, I didn't want it to be game over, but her wet little mouth felt so good around my cock. My hand grabbed the back of her head, holding her still while I throat fucked her. I grunted, my body tensing as she took me like the queen she was. Her small fingers wrapped around my girth, pumping them up and down to match the rhythm of my thrusts. My free hand glided across her hardened nipples, tweaking and pulling before they slipped between her legs. Pushing a finger into her pussy, I fucked her with my fingers.

She moaned and groaned, but they were stifled because my dick had her mouth filled to the hilt. I felt my cock twitch as she drew me out to the tip, flicking her tongue across it before swallowing me and taking me deep.

"Baby," I spat through gritted teeth, pushing my hips deeper into her hot, wet mouth. She felt so fucking good.

Fuck it.

Maybe I will just come in her mouth. I'll be ready for round two in about ten...

I felt my balls tingle as her small hand cupped them, massaging them gently before her nails softly tickled them. They tightened and constricted as my cock jerked in her mouth. Her pussy was soaked, she was so turned on by this which turned me on even more.

Pulling my fingers to the tip, I plunged them back into her. Her pussy tightened around me.

"You going to come for me like the good girl you are?" my jaw clenched, my hand gripped her hair and tugged it at the roots.

She moaned.

"Such a good girl," I pumped into her mouth, her eyes watering as she took me deep.

She was a fucking pro.

Her hand that was massaging my balls moved round to my ass where she pushed against me, pushing me deeper into her mouth, her cheeks hollowed out as she held me at the back of her throat, deep throating me, her lips pressing against my pubic bone. She slowly shook her head from side to side, the feeling was indescribable. My whole body tingled as a shiver danced over my skin, shuddering I exploded.

"I'm going to come," I growled as I emptied myself into her innocent mouth, she moaned as she swallowed down, not leaving a single drop untouched. Pulling me slowly out of her mouth, she licked the tip before wiping the corners of her mouth with her ring fingers.

"Fuck," I groaned, my fingers wrapping round her throat as I fell to my knees and fucked her hard with my fingers.

"Come for me, I want you to come all over my fingers," I whispered against the shell of her ear before I rocked back onto my knees and watched as my fingers slipped in and out of her.

"Good girls listen, now come," I ordered, tightening my grip on her neck. Her hands reached for her breasts as she kneaded and squeezed them, one of her hands carried on sliding down her body as her fingers landed on her swollen clit. She rubbed in circular movements, her hips rocking into my fingers. I felt her pussy contract and tighten around me before her head fell back, her fingers rolling her nipple, her other fingers rubbing her clit harder as she shuddered, an orgasm blowing through her. I gave her a moment to come round, then slipping my fingers out I pushed them between my lips and sucked them clean.

She looked spent.

"Oh, baby... I am nowhere near finished with you yet."

Rolling her on her front, I climbed over her. Pushing her hair over her shoulder, I ran my fingertips down her spine, my lips following the trail.

My fingers danced over the skin on her peachy ass, my lips planting sloppy, wet kisses. I was drunk on her.

I felt myself harden once more; my hands moving to her little waist as I rolled her over. She smiled, her eyes drinking every ounce of me in.

"Wow, ready already old man?" she taunted, nibbling her lip as she pressed her thighs together. I roared a laugh, kneeling on the bed, my hands gripping her knees.

"I'll show you old man," I winked. I loved that she was laying spread over my comforter, completely naked and ready for me to play with again.

But this time, we weren't going to fuck... we were going to make love.

Slow, passionate, deep, meaningful love.

I began to press her knees open, Reese giggled as she closed them again.

"Let me in, brat," I whispered, pushing her legs open wide for me.

She gasped as I lay over her, not letting her shut them again.

"Don't play hard to get, Buttercup... you know you want this as much as I do."

She panted, nodding.

"I do," she whispered, "but I know that once it is over, this is over between us."

I sucked in a breath through my teeth. I didn't want to think about that now, shaking my head side to side, I fisted myself, lining myself up at her dripping wet pussy. Edging the tip in, my swollen head pressing into her tight cunt.

Her mouth formed a small 'o' as her body stretched in the most delicious way for me.

"That's it, take me like the good girl you are," I praised her as I slowly rocked my hips into her, filling her to the hilt.

Low moans escaped her and filled my room. Laying over her, my hands moved to her face, my fingers entwining in her hair, our eyes locking.

"Look at me baby," I say softly. Her legs wrap round my waist allowing me to thrust deeper into her, the tip of my cock rubbing her g-spot.

I never wanted to forget this moment. She was so pure and beautiful. Slipping my cock out to the tip, I still for a moment before sliding back into her hard.

She whined. I loved making her mewl for me, so I do it again.

"You like that?" I coax her, her eyes glued to mine.

"Yeah," she breathes out, her fingertips digging into my chest, her nails marking me. But not once did her eyes fall to my scar. It didn't even seem to bother her.

Craning my neck down, my lips hover over hers for a moment. Her sweet breath on my face, her pussy tightening around me.

Her hand glides up from my chest and wraps round my neck as she pulls my mouth to hers. Our lips connect, our tongues swirling and dancing together. Thrusting my hips faster now, my pace getting messy as my impending orgasm begins to heighten.

"I'm not going to last much longer," I whisper against her mouth.

"Neither am I, make me come Killian," she begs before kissing me again.

Pulling away, my hands leave her hair and grab onto her hips as I rear up. Lifting one of her legs over my shoulder, I slip out to the tip and hold it for a moment. Her fingers graze down her body and rub her clit gently. Spearing in and out of her, her pussy clenches around me. The sound of our bodies hitting together, my pace is messy and sloppy but I don't care. Tipping my head back, my eyes closing as I try to slow my orgasm.

"Oh fuck, Killian, fuck me harder," she cries out. I pound into her now, hard and fast like she asked, my skin tingles as I feel my orgasm brimming, I can't stop it.

"I'm going to come," I grit out, my eyes falling between our bodies as I watch my thick cock fuck her with ease.

"Shit," her teeth grit, her hand reaches up as she pulls me down and slams her lips into mine, her teeth sinking into my bottom lip as she comes. Her body trembles and my cock jerks as I empty inside of her before I collapse on top of her.

We lay in silence, her head on my chest with her hair fanned out behind her. My fingers trailed up and down her bare spine. No words were needed. This right here was perfection; it was the perfect goodbye.

CHAPTER 28
REESE

Fluttering my eyes open, it took me a moment to register where I was. Killian was snoring softly, my head on his chest. I slowly pushed myself up, careful not to wake him. My finger skimmed across his pink scar, tracing it down to under his ribs. My brows furrowed as I wondered what happened.

Lifting my finger, I slipped out of bed quietly and dressed myself before sneaking out of his apartment.

It was the perfect goodbye. No other words needed to be exchanged.

I rushed down the hallway and into the lift, continuing until I got to my apartment.

Locking the door behind me I didn't even undress, I just fell into bed. Exhaustion sweeping over me before I fell into a peaceful slumber.

It had been a week and Killian had kept his word. I hadn't heard from him, not even on a work basis. He cancelled the work meeting he arranged, saying it was for the best but if I needed to, I could always go and see him. He put the distance between us and for that, I was grateful.

I was at the office bright and early every day, hoping that each day was the day that Adele promoted me like she said. But up until now, she had hardly said two words to me. I don't know what I had done to upset her, unless Killian told her that we had an out of work relationship. Well, we couldn't really call it a relationship.

We fucked a few times. It wasn't a real relationship.

Sighing, I typed out a reply to some emails that Adele couldn't be bothered to reply to because replying to her clients was obviously beneath her now, she had her dogsbody to do it all for her.

After an hour, I pushed away from the desk to make a cup of coffee. It tasted like shit, but it was better than the twenty different flavoured teas they had. When I walked back towards my desk, I heard light chatter coming from Adele's office. Her door was cracked open, I shouldn't eavesdrop but I couldn't help it. Walking slowly to her door, I stepped aside so she couldn't see my shadow through the frosted glass.

"Well, she is going to have to get over it," I heard her harsh tone. "I know I did, but she played into my hands. I knew she was good, she got us what we wanted and now I have no use for her."

My heart raced.

"That's my final decision, she isn't getting the promotion. I'm not going to be at a loss if she walks out. In fact I'll be glad to wash my hands of her, I'll be asking her to leave sooner rather than later anyway."

I felt my heart drop out of my chest. Staggering back, I knocked into my desk, spinning around and placing my cup on the surface. I wasn't sticking around.

Throwing my belongings into my bag, including the photo frames of me and Connie and my parents. Grabbing my coat, scarf and hat, I threw them over my arm. Rushing past the turnstiles, I yanked my lanyard off and slapped it down on the front desk.

I didn't stop when the receptionist called me name, I held my hand up and flipped her off before pushing through the rotating doors into the soft snow blizzard. I was freezing, but I didn't want to stop. The cold air burned my lungs, my eyes streamed with hot tears, but I continued walking through the snow. I needed the air; I needed the time to think.

I just wanted to go home.

I SAT ON MY SOFA IN MY COMFORT CLOTHES OF LEGGINGS AND AN oversized jumper as I sipped on a proper cup of tea. What the fuck had just happened.

She was going to let me go? After getting her Lordes' biggest fucking signing to date she couldn't follow through on her word.

To say I was pissed off was an understatement. Snatching my phone from beside me I tapped on Connie's name.

ME

> Guess who walked out of her job today. That fucking woman is an ogre.

The three dots popped up to show me she was replying

CONNIE

> No. Fucking. Way. What a dog. What happened??????

I rolled my eyes, I could feel the heat pumping through my blood, the rage consuming me.

> ME
>
> I overheard her on the phone, no doubt to your dad, telling him that she wasn't going to follow through with what she said and that I wouldn't be getting the promotion. Whoever she was talking to must have asked her why, and she said I played into her hands and got what she wanted. She didn't care if I walked, she would be glad to wash her hands of me and would be getting rid of me soon anyway.

I tapped my phone screen so hard I was worried I was going to break it.

> CONNIE
>
> That bitch.

I saw the three dots appear as she began typing again.

> CONNIE
>
> Want me to speak to my dad?

I shook my head as if she was here as I typed out my response.

> ME
>
> No, no no!!! No speaking to your dad. It's done. I'll sort something out. Shit, this close to Christmas. Fuck it. Maybe I shouldn't have walked out.

I sent the message before dropping the phone into my lap. What had I done? My phone began ringing, making me smile when I saw Connie's name.

"Hello?" I asked a little apprehensive.

"Are you okay?" she asked, her voice low.

"Yeah, why are you talking so quietly?" I asked.

"I'm at work, shouldn't be on my phone... I just wanted to see if you were okay."

"I am fine, just annoyed but more annoyed at myself for

walking out without saying anything." I rolled my eyes to the empty room.

"Then go back over there and give her a piece of your mind," I heard Connie snigger. "If I wasn't at work, I would totally be there with you."

"I know you would."

"Do you really think she was on the phone to my dad."

I shrugged as if Connie could see me, "I just assumed."

"I couldn't see him being okay with that."

"Well, people surprise you when it comes to business and money." I felt the agitation brewing, "I am just annoyed that I worked so hard to get Harlen on board and now I've been disregarded."

"I know hun, it's a real low thing to do," I heard Connie sigh, "look, I've got to go. I could possibly get you some shifts if you want some… just let me know."

"Thank you," I whispered before cutting the phone off.

I didn't want Connie getting in trouble, that's all we needed, two of us out of a job.

I sat festering, playing the scenario over in my head. I should have said something, instead I have just slipped out like a coward. I loved my job, I loved doing what I done, I just didn't enjoy working for her.

Pushing off the sofa, I began to pace.

I swear, if she was on the phone to Killian and that twat hadn't called me or messaged… that's when I realised I had him blocked still. Fumbling with my phone, I unlocked it and found Killian's name, unblocking him. I gave it ten minutes, a few missed call notifications, and messages but nothing in the last week. What an arsehole. Did he know about this? Did he know I was going to be asked to leave?

Launching my phone onto the sofa, I walked for the door. Grabbing my scarf and coat on my way out, I wrapped myself up before slamming the door.

I was more than angry, I was raging. How dare he not even have the decency to give me the heads up.

Connie told me where he worked, it was close to my office. Hailing a cab, I jumped in and gave the driver Killian's address.

The drive took longer than expected, there were taillights most of the way which gave me even more time to let my anger stew. Throwing the driver his money and not waiting for the change, I opened the door and flew for the main door of his office. Barging through the reception, I didn't stop when asked where I was going. Pressing the lift button continuously, I watched as it dropped the many floors. Letting out an irritated huff, I stepped into the lift and pressed the top floor. Of course, he would have the top floor. Pretentious prick.

Tapping my foot on the floor, I watched as the arrow moved up the floors.

"Come on," I groaned to the empty lift. Finally, the doors pinged open. I barged through a couple of people that were waiting for the lift. I stalled for a moment as I looked down the hallway. Left or right?

I decided right.

Storming down the narrow hallway, I passed a sign that said *PA to Killian Hayes*.

Bingo.

"Sorry, you can't go in there," a young man said as he stood up from behind a desk.

"Bite me. I'm his wife." I snapped, flipping him off and pushing the door open, the door swinging and hitting the wall. I winced.

Oops.

I scanned the large office, there were floor to ceiling windows behind his desk, large bookshelves sitting on one wall, on the other there was, no doubt stupidly expensive, art. Well, I thought it looked shit. He even had his own dressing room in here and a bathroom. Of course, he did. I turned to face the young PA who was looking at me wide-eyed as if I was a crazy woman. I smiled a sickly smile, pushing my index finger to my lips as I told him to keep quiet.

He nodded.

Stepping back, I closed the office door and sat on the sofa waiting for the dickhead himself to arrive.

I don't know how long I had been sitting there when I heard the distinct click of his shoes, followed by high heels.

Fuck.

Standing up, I went to rush for the door, but it was too late. I was out of time. I looked round the room and saw Killian's boxed desk. Running for that I hid under it.

I heard Adele's laugh, as the door closed. Adele's heels clicked along his floor as she took a seat opposite where Killian was no doubt going to sit. I saw his shoes as he pulled out the chair, his eyes falling to under his desk where I was on my knees, my hands pressed to the floor. His eyes widened as he saw me, my own eyes mirroring his.

Then a hot as sin smirk crept over his face as he took a seat, his legs parted. I tried to stay as still as I could, I didn't want Adele knowing I was here.

She was droning on about work but to be honest, I lost interest. My anger was still brewing, but I couldn't have it out with him while she was in here. I didn't want her knowing what goes on between me and Killian.

I nibbled my bottom lip, my eyes focusing on the evident bulge in Killian's suit trousers. Was he turned on?

I ran my fingertips up his thighs, causing him to fidget in his chair. I smirked. I continued, edging closer to him. My fingers fumbled with his button, tugging them down. He didn't stop me.

Licking my lips, I pulled his hard cock out of his restricting boxers and shuffled on my knees closer to him.

Should I be doing this? No.

Was it going to stop me? Also no.

Pressing my lips over the tip of his cock, I pushed my mouth slowly down his length.

He sucked in a breath through his teeth. Holding him at the back of my throat for a moment, his hand slipped down his thigh before grabbing a handful of my hair, pulling my head up then pushing it back down again.

Adele was still talking; Killian obviously wasn't paying attention. He was enjoying having his cock sucked by me.

It turned me on knowing that she was sitting on the other side of the desk while I pleasured this beautiful man.

I felt him jerk in my mouth, a low guttural groan vibrating in his throat.

"Are you okay?" I heard the concern in the bitch's voice.

"More than okay, continue," his voice was low as he tried to contain himself.

His fingers pulled at the root of my hair, I stifled my moan as I took him deep, his balls contracting as he came, it didn't take him long. He banged his fist on the desk.

"Did you hear what I said?" Adele's laughter died down as her voice projected across the office.

"No," Killian panted, his hand moving from my head as he popped his cock back into his trousers discreetly, I wiped my mouth with a smile on my face.

"The news, what happened this morning?"

"What news?" Killian's disinterested voice made me smile.

"I got rid of Reese."

I saw and felt Killian tense as my fingers dug into his thigh. I froze under the desk, my eyes widening.

She wasn't on the phone to him this morning.

"You what?" he snarled at her.

"Reese, I got rid of her," her tone completely unbothered, "well, she walked... but I was going to get rid of her."

"Why would you do that? She got you Harlen fucking

Laufer?! The best signing the company has ever had!" He spat, his tone was angry. I could just see his face now in my mind. Beautiful jaw clenched, eyes wide and bulging. His pulse would be racing, the vein throbbing in his neck. "And you wanted rid of her?!" He slammed his hands down on the desk as he stood up.

"You're going to give Reese her job back."

"No," Adele said too calmly for my liking, you could hear the smile in her voice.

"Adele," he gritted.

"I'm surprised you didn't know actually…" she drifted off for a moment.

"And why is that?" I could tell he was clenching his jaw even tighter now, his tone aggravated.

"Give me a little credit," she snorted a laugh.

Killian didn't answer, I could see his hands balled at his side.

"I know you're sleeping with her. She knew from the get-go that I didn't take kindly to my staff sleeping with clients or investors." She laughed, "what a slut, I didn't think she would be such an easy lay."

"I never want you to say that word and Reese's name in the same sentence again. Besides, we're not sleeping together." His voice was steady, my heart dropped. Was he actually going to lie to her?

"We're married."

I gasped at the same time as Adele.

"You're what?"

"You heard me, now, do yourself a favour… pick your bag up and get the fuck out of my office," he growled.

Adele didn't move.

"GET OUT!" He bellowed, his voice bouncing off the walls. I jumped; angry Killian was not someone I wanted to get on the wrong side of.

"Killian," Adele said a little taken aback.

"Get out now Adele, before I call security and have them march you out."

"You wouldn't do that; this is your name on the line as well Killian. You need to remember that."

"Last warning…"

"I'm leaving," she said quietly, the chair scraped across the floor, followed by her heels clicking quickly.

Once the door was shut, Killian crouched down, smirking at me. Angry Killian had left with Adele, and now playful, beautiful Killian was here.

"Hello, you."

His hand reached under the desk as he helped me out. Standing tall, I brushed myself down.

"Hey," I breathed, tucking a loose strand of my hair behind my ear. "It didn't take you long, did it?" I teased, "Missed me that much?" I blushed.

"With your dirty little mouth, it never takes me long."

I swatted at him in the chest.

"Not that I am not pleased to see you, but why are you here?" he sat in his chair, kicking his feet up on his desk. I walked slowly round to the other side, knotting my fingers together.

"Well," I breathed out, "I was coming to shout at you." I nibbled my bottom lip as my eyes cast down to my hands that were sitting in my lap.

"And why is that?" he said trying to stop himself from smirking.

"Because of what happened at work this morning, I've been getting in early, you know… to try and keep occupied and my mind busy." I heard him sigh but I didn't look up, "I went to make myself a drink and when I came back, I heard Adele on the phone. I didn't even know she was in. Anyway, she was on the phone to someone telling them that she wasn't going to promote me, and she was going to let me go sooner rather than later." My eyes lifted and met his, a scowled look on his face, his brows pinched and furrowed as he listened.

"But now I know that she wasn't on the phone to you…" I shrugged, "I was annoyed because I thought after everything we had been through that you would have had the decency to give me a heads up or at least make sure I was okay… but that anger and rage have gone now because it wasn't you on the other end of the line."

"Reese, you should know me better than that…" he dragged his feet off his desk and leaned forward in his office chair. "I wouldn't have even entertained the conversation."

The room grew with thick tension, I felt choked as our gazes locked.

"You're going back, right?" Killian finally broke the silence.

I shook my head from side to side. "How can I go back after walking out? And you told Adele about us… we're getting annulled in a little over a month. She is going to hate me even more now."

He didn't say anything, just rubbed his index finger and thumb across his stubble.

"I just wanted the fresh start. I wanted to make something of myself here… yet nothing has gone to plan. I've lost my job, I accidentally married my best friend's dad… And just sucked him off under his desk because I liked the fact that Adele was sitting there, and I could do that to you." I face palmed myself, agitated suddenly.

"I liked that you done that…" he winked, his tongue darting out to lick his top lip. "It's just a shame I won't be able to return the favour since we have both agreed not to do this anymore…" his voice was raspy, his eyes hooded as he shuffled to the edge of his seat.

"I know…" I breathed a whisper, "it's for the best." I swallowed, praying that I could feel some saliva back in my mouth.

"It is," he nodded.

Pressing my legs together to dull the ache from my throbbing sex. I knew we couldn't, we had to refrain from doing anything.

He was my best friend's dad.

We had to put a stop to it, we both agreed.

I had to take myself out of this tempting situation. I ached for him, I wanted his hands and mouth all over me. It was forbidden now.

He was a temptation I couldn't give into.

My whole body hummed as I stood, my skin alight with a burning sensation from his gaze. It was hard to step back, his penetrating gaze pinning me. I caught my breath as I stepped back towards the office door.

"Where you going?" he asked, standing from his desk and walking towards me cautiously.

"I've got to get out of here... one of us needs to be sensible." I swallowed, my back hitting the door.

He closed the gap between us, one of his hands pushed against the wall beside my head, the other was deep in his pocket.

"Are you sure there isn't anything else I can do for you?" seduction laced his voice.

"Very sure." I nodded quickly, breaking eye contact and ducking under his arm.

Opening the door I stepped over the threshold, I felt like I couldn't breathe.

"Hey, Hey... Reese!" he called as he stood in opening of the door and grabbed my arm so I couldn't run.

"What?" I whispered.

"Are you going back to Lordes?" his voice was low, his beautiful brown eyes volleying back and forth between mine in that way he had.

I inhaled deeply before shaking my head side to side, "No, " I breathed.

"You can't let her win."

"I'm not letting her win, Killian. I just don't want to work with her anymore. I deserve better," I pulled my arm from his tight grip. "I'll be fine, Connie said she can get me some shifts at the hotel if needs be," I shrugged my shoulders up, "I've waitressed before, it's easy money."

Killian shook his head quickly, "No, no," his tone stern. "You can work with me until something more permanent comes along. You can help me with any loose ends that I just don't have time for," his eyes begged me to say yes.

"Can I think about it?"

He nodded.

"Come to dinner Friday night with Connie, a little drink and catch up before Christmas break. It'll be nice to see you," he stepped back inside his office, "please say yes."

I nodded.

"That would be lovely."

He beamed at me.

"I'll see you Friday."

"I'll see you Friday." And with that, I left.

CHAPTER 29
KILLIAN

Sitting at my desk, I drummed my fingers against the hardboard of my solid, black oak desk. I was distracted. Ever since Reese showed up and gave me a phenomenal blow job under it, I couldn't stop thinking about it.

Everything about her is a temptation.

Adele had tried to call me numerous times throughout the week, but I didn't have the energy to speak to her. The mood she put me in would only make me act and do something I would regret.

I had to keep level-headed regarding the business. I had to take my personal life out of this.

Should I have told Adele that me and Reese were married? No. I should have kept my mouth shut but she made me so angry. I don't think my blood has ever boiled so bad.

My eyes flicked to the time on my computer monitor, it had just gone three. I was so ready to leave and go home.

I had Connie and Reese over tonight, I didn't know if I would see much of Connie over Christmas so decided on an early dinner tonight. Connie was always hesitant about wanting to come over, but her knowing Reese will be there makes her decision a lot easier.

"Screw this," I huffed, pushing off the desk and shutting my computer down. I grabbed my suit jacket and coat before walking out of my office.

"Ben, cancel my calls. I'm finished for the day." I didn't stop to hear if he said anything, I walked towards the elevator, shrugging my jacket and coat on before stepping into the snow.

My car was sitting kerbside, thanking Colin, I slipped in the back and let him drive me home. I felt tense. Work wasn't bothering me. Yes, Adele had got under my skin, but I think it was more the fact that I had to fight the urge every minute of the day to stop myself from going to Reese. She was like a magnet. Constantly pulling me towards her.

We would never work. I couldn't do that to Connie. I couldn't be selfish, and if I pursued a relationship with Reese, it would be for selfish reasons.

I didn't even want the annulment, but I couldn't expect Reese to stay married to me just because deep down, I didn't want to let her go. The papers were still sitting unsigned in my office, it would take merely a minute, yet I couldn't bring myself to do it.

I had this constant battle in my head. The voices from my head and my heart constantly arguing about it.

It would get easier; I knew it would.

I just had to be patient.

Walking into my apartment, I hung my coat and scarf up in the cloak room before heading to my bedroom. I needed a shower. The winter air was bitter.

Tugging my tie out of my shirt collar, I tossed it onto the bed. Unbuttoning and discarding the shirt on the floor, I stepped over it and pulled down my suit pants. Turning the shower dial, I slipped my jocks down and stepped into the hot water. It felt good against my tense skin, my muscles rippling as I lathered myself up then washed my hair. The smell of mint wafted through my nostrils, smiling as I rinsed it off.

I felt the bubbles of excitement surface in my stomach before they popped. I was excited to see Reese. I almost felt wrong for feeling the way I did, my stomach churned and coiled constantly at the thought of her being here but being unable to touch her because of Connie. I sometimes wish I could switch them off, but it wasn't that simple was it. Because believe me, if I could, I would.

Drying myself off, I dressed in jeans and a t-shirt. I ramped the heating up to take the chill out of the apartment then slipped a couple of bottles of wine into the fridge. Padding back into the bathroom I brushed my teeth then styled my brown hair, messing it up and pushing it back away from my face. Running my hand over my chin, my stubble felt rough, but it wasn't long enough to tame or style. I never intended on keeping it, but the sultry look and little lip bites from Reese when my stubble grazed across her sensitive skin made me want to keep it. So, it stayed.

Looking at myself in the mirror one last time, I walked into the lounge area. I felt restless, I didn't know what to do with myself. I couldn't relax. Walking towards the sound system, I turned on the music, Lionel Richie filled the room. Nice, mellow music. I paced the width of my penthouse, walking back and forth as I fought with my thoughts.

Stopping outside the kitchen, I checked on my housekeeper. She was cooking Connie's favourite. Salmon, white rice and asparagus. It smelt amazing. She liked it with a lemon dressing, but it had to be on the side. She didn't like it running into the other food on her plate. Then we had traditional New York cheesecake with raspberry ice-cream. All homemade, just not by me.

I had bought some cookies, Connie used to like to have them as a little snack while waiting for dinner while dipping them in milk. I also bought English tea, tea bags for Reese. I wasn't that great at making tea, but I would give it a go for her. I even had my housekeeper buy an electric kettle. I have never used a kettle, if I wanted a flavoured tea, I would always warm my cup of water in the microwave, but after looking online it's what Reese would use to make a tea.

Why was I so nervous? I rubbed my hand through my hair, the cool metal from my wedding band scraping across my scalp. My skin prickled in anticipation; my heart drummed at a steady beat but a little harder than normal.

Checking the time, it had just gone six pm. They would be here soon.

Pacing back and forth, my gaze alternated between the clock and the door to my penthouse. Running my hand through my hair and messing it up slightly, I stilled when I heard a knock on the door.

I strolled towards the noise, my fingers gripping the doorknob with my sweaty palm, my fingers locking firmly round it. As I twisted it, I plastered a smile on my face. Swinging the door open to see Reese standing there holding a bottle of wine and a card.

"Hey," she beamed. Her smile lighting up the room instantly, her blonde hair was sitting in waves and cascaded down to her ribcage. Her green eyes glistened as they took me in, our gaze locking. My heart skipped a beat at the intense gaze we held with each other, my breath catching but I disguised it with a clear of my throat.

My eyes skimmed down her body as I looked at what she was wearing. Jeans and a v-neck loose tee. Simple. The tee plunged in deep, stopping just before her breast bone, revealing her glorious, tanned skin. She was petite and slender, I liked that she could wear tops like that without seeing her pert little tits spilling out.

My lips twitched with a smirk.

"Hey," I breathed, stepping aside to let her in.

"This is for you; I didn't know what wine you liked so I just grabbed my favourite," she winced a little and shrugged her shoulders up as she placed the bottle and the card on the black side table.

A gentle laugh bubbled out of me.

"Thank you, but you didn't have to get me anything," I closed the door softly as I turned to watch her take her sneakers off, placing them neatly by the door.

Scoffing when I saw she had white, fluffy socks on. They looked like clouds and seemed to have little rainbows stitched into them.

Cute.

She turned to face me, giving me an awkward smile. She pushed her hands into the back pockets of her jeans, then licked her lips. Her chest pushing forward as silence fell over us.

Why was this so awkward?

"When do your parents land?" I asked as I reached for the wine and the card strolling towards the wine chiller.

"Day before Christmas Eve," she sighed a little, "the snow doesn't seem to be letting up and I am worried their flight will be grounded back home."

"I am keeping everything crossed for you," I offered her a weak smile as I put the wine away.

"I don't know how it works here, but England comes to a complete standstill if there is even a flurry of snow, I mean if we had the same weather here as we did back home, England would go into meltdown." She laughed as her fingers drummed on the worktop

I laughed with her, my eyes down casting to my wrist. *Where the bloody hell was Connie!?*

Being this close to her and having to stay away is torture. All I want to do is take her in my arms, inhale her scent then take her plump lips between my teeth before grazing my teeth over her jaw line before dragging my lips back to hers and kissing her.

"Have you heard from Connie?" I asked as I stepped forward towards the centre island.

"Yeah, she said she was running a little late," I saw her eyes widen slightly, "should I have waited? I'm sorry, I'll go and come back. I didn't even think," she began to ramble, her hands flying around as she spoke. Biting the inside of my lip hard, I tried to stop my laugh.

"It just gets lonely on your own..." her voice fell for a moment, her eyes found mine.

"Yeah..." I nodded; I knew exactly what she meant. The evenings are long when you're home alone every day.

The silence fell between us, the tension crackling in the air that surrounded us.

Her breath caught in the back of her throat, her chest rising a little faster now. If you looked close enough, you could see her heart beating through her skin.

"Do you want a tour?" I asked her, I had to keep moving. I had to try and put some physical distance between us.

"Sure," her voice was high pitched, and deep down I think she was grateful too.

Pressing my lips into a thin line, I rushed past her to try and soften the gravitating pull that I felt every time I was close to her.

She followed a few steps behind, keeping her head low as she walked.

"So, you know the seating area..." I smirked, holding my hand out. She smiled back at me before I continued. I walked towards the bathroom that overlooked the city, a gasp passing her lips as she took in the views.

"How do you ever leave?" she asked.

"Believe it or not, you do get used to it and before you know it, it's just another room in the apartment with a view." I shrugged my shoulders up, my tone flat and dull. It was the truth. Yes, my apartment penthouse was made of dreams, but at the end of the day, what's the point in all of this when you can't have the person you want to share it with.

I quickly escaped my head before turning on my heel and heading towards the stairs, my hand glided up the handrail, I heard Reese's soft footsteps hitting the oak stairs behind me.

"Okay so up here we have three bedrooms, three bathrooms and one of the bedrooms has an en-suite." I turned, rubbing my hands together as I walked backwards.

"You missed three rooms downstairs," she pointed out, looking over the glass that was the stair rail.

"Don't be impatient, I'll show you them next," I rolled my eyes in a playful manner.

"Erm, sorry…" I heard her quip as she stepped in front of me, crossing her arms across her chest.

"Can I help you?" I smirked; I knew where she was going with this, but I loved teasing her. She always made me want to be in a playful mood. I liked who I was with her. She made me forgot the grump I was before her.

"You rolled your eyes…" she tapped her fluffy covered foot on the floor beneath her.

"And?"

"Well, you always threaten me… so… I'm going to threaten you," I saw a hint of a smile play across her lips before she went back to pouting.

"Go on then, Buttercup," I licked my top lip slowly as I held her steady gaze.

"Roll your eyes at me again, I'll bring you to your knees."

"To do what?" I stepped towards her, the air crackling loud between us, the tension thick.

"I'll let you know," she winked, shoving me away as she walked past. "Come on then husband, show me your room." She twisted round and smiled at me before hovering outside the closed doors, "Again."

My cock hardened at the thought of our last night in my room. It was delicious, amazing, earth shattering.

After a quick whizz round of the upstairs, we headed back downstairs. I padded to the first closed door, opening it quickly to show a gym area. It had all the equipment you could ever need.

"Huh," she scoffed, "didn't have you for the work out type of guy," she said lightly as she popped her head round the door before nudging me. "Next." She called out.

Oh, she was in a playful mood too by the looks of it.

The next room was a library, floor to ceiling bookshelves filled with every single book you could think of.

"Wow," she whispered, stepping into the room and looking around it in awe. "You like to read?" she asked.

"I do," I nodded.

"I don't have much time at the moment," she stopped suddenly as if the words choked her. She spun to look at me, lifting her shoulders up slightly. "Well, I suppose now I do… seeing as I don't have a job anymore."

I felt myself tense. I needed to sort it with Adele, it wasn't on.

"You will have a job, whether it is with me, back at Lordes or with Connie…" I stepped towards her, pressing my forehead against hers as my hands automatically wrapped round her slender frame, "I promise." The words left my lips in a whisper. Her wide eyes found mine, the hint of a glisten that ran through them made my heart hurt. I hated that she was sad, I hated that she was hurting, and I hated it even more that I couldn't do anything to stop her feeling that way.

She simply nodded, her hands pressing against my chest like she did before, but this time she left them there for a moment before her head dropped. A deep sigh left her and then she pushed herself off me and headed for the door.

I stood, my back to her as I tried to calm my racing heart.

"You coming? There is still one more room..." her sweet voice echoed round me.

"Sure," I spun, pinning the smile back on my face and following her out.

Opening the last door, she smiled as she stepped in. My office.

The desk was mahogany, the room a deep biscuit beige colour. I had shelves stacked against the wall, but they were filled with a different kind of books to the library. They were self-care and self-help books that have helped me grow over the last few years.

She stepped towards the desk, her fingers skimming across it.

The chair that sat behind was a deep, cherry red leather. Not quite sure why I chose that, just liked it if I was being honest with myself.

The room smelt of leather and polish, the soft scents floating through the room.

To the left of the desk was a gold globe, but it wasn't just a globe.

"Open the globe," I said softly as Reese stopped by it. She looked over her shoulder at me before turning her attention to the globe. Her fingers skimmed across the high gloss coldness before undoing a catch at the side. Using both her hands she opened it gently to see two crystal tumblers and an etched crystal whiskey decanter.

"Typical businessman..." she teased as she reached for the glasses and placed them on my desk. Next, she reached for the decanter, the lid pop echoing round the room as she poured out.

She placed the decanter back into the globe and grabbed both glass tumblers. I stepped towards her, taking one off her and holding it up.

"Typical businessman?" I repeated her last words stalking towards her.

"They always have to have a decanter of whiskey in their office."

I tsked, rolling my eyes as I let out a deep laugh that rumbled through me.

My laughter soon stopped when I realised what I had just done.

I had just rolled my fucking eyes.

Reese was looking all smug as she rested her pert little ass on the edge of my desk. She looked good there. One of her arms pressed against her chest, her legs crossed over each other as she put all of her weight on the desk.

"Tut tut," she said, her eyes looking at the deep amber liquid in the bottom of her glass, bringing it to her lips and taking a mouthful. I watched intently for the wince, but it didn't come.

I mirrored her, bringing my own glass to my lips all the while keeping my eyes on her as I knocked the burning liquid back in one. I let my arm fall to my side, my finger tapping on the now, empty glass.

"What a waste, surely bourbon this good needs to be savoured… enjoyed…" she licked her lips, her eyes finally meeting with mine and I swear I felt the fucking ground move beneath me. I stepped towards her, my body pressing against hers as I placed the glass on the desk behind her.

She took another mouthful, trying to put on a show to try and convince me she wasn't affected by me.

But I could see right through her bullshit.

Picking the glass from her hand, I finished hers and slammed it on the desk behind her a little harder this time which caused her to flinch.

I could hear her quivering breath; her eyes didn't move from mine as I gazed at her. My hands wrapped around her hips as I pushed myself onto her. Our bodies flush.

"Killian," she whispered, her fingers wrapping round the edge of the desk behind her as she steadied herself.

"Yes, wife," I whispered back as my fingers trailed along the waist band of her jeans and stopped at her buttons. Popping the button out, I hooked my fingers on the inside of her waist band and tugged them down her thighs in one swift move.

Her breath caught at the back of her throat as I sunk to my knees in front of her.

"Is this what you meant when you said I would fall to my knees?" I asked, my lips pressing against the soft skin of her thighs, the waft of her scent rushing through me. I dragged my lips across her sensitive skin before stopping at the apex of her thighs. Pressing my lips at the thin, silk material, I licked and nipped her through them. Her breath shook.

"Killian," she breathed; her head dropped forward as she looked down at me.

"Tell me, Buttercup... is this what you wanted?" I ask, my fingers slipping into the side of her panties, curled round and ready to pull to the side.

She didn't answer, her fingers tightened around the edge of the desk. I could see the wetness pooling on the white, silk material. I let my fingers brush gently over the front of her bare pussy, causing a small moan to escape her.

"Brat... tell me," I groaned as I edged my mouth to her panties, nipping at the material and grazing her skin with my teeth.

"Yes," she finally breathed out.

"Good girl." Looking up at her, I pulled her panties to the side and my mouth was on her. Two of my fingers spread her pussy lips open, giving me better access to her clit. She hung her leg over my shoulder, edging herself a little further back on the desk.

"This has got to be quick, Buttercup," I groaned, sucking on her clit then letting my tongue glide up and down her folds. Swirling my tongue at her opening, I dragged my tongue slowly up to her clit. Circling her nub gently, my spare hand skimmed up the inside of her thigh as I pressed my fingertip at her opening. Bucking her hips forward she moaned, her fingers tightening.

"Yes, please," she panted as I teased her. Smiling against her sensitive skin, I pushed two fingers inside of her with ease. Her greedy little cunt stretching as I pumped them in and out of her. My tongue swirled and sucked on her clit as her sweet moans filled the room.

"You taste so fucking good," I lift my lips from her, licking her arousal from my mouth. "I am addicted to your taste, I'm addicted to you," I groan, my eyes falling to watch my thick fingers fuck her tight little pussy. Slipping them out slowly, I pause just at the tip. Her pussy clenches my fingers. I do it again, my own breath shaky as I watch.

"Oh," she cries out.

I slip my fingers out hastily, wrap my hand round her throat and push her back onto the desk so she is sitting on it completely. Falling back to my knees, I push both of her legs up onto the edge of the desk.

"Hold them there," I demand, my eyes falling to her glistening cunt.

Rubbing her clit fast with my fingers then gliding them between her folds before pushing them deep inside of her.

"Now watch me brat, watch me finger fuck your pussy," I groan, my eyes lifting to her for a moment to make sure she does what I asked.

"You're such a good little girl," I praise her as she pants. Her eyes watch as I pull my fingers out to the tip, holding then pushing in. My eyes darken as I hover my spare hand over her pussy and slap her clit, hard.

"Fuck," she whispers as I do it again.

I am so turned on; I would do anything to fuck her, but I can't. I palm myself through my jeans while I watch. I feel the burn inside me, the need to erupt and explode so I stop. My hand moves to grip the inside of her thigh, my fingers digging into her skin as I move my mouth over her clit. Licking and sucking hard I bite her causing her to scream.

My fingers are soaked, coated in the only honey I ever want to taste in this lifetime. I press a third at her opening, worried it will be too much but her greedy cunt takes me with ease. Slipping my fingers back and forth faster now, giving her the friction and speed she needs. Her hips thrust forward as her pussy rides my fingers, my tongue is buried deep inside of her cunt as I eat her.

"Killian," she moans, her head tipping back.

"Dad?" We hear Connie's voice echo through the apartment as the front door shuts. Reese freezes, trying to get away from me but I don't let her. Instead, I move my hand from her thigh to her waist and hold her their tightly, digging my fingers into her skin.

"You're going to come all over my fingers like the good girl you are, do you understand me?" My voice is low so only she can hear.

She nods.

"There's my good girl."

My fingers pump in and out of her with ease as I tease my ring finger at her tight little asshole. She likes it, she just won't admit it just yet.

My tongue still works on her clit as I press my finger into her, her whole body tightening and clenching as I do.

"Let me in," I whisper, "relax baby."

And she does, my tongue sucking her clit softly now as I fuck her with my fingers.

"Oh fuck" she calls out, her eyes moving from me to the door.

"Dad?" Connie calls again.

"She's going to find us," she whispers.

"Shhh," I soothe her before taking her clit between my teeth. Slowing my fingers inside of her, I slip them out to the tip, holding them there while my ring finger is still buried in her tight ass. My tongue glides over her clit slowly as I suck and nibble it.

I feel her pussy clench, her hips moving involuntary to try and get the fullness she needs from me. Her breaths fall short but fast as her chest heaves, her head rolls forward as she watches me work her to her orgasm.

"Dad? Reese? Where are you?" Connie calls out, her voice getting louder as we hear the impending footsteps.

And that's all it takes. The fear of being caught.

I push my fingers into her soaked cunt fast and hard as she comes hard, my hand slamming over her mouth to stop the screams leaving her as she rides out her orgasm.

I smirk, slowing my fingers and slipping them out before sucking them clean. I push to my feet quickly, lean in and kiss Reese on the forehead and whisper, "Such a good girl for your husband."

I step back and walk for the door, leaving Reese to compose herself.

"Hey, Connie darling... I'm here." I shouted out, closing the study door just before Connie reached it.

"Hey dad, sorry I'm late. Where is Reese?"

"Just on the phone to her parents," I lied, but Connie bought it.

We stepped away towards the kitchen where I poured three glasses of wine. The taste of her was still on my tongue, her scent still on my fingers. I loved the rush she gave me; and tonight only confirmed what I already knew.

I wasn't ready to give her up yet.

CHAPTER 30
REESE

We had just finished dessert, Killian's housekeeper cleaned our dishes away before bringing a tray of cookies, milk and a cup and saucer.

"I thought you would like a cup of tea?" Killian smiled opposite me, I blushed at the thought of his mouth and what it done to me a couple of hours ago. My insides were still reeling.

"Oh, thank you," I smiled, "I would love a cup of tea."

Killian sat back beaming, he looked like the cat who had got the cream.

No pun intended.

Reaching for the teacup, I saw a tea bag floating in scalding hot water.

"I'm impressed," I wink at him.

"I went and bought a kettle just for you."

I felt the burn in Connie's stare volleying back and forth between me and her dad.

"Am I late to the party or something…?"

"You were, yes," Killian laughs before reaching for a cookie, then passing the plate to Connie which she takes along with a glass of milk.

"No, I don't mean literally," she rolled her eyes, "you two... You're acting all weird."

I widen my eyes as I look at Connie then back to Killian.

Killian pipes up.

"No, my God Connie. Don't be so disrespectful. Me and Reese work together, I know she likes tea and, I am trying to cheer her up a little seeing as she lost her job."

"She walked out," Connie interjected, a sly smile on her face.

"Fine, she walked out, but she would have lost her job anyway."

Connie nodded and shrugged at the same time as she dipped a cookie into the milk.

I lost myself amongst their chatter... I didn't want Connie knowing. What we done earlier was reckless and too risky. You don't play with fire, especially not that close to home.

I leaned and grabbed the small milk jug and added a splash to my tea, stirring the milk in and watching it change colour. Straining my tea bag against the side, I spooned it out and put it on the tray.

"You don't leave the teabag in?" Killian asked, he sounded a little dumbfounded.

"No," I laughed softly, shaking my head as I grabbed a teaspoon of sugar. I don't normally have sugar but I fancied it tonight.

"Have you never had a tea like this?"

"No we haven't," Connie said, Killian just smiled.

"Well, you're missing out," I smirked at both of them then, brought the china teacup to my lips before blowing softly and taking a mouthful.

"Mm," I hummed in appreciation, "I can't remember the last time I had a decent cup of tea, so thank you Killian, and pass thanks on to your housekeeper."

Grabbing a cookie, I dipped the cookie into my tea and let it soak for a second or two then pulled it out and eating it.

The chocolate chips were already softening, and the buttery cookie literally melted on the tongue.

"What the f—"

"Language," Killian scolded.

"You're dipping your cookie into tea?" Connie looked utterly disgusted with me.

"It's just the same as you dipping cookies into milk…" I raised my brow while going in for another dunk.

"But the milk is cold."

"And my tea is hot, don't turn your nose up at it before you've even tried it. Back home, biscuits and tea are a delicacy," I giggle, "even the queen likes a little dunk in her tea."

They both stare at me.

"Well, your biscuits are different to our biscuits. We don't just have cookies; we have all ranges of cookies for tea dunking, we call them biscuits." I was rambling and I am sure they thought I was certified insane. "Just don't knock it till you try it," I shrugged, reaching for another cookie before dunking. "I could go on about the stuff you say for different things, but I think that'll open a can of worms."

Killian nodded in agreement as he laughed, Connie soon joining in.

"What are you going to do about your apartment now that you've left Lordes?" Connie asked as she took a mouthful of milk.

The sheer panic that coursed over me made me sweat, the shiver of fear that danced up and down my spine made me nauseous.

"Shit," I stammered out, my eyes moving to Connie. "I didn't even think of my apartment." Gasping, I moved my hand over my mouth. "I think I am going to be sick." Closing my eyes, I tried my best to push the feeling down. It was just my anxiety, we hit panic mode and that isn't good for me or my body.

"I'm sorry Reese, I didn't even think," Connie pushed away from her chair as she wrapped her arms around my shoulders.

"Don't say sorry. It's my fault, I have been so consumed in everything else that I forgot the most important thing. If I don't find a steady job, I'll have to go back home." I felt my throat tighten, the burning lump lodging itself there.

"You won't have to go home." Connie stroked my hair, "you can move in with me and my moms, plus we will find you a job."

"She has a job," Killian interjected. "If she doesn't want to go back to Lordes, she has a job with me... as with moving, I have a spare bedroom here for you."

I sniffled, hugging Connie.

"Thank you," I whispered, "and thank you Killian, that's very kind of you. If you're happy with me working with you I would be honoured, but just until I find something else, I don't want to be a charity case." I smile and he nods firmly, but I know how Killian works.

"And with the moving, Connie, I would love to move in with you and your mums, if they would have me of course."

I saw Killian clench the tablecloth.

"No, no," Killian shook his head, "I insist you stay here, I own your apartment, but it's tied in with my finances with Lordes so I can't rent it out to you, unless you are a Lordes employee. Some bullshit with the contract, so I insist, that you stay here until I can figure this out and get your apartment back."

"Dad!" Connie shouted at him, pulling away from me and crossing her arms across her chest. "She is staying with me, stop trying to be the hero," Connie huffed.

"If you say so," Killian's lips twitched as he took a mouthful of his drink.

I rolled my eyes, gaining a clenched jaw and a sly smirk to cross Killian's lips.

I loved that it turned him on.

CHAPTER 31
KILLIAN

I padded through the apartment; it was quiet. Reese was still asleep; it had just gone five am. I had a ritual, get up, head to the gym then have a shower and a light breakfast. It took me a few weeks to get used to living with a woman. I had never lived with anyone else before, so this was a new thing for me. But I was enjoying it, in fact, I was loving it. I loved her being here and the thought of her leaving soon made my heart thump against my ribcage. I didn't want her to leave, if I could, I would keep her locked away in here with me forever and throw away the key. A sadistic smirk spread across my lips; I could do it... possibly.

My cock twitched at the thought of keeping her all to myself. *Stop it*.

Tsking, I walked towards the bathroom to wash off after my work out from the gym. I had to keep my mind busy, because if I didn't, I wouldn't be able to leave Reese alone. She prances around in short-shorts with her toned little ass cheeks hanging out the bottom and her cropped tops. If it's not booty shorts, it's my tees that she prances around in. All long legs, and slender body as she pads around my apartment bare foot.

My cock restricts against my shorts. Rubbing my palm over myself to try and ease a little bit of the tension I was feeling. It was no use, it just turned me on even more.

The first few nights I used to sneak into her room, just to watch her. I couldn't get enough of her. I didn't have to touch her; I didn't have to even talk to her. I just needed to be close to her to get my hit. She was like a fucking drug to me, constantly high when I am around her and as soon as she's not near, the withdrawal kicks in. I am not a needy man, but fuck with Reese? I have never been needier in my life.

Pulling my top over my head as I walk into the bathroom, I scoff as I look around my bathroom. All little bits of Reese scattered around. She had her own bathroom, but of course she wanted to use mine. I was ninety-nine-point nine percent sure she done it to tease me.

I smirked at her little cream bath towel that had a light pink piping. She replaced my old, low pile bathmat with a fluffy bathmat. And being honest, I wasn't mad about it. It felt like I was stepping out onto a cloud every time I left the shower. Her tampons sat on the side like a fucking trophy, she could have put them away but for some reason, they were on show. It didn't bother me, kind of got used to seeing the little vagina plugs there.

Pulling my shorts down along with my jocks, I discarded them into the wash basket before stepping under the hot shower. The steam filling the room as I reached for the shower gel and lathered myself up. The fruity scent taking over my senses as I cleaned myself, her products were a lot better than mine. Rinsing the suds off, I reached for her shampoo quickly. Flipping the lid open, I bought it to my nose and inhaled it deeply. My whole body erupted in goosebumps at the familiar smell, it was like home to me now. It was my favourite smell in the whole wide world, it smelt good straight from the bottle… but my kryptonite was this scent on her. Intoxicating me, filling every sense of mine to the hilt.

She was no good for me.

I was no good for her.

But she was my kryptonite, and you can bet for sure that I was hers.

Squeezing a small amount of the creamy, thick liquid into my palm I rubbed it into my hair and massaged my scalp. I began humming, closing my eyes as *Taylor Swift's – Blank Space* came into my mind. The lyrics swarmed me as I began singing a little louder as I broke into the chorus. Stepping under the shower, I dropped my head forward and let the rainforest shower cascade over me, the scent wafting round me. I groaned before breaking into song again.

Turning the shower off, I stepped back and reached for the large bath sheet and wrapped it around my waist. Turning, I continued whistling the tune. My eyes flicked open, a smile on my face when I saw her standing there. Messy bed hair, my oversized tee and her long, glorious, fucking legs. She had a playful smirk on her lips, her brows lifted high as her eyes stalked up and down over me.

"What a lovely voice you have…" she scoffed, sarcasm lacing her voice. "Never knew you were one of the Swiftie fan girls…" she giggled and fuck, the sound of her laugh filled the room and swarmed my heart.

"No one knows…" I winked, I felt a small blush creep onto my cheeks, but she would never know… the room was so hot and filled with steam that my skin would be slightly redder anyway.

"I'll keep it our little secret," she smirked, pretending the lock her lips and throw away the key.

I smirked, my eyes trailing up and down her body. I needed to walk out before I picked her up and took her back in the shower with me and fucked her.

As much as living with her is like a piece of heaven… it's also like living in my own, personal hell.

Like a child in a sweet shop not being able to touch all the things I want.

It would happen… we were destined.

"I'll go put the kettle on," she said sweetly, her eyes glistening before she turned her back on me and walked out of the bathroom, shaking her hips side to side. She reached up, pulling her hair into a messy bun. The tee she was wearing rode up over her thighs and revealed her little ass cheek creases. I dipped my head, nibbling my bottom lip, I felt my cock harden again.

She was a cock tease, but I fucking loved it.

Once I knew she was out of sight, I slipped back into the shower and took care of myself.

It's the only way I could get through each day with her living here. I was like a horny teenager all over again crushing over the girl that didn't give me the time of day. Sure, my hand done the trick, but I would much rather be sinking my hard cock into her tight little cunt.

My head fell back as I groaned. Snapping my head forward I watched as I stroked myself. My hand pumping up and down slowly. Slamming my hand against the tiled wall, I felt the shiver cover my skin, my orgasm teetering before it crashed over me.

Cleaning myself up, I got dressed quickly and walked towards the kitchen to see my little brat.

Mine.

CHAPTER 32
REESE

Our annulment was tomorrow. I had this ache in my heart that wouldn't leave and a sickness in my belly that filled me with dread every day.

I had been living with Killian for just a little under a month now, of course he got his own way. I am sure he made Connie's mums say no. Nothing surprises me with that man.

Reading over the annulment papers for the millionth time, every 'I' was dotted, and every 'T' was crossed.

Killian kept his distance and nothing sexual had happened between us since we all had dinner together. The risks outweigh the pleasure, and I don't want to lose either of them as friends, especially Connie.

I felt like I had hit a low over Christmas. My parents couldn't fly due to England getting a freak snowstorm and grounding them. I was heartbroken but Connie's mums welcomed me with open arms.

And like it does every year, Elijah's death crippled me. After eating dinner, I excused myself back to Killian's and locked myself in my room. I ignored him and Connie for four days.

I needed to cry it out and let myself heal in my own time and they understood that. Is it weird that I have a close relationship with my best friend's dad? A bit yes. Do I care? No.

Killian has helped fill a huge, gaping black hole in my heart that I was worried never would close again.

I didn't ever want to lose him, and I was going to try and do everything to make that not happen.

I felt awkward being here the night before the annulment, and to be honest, I didn't want to go through with it. Things had drastically changed between the two of us, but it was the right thing to do. We had been plodding along for far too long as husband and wife. It was a drunken night that neither of us remember so why are we still married?

I started working this week with Killian at Hayes Investment. I was apprehensive mixing pleasure with work but it was just a stopover. A fill gap until I found a job that worked for me. I was just grateful for the opportunity plus the job security. Killian kept re-assuring me that he would make it right at Lordes but I didn't know if I wanted to go back there. I couldn't work with Adele again. She would make my life hell, even more so now knowing that we were actually married. I wanted to ask Killian what the deal with him and Adele was, but I just couldn't find the words to ask him.

It was none of my business anyway, after tomorrow we were no longer legally bound to each other.

Killian wouldn't take any rent off me, so I made a point of helping round the house. Not that I could do a lot because his housekeeper was here, but I managed to make the odd dinner here and there and tonight was one of those nights. I wanted to make him a traditional English dinner and lucky for me, my mum sent me a care package just after Christmas, so I had a lot of goodies and all I needed for this dinner was my gravy granules.

Checking the oven through the glass, the batter was rising nicely, and the sausages were browning off.

Poking my knife into the potatoes they were still a bit hard, so I increased the heat on the hob slightly and popped the lid on.

My hips were sashaying to my earphones, *talk dirty to me – Jason Derulo* was blasting. I was miming, while trying my best to dance seductively. Flicking my eyes to look at the time, Killian should be walking through the door in the next fifteen. Making sure everything was okay, I quickly ran upstairs to use the loo. Stopping to look in the mirror, I smiled. I looked different, but in the best way. I had a slight glow to my skin that I hadn't seen in a long while. My eyes scanned my outfit, I should really change but I was comfortable in my short cotton shorts and one of Killian's tees that I had nabbed out of the laundry. It was clean, but I could still smell the hint of his scent on it.

My golden hair was pulled into a messy bun with a few loose strands. I felt like me, this was me. Finally pulling myself away, I used the loo, washed my hands then headed back downstairs.

Draining the potatoes, I added milk, salt, pepper and a knob of butter before I mashed them. The toad in the hole was cooling on the rack of the hob and the greens were buttered and plated up.

Scooping two huge mounds of mash next to the veggies because I don't know how to make a reasonable amount of mash, I then cut into the toad in the hole, the batter golden cracking as I slice through. My stomach grumbled. I was famished.

I plugged the kettle in that Killian bought and filled it up with water before flicking it on and letting it boil. I poured an unhealthy amount of gravy granules into the bottom of a mixing jug because I liked my gravy thick. Once the kettle was boiled, I mixed the water with the granules to make the right consistency before pouring it over my plate. I didn't want to do Killian's as I didn't know if he would actually like it or not. Walking over to the large dining table, I placed the plates down then went back for the gravy and cutlery.

I heard the door click before watching the round doorknob twist.

"Baby, I'm here," he calls, his smile lighting up the room before stilling and seeing me sitting at the table. He has done the *baby I'm here* since I have lived with him, it started as an annoyance, where now I adore it. I would definitely miss it once I move out.

"Hey," I hold my hand up to wave as he drops his briefcase on the floor by the side table, then pushes the door shut.

"Smells amazing," he says as he steps towards me and takes a seat, "what is it?" he laughs.

"Toad in the hole," I look down at my homemade dinner then back up at him.

"Toad in the hole?" he repeats, a little confused.

"Mmhmm, it's basically sausage in batter... not quite sure where it comes from... well I could google it but yano..." I shrugged, picking up my knife and fork.

"I was going to get changed but decided against it. I can't wait to taste this sausage in the hole."

I rolled my eyes. "Toad in the hole," I giggled.

"Oh, shit yeah, toad." He laughed with me as he picked his knife and fork up.

"Do you not want gravy?" I asked, my hands hovering over my full plate.

"Do I want gravy...?" he asked me.

I nodded, "You can't have toad in the hole without gravy..."

"Okay, yes please, may I have some gravy, wife." My smile fell for a moment as I reached for the jug before I plastered it back on and covered his food. As much as we were an accident, a mistake, I couldn't deny the pain that crushed through me, the wave of emotion that crashed over me at the thought of us not being together anymore.

Even if it was just pretend.

"There you go, husband. Bon appetite."

CHAPTER 33
REESE

Closing my eyes, I inhaled deeply and tried to calm my erratic heart. After a moment, I opened my eyes and pulled the door of the courthouse open. Killian had already left this morning by the time I had woken up, so we never got a chance to speak after last night. I tried my hardest to keep away, but after a couple of glasses of wine we both were like moths to the flame. Unable to stay away from each other. It was because we knew we couldn't be with each other that we craved it more. You always want what you can't have. We both agreed it was the perfect way to say goodbye. We made love until the early hours of the morning before I slipped out and slept in my own bed.

I also needed to look at moving out, I couldn't stay living with Killian much longer. I had to get on with my own life, I had my own plans to keep and my own dreams to follow and I couldn't allow Killian to put them on hold any longer.

My legs felt heavy as I walked down the aisle towards the judge. I looked to the left to see Killian's lawyer, but no Killian.

I had prayed and begged silently last night that Killian would want me, would want what I did, and we could stay married and live happily ever after. But he made it clear he didn't want that, Connie was his priority, which was right. One hundred percent. But a small, teenie weenie part of me hoped he wanted me as a priority too.

But he didn't.

He wanted the annulment, and he wasn't here.

I nodded curtly to his lawyer who gave me a grave smile before turning to face the judge.

"Morning," the judge said to both of us, "we are here today for the annulment of a Ms Reese Hernández and a Mr Killian Hayes, is that correct?"

"Yes, your honour," me and his lawyer said in unison.

"Let's get started." She smiled, turning to face the lawyer.

"Your honour, before we get started, I need to let you know that my client, Killian Hayes will not be present today, but he does have the documentation signed by himself and Ms Hernández."

"And why couldn't Mr Hayes be here today?" her brow raised as she leant forward.

"Personal issues," his lawyer's voice was tight, "but I have full control over Mr Hayes' personal affairs as well as his finances. I am fully aware of everything that needs to happen today."

He wasn't here.
He couldn't even have the decency to turn up to our annulment.
He didn't want to be here.
He didn't want me.

The harsh reality seared through my heart like a samurai sword, destroying all of the patches he had covered. But that's just it. They were patches. Small repairs to try and fix my obliterated heart. He never saw a future with me. He never wanted it to be any more than what it was. A booty call.

A forbidden love affair.

The tears stung behind my eyes, my throat constricted and tight as the burning lump lodged itself in my windpipe.

My breath ripped from my lungs.

He wasn't coming.

"Ms Hernandez?" The judge said a little louder now.

"Sorry, yes your honour."

"Welcome back," a small smile crept across her lips. "I will repeat my question, are you happy for Mr Hayes' lawyer, Colin, to act on Mr Hayes' behalf and represent him for your annulment."

The breath caught at the back of my throat, rendering me speechless, a lone tear escaped as it rolled down my cheek. Swiping it away quickly, I nodded.

"Let's proceed."

THE OVERALL PROCESS WAS SHORT AND SWEET, A BIT LIKE MINE and Killian's drunken marriage. He had taken care of everything. His statement advised it was a drunken mistake, no consummation of marriage was ever had and the reason it took us a few months to get our annulment was because our clash in work schedules. I was also given my old apartment back as part of the arrangement, even though I didn't want it.

It was official.

We were over, he didn't want me living with him anymore.

I was angry, I was upset and most of all, I was disappointed. I thought I meant more to him than that, I thought we were friends.

He signed the papers and gave the lawyer his ring to pass on to me, but I respectfully declined. Why would I want that?

I walked home in a daze, my mind flooding with why he didn't show, but it didn't matter anymore. We didn't have any ties. The air was still cold, nipping at my skin as I continued walking towards Killian's. I was numb. Emotionally and physically. Passing Frank, I didn't even respond when he wished me good afternoon, just carried on towards the lift.

Once I was in Killian's apartment, I felt sick to my stomach at being here. He didn't want me anymore. He didn't want me here anymore.

I slipped the lock across the front door and slipped my heels off, padding over to the sofa I sat down and rubbed my tired, aching feet. This is why I didn't like wearing heels, they were uncomfortable. How women wear them all day, every day, just baffles me. Give me a pair of flats or trainers any day.

Letting my foot fall to the floor, I tipped my head back onto Killian's sofa, my eyes pinned to his ceiling. Why was this gutting me? Why did I have this burning pain searing through my heart? Why did I have this constant sickly feeling? I didn't want the marriage, we both agreed to call it quits. Yet, why when he didn't show has it broken my heart? I rubbed my chest with my palm to try and ease the ache that was so prominent it was scaring me.

We were never going to work.

I knew that.

Deep, deep down I knew that.

I would be okay; I just needed to hide away and lick my wounds. First things first, I needed to move out. I lifted my head when I heard my phone ping from near the front door where I dropped my bag. I couldn't be bothered to get up, I didn't move until I heard it ping again. Rolling my eyes, I pushed off his sofa and headed towards the door. Grabbing my phone from my bag, I stilled on the spot when I saw Killian's name.

> KILLIAN
>
> Won't be home tonight. Glad all is sorted with annulment. K

No 'x'.

I felt the tears prick behind my eyes, my skin covering in a cool sweat, even though I felt like I was on fire.

What the fuck was going on?

I dropped my phone on the side unit and walked towards the bedroom slamming the door behind me.

After a well needed bath and hair wash, I felt a little calmer. I padded across the quiet apartment and grabbed my phone to see a key next to it. It was the key to my apartment.

Swallowing hard, I looked around to see if he was here, but he wasn't. I was alone.

Picking up his keys and my own, I walked for the door and locked it behind me. Slipping out of the lift, my heart rate spiked as I headed towards my apartment. I stood outside for a moment before trying the key in the lock, a smile spreading as I heard it unlock. Opening it slowly, I stuck my head round first – just to make sure there was no one in there that shouldn't be. Could you imagine? Walking in and the apartment had been rented out?

Closing the door behind me, I noticed a small bouquet of roses sitting on the worktop. My brows pinched as I cautiously walked towards them. Placing the keys down next to them, I plucked the card that was sitting nestled between the red roses and read it silently.

Welcome Home
K

Still no 'x'. Arsehole.

Slipping the card back in the flowers, I skimmed my finger along the edge of the worktop, my cheeks flushing at the memories of when we were last together in here. Me on the worktop, him between my legs. I had never had sex like that, and I felt so fucking guilty for even thinking that. I mean, what sort of fiancé was I to Elijah to think thoughts like this.

But it was the truth, I couldn't deny that. The connection between me and Killian was explosive. I had never felt a tension or chemistry like that, sure I didn't have much experience, but it couldn't get any better than what me and Killian had.

I flopped down on the sofa and tapped my foot. I wanted out of Killian's apartment tonight, I haven't got that much to move. All the furniture is still here, it is literally my clothes and a few odds and sods. I could do it.

And I was going too.

Standing from the sofa, I swiped the keys off the work top and headed back towards Killian's to start packing my suitcases.

It had only just gone two, I had plenty of time.

Lugging the last suitcase full outside of Killian's apartment, I left my copy of my key on the side table, lingering for a moment as my fingers tightened round the door handle.

This was the end of this chapter.

Another life lesson done.

One more experience that has only bought me pain.

And I was done with being hurt.

Dipping my head, I closed the door behind me, my fingers still wrapped around the doorknob. I wanted to let go; I was just struggling. But the truth was, I don't think it was my hand, it was my heart.

I didn't want to admit it, but I had fallen.

Hook, line and fucking sinker.

I had fallen for my boss.

My best friend's dad.

My now ex-husband.

CHAPTER 34

By the next morning I was unpacked, and I felt so much better about being back here. It felt like home and I didn't mind the quietness here.

I was wrapped up under the fur throw from the sofa as I looked round my living room. I had only just decorated when I had to leave. The walls were off white, black photo frames hung around the cosy, open planned space. I had pictures of me and Connie, my parents, my grandparents who had passed and of course, I had Elijah. He was always going to be a part of my life; he would always be with me.

I smiled at his photo; we were in Cornwall. Standing at his favourite cove, our favourite cove. It was the morning before he proposed. It was beautiful and completely unexpected. But that's the thing about moments, they can be so sudden, so random, so overwhelming… so unexpected.

We have no control over these moments, we just need to live in them and enjoy every second of it as we never know when we will get a moment again. Sighing, I reached across and grabbed my diary. Opening it, my fingers skimmed across the pages. I had been writing in this since Elijah died, I hadn't written in it as much as I would have liked, but you know… life has been a little crazy.

I flicked the pages, reading small snippets and most of them were about Killian.

How crazy he made me.

How pissed off he made me.

How loved he made me feel at times.

How beautiful he made me feel.

And most of all, how he believed in me. Even when he was being a possessive prick.

He was my possessive prick.

Was.

He *was.*

I turned to the next blank page and began writing.

Dear Diary,

I don't even know where to start.

I feel like I have fucked up on so many levels, but I couldn't tell you why.

Okay so maybe, first off, I shouldn't have got intoxicated and shagged my best friend's dad. Even though I didn't technically know he was Connie's dad.

That was a pleasant surprise on thanksgiving.

Killian drove me insane. He was possessive. He was controlling. He was a walking fucking red flag.

But, I couldn't stay away from him.

I felt a rage like I had never felt before

with him, but the pull that I felt towards him was indescribable.

And that's the truth.

I can't even explain how he makes me feel.

I love who I am with him.

I am carefree, I am excited about life again and most importantly... I am happy.

Yes, I have a plan.

I want him in my plan.

I want him in all of it.

But he doesn't want to be in it. He doesn't want children, I mean, I can't blame him. He has a twenty-one-year-old daughter, he is late forties so why would he want to start again...

And kids are one thing I am not willing to negotiate on.

They're a deal breaker for me, and him for the matter.

We were always a losing game. We were over before we begun. We both knew that, yet we couldn't stop the catastrophe that was unfolding in front of our eyes.

We were never going to work.

I knew that.

He knew that.

But lately I didn't want to believe it, I wanted to believe that we could make this work.

And then today, the annulment...

I dropped my pen onto the pages for a moment as I closed my eyes for a moment, and when I opened them, a tear rolled down my cheek and fell into my diary. I choked out, a scoff of a laugh leaving me as I realised how pathetic I was.

Why was I crying over him? Why was I even letting that arsehole have any more of my thinking time? Why was I letting that self-absorbed, selfish prick even have any of my tears? Shaking my head from side to side, I picked my pen up again and began to write.

The cunt didn't show.

Yes. I used the worst swear word in the history of swear words.

But he deserves it.

He left me there, alone.

He signed the papers and left his ring with a lawyer.

You want to know why? Because he is a fucking coward.

A coward that I am no longer married to... and thank fuck I got out when I did.

Now, he is out of my personal life... except with Connie. But let's be honest, I just will avoid anything with Killian. And IF she asks, I'll just tell her that her father is a cock womble and I don't want to see him.

I'll just blame it on Adele.

Yes. Perfect.

The bitch Adele.

I bet she is behind it. She hated that me and Killian were together.

I just need to sort work. I'll stay professional. But I'll be looking elsewhere.

I stopped for a moment, taking a breather and shaking my hand out. I had cramp from how quick I was writing.

"It just doesn't make sense…" I whispered to the room, "No sense…"

Picking my pen up I scribbled a few more words.

He didn't show.

And that was the sucker punch straight through my heart.
The realisation.
The reality.
He didn't show.

CHAPTER 35

Today was the start of a new chapter.

It had been two weeks since the annulment, and in them two weeks I had seen Killian twice.

Honestly though, I was fine with it. It actually worked better for me this way. It gave me a chance to get over him. I have been tempted to ask Connie what has gone on, but then I would have to indulge in our past and me and Killian both agreed it would never be spoken about. So, my mind is the only place for me to dump it all.

I sat at my desk; my fingers wrapped round my cup as I drank my tea. My eyes were fixed on the date on the calendar of my computer.

I had a gynaecology appointment this afternoon. I had been to meet Connie's mums' fertility doctors, and everything looked good for me to go ahead and find a donor. I knew this is what I wanted. What I have always wanted.

A baby.

I didn't need a man. I was an independent woman.

I had savings, I had a job… *okay so it wasn't permanent, but it was a job. And Killian wouldn't kick me out.*

Well, he did basically kick you out of his apartment- my subconscious so kindly reminded me.

Rolling my eyes, I closed the calendar and turned my attention to my ever-growing inbox.

Grabbing my coat, I pulled it on and wrapped my scarf around my neck. I was excited but nervous. I just prayed that after today, things were going to start looking up for me. I rushed out the office before I was stopped by an office junior asking me questions that I didn't need to answer. Pushing through the door, I inhaled the cold air, filling my lungs. Damn, it felt good. Holding my hand up, I stopped the first taxi I saw and climbed into the back.

"1016 5th avenue please," I asked nicely as I shut the door.

The driver grunted, turning his light off and pulling into the busy road. My heart was racing but in the best way, my whole body tingled with anticipation.

This is what I needed.

What I had been waiting for.

Throwing the taxi driver some notes after the short taxi ride, I hopped out and practically skipped up the steps of the doctors.

The heat blasted me as soon as I was in the office, taking in the light and airy reception area. These were a lot posher than our doctors back at home.

"Afternoon, welcome to Doctor Kyra's office, do you have an appointment?"

I smiled at the friendly lady sitting behind the desk, her bobbed brown hair was styled to perfection. Her cheeks had a rosy glow, but I wasn't sure if it was her make-up or whether it was from the belting heating that was on all day.

"Yes, yes…" a nervous laugh bubbled out of me, "I do have an appointment. My name is Reese Hernández, I have an appointment at two." I said quietly, unsure why.

"Lovely," she smiled as she tapped the keyboard, "take a seat Ms Hernández, Doctor Kyra will be out in a moment."

My smile was still sitting on my lips as I stepped back and sat down in the pristine and modern waiting room. I looked at the magazines on the coffee table in front of me.

Baby, baby, baby.

My heart warmed, fuzziness spreading through me. I wanted this so bad. I felt desperate. It was so close, my grasp millimetres away from grabbing it and holding onto my dream for dear life.

"Ms Hernández?" a young blonde woman said as she stood in light pink scrubs and a long, white doctor's jacket. The waiting room was quiet, a few couples sitting and here I was sitting alone.

Again.

I stood up, grabbing my bag and following her into her office.

"Please, take a seat," she said as she sat behind her desk, her hand opening and gesturing for me to sit down opposite her.

She was British, I felt a little more at home suddenly.

"Okay, so I have your file here. Everything looks great." Her eyes were cast down as she looked at the paperwork tucked in a light brown folder. "You're healthy, you're young..." her eyes found mine as she smiled. "You're sure you want to go ahead with this?" she sat back, her fingers pressing into her chin.

"Why wouldn't I be?" A bubble of a laugh left me.

"Because you are young, there is still time for you to settle down with someone…"

I shook my head from side to side fast, "no, no," I continued. "I don't want to wait for someone, I had someone… he died. I can't go through that again. I know this is what I want… I can do this… don't take this away from me." My voice was more of a beg now.

"Reese, I'm not going to take anything away from you. I just wanted to check; I have to ask…" she smiled softly as she closed my file. "I'm sorry for your loss."

I nodded solemnly at her acknowledgment.

"Okay," I whispered, "I'm sorry, I just…"

"I know." She nodded gently, pushing back away from her desk, "let's do an ultrasound, see how things are looking, then we can go from there," she said as she sat at the ultrasound desk, slipping on some gloves and holding the probe in her hand.

I walked over cautiously, the nerves suddenly putting out the excitement that I once felt. *Did I want this? Did I want to do this alone?*

"Lay on the bed and lift your top for me please."

I did as she said, my heart was thumping in my chest.

"How long have you been here in the city for?" she asked as she applied a cool gel, making me jump a little. "Sorry, it can be a little cold."

"Erm, a few months."

"Enjoying it?" she asked as she pressed the ultrasound probe into my lower stomach. I should have peed before I had this done.

"I am, I came here for work. It's been a little hectic and things haven't gone quite to plan but I am hoping that after today things will be back on track." I smiled, turning my head to look at her but my words fell on deaf ears. Her eyes were fixed to the screen as she studied whatever was on there.

"When was your last period?" she asked as she pressed some buttons on her keyboard while pushing the probe harder onto my stomach.

Her question threw me.

I couldn't think, I had complete mind fog.

"I, erm… I'm on the pill, I track them… I just can't think off the top of my head," I confessed. Panic covered me at her words.

I didn't even know when my last period was. *Shit. Fuck.* Leaning up on my elbows to try and see the screen but it was useless. It was turned towards her; I couldn't even see it if I craned my neck.

"Is everything okay?" I asked, concern lacing my voice now. Was something wrong?

"Everything is perfect," she smiled, turning the screen to face me. "Con…" her voice was cut off when the door to her office flew open.

"Sir! I said you can't go in there," I heard the receptionist call as a heavy breathing, hooded eyed Killian stood in the doorway.

"Excuse me," Doctor Kyra said as she spun in her chair to look at Killian. "Who are you? I am with a patient. I am going to ask you to leave before I have Patricia here call security," her voice was stern, her accent thick. Her eyes darted to me for a moment, "I am so sorry," she whispered.

"It's fine." I reassured her, my head turning to look at Killian.

"I'm with her," Killian snapped as he stepped into the room.

"He isn't," I shook my head.

"Reese, now is not the time to be a brat," he growled; his jaw clenched.

"Don't you dare. Get out Killian. You're not going to ruin this for me."

"I'm staying." He stepped closer to me now, Patricia was hanging back, her eyes volleying from me to Doctor Kyra.

Kyra held her hand up to still Patricia for a moment as she watched me and Killian.

"The fuck you are. You lost all right to be here two weeks ago, now please… leave." My voice was a plea, my eyes brimming with hot unshed tears. I was frustrated and infuriated that this man made me feel like this.

"Do you want me to call security, Reese?" Kyra's eyes

pinned to mine; her voice was quiet. I got it. She thought I was in trouble.

I shook my head, "It's fine..." I tried my best to reassure her. "Honestly, he can stay." You could hear the defeat in my voice. I just wanted to know what was wrong, I would deal with Killian later.

"Is something wrong?" Killian sensed the mood in the room. His voice was softer now he saw the tears in my eyes, his hand rubbed over his chin. His other was deeply fisted in his pocket.

"I don't know," I whispered, turning my head to the doctor. "You burst through the door like a mad man before I could find out what was wrong."

I saw Kyra nod to the door to let Patricia know that everything was okay. She nodded and shut the door behind Killian.

The three of us waited in silence for a moment, Killian was by my side, his brows furrowed at the screen that I still couldn't see.

"Is that a..." Killian paled, his eyes wide and bulging.

"It is." Kyra grinned before she turned from the screen to face me. "Congratulations Reese, it seems you are already pregnant," her voice was gentle and full of happiness, her pitch heightening slightly. "I would say around ten weeks, but that's just a guess at the moment."

Oh shit.

"Pregnant," I whispered, my eyes glued to the screen at the little jellybean that was floating around in my stomach. It's legs moving as it somersaulted.

My little jellybean.

"I will schedule your next scan and update your file, congratulations again Reese." She pulled the probe off my stomach, but the screen was frozen with the baby.

I felt Killian's thumb pad against my skin as he swiped a stray tear that was rolling down my cheek. My eyes were pulled from the screen when Doctor Kyra stood next to me, wiping the gel off my stomach then holding her hand out for me to take. I did, my trembling hand sat in hers as she helped me up.

"You okay?" she asked, her head dipping slightly as she looked for our eyes to meet.

I nodded, "Yeah," I said breathless, "just a little surprised that's all."

"Good surprise?"

I nodded again, "It's a wonderful surprise."

Pulling my hand from hers as I tugged my top down with force and stepped away from her, taking my files and walking for the door.

"I'll call you with your new dates." Kyra called out as I stepped outside the door and not looking back. I didn't stop, I just carried on walking down the pavement.

"Reese!" he called out, but I ignored him. "Reese!" he shouted louder now.

I kept marching on.

"Damn it, stop!" he screamed but I couldn't hear him. I was too lost in my own thoughts whirring and whizzing round my head.

Killian was hot on my tail, grabbing my wrist he tugged me back to a halt.

"Reese!" he sounded exasperated as I finally stilled.

"What!?" I snapped, "What!?"

"Just stop for a minute will you," he groaned, his hands wrapping around my waist as he held me in place.

"Why, Killian?"

"Because you have just found out you're pregnant and you're running around like a headless chicken." My chest was rising fast, my breath heavy as my eyes volleyed back and forth. "Is it mine?" I saw the wince creep across his face as the words left his mouth.

"Fuck you," I screamed at him, slapping his cheek hard.

His head cocked to the side, his large hand rubbing his skin. His tongue darted out, resting at the corner of his top lip before his blazing eyes found mine. His eyes hooded, looking down at me. The spark that coursed through me from his intense stare made my steps falter as I slipped back. I ignored the swirling heat that stirred in my stomach, the ache between my legs growing. I was angry with him. Super pissed off.

He stepped towards me. I stilled, holding my hands up and hitting them against his chest repeatedly. Turning quickly, I rushed away from him, but I could hear him behind me. Picking up the pace I tried to lose him, but with his long legs and his big strides which equated to two of mine, it was useless.

I spun round, pointing my finger at him.

"Don't you dare," I warned, my hand shaking through anger and nerves. My voice was hoarse as I tried to keep the burning lump at bay as my tears stung my eyes, but I wouldn't let them fall. I was sick of crying. I was sick of being angry. I was sick of feeling like this.

"Reese…"

"Just leave me alone. Leave *us* alone," my hand automatically moving to my belly. My head dropped, my eyes landing to where my hand was resting.

"We don't need you. You didn't want me anymore, so now you lose the both of us." And with that, I turned and walked away from him. Not once looking back.

I couldn't do this.

I needed to put the distance between us and now was the perfect time.

CHAPTER 36

I locked my door behind me, then slipped the safety chain across. I didn't think he would turn up, but I could never be sure with him. He was unpredictable. The fact he had a spare key for my apartment meant he could let himself in at any time. *Weirdo.*

My skin swarmed in heat, I felt clammy and sticky. Unwrapping my scarf, I pulled it from my neck and threw it on my sofa, next I shrugged my coat off and threw it in the same place as my scarf. Why was it so hot in here? Pushing my fingers through my long blonde hair, I wrapped it round into a high bun and pulled a toggle over it. I needed air, yes. Air. Opening the window to my apartment, I leaned my top half out and inhaled. The ice-cold air hurt my lungs, making them burn but it felt good in some weird, kind of way. The air was far from clean in New York City, but it felt good having the fresh air circulating inside of me.

I must have been hanging out the window for a while, my mind wandering too earlier today. I went to find out when would be good to be inseminated, and I came out already pregnant.

With Killian's child.

That he wants nothing to do with.

But why does that matter? I was going to do this myself all along. I didn't need him or anyone for that matter.

Goosebumps smothered my skin, the chill spreading across me now. Slamming the window down quickly, I walked into the bedroom and tugged my jeans off. I felt constricted, I needed something loose around my non-existent bump.

Grabbing some oversized tracksuit bottoms, I rolled them over a couple of times then reached into my drawers for my grey *Nirvana* tee.

That felt better. I smiled in the mirror, turning to the side and placing my hands over my lower belly.

It still didn't feel real, it still hadn't sunk in that I was growing a baby.

I was going to be a mum in a little under seven months.

Now it really was time to get my act together.

I sat on my large, black sofa. My eyes just danced round the room. I had a small television in the corner of the squared, open planned lounge. I wanted some plants scattered around, but I only went for pretend ones. I could never for the life of me keep plants alive. A familiar fear pricked at my skin, the sweat beading on my brow.

I couldn't even look after a plant... how the hell was I going to look after a baby.

Edging forward on the sofa, my fingers tapped against the china of my mug. I wanted to nibble my skin on my nails but tapping my fingers would help contain the anxiety that was ripping through me.

I'm going to need a bigger apartment, my head spun as I looked behind me and looked round my spacious one-bedroom home. I loved it here.

I didn't have to panic, we had time.

Turning my head quickly I spun to look at the photos on the wall, Elijah's eyes finding mine.

"I'm so scared," I whispered.

My eyes fell to my half full cup of tea, swirling it round gently. I jumped when I heard a knock on the door.

"Bitch tits, you in?" I heard Connie's voice. I let out the small breath that I had been holding. I could really do without this, but on the other hand I needed my friend more than ever. I just couldn't tell her yet.

Rushing for the door, I slid the safety chain across and let her in.

"Hey," I smiled at her, she had wine in her hand and Chinese. She was an angel.

"Hey, you," she smiled back.

I stood aside and let her in, she smiled as she rushed past me and placed the cartons of food on the work top and set to quick work to get the cork out of the wine. Reaching up for two glasses and pouring a glass. My eyes widened as it sunk in. Moving quick, I covered the top of my glass and shook my head side to side.

"Not for me," I tried say it in a joking manner, but I was worried she would see through my shit.

"Why?" her eyebrow lifted.

"I'm not feeling very well, I have had a terrible migraine…" I laughed, even I wasn't convinced.

She rolled her eyes.

"Bore," she smirked, "more for me."

"Dish up, I just need the loo," I said quietly, rushing off and closing the door. Washing my hands, I walked back into the kitchen area, smiling.

"I am starving, what did you ord…" I was cut off, stilling when I saw what was in Connie's hand. *The pregnancy leaflets. Shit.*

"You're pregnant!?" she gripped onto one of the leaflets tightly in her grasp, her wine glass was in her other hand.

"Connie… I…" and just before I could finish what I wanted to say, the apartment door burst open. My head snapped around to see Killian, my eyes widened, my heart thumping against my ribcage.

"If you think for one minute that I am not going to be part of my baby's life, then you've…" his voice boomed around my apartment when I heard the glass smash. Everything moved in slow motion as I turned my body to face Connie. I watched the wine cover Connie's feet, the glass shattering across the highly gloss, tiled floor.

No words were spoken. Connie's eyes were pinned to her dad, her mouth slightly open, her eyes filling with tears.

"Darling," I heard Killian say, but he wouldn't dare to step forward.

"Don't." She hissed at him before her stony, cold gaze found mine. "And you," she spat, "sitting here pretending we are BFFs!? And you've been fucking my dad the whole time!! What else have you been keeping from me?" her voice was loud.

"Connie, it's not like that…" my voice was a whisper in comparison to hers. I was devastated.

"No? Because I am sure I have just found out that you're pregnant with my dad's baby, or have I got that wrong?" Her arms crossed against her chest as she pinned her stare to me.

I didn't have the words for her. Everything she said was the truth. I felt the sting at the back of my throat, my eyes pricking with tears. I felt the betrayal in her eyes slice through me and it was one of the worst feelings I had ever felt.

"Why him?" she asked me, "why out of all the men, in all of the city did you have to go for him?"

"It wasn't out of choice. It just happened…" I turned to look at Killian, the look of remorse masking my face. We were fucking fools for thinking we could keep it from her.

"So, you only slept together once?" this time she directed her venomous tone towards her father. I felt like we were facing a firing squad.

"No." Killian said sternly, his eyes dropping to his feet,

one of his hands fisted in his pocket and the other was rubbing round the back of his head, before it moved towards the nape of his neck. He was tense.

"More than once then?" she continued; her tone sharp.

Killian nodded, I saw his jaw twitch and clench as he gritted his teeth. Connie turned to face me, her eyes dragging up and down my body.

She stepped towards me, her boots crunching through the broken glass. She stopped in front of me, her eyes steady as they bored into mine.

"I never had you for a gold-digging whore," she spat, pushing past me, her shoulder knocking into mine. "Screw this," throwing her hand in the air, she stormed to the front door and slammed it behind her.

As soon as she was out, I stumbled over to the sofa before crying. My head fell into my hands as I let the tears fall. How the fuck had I gotten myself in this situation.

How could have I been so stupid.

It wasn't my heart that screwed me.

It was Killian Hayes.

CHAPTER 37
KILLIAN

I STOOD IN THE CHAOS THAT SURROUNDED US, A DEVASTATING fire that ripped through the three of us within seconds.

We were a disaster. We both knew that. Yet, we couldn't stay away from each other because we were too fucking selfish.

And now we have done the one thing we didn't want to do. The one thing I didn't want to do. I had hurt Connie.

I finally lifted my eyes to see Reese a trembling mess on the sofa. Her whole body shook as the tears left her body.

I could have done more; I *should* have done more. Stepping back, I moved into Reese's kitchen and saw the Chinese take-out still sitting on the countertop. I felt my cell buzz in my pocket, slipping it out I saw Lara, Connie's mum flashing on the screen.

I cut her off and switched it off. I didn't need her screaming down the phone at me tonight and telling me how much I had hurt Connie. I didn't need her telling me, I already knew how much I had hurt her. I didn't need her telling me and making me feel even more worthless than I already did. Looking at the plug-in kettle, I twisted it to see it had water in it. Flicking it on, I waited for it to boil. Reaching for a mug, I threw a teabag in the cup and filled it with boiling water. Did I add the milk now? Pulling the refrigerator door open, I grabbed a carton of milk and added a dash.

I turned my nose up, I wasn't sure if this was right, but I would hope she would appreciate the gesture, or if she didn't, I am pretty sure I would be wearing it. The temper in her was something else. She just snapped. One little thing to push her over the edge.

I walked cautiously over to her. She hadn't moved.

I felt like an ass.

I crouched down in front of her and placed the mug on the coffee table in front of her.

"Baby," I whispered, my hands gripping onto her thighs as I steadied myself.

She didn't look up, her head was still buried in her hands.

I was at a loss. I didn't know what to do.

"I'm sorry," my voice was still low. She lifted her head, her beautiful opal eyes that were the most beautiful I had ever seen, rimmed in red, swollen and glassy.

"You're *sorry*? she hissed before a laugh ripped through her, shaking her head from side to side as if in disbelief.

"I am," my hands rubbed up and down her thighs.

"You don't even know the meaning of the word." She spat, pushing my hands off her then standing up and slamming her bedroom door shut.

I stood slowly, sitting on the coffee table and dropping my own head into my hands. How the fuck am I going to fix this?

I don't know what to do, I feel like I am being pulled in opposite directions. I needed to sort it out with Connie, but I also needed to sort it out with Reese. I couldn't leave it like this. She was pregnant with my baby, and I needed to be here for her.

Now.

Rubbing my face with my hands, I dragged my fingers over my stubble then slapped my palms onto my thighs. Standing, I shrugged my suit jacket off and folded it over the arm of her sofa where her coat and scarf was. I looked around her apartment, it was cosy and warm. Not like my apartment. My apartment was cold, it had no warmth in it at all. I paid someone to come in and design it, I didn't choose any of the décor or the furniture. It wasn't home to me. Just somewhere for me to lay my head.

I knew where I wanted to be. I knew where I wanted home to be.

But I wasn't sure if home wanted me anymore.

Grabbing Reese's coat and scarf, I held the cream cashmere scarf and held it under my nose and inhaled her scent. The familiar vanilla and peach tones awakened my senses, like a hit of a drug I so desperately craved. My skin pricked and tingled as I continued to sniff, I just couldn't get enough.

She was my favourite scent.

My favourite taste.

My favourite everything.

It took all the strength in me to let go, to make my legs move to where I wanted them to go. I hung her coat and scarf up, letting the soft cashmere material slip between my index and middle finger.

Turning, I moved back towards the kitchen, putting the cartons of the still warm Chinese into the empty oven in the hopes to keep it warm for when she was ready. If she didn't want it, I would go to wherever she wanted me to so I could get her food.

I picked up the broken glass from the floor where Connie had dropped it, making sure that the floor was cleaned of the spilt wine too. Then spraying the countertops down, I gave them a quick wipe over. I don't know why, but I felt useless and thought it would help.

Thought it might make her feel a little better.

But then again what did I know… I was doing a pretty shitty job of making her feel good at the moment. But truth was, I needed to put the distance between us.

There was stuff going on behind closed doors that no one knew about and that's how I wanted to keep it.

Once the sides were wiped down, I walked slowly back over to the open planned lounge and stood at the floor to ceiling window as I looked out at the people huddled together trying to shield themselves from the arctic rain that was pounding down onto the sidewalk.

Sighing, I pressed my forehead against the windowpane as I stilled. I turned my head behind me, my eyes skimming up and down the closed door. The single pane of wood between us. I hated it.

Turning my body slowly, my hand pushed into my pocket as I fiddled with the inner material of my suit trousers. I was nervous and no one ever made me nervous except her. She made me feel things I have never felt before.

I lifted my other hand which was balled into a fist and lingered over her bedroom door. I wanted to just walk in, stick my head round the door and say, *'baby, I'm here.'*

But I lost that right. She was angry with me; I had hurt her and she had lost her best friend because of my lack of self-control around her.

She wasn't just some drunken mistake for me, she was so much more, but it was too late now. The damage was done.

My head dropped as I looked at the floor, my fist still hovering. I inched it closer to the wood before pulling it away slightly.

Inhaling deeply and squeezing my eyes shut I knocked gently on the door and waited. She never responded. My fingers skimmed down the wooden panel and curled around the silver doorknob, twisting, I heard the latch click. Pushing the door gently, craning my head round the door frame and calling out, "Reese," keeping my voice low and soft.

My heart dropped, my throat thick suddenly as I saw her curled up on her bed. Her knees were tucked into her chest, her hands resting under her cheek as she let out soft snores. I saw her body shudder as she took an intake of breath, her breath catching. She had cried herself to sleep. It sounded like she was still crying while in her sleep and that broke my heart. I had screwed this all up. I had to fix it. Or at least fix her and Connie. I owed them both that much.

I tiptoed quietly over to the side of her bed, my eyes falling to her. Her golden blonde hair surrounded her face, her lips parted as the shallow breath left her. My hand hovered over her face, my brows pinching as I stilled for a moment. She truly was breath-taking. I knew she was beautiful, but I have never seen her this close and this still before.

Gently pushing her hair out of her face, I leant down and pressed my lips to her forehead, lingering for a moment. Her scent filled my nostrils, intoxicating me. I always wanted her, always craved her.

My lips brushed along her temple, they glided across her cheek bone before my lips pressed to the shell of her ear.

"I'm sorry," I whispered, kissing her again, "I'm so sorry..."

It took all the strength I had to step away from her, to leave her on the bed asleep when all I wanted to do was wake her up, climb on the bed behind her and pull her into my arms then never let her go again.

But it was too late.

We were always a losing game.

Some people are written in the stars, some their souls are linked and entwined from the very beginning and for some, love is nothing but a disaster. I was the gasoline; she was the flame. We were always going to cause a catastrophic wake in our paths.

I had found my person. Just at the wrong time.

And it killed me to walk away.

But I had to walk away.

CHAPTER 38
KILLIAN

I was up and out early the next morning. I sat in the back of my car as I was driven towards Connie's townhouse. Reaching for the cashmere material next to me, my fingers twiddled with the small strands that hung from Reese's scarf that I had taken the night before. Lifting it to my nose, I inhaled deeply. If I was going to walk away from her, I needed something of hers to remind me of the one I lost. The one that would eventually get away and find the one person she was destined for.

My heart ached at the thought that she would move on one day without me.

Connie flooded my mind in an instant and I felt my stomach flip, I hated upsetting her, but this was more than a taboo fling with my daughter's best friend. My index finger rubbed the indentation mark from the wedding band that was a little too tight on my finger. I felt the pain crash through me at the thought of it not being there anymore, and for some strange reason, I missed it more today. Funny how a little bit of metal could mean so much.

But now there was nothing but emptiness. My chest hollow.

Pulling up outside Connie's home, I told my driver I wouldn't be long and if he had to move then to text me.

Pushing the button through my charcoal suit jacket I climbed the steps and knocked on the door.

I wasn't on the doorstep long when a very annoyed Lara opened the door.

She crossed her arms across her pristine, white pant suit. Her short brown hair sitting on her shoulders. Her lips were pouted, her perfectly shaped brows raised.

"Well, you fucked up," she sighed, stepping aside and letting me in. I nodded, sighing as I stepped over the threshold.

I held my hands up in surrender. "I know, I know… okay?" my voice hushed as we stood at the bottom of the sweeping staircase. I bought this house for Lara and her wife Katie once Connie was born. They wouldn't take money from me at first, so I bought them a house for Connie. They couldn't say no to that.

"Why, Killian? Why Connie's friend…?" she dropped her arms, one of her hands clutching onto the stair rail.

"I didn't know she was Connie's friend until Thanksgiving. If I did, I would never have come onto her." I winced at my words.

"Classy," she scoffed softly, "Connie is really upset…" her voice trailed off as she looked up the stairs, "not only is she her best friend, but she is going to be a big sister… it's one big fuck up Killian!" Lara's voice was a little sterner now as she crossed her arms against her chest again.

"I know, I'm here to make it right… let me go up there please," I said exasperated.

"Be my guest, I'm not sure she will want to see you, but you know where her room is. Me and Katie will have a glass of whiskey on the table when you're ready," she laughed, "you're going to need it I feel…"

I pushed the sleeve of my suit up ever so slightly and

looked at my watch, my head snapping up as I looked at Lara. "It's ten am in the morning." My brows pinching.

"It's five o'clock somewhere." She shrugged her shoulders up before sashaying her hips down as she walked down the hallway.

She was right. I was going to need it.

Connie was stubborn and strong headed. If she didn't want to hear me out, then she wouldn't. She could quite easily turn a deaf ear on my words if that's what she wanted to do. You didn't cross her; she wasn't big on giving second chances. I just hoped I hadn't burned the rickety bridge that I had spent so hard re-building over the last few years.

Pacing the stairs slowly, I didn't know what I was about to walk into. I was hoping it was a full on, bull raging Connie instead of a calm and nonchalant Connie.

She was much worse.

I knocked gently with my finger, then pushed the handle down when she called for me to come in. I am sure if she knew it was me, she would have told me to go die.

I sighed, putting on my best smile for her as I stepped into her room. The walls were a light lemon, her wooden framed bed situated in the centre of the room and sitting under the large, sash window that overlooked the large back yard. She had the odd boyband poster hung on her walls, as well as the dream catchers she collected over the years for her bad nightmares that used to cripple her of a night. We never knew if it was the dream catchers that worked or if it was just the thought of them, but they worked.

She was laying on her front on the bed, her legs up and crossed at her ankles as she texted from her phone, not even lifting her eyes to look at me.

"Hey," I said quietly, running my hand round the back of my head and giving it a gentle rub.

"Go away." I heard the irritation in her voice at just my presence.

"Connie… I –"

"I don't want to hear it, Killian, I don't want to hear your lame excuses."

She fucking Killian'd me.

"It's dad," I coughed, clearing my throat as I took another cautious step towards her.

"No," she shook her head, "no it's not. You lost that title when you fucked my best friend and got her pregnant." She scowled, her tongue sharp and laced with a poisonous venom. I could feel the hate spilling out of her.

"And I'm sorry Connie, if I would have known—"

"Yeah yeah, you wouldn't have slept with her blah, blah, blah." She rolled her eyes as she picked her phone up again and scrolled her finger up the screen.

"Can you just hear me out?" My voice was more of a plea now, rubbing my hand against my stubble.

"You can talk, I won't listen… so if that's how you want to waste your breath today then please do," her condescending tone was starting to piss me off.

I clenched my fist at my side, closing my eyes as I inhaled deeply.

She is angry with you. She feels betrayed. She feels singled out. She is twenty-one. Just a kid.

My subconscious reminded me repeatedly.

"Want me to start from the beginning?" I asked, pushing my hand through my hair. She shrugged her shoulders up, her eyes still pinned to that fucking phone.

"If I knew she was your best friend, it would never have happened," I sighed, she begun to hum as I continued. "I met her in the champagne bar at the hotel one evening, she caught my eye, so I sent her a bottle of champagne. I had been with Adele, and we decided to stop for one drink, but something about Reese intrigued me." I swallowed hard, trying to coat the dryness that was taking over my throat and tongue. I felt like I had swallowed half of the Sahara Desert. "One night, we ended up having a drink together, one led to five, five led to ten…" I stopped talking when her eyes connected with mine. A flash of forgiveness struck through them.

Keep going Killian.

"I don't know how, or why, or even who's idea it was but all I knew was the next morning we were at Reese's apartment, married." I took another step forward. "We have no recollection of what happened… well… so Reese thinks." I sighed as I dropped my head.

"What do you mean *'or so Reese thinks',*" she pressed up from her front, swinging her legs underneath her as she sat crossed legged on the end of her double bed.

"I was drunk, but I wasn't blacked out drunk. I remember most of the night, just not why we decided to get married. That bit is still a distant memory."

Connie didn't say anything, just kept her icy glare on me.

"I never meant for this to happen, and if I knew she was your friend, believe me Con, I never would have gone there. But I can't lie to you and say I don't feel something for Reese. It's wrong, so fucking wrong. She is nearly twenty years younger than me, but she makes me feel things I have never felt before. She makes me happy, I forgot what happiness felt like before her. I have never wanted to work on a relationship before, I have always been able to cut someone out of my life when I need to. But with Reese, I can't do that. I crave her constantly, I know I need to stay away from her, but I can't. And that's what hurts me the most, the one woman I have fallen head over heels in love with is forbidden. I can't go there; I can't do that to you Connie. Because you are everything to me. I know I have been a shitty dad; I could have done so much more but I was selfish."

"Dad," she whispered, her eyes glassy when mine finally met hers.

"I can't be selfish anymore, darling. I've got to do what is right for us all and that's to walk away from Reese." Saying the words made my heart lunge, my breath catching as my throat burned as if a burning hot pole had been pushed into my windpipe. My stomach flipped, my skin smothering in goosebumps as the realisation had finally kicked in.

I had to walk away. Dropping my head in disgust, I couldn't even bring myself to look at Connie. I was disgusted with the whole situation.

"Dad…" Connie's soft voice crashed through me. I didn't look up; I fought the urge to give into the pull that was trying to drag my head up.

"You were never a shitty dad," she repeated my hateful words, but for some reason they didn't sound as nasty on her tongue as they did mine. "You never asked to be a father, you were a donor. That was it." Her tone was clipped suddenly, the ache in my chest growing by the second at the truth of her words. "You gave my mums something they had been wishing for, you done that for them," I heard her bed creak and her feet hit the hardwood floor. "You never asked to be a father, dad… you *chose* to be a father." I tensed, my heart thumping in my chest. A ripple of uneasiness crashing over me like a tidal wave. "You made the selfless decision to be in my life, even though you didn't *need* to. That's the difference dad, you *wanted* to be in my life." I heard the thickness in her voice growing, I never thought this conversation was going to get as emotional as it was. I swallowed the apple sized lump down my throat, pushing it back down and blinking back the tears that were forming in my eyes.

"Sure, okay, it took you a few years, but you called Lara as soon as you knew I had been born, you bought them this home, you set me up for life and yet you call yourself selfish…" she sniffed as she closed the gap between us, her arms wrapping around my torso as she hugged me, her head on my chest, "you're the most unselfish person I know, you have given me everything and more. That's why I never accepted your job offer, because I want to make you proud dad, by making something for myself someday." I heard the sniffle again, her voice trembling. "Don't give up on Reese dad, and please don't give up on that baby." Her choked sobs left her now, her tears soaking through my thin, white cotton shirt. I cocooned my arms around her tiny frame and held her tight, dropping my head as I placed my lips on the top of her head. "It deserves to have an amazing father in its life, and Reese deserves to have happiness too dad." She sighed, pulling back and looking at me with her red, rimmed brown eyes. "Her happiness is you. And not that I need to give it, but this my blessing dad. Don't give up on her, don't give up on the one you love because you think you're going to hurt me. I'm a big girl. Sure, it'll take some getting used to, but I'll manage." She smirked as I laughed, causing her to laugh as well. "Just give her some time..." She whispered. I nodded, even though all I wanted to do was to rush to her apartment, clasp my hands round her beautiful face and kiss all of this away.

"And seeing as we are on delicate subject matters..." her voice pulled me back into the room. Connie stilled, stepping back as she locked her fingers together.

I paled, my eyes widening as I stepped towards her, "You're not pregnant, are you?" I scowled, trying my best to contain the rage that was coursing through my blood.

"Oh my god, no!" she blushed but clearly shocked by the question that just left my lips. "Jesus," she shook her head, "no, nothing like that." Her hand pressed against her forehead, the other hand on her hip.

"Then what?" I asked, my voice softer now as I waited for her to tell me.

"I'm back with Tryst..."

"Tryst?" I scrunched my nose, my brows pulling into the middle and digging in causing the wrinkles in my head to be more prominent.

"Tryst from school..." her voice was barely a whisper now.

Tryst.

"The little nerdy kid who used to pick you up, take you to underage drinking then bring you home and break curfew?" I could feel my temper rising, but I inhaled deeply, closing my eyes as I contained it.

"Yup. Him." She rushed out before she began stammering, "but honestly dad, it was more me than him. He was always the good one. He never forced the alcohol down my throat, he never made me stay out late, it was always me making *him* break the boundaries..." she stilled for a moment as she saw the rage flash through my eyes.

"You put your moms through hell!" my voice was a little louder than I intended.

"Excuse me," she crossed her arms against her chest, the fire igniting in her eyes. "You cannot say anything, I will always win this battle now. You married my best friend, kept your affair quiet and then knocked her up! So yes, dad, I am with Tryst. I was a shit when I was younger, but you have no right to be angry at me." She huffed, tapping her foot on the floor.

But she was right.

My lips twitched as I tried to fight my smile before I lost the will. I chuckled softly, reaching out and pulling her in for a cuddle.

"Not that you need it, but you have my blessing," I winked at her, chuckling again as we walked to go and see her moms.

One girl down, one to go.

CHAPTER 39
REESE

It had been a week.

One week since I found out I was pregnant with Killian's baby.

One week since Connie found out about me and her dad.

One week since I last saw either of them. The pain in my gut and the searing pain in my heart was a constant reminder of how much I missed them both.

I hadn't left the apartment, the thought of seeing either one of them was too much. I didn't even know where to begin with Connie. Sure, Killian hating me I could deal with, he will soon move on and out of my life, but Connie was meant to be here for life. We were best friends. Elijah sent her to me when I needed her, and I didn't want to lose her.

I felt like I could cry a thousand tears, but I had nothing more to give. Every ounce of sadness was ripped from my soul that first night. When I woke the next morning, I really expected to see him sleeping on the sofa, his bed hair messy and the pillow crease from the scatter cushions on his face.

But he had gone. Just proving to me that he didn't want me once more. I felt hurt and betrayal like I had never felt before. I couldn't even compare it to the pain of losing Elijah because the pain of death and the pain of someone not wanting to be with you is completely different. With Elijah, that pain will never ease, it will never fully disappear. I will always be constantly reminded of him.

But with Killian? That pain will eventually ease before disappearing completely and all he will be is a memory. A drunken, beautiful memory. Well, that would be the case if I wasn't pregnant with his child. I will be reminded every day of what I felt for him. I was a fool to think that I felt nothing towards him, and maybe if I told him just how much I had fallen for him he would still be here. But how do you tell someone you love them when they don't want the same things you do. He never wanted this baby.

He never even wanted me.

He liked the idea.

The taboo and forbidden of our relationship.

You always want what you can't have. And now he can have me, he doesn't want me.

That was okay, I will get over him in time. I will never beg him to be in my child's life, that's down to him if he wants to be part of it or not.

I will never beg anyone to be in their life.

Padding out to the lounge, I fell onto the sofa and switched the television on. I needed some background noise. Normally the quietness of this apartment I found comforting, where now I just found it too loud. All I could hear were my own thoughts, how I could have changed the outcome of this situation, but the truth was. I couldn't.

Connie was always going to find out and react the way she did. Even if we sat her down and told her face to face, she still would have reacted that way.

Me and Killian were never going to work. We were wrong for each other; we should have never met. We are both on completely different paths in life and yet, for some reason the universe thought it would be funny to force us with each other like it was some sort of sick joke for its own, selfish gain.

The hours slipped by, and I hadn't moved from the sofa. I eventually pulled myself up when I realised I had to eat. I didn't want to eat, but it wasn't about me anymore. It was about my little jellybean. My hand moved to my flat stomach, my heart thumping in my chest as I felt a warm buzz course through me. I loved this little one so much and I hadn't even met them yet.

Standing, I walked over to the fridge and pulled it open. It was empty.

My stomach grumbled.

Sighing, I slammed it shut and headed for the front door. Grabbing my coat, I wrapped it round me then went to grab my scarf only to find it missing. I groaned, dropping my head back as I looked at the ceiling.

"For fuck's sake."

Inhaling deeply, I blew the air out past my lips, my cheeks puffing. I was grateful it wasn't snowing anymore, we now just had grey, miserable skies. A bit like my mood. The air was still on the chilly side, but I was only running to the corner shop. My coat would be enough for now. My scarf has got to be here somewhere, I'll turn the apartment upside down when I get home.

Grabbing my keys off the hook, I shut the door behind me and headed for the lift. The fresh air would do me good, I told myself. I needed to get out that apartment for a bit anyway. It was just a constant reminder of everything that had gone wrong in my life since I had been here.

Breathing the air deep into my lungs, I held my breath before exhaling. I managed to duck past Frank without him seeing me. I didn't want to be stopped by him and be asked about Killian. It was bad enough that I was carrying a constant reminder around with me.

I would be at the shop in about five minutes, or in five

blocks as Connie would say. A weak smile crept on my face before I stopped it. I didn't want to think about either of them at the minute. I wanted a clear head, I wanted to think about anything other than them.

Pushing through the door of the shop, I walked aimlessly up and down the aisles. I had a few looks off fellow shoppers, but I was hardly surprised. I was wearing five-day old tracksuit bottoms, crocs and a beige trench coat. And I don't even want to think about my hair. It was so greasy; I was worried if I took it out of its messy bun it would stay in the same style.

I was gross. Turning my nose up in disgust, I needed to shower.

I picked up the pace and threw all sorts into my basket. I didn't even know what I fancied, but at least if I had the essentials, I could make something.

I paid the cashier and walked with my brown paper bags back towards my apartment. My mind was elsewhere when I got a whiff of a strong lavender and sage scent. Turning my head down a small alley, the sound of wind chimes pulled me down there. I walked cautiously, following the sound until I came to a small shop between two buildings. It was tiny. I looked at the beads hanging across the door, the wind chimes hung in the corner of the doorframe. I smiled. Stepping into the shop, I saw an older lady sitting at a round table. There was a doily tablecloth hanging over the round edges. My eyes scanned the room, there were crochet rainbows pinned to the walls, tarot cards and beautiful dream catchers. I heard the gasp leave my lips before I looked at the woman. She had a lilac bandana cloth wrapped round her head with small, gold coins hanging from each of the tassels. Her caramel skin was glowing as she flicked through a stack of cards. Her shoulders were covered in a pink, satin shawl that seemed to cover a beautiful white dress. She reminded me of Esmerelda from *The Hunch Back Of Notre Dame*.

She was beautiful.

"Can I help you child?" she asked, her crystal blue eyes finding mine and I swear I felt our souls connect in some spiritual way.

"Erm, no, no..." I smiled, pulling away as I stepped back, "I smelt your incense and heard your wind chimes and before I knew it, I was standing here." I admitted. I must've sounded crazy.

"Then somebody wants you here," she said softly, smiling as she gestured for me to sit down.

"Oh, no, really... I should get going... I have no cash on me," I said with a grimace, my cheeks flushing a crimson as I thumbed behind me. I did have some notes, but not a lot.

"Sit down," her voice was still kind but had a little more sternness to it now.

"Okay," I whispered, placing my bags down beside me and sitting in the old, rickety chair.

"You don't want to anger the spirits beyond this earth plane. You were called here for a reason, and now I am going to see if I can connect to you to find out who it is," she smiled, reaching over and taking my hands in hers as she looked at the lines on my palms. After a moment or too, she closed her eyes as she began to hum.

I don't know why, but my heart was jack hammering in my chest. I was apprehensive but also excited. I had never done anything like this before.

"Spirits, I call upon you to find the soul who brought this young lady to me," her voice echoed around the room, my eyes were glued to her.

"Come forward, my child," her voice was soft, quiet, calm which instantly stilled my racing heart as I waited with bated breath.

"Yes, I can hear you." She smiled before her eyes opened, but something was different. They were still a crystal blue, but I felt the connection. I gasped, my breath catching at the back of my throat. My eyes widened, my face moving closer to the lady.

I knew those eyes.

"Elijah," I whispered.

"Yes, my child. I have Elijah here with me. So young to have crossed over onto this side." I heard the tightness of her voice, her head cocking to the side as she studied me.

"Okay my darling, okay..." she nodded as she listened, "slow down, we are in no rush." Her lips lifted at the either side. She dropped her head for a moment, her eyes closing. Once her head lifted, her eyes opened, and the connection had gone.

"Your Elijah wants you to know that he is at peace, and he is okay. He didn't feel anything when he passed over, but he feels the gaping hole in his heart at the loss of you." Her brows furrowed slightly as she looked at me, "but he doesn't want you to be sad anymore. You have a much bigger reason to smile now and that's because of the baby that is growing inside of you. You need to let go of your past, let go of Elijah and move on with the life you deserve."

"I don't want to let go. I don't want to forget," I whispered, her hands still holding mine. I felt the gentle squeeze.

"No-one said anything about forgetting my child, just about letting go of the pain that you're harbouring. Elijah is working hard to give you the life you want and need, and the first step towards that was Connie."

I knew it. I felt it.

My eyes began to glass over as I nodded, nibbling the inside of my lip.

"And the second is Killian."

I froze.

"He is your next path, the path that Elijah has paved for you to follow. He told me to tell you to let go of your stubbornness. The last thing he said to me was that it was time to chase a new end of the rainbow. Mourn Elijah, remember him, talk out to him but don't get so lost and consumed with your past that you forget to look forward to your future. That's all he wants for you," she smiled as I pulled my hand from hers and palmed away the tears that were rolling down my cheeks.

"He loved you very much, and he knew how much you loved him but now it's time to find a new person to love, a new heart to hold onto… and he told me to tell you to trust him, everything will make sense soon."

I nodded, taking the tissue she handed me as I wiped my tears away and blew my nose.

"Thank you, I didn't know how much I needed that," I choked, the tears filling my eyes.

"But he did," she bowed her head.

"Thank you," I whispered, pushing off the chair and reaching into my purse. She reached forward, grabbing my hand and shaking her head. I smiled, as I stepped back.

"Now go, take care of you and that beautiful little girl that is growing inside of you."

"Girl?" I whispered, looking down at my flat stomach. "I'm only early…" confusion laced my voice.

"I have it from higher voices, she was sent to you at a time you needed her most…" her voice was quiet as she began to lay cards out in front of me.

The first card was death.

The second was the star.

And the third was the sun.

I looked up at her, my eyes scanning the three cards.

"Death, as much as this seems a scary card. It doesn't mean what it says. You're transforming, moving into the next stage of your life after a dark time. Death is here to make way for new things to come into your life." Her hand moved to the right and hovered over the next card on the table. "The star," she smiled, "after every storm, must come a rainbow." Her eyes lifted as they landed on my stomach, "this card is all about healing, purpose and wholeness. This card normally comes up if the person has gone through a deep and emotional turmoil in their life… which you have. This card is showing you there is hope and recovery. This is a sign from your guardian angel that everything is moving in the right way. And last but not least," her hand hovered over the third card, "the sun…" she smiled, "happiness. Life is good, the sun is shining on you and the path you need to be on… and I believe the sun is Elijah."

The smile was spread across my face, my heart felt so full but still broken at the same time, but I felt content. I felt whole.

"Thank you," I nodded, the happy tears streaming down my face.

"Now go, my child. Find your happiness."

I bent down to pick my bags up, thanked the tarot reader again and walked back into the alley.

"Thank you, Elijah," I whispered to the sky, and suddenly the clouds parted, and a beam of sunshine beat down on me. He was always with me.

CHAPTER 40
REESE

The first thing I done when I walked through my apartment door was put my food away, then I stripped down, dropping my clothes behind me as I did then slipped into the shower. It felt good to wash my hair, the water cascading down over my skin. Wrapping my towel around me, I padded to the bedroom when I heard a knock on the door, rubbing the towel that was in my hands at the root of my hair, I looked through the peep hole.

Connie.

Stepping back, I clung onto the towel around my torso and holding onto the small hand towel. Inhaling deeply, I slipped the security lock across the door and opened it slowly. She smiled, holding a bag of Chinese food and a non-alcoholic champagne.

"May I come in?" she asked a little hesitant as she stood in the doorway.

I nodded, stepping aside to let her through. I could feel the awkwardness and the tension crackle in the air. Closing the door behind her, I turned as she put the food on the countertop.

"I'm just going to… ya know…" I pointed to my lack of clothes.

"Yeah cool." She smiled, her hand in her back pocket as she rocked on the balls of her feet.

I gave her a thumbs up before walking into my bedroom and shutting the door behind me.

A thumbs up!?

I face palmed myself. Dropping my towel to the floor I grabbed some leggings and an oversized tee before pulling my damp hair into a messy bun. I hung my towels up on the towel rail in the bathroom before walking back out towards Connie. She had put the cartons out and opened them with both pairs of chopsticks sitting in the noodles. We always ate the noodles first. We didn't need plates, we just dug straight in.

I walked slowly over to her, giving her a weak smile as I did.

"Hey, look…" she said as she broke eye contact suddenly, looking at the floor then bringing her deep brown eyes back to me.

I inhaled deeply; my heart was thumping against my chest. I felt so nervous. I never wanted to fall out with Connie. That was the last thing I wanted to happen.

"I didn't want to fall out with you. It was just a huge shock to the system as you can imagine. To find out that not only you were sleeping with my dad, but you were also married and pregnant with his child…"

"No, I get it…" I breathed, my hands on my hips as I looked at the ground.

"I don't want to lose you Reese," she whispered.

I sighed, licking my lips before rubbing them into a thin line. Of course, I was going to forgive her, I just wanted to make her sweat a little.

"How much do I owe you for dinner?" my tone was

clipped, nibbling the inside of my lip as I tried to suppress my smile.

"You don't owe me anything," she glared at me.

"Nah, I want to give you my money, you know, pay my way, out of my *own* money." I walked towards my purse that was still laying on the countertop. "Don't want you thinking I am giving you any of my gold digger money."

"Reese…" I heard the exasperation in her voice.

"Nah, it's fine…" I twisted my lips as turned my back on her, but I couldn't hold it anymore before I burst into a giggle.

"You fucker," she laughed as she lunged herself at me, her arms wrapping around my neck and kissing me on the cheek. "My bad."

I continued laughing as I turned to face her, "It's fine, just don't call me a gold-digging whore again," I warned.

"You know I didn't mean it, I was just angry."

I nodded. "I know, it just hurt me a little." I saw Connie's smile fade, "but not as much as it hurt me watching you storm out the door and out of my life."

"You would never lose me," she smiled, "you're stuck with me for life now."

"Good."

We sat in light chatter whilst we ate. I had to stop myself so many times from asking how Killian was. I don't know why I wanted to know; I was just torturing myself.

I took a mouthful of the champagne that Connie brought and turned my nose up at the taste as I pulled the glass away from my lips. "This tastes like cat piss," I snorted.

"What do you expect? It's some cheap, non-alcoholic shit I had to pick up cos you got knocked up," she winked.

"It just happened… okay," I rolled my eyes.

"I don't need to picture it any more than I have thank you," Connie stood, taking my glass and putting it on the countertop. She spun round to face me, her face aglow, her eyes glistening with something.

"What is it?" I asked as I leant over the arm of my sofa.

"I told my dad about Tryst," she squealed.

"You did?" my eyes widened, my mouth agape.

She nodded.

"How did he take it?"

"Pretty well, but then again," she shrugged her shoulders up, "he didn't have a choice did he? He couldn't be mad at me after what I had found out."

I felt my stomach flip.

"I suppose not." Plastering a fake smile back upon my face, "That's great Connie, I am so glad that it's all out in the open now."

"Me too, feels good getting it off my chest," she skipped back towards me and jumped on the sofa next to me. I spun round to face her, laying my legs out and resting them on her lap. She leant into me, her hand resting on my non-existent bump.

"How is my little brother or sister?"

I snorted a laugh, my head tipping back before I looked back at her, "It's a jellybean at the moment."

"But it's my jellybean," she beamed.

I sighed happily as we fell back into easy chatter. And for the first time in a long while, I felt like I was becoming my old self again. I felt content, but as soon as my mind drifted to Killian that gaping hole came back.

Me and Connie arranged to have a little sleepover, I can't remember the last time we spent the night together. Plus, it would be good having her here with me. It would stop my mind from drifting to the place I didn't want it to.

Cosied up under my duvet, or comforter as Connie called it, we put the tele on for some background noise. Connie rolled onto her side; I felt her eyes burning into the side of my head, but I chose to ignore her while I stuffed my face with ice cream.

I heard her sigh.

"What?" I snapped as I kept my eyes on the television.

"Oh, nothing…" Connie's voice drifted off.

"It's obviously not nothing, as you have been staring at me waiting for me to ask you what you want," I laughed, turning my head to face her.

"Okay fine, fine," she smirked as she laid next to me. "Have you spoken to my dad?"

"Nope and I don't plan to." I turned my face away from her and glared at the tele. The ache in my chest was prominent now.

"Why?" she propped herself on her elbow and let her head rest on her hand.

"Because he left just after you the night I found out I was pregnant, and I haven't heard from him since. Okay, sure, I haven't messaged him, but to be honest I feel like he owes me a message and not the other way round." I sighed, dropping my spoon into my nearly empty tub of ice cream, my appetite disappearing in an instant.

"I have spoken to him," Connie's voice was hushed beside me.

"Of course, you have," my eyes automatically rolling. I turned my head to face her, "Con, is there any chance we can do this tomorrow? I really don't want to talk about it now. I am trying so hard to move on…" I swallowed hard.

"But that's just it, Reese, you don't have to move on," she smiled.

"And why's that?" I smirked at her.

"Because he doesn't want to move on either. He knows he fucked up."

"Then I need to hear it from him, not you…" I grimaced, a little sigh leaving me.

She nodded, turning on her back as she looked at the ceiling.

"Don't think I am being ungrateful or selfish," now it was my time to roll on my side and face her.

"I know you're not; I just think you need to both get over yourselves and one of you needs to make the first move. I told him to give you time, you have had time now get off your ass and ignore that stubborn streak that flows through you," she snapped her head towards me and smirked.

"I'm not being stubborn, just being a realist." I pulled my eyes from her, wiggling into my pillow as I began spooning more ice cream into my greedy mouth.

"Whatever you say, you stubborn mare."

I scoffed, but kept my mouth shut. She was right, but I wasn't going to tell her that.

She snuggled down under the covers as we stay silent while watching the tele.

I WAS AWOKEN BY A LOUD THUD. SITTING UP QUICKLY, I LOOKED round the room to see Connie snoozing next to me. I let out a sigh of relief. Pressing the screen of my phone, it was two-thirty am.

Laying back down and waiting for my erratic heart to still, my eyes were pinned to the ceiling. I was trying to ignore the thoughts that were whirling around in my head, I didn't want to start thinking because then I wouldn't be able to fall back asleep.

I forced my eyes shut, squeezing them tightly as I silently begged for sleep to take me, but I heard another thud.

"Fuck," I whispered. "Connie," I nudged her, trying to wake her but it was no good. She was out of it.

Throwing the covers back, I stood on shaky legs as I walked out of my bedroom. I had a baseball bat behind my front door that my dad made me promise I would leave there. I thought it was ridiculous until now.

Thud, thud, thud.

My heart was beating so fast in my chest, it was skipping beats causing my breath to catch. As I approached the apartment door, I reached for the bat and held it tightly in my hands. Edging closer, I stopped for a moment, closing my eyes and inhaling deeply. It's fine.

Thud, thud, thud.

My eyes pinged open.

This is how you're going to die, in your big, granny knickers... you could have at least worn your nice ones- my subconscious whispered but I chose to ignore her.

Taking one last step towards the door, my whole body was trembling as I looked through the peep hole, my eyes rolled so far in the back of my head when I saw Killian on the other side, his eyes pressed up to the peep hole.

I heard him mumble, "oh shit," he groaned.

Stepping back, I let my head hang as I placed the baseball bat back in the corner behind the door.

Rubbing my hand over my lips I contemplated what to do. If I ignored him, he would continue banging on the door.

"Reeeeeese," he called, "stop being a brat and let me in."

I scoffed a laugh as I shook my head from side to side. My hand hovered over the handle. I could just ignore him, leaving him out there and he would soon get bored. Or I let him in and hear him out.

Thud, thud, thud.

I pulled the door open until the safety catch wouldn't let me do it anymore.

"What do you want?" I hissed.

"I want you to let me in," he slurred, his hands grabbing onto the doorframe to steady himself. He was drunk. Great.

"And what if I don't?" I challenged him.

"Then I'll keep knocking," he smirked as he leaned closer, trying to press his head through the gap in the door. "And when you still don't answer, then I'll sleep on the floor out here and knock again."

"Why would you do that when you live just above me?"

"Because I want to see you…" he stuck his bottom lip out

and tried giving me his best puppy dog eyes as he leant into the door. And damn it, it worked.

I sighed, slipping the chain across and swung the door open then watched Killian fall through and onto the floor.

"Oops," I giggled, closing the door behind him and locking it. I stepped over him and flicked the kettle on. I'll make him a coffee and hopefully he can sober up a little. Then he can sleep and be gone before Connie wakes up.

Once the coffee pot had warmed, I poured him a cupful. Turning to see Killian standing by the large window, his head pressed against the glass.

My heart ached, I hated him being here and not being able to kiss him like I wanted to.

"Hey," my voice was soft as I tapped him on the shoulder. He turned slowly, a little off balance as he spun. His eyes were bloodshot, his skin grey looking as his empty, hollow eyes struggled to focus on mine.

"Here, take this…" I pushed the cup into his hand and walked him over to the sofa, helping him sit down.

"Thanks," he muttered, his eyes looking forward and his legs parted as his elbows rested on them.

I stayed standing, I didn't know what to do with myself. I looked around my room, noticing the door to my bedroom wide open. Walking over, I quietly and gently pulled the door to. I didn't want Connie to wake up. I didn't want there to be any issues, not that I thought there would be, but I needed to sort things out with Killian by myself. I didn't want Connie being involved and swaying our conversation in any way.

This wasn't going to work between me and Killian. We were too different; he was nearly twenty years older than me… he was my boss and he was my best friend's dad. We could be amicable for our baby's sake, but that was it. He could be in our child's life as little or as much as he wanted. I would never force him.

Padding back over to where he was sitting, I knotted my

fingers together. I wish I had more suitable pyjamas on. I tugged my oversized tee down, trying to cover my little short-shorts.

The tension crackled between us, the air was thick with the unspoken words we both wanted to say but were too scared to mutter.

"I should get to bed..." I thumbed towards my bedroom door; my voice was low as I looked over my shoulder.

"Don't," he whispered, but he didn't pull his eyes from the wall. I looked to where he was staring, his eyes were fixed to Elijah.

I hugged myself as I stood meters away from him.

"Okay," I whispered.

Say something, I begged silently.

I watched as he took a mouthful of his coffee, then let his head fall forward, his shoulders sagging.

He looked broken.

I stepped towards him, standing closer to him now as I looked down at him. He didn't lift his head to look at me, just leaned towards me and wrapped his arms around my hips and bum and held onto me, not letting me go. I don't know how long we stayed like this for, but it felt like hours, when in reality, it was probably only minutes.

"I'm sorry Reese," he whispered, eventually lifting his head up to me. His red rimmed eyes locked with mine causing the breath to escape me, the air being knocked out of my lungs. I could see the pain he was feeling, the flash of fear that flickered in his deep, brown eyes made my soul ache and my heart shatter.

I could feel the remorse seeping from him, he was waiting for his redemption, but the truth was I don't think I was ready to forgive him fully.

Was I being petty and over the top? Maybe.

But I have been hurt before, I needed to guard my heart. If we were meant to be together, then we would.

"I know," I whispered back, my own eyes brimming with tears, but I wasn't sure why I was getting upset. I felt such a rush of mixed emotions consume me instantly. Grief, anger, sadness, emptiness, fullness, love, unwantedness and loneliness... all at the same time. I couldn't pinpoint one emotion that was stronger than the other.

I was in the wake of destruction, and Killian was the final obstacle to send me into a catastrophic disaster.

"Forgive me?" he asked. He looked so vulnerable and small as he clung onto my body as if a fear consumed him that when he let me go, he would lose me forever.

"Let's talk about it tomorrow." My voice was almost non-existent as the lump in my throat crept up and lodged itself where I didn't want it.

He nodded before his head was resting on my stomach, his ear pressing against my t-shirt.

"I promise I won't fuck this up, I promise I will be the best father I can to you," he choked out, talking to our jellybean. "I missed out the first time, I'm not going to miss a second this time round."

I sniffled, my hands moving to his shoulders as I dug my fingers a little into his skin as I pushed him away.

"Go to sleep," I whispered. He sat back into the sofa, his head tipping back as he looked at the ceiling.

"Kiss me," he whispered as I began to walk away. I stilled, turning to look at him. He didn't face me, just continued to look above him. I couldn't. As much as I wanted to walk over to him and climb into his lap, link my hands around the back of his neck before running my fingers through his luscious brown locks and tug his hair as our lips connected, our tongues moving together... I couldn't. Because I knew once I started and once, I got another taste of him, I wouldn't be able to stop.

"Goodnight, Killian," it took everything in me to walk away.

He didn't respond, with a curt nod to myself I slipped back into my bedroom and closed the door.

I HEARD CONNIE'S VOICE COMING FROM THE LIVING ROOM, groaning I rolled over to look at the time.

Eight am.

I sighed as I rolled on my back. My eyes felt like they were full of grit, they were dry and sore. Once I got back into bed last night I just couldn't settle. All the unspoken words spun in my head, all the different scenarios that played out kept me awake for what felt like hours. I was continuously fighting with myself. Should I have just kissed him? Should we give this a go for our own happiness, but more importantly for the happiness of our child?

Grabbing the pillow beside me, I pulled it over my face and held it there while I screamed into it.

It shouldn't be this complicated, it shouldn't be this hard but yet it is. I don't know what to do, I can't differentiate right from wrong, and it was frustrating as hell.

Tossing the pillow to the side, I threw back the duvet and headed to the bathroom. Killian was obviously still out there, otherwise I am sure Connie would be back in bed with her coffee. Padding to the small en-suite that was in my bedroom, I slammed the door.

I stood and looked at myself in the mirror, my dark, puffy eyes were the first thing I noticed. I felt exhausted. Ever since Killian Hayes had been in my life, I didn't feel like I had slept properly.

Splashing my face with cold water and brushing my teeth I inhaled deeply as I walked towards the lounge. Pulling the bedroom door open, I saw Killian and Connie in hushed chatter that soon dwindled to nothing as they both turned to face me. Connie's menacing smile crept on her face, while

Killian's blazing, brown eyes roamed up and down my body. I blushed under his gaze, but soon brushed it off as I quickly stepped towards the kettle.

"Morning," I smiled but not looking at either of them as I flicked the switch, the low rumbling of the boiling kettle filling the deafly silence.

"What are you doing today?" Killian asked, snapping me from my trance.

"Oh," I smiled, turning to face them both, my fingers curling round the edge of the worktop. "Not a lot really. I have to call my parents, then I might take a walk…" I shrugged.

"Sounds exciting," I could hear the sarcasm dripping from Connie's tone.

I laughed, spinning back around and making myself a cup of tea.

"What about you two?" I asked, bringing the cup to my lips as I blew softly on the steaming brew.

"I have work and then I am out with Tryst, date night," she wiggled her brows up and down, the realisation slapping her hard in the face when she remembered her dad was standing there.

I snorted a laugh but quickly composed myself as I took a mouthful of my tea. Killian let out a low rumble of a groan beside her, shaking his head side to side.

"And you?" I asked him, trying not to spend too long staring at his handsome face.

"Not a lot," he sighed, "I was wondering if you would like to go out for lunch with me?"

He moved from foot to foot before fisting his hands into his pocket. He was nervous. I see Connie's lips pull into a smile as she watched her dad, then averted her gaze to me. I felt the butterflies swarm my stomach, my heart pumping fast in my chest as I kept my eyes pinned to Killian.

He was waiting with bated breath for my answer. I was

trying to think of a million and one reasons why I couldn't go, but in the end, I let out a happy sigh and nodded, "That sounds lovely."

CHAPTER 41

THREE MONTHS LATER

I rushed around the apartment as I grabbed my bag and light weight jacket. Spring was blooming and it felt nice to have the warm sun on my skin. I smiled as I looked down to my small bump, my hand resting on it as I felt the baby kick softly against my hand. Today was our twenty-week scan, even though I was a little over twenty weeks, Killian schedule kept clashing with mine so it took a while for us to pin a date for the both of us to attend. I was excited but nervous. I couldn't wait to see my little jellybean again and see how they were growing. Stepping outside the apartment, I locked the door behind me and waited in the hallway for Killian. After his drunken sleepover, we went for lunch to discuss how we were going to move forward. He tried to explain why he hadn't shown up for the annulment, but I stopped him. I didn't want to know. We were trying to move on from then and us going over it and trying to hash it out just seemed pointless; by doing that we would just be re-opening wounds. We agreed to stay friends for the time being. I cared a lot for him, and I couldn't just switch off the new feelings that consumed me. But I had to try. I couldn't get hurt by him. I had a lot more at stake now. He promised me the world and more, but I told him we had to take it slow. See how things progress.

Of course, I wanted to be with him and honestly, I was annoyed at myself for being so cautious, but it felt right. I had to listen to my gut, because my head and heart were screaming at me telling me I was a fucking idiot.

But my gut was always right. It was always the one I listened to most because it never steered me wrong… *yet*.

If we were meant to be, we would be. But it just didn't feel right between us yet.

I smiled as I turned to see him strolling down the hallway, he looked so beautiful. He was wearing black suit trousers with a white shirt. His top two buttons were undone, his eyes glistening as they saw me, his lips turning at the corners as he approached. I was so used to seeing him in a tie and suit jacket at work, that seeing him in anything other than that attire seemed strange to me.

"Hey brat," he winked, his arm wrapping around my shoulders as he pulled me into him and placed a soft kiss on my temple. My heart raced but I composed myself well.

"Hey," I smiled back at him, ignoring the bolt that shot through me making my blood heat and my cheeks blush.

I gently pulled away from him, putting a small bit of distance between our two bodies. Being that close to him was torture. I was constantly fighting with myself to stop me acting the way I really wanted to.

Our fingers brushed, barely skimming as they touched. The spark coursed through me making me gasp; I pulled my hand away as if he had burned me.

"You okay?" he asked.

I nodded, pressing the button for the lift.

"I am," I smiled at him before snapping my head round quickly to face the lift.

"You excited?" he asked, his hands sunken in his suit trouser pockets.

"I am, a little nervous but excited," a nervous giggle slipped out of me, "how about you?"

"About the same," he laughed, his eyes burning into the side of my head as he looked at me, but I ignored the magnetic pull to look at him.

Pulling up outside the doctor's office, Killian parked and then took my hand as he helped me out the car.

"Here we go," he beamed, I could see the glint of excitement flashing through his eyes.

"Mmhm," I agreed, taking his hand before he shut the car door behind me. "You're going to have to get a bigger car, that one is too low," I groaned, looking at the Porsche.

"I know," he agreed as he let go of my hand but now placed it on the small of my back. He pressed the buzzer and waited for the door to unlock. "If you're free after, I was wondering whether I could show you something…" his voice trailed off as he looked down at me smiling. Our gaze locked, my heart thumped. I nodded yes.

"Good," he mumbled as he placed a kiss into my hair.

"Killian," I warned, slightly breathless.

But before he could reply, we were buzzed through. A few moments later we were booked in and waiting in the pristine waiting room. We weren't waiting long before Doctor Kyra came out, smiling as she saw me.

"Ready?" she asked.

I smiled, standing with Killian close behind me.

After we went through the paperwork, I lay on the bed and waited for the probe.

"Do we want to know the gender of the baby today?" she asked.

"We do," I smiled at her before turning to face Killian. His hand scooped up mine as he pressed the back of it to his lips, holding it there. I felt my heart constrict.

Killian wasn't sure if he wanted to know the gender, but I had to know if my reading was right. Connie had arranged a gender reveal as well as a birthday party for me so thought we could do one little party with both.

It wasn't going to be a massive get together, just her mums, Killian and a couple of the girls from work as well as Julianne.

We were hoping my parents could get over, but Connie is trying to deal with it and surprise me, but I can't see it happening.

"Okay, let's get started. We will find gender of the baby first then I will do all our checks." Doctor Kyra said as she put gel on my tummy then pressed the probe.

"Any guesses?"

"I would love to say boy," Killian said with a smile, "but let's be honest, I've already had a girl, so I think it'll be another girl."

I shrugged as I laid down, looking at the screen, "I really don't know. Every craving is savoury, I've had no sickness… I haven't had any of the tell-tale signs for a girl so who knows."

"Well, I do," she smiled, turning the screen so we could see, "say hello to your daughter."

I felt my eyes fill, my bottom lip trembling as I watched my baby girl kicking around on the screen. Killian stood, clasping my hands in his as he kissed me on the forehead then swiping my tears away with his thumb.

"A little girl," I choked through my happy tears, "I'm really going to be a mum."

It had just hit me. An overwhelming love that crashed through me, bulldozing anything I ever knew or felt. "You're going to be a dad," I whispered loudly. Killian's thumb stroked the back of mine, as he sat back down.

No one could take her from me. No one could ever take my love for her away because I was always going to love her, like she was always going to love me.

"I've taken some screenshots for you ready to be printed when we have finished." Doctor Kyra said as she began the examination, but I wasn't really listening. I just watched in fascination as she measured the baby and checked her heart. She spent a little longer on the heart as she checked the baby's chambers and valves. My pulse began racing faster as she continued looking.

"Is everything okay?" I asked, I couldn't help the panic that was coursing through me.

"Yes, everything is fine," she gave me a reassuring smile before her eyes were back on the screen.

"Is something wrong with her heart?" Killian asked, his own voice full of concern now. His hand was still clinging to mine, but now he squeezed it tighter.

"There seems to be a slight flicker on it, it could be nothing but it's very hard to get a clear look as she is fidgeting," a small laugh left her, which didn't seem to match the stern look on her face.

I turned to face Killian, my eyes scanned his face trying to read his expression.

"Killian, what is it?" I whispered, my skin pricking in fear. A shiver dancing down my spine.

He tore his eyes from the screen, looking down at me.

"I have heart issues, well... *had* heart issues," his voice was low before looking back at Kyra. "I didn't mention anything because of my transplant. When I had my first daughter, twenty-one years ago, I was as healthy as a horse." His voice faltered for a moment, "but three years ago, I fell ill with a viral infection which caused cardiomyopathy." He took a sharp intake of breath; his eyes fell back to me as I looked at him wide-eyed.

"What's that?" I whispered, suddenly terrified for him and our baby.

"It's a disease of the heart muscle... never had heart issues until I got unwell. Doctor said it was the viral infection that caused it." Killian's head dropped, "we tried to manage it, but that all changed very quickly and suddenly. I was in London on business when I fell extremely ill. I was admitted into hospital and before I knew it, I was on the transplant list." He stopped talking suddenly when I gasped.

"Your scar," I whispered.

He nodded. "I got lucky..." he rubbed his lips together.

"Killian," Kyra's voice distracted us, "I need you to write all this down for me please." She said to him before she turned to face me, "we will rebook you in for a weeks' time, hopefully madam will play ball and please try not to worry Reese, I know it's easier said than done but what Killian had was caused by a viral infection, not through genetics. But if when we do your next scan the flicker is still there then we will book you a cardiology appointment."

I nodded, my throat burning as I tried to ignore the fear that was flooding through me now. I didn't want to focus on what might be wrong with our daughter's heart, because I would just spend the next week panicking and googling it. And google is not the place to go when it comes to wanting to know medical information.

I was concerned for Killian. I wanted to ask how he was, what he went through was traumatising. I should have asked him before all of this, but how could I? I felt out of place asking him something so personal. Even though I was pregnant with his child, I felt like I had no right to ask him.

We sat in the car, neither of us saying a word. I felt numb. I had so many questions I wanted to ask but I just couldn't muster the words. I let out a heavy sigh as Killian pulled up outside a three-storey townhouse. "What's wrong?" he turned the car off, turning the top half of his body to face me. My eyes pinned to him, my heart racing.

"Talk to me," he whispered as he leant across the centre of the car, resting his hand on my thigh.

"I'm freaking out a little," I admitted, my voice shaky as the words left me.

"About the baby?"

I nodded, "But not just about the baby. I'm also freaking out about you. Why didn't you tell me?" my words came out bitter, I didn't intend for them to.

"Because I didn't want to burden you with that." He smiled softly, his eyes creasing slightly in the corner. I felt a surge of energy course through me as his fingers skimmed along the material of my dress on my thigh.

"Killian, you would never burden me. You must have been terrified," my breath caught.

"I have never been more scared than I was back then. I was alone, I honestly never thought I was going to be lucky enough to get my transplant." I heard his voice crack, his eyes falling from mine as he looked to his lap. He scrunched his eyes shut; I could feel the emotions coursing through them. I could see how hard this was for him to talk about.

"You okay?" I asked, now it was my time to comfort him. I leaned over, wrapping my arms around his neck and let him bury his face in my hair.

He didn't answer, just held me tightly until he was ready to let me go.

I looked through the car window in awe at the house in front of us. The front door was cream, with a square piece of glass. Six steps led to the front door, black railings running either side of it. The beautiful, Georgian glass sash windows made me smile. It was pretty, so understated but so prestigious.

"Where are we?" I asked as Killian helped me out of his Porsche.

"Greenwich Village," he smirked, his lips twitching as he had a childish glint in his eye.

"Okay... and why are we here?" I stood at the bottom of the steps and looked up and the spectacular house.

"Because..." he smiled, standing behind me and wrapping his arms around my waist, his large hands cradling my small bump. I heard the breath catch in the back of my throat, my skin alight and smothering in goosebumps at having him so close. He rested his chin on my shoulder and pressed his lips to the shell of my ear, "this is your new house, or ours if you wanted to move in with me," he joked, letting go of me and pulling a single gold key out of his suit trouser pocket.

"Killian," I whispered, my hands covering my mouth at the shock of what he just said. "I can't accept this. It's too much..." I shook my head from side to side as I looked at him.

"You can and you will. It's the least I can do." He winked, "welcome home baby."

My lips curled into a smile, my eyes glassing over from the tears that were filling them.

"I hope they're happy tears?" his brows sat high as he gazed at me.

"They are." I snorted a laugh as I followed him up the stairs and into my new house.

Our new house.

My heart warmed at the idea of living here with Killian, as he opened the door. My eyes widened. This house was out of this world. It was one of those houses you saw in home magazines, houses you were never meant to live in. My eyes scanned the hallway slowly as I took in every, single, detail. My mind flashed with little snippets of our future daughter; she would be here taking her first steps in this hallway that led down to the kitchen. Killian would have his own office and so would I. She would have a large bedroom overlooking the long garden that sat at the back of the house. Her toy room would be filled with everything you could have ever dreamed of and more. Our bedroom was just across the hallway, a large bedroom with a walk-in wardrobe and huge en-suite that had his and her sinks and a large, walk-in shower.

And if we weren't living together, we have three spare rooms that Killian could stay in.

"You like?" he asked as we walked into the large, high ceilinged living room. The room had coving wrapped round the top of the wall, the walls were half panelled and painted in a light grey, the top of the walls a crisp white.

"I love," I turned to face him as I threw myself into his body, wrapping my arms around his torso never wanting to let him go.

"Thank you," I whispered.

"You don't need to thank me," he muttered into my hair, his voice low as he accepted my embrace. It took him a moment before he wrapped his arms around me and held me tightly.

"We have a couple more stops," he whispered as he let me go, "ready?"

I nodded, too stunned to even speak.

He done this for me, for us, and I would never be able to repay him or show him how appreciative and grateful I was.

But I was going to try. I would spend the rest of my life showing him.

That was a promise.

CHAPTER 42

We sat in the restaurant that Killian had booked called Per Se. We were waiting for our drinks while scanning the menu. Killian had taken me to a car show room to show me his new car he had bought. He had chosen a Range Rover SVR. I wouldn't have said it was particularly practical when it came to fuel, but who was I kidding. He obviously had more money than sense.

"I'm proud of you," I said quietly, I didn't want to come across as condescending, but I was proud of him.

I watched as his eyebrows pinched, his jaw clenching as his lips twisted into a smile. "And why is that?"

"Because honestly…" I played with a breadstick, tapping it on the table then rolling it between my fingers, "I didn't think you would want anything to do with me, or our baby." I winced a little as I said the words out loud.

"Reese," he sighed, "even if we were enemies who hated each other, I would have still wanted to be there for you both." He reached over and took my hand, "but we don't hate each other, do we?"

I shook my head from side to side. "I just wanted you to know."

"I am grateful, thank you," he let go of my hand as he sat back and accepted our drinks from the waiter. Killian had a red wine; I had a soda and lime.

Once he disappeared, I leant forward, stirring my straw into my drink. I felt my cheeks flush as Killian's gaze burned into mine. My stomach flipped; my heart raced.

"I cannot get the memory out of my head of you sucking my cock under my desk while Adele was sitting on the other side."

"Killian," I whisper-hissed at him, looking around the busy restaurant. He let out a throaty laugh, his shoulders shaking as he continued. I slapped his hand, blushing out of embarrassment now.

"Oh, come on, baby. Don't get embarrassed, it was the best blow job I had ever had. I jerk off to that memory."

"Oh my god," I mouthed, covering my face with my hands which only caused him to laugh louder now.

"And then in my house, you on my desk with my tongue buried—"

"Okay! Enough!" I said loudly.

He sat staring at me, his glass pressing against his bottom lip hiding his beautiful smile.

"We shouldn't be talking about that; we've moved on from that… we're just… friends."

"Are we?" he asked, leaning forward as he placed his glass on the table.

I swallowed hard, nodding.

"I don't think we will ever just be friends." He shook his head, "You can't deny that you feel the pull and connection I do…"

I ignored him, my breathing fastening; my chest heaving up and down.

"Look how you react to me, how your body reacts… you can't deny this forever Buttercup," he pulled his bottom lip between his teeth, moving in his chair. His brown pools filling with fire and desire. I pressed my legs together, trying to dull the ache that was growing.

"We said…"

"I know what we said, but that doesn't change anything between us," his voice lowered as he leant across the table, "I bet your little panties are soaked just thinking about me, about what I would do to you if we were in this restaurant alone." His voice was so low it sounded like a hum that vibrated through me, waking my senses. "I would eat your pussy as if it was my last meal, licking and drinking every bit of your cum from you." His tongue darted out, licking his bottom lip before he slowly brought the glass to his lips again, drinking it ever so slowly, trying his hardest to tease me. *Holy fuck.* My cheeks blazed.

I had to stay strong, because I knew if I gave in just a little… it would be game over.

"Let's order, I'm starving," I groaned, dropping my eyes to the menu. I had to distract him. My eyes flicked up, I tried to ignore the pull, but I couldn't.

"I'm only hungry for one thing," his eyes darkened as they fell to my lips.

"Killian," I whispered.

"All I want to eat is your pussy. Nothing else will satisfy my hunger other than you."

Swallowing, I managed to pull my eyes from his and hide my blush with my hair. My head dropped forward as I focused on the menu creating a wall of hair to hide behind.

"I think I'm going to go for the chicken," I muttered, lifting my head and ignoring Killian's heated gaze as I tried to get the waiter's attention.

I heard him laugh but I didn't look round. I saw the young waiter walk towards us, and I was internally grateful, I felt my shoulders relax suddenly.

"Yes, what can I get you both?" the waiter asked, his eyes moving from mine to Killian's.

"I'll have the chicken, but can I have it with chips…" I sighed, "shit, sorry, fries." I grimaced, "and a side of mac 'n' cheese please."

"It's fine," the waiter reassured me with a smile. I couldn't stop the blush that was reddening my cheeks.

"And for you sir?" his smile faltered slightly as he looked towards Killian who hadn't taken his eyes off me for a second.

"I'll have the salmon."

"Excellent choice, thank you," the waiter said as he took the menus from us. He didn't say another word before disappearing towards the kitchen.

"Now where were we?" Killian asked, his eyes hooded as they darkened.

"Baby names?" I shuffled in my seat, "any ideas?"

"Why are you trying to distract me?" he wiggled his eyebrows as he lifted his wine glass off the table.

"Because we're not doing this," I smirked, reaching for my own drink. "We're in a really good place, we are getting on well and I don't want to ruin this."

I saw the realisation hit, his eyes losing their darkness in almost an instant.

"You know I am right…" I winked, trying to show him my playful manner. He smirked, sitting back in his chair. It worked.

"You're right," he sighed as he swirled his wine in the glass, "baby names?" he asked before taking a mouthful.

"Baby names," I smiled back at him.

Killian drove us home, pulling into the underground carpark of our apartment block. I felt my stomach coil.

We walked side by side as we made our way up to my floor. I felt his eyes on me, first they were on my eyes then dropping to my parted lips before they were on my heaving chest.

Fiddling with the key in the lock, I let myself in. Killian stood in the doorway waiting to be invited in. I felt constricted. I knew I wanted him to come in, but once we were behind closed doors and away from an audience, I wasn't sure how much self-control I would have. Before I had a moment more to think about it, my mouth started moving before my brain caught up.

"Would you like to come in?"

He smiled, his eyes alight as he stepped over the door threshold and walked into my apartment. He closed the door behind himself as I headed towards the kitchen and flicked the coffee machine on.

I felt him close to me, his hands skimming around my hips and as he tightened his grip, his body pushing into me, pinning me to him. I felt his hard bulge pushing against my bum.

My breath hitched. I could feel my heart racing as it thumped in my ears. His lips pressed to the shell of my ear, his tongue darting out and licking my lobe before he sucked it into his mouth.

I couldn't stop the moan that left me. I have been dying to feel his hands on me like this again, his lips on me…

"Killian, we can't," I breathed out, even though I didn't do anything to stop him.

"I know… I know," he whispered.

His lips trailed down from my ear, skimming along my jaw line as he nipped.

"Just one last time…" he panted, his own breath ragged and fast as he tried to control himself. I was incredibly horny, and being honest, my little silver vibrator just didn't hit the spot. Killian would make me come and satisfy my craving, but I couldn't go there.

I dropped my head forward, my palms pushing flat on the countertop as his hands continued to move round to my bump.

His left hand glided down to the hem of my dress, tucking his fingers underneath and drawing soft circles over my skin. He lifted the skirt of my dress a little higher, exposing my thigh. His fingertips leaving a blazing trail along my skin. Tipping my head back so it was on his chest, my throat exposed. His lips crashed down and pressed against my sensitive skin, his fingers slipping higher, tugging my dress up and over my bum. His large hand palmed my bare bum cheek. I felt his body stiffen, he gasped, jumping back and dropping his hands and lips from me in an instant.

"Did she just..." he whispered.

"Kick?" I giggled, my hands on my tummy.

"Yeah?"

"Yeah, she did," I smiled as my eyes fell to my bump.

I heard Killian laugh out loud, spinning me to face him before he dropped to his knees. His large hands covered my small bump, his lips pressing against my skin through my ribbed dress.

"Daddy's little princess... already trying to stop me from kissing mommy." He cooed, I saw his smile as he continued talking, "we can't wait to meet you," he whispered, "I can't wait to meet you."

He stayed there for a moment, his eyes closing as he fully embraced this moment. I felt my heart swell in my chest, a lump growing in my throat as I watched. I cared for him so much, my feelings consumed me sometimes. I couldn't quite describe them, but one thing was for certain. I knew I had fallen for him.

But it wouldn't last forever. It was just a crush. We don't work. We wouldn't work. It was just a chemical reaction between us. Growing sexual tension.

Tonight, was a close call, it couldn't happen again. I needed to keep my head in the game. We were friends. We agreed to be friends, co-parents, and that's all we could be.

Whether I wanted it or not, that's the way life had to be.

CHAPTER 43

Twenty-eight.

I couldn't believe it was my birthday, I was pregnant, and I was spending it in New York with my nearest and dearest.

Connie told me that my parents couldn't make it and I was devastated. What with them missing Christmas, and now missing my birthday, it just felt like another blow to the heart.

Everyone else was coming, but I wanted my parents there. I couldn't help the feeling of a shimmer of hope that Connie was keeping it a surprise, but then again, I don't think she would do that to me because she knows how much I *needed* to see them.

I slipped a pair of small gold hoops through my ears, then ran my fingers through the curls to loosen them up a bit. I wanted more of a beach wave, but at the moment I felt like I had more of a poodle look going on.

I pinched my brows as I grabbed the brush and dragged it through to loosen them a little more.

"How are you doing? We're going to be leaving soon," Connie chimed from the kitchen as I fussed with my make-up. I swiped my lips with a red matte lip gloss and sprayed my wrist and neck with perfume.

"I'm just getting my bag," I called back, as I walked over to my bed and grabbed it. I checked my phone to see if I had a response from Killian, but there was nothing. I blew my frustrated breath through my lips, tossing my phone back into my bag. I had texted him last night and this morning to just remind him. He had a lot going on over the last few weeks to do with work, and he had been extremely stressed. He kept mentioning something about a merger, but I didn't want to pry. One thing I've learned with Killian was if he didn't want to talk, he wouldn't. He had been in and out of work, but I hadn't seen much of him even though I was now his personal assistant. We had decided that I would stay working with him until the baby was born and I knew what I wanted to do after my maternity leave. If I didn't want to go back to work, he would support me, and if I did, I could go back to work with him or find a new job.

He'd text me letting me know that he would be at the party yesterday morning and that he just had some work bits to finish up.

He promised me.

He promised he would be there.

Of course, he would be there. I didn't have to doubt him. Why was I doubting him?

It was my birthday, and it was also our gender reveal for our friends. I pushed the invasive thoughts from my mind, turning on my heel and looking at myself in the mirror. I smiled.

I was wearing a black, ribbed midi dress that came down past my knees and wore chunky soled Dr Marten's that gave me a little more height.

Placing my bag over my body, I walked out to the kitchen to see Connie smiling at me.

"Well, look at you... hot little mama," she smirked, her eyes trailing up and down my body.

I laughed, dropping my head as I shook my head from side to side.

"Thanks," I smiled, heading towards the door. "You ready?"

Connie jumped off the worktop counter and skipped towards me. "Yup! Let's go celebrate you, little granny. Birthday and time to prove that I am right…"

"Right about what?" I asked, swinging the front door open as I stood with my keys in my hand. Connie bound towards me like an excited puppy. "About it being a boy," she winked, passing me and waiting in the hallway.

I laughed, pretending to lock my lips with a key then shrugged my shoulders.

I locked the door behind us and headed for the lift.

Oh Connie, if only you knew.

Connie had hired out a little function room in the plaza. It was decorated with banners and balloons. There were big number balloons documenting my age which was not what I needed, but it was still thoughtful. There was a huge arch with pink and blue balloons that sat in front of a backdrop sign that said *'Baby Hayes, Pink or Blue? Either way, we can't wait to meet you!'*

I smiled at all the little details. She had really gone to town. There was a table of food, sweets, cakes, and little party favours in plastic baby bottles.

"Connie," my eyes began to tear up as I looked up at her, she was fussing with a few of the table decorations.

"Yup?" she smiled as she faced me.

"This is amazing, thank you so much," a sigh leaving me as I marched towards her and wrapped my arms around her body.

"It's the least I could do. You're my best friend, you're carrying my brother…"

"Or sister," I laughed, still hugging her.

"Or sister," she repeated, letting go of me and rolling her

eyes. "But it's your first birthday here, I wanted to make it special."

"You have succeeded in that!"

"Good," she nodded curtly, then clapped her hands together as she pulled a large bag out from under the tablecloth.

"Here," she handed it to me. I lifted a brow, eyeing her suspiciously as I looked inside the bag and saw a tiara, a 'mom to be' sash and some goodies in there for me.

I lifted the silk sash and smiled as I put it over my head.

"I tried to get you one that said 'mum' but it was hard, and the stuff coming from the UK would never have turned up in time."

"This is perfect, they will call me 'mom' anyway, so it makes sense." I gently rubbed my bump as I felt her move around, smiling. I loved feeling her, it's a sensation I will miss dearly once I have her.

I heard the big doors go to see Connie's mums walk through with bags of presents.

"Mom!" Connie called out to the both of them as they embraced.

"Hey!" I smiled as they welcomed me with open arms, "Thank you so much for coming."

"We wouldn't have missed it for the world," Lara said as Connie and Katie walked over to the gift table.

"It means a lot, especially with my parents not being here…" my voice drifted off, I rolled my eyes at myself. Waving my hand in front of my face as I felt the prick of tears that were threatening to fall.

"Oh, darling…" Lara said as she threw herself at me and wrapped me in a motherly embrace. "It's okay to cry, don't be ashamed or embarrassed."

I held onto her for a little longer, it felt good to be held like that. I was desperate for my parents to be here; I was desperate to cuddle my mum and for her to tell me that everything was going to be okay.

It wasn't long before the room started to fill with my old work colleagues, Julianne burst through the door and she kissed both of my cheeks. Connie soon whisked her away to drop her gifts on the table. I tried to not focus on Killian not being here, but it was still early. We still had time. I tore my eyes from the door as I looked round the room at my nearest and dearest, but I couldn't stop the ache in my heart and the wave of sadness that threatened to drown me.

I felt such mixed emotions about this all. It felt weird that I was sharing this moment with these people and that I was even pregnant with another man's baby other than Elijah's.

But I was happy. So incredibly happy.

Connie spoke to the room as she clapped her hands together to get everyone's attention.

"First of all, I want to thank you all for coming to my girl's special day," she turned to face me, smiling as she flicked her long brown hair over her shoulder. "I'm sure you will agree that our Reese is one of a kind, and such a beautiful and caring soul. And not only is she my best friend and a wonderful friend to all of you, but she is also going to be an amazing mom." Connie continued as her smile grew, "now before we get into the rest of her party, can we all take a moment to wish our main girl a very, very happy birthday."

The small crowd erupted as they all shouted happy birthday. I blushed. I hated being the centre of attention.

"You all sounded great," Connie laughed, "but before we do actually move on, I do have a little present for her that I am just bursting to give her." She walked over to me and took my hand. She gave me a reassuring wink before leading me to a door in the corner of the room. I couldn't still my heart, it was racing under my skin and making me nervous but excited. "Close your eyes," she whispered.

I felt daft, but I done it anyway.

"No peeking."

I heard the handle click on the door as she opened it, her hands gripping onto the top of my arms.

"Open your eyes," she whispered in my ear. My eyes pinged open, moving from person to person when I saw my mum and dad standing there, their smiles so big, their eyes glossy and glistening from their happy tears. I heard the gasps, and 'ahhs' and the 'oh my Gods' echo around the room.

"Oh my God," I whispered, "you're here!" I cried out, throwing myself at them as they embraced me and wrapped their arms around the top of my shoulders. I don't know how long we stayed like this for, but it felt so good to be near them. It felt like it had been forever since I had last seen them, and I hated every minute of it.

"Mi amor," my dad's voice was soft as we pulled back from our cuddle. His hand cupped my face as he wiped my tears away, "No llores en tu cumpleaños."

"English," my mum swatted him which made me choke out a laugh.

I heard my father tsk at my mother before he focused on me again. "No crying on your birthday," he smiled, leaning in and kissing me on the forehead.

I nodded.

"They are tears of happiness; I promise," I reassured him as we walked back towards the party.

"Where is Killian?" my mum asked looking round the room.

"He should be here soon," I nodded, looking at the door behind me before looking at my watch. He was late. Furrowing my brow, I whisked my mum over to Lara and Katie.

"Mum, Dad, this is Connie's Moms… Lara and Katie." I smiled, "Lara, Katie… this is my parents Patricia and Mateo," I smiled.

"Oh, it's so lovely to meet you! Thank you for taking such good care of our little girl," my mum cooed as she gave Lara and Katie a kiss on the cheek.

"And please, call me Matt," my father insisted as he shook their hands.

"It has been our pleasure; she is part of our family," Katie grinned at me.

I stood as they spoke amongst themselves, but soon saw my window to leave. "Please excuse me a moment," I interrupted my mum and Lara's conversation as I headed towards Connie.

"Have you heard from my dad?" Connie asked as she held her phone to her ear.

I grabbed my phone out my bag and frowned at the blank screen, "Nope, not a word."

"He isn't answering," she sighed, as she cut off.

My skin prickled, my heart dropping from my chest to my stomach as the fear began to smother me.

Flashbacks of the night Elijah died soon flood my memory. What if something had happened to Killian like it did Elijah? I couldn't lose him too. Maybe I was cursed, maybe everyone I fall in love with is taken away from me.

I shook the thoughts from my mind. No, he was just running late that's all.

"We need to get started, we only have this room for another hour and a half," Connie muttered as she angry texted on her phone.

Sucks to be Killian right now.

I nodded, sighing. But she was right. We couldn't hold off any longer.

AFTER A FEW PARTY GAMES AND BABY GAMES EVERYONE WAS writing down their guesses on the baby's gender. There was a big, black balloon that had 'he or she, it's time to see…'

written on it that sat on a white ribbon before being anchored to the floor with pink and blue balloons.

I stood with my sash over my bump, the needle in my hand as I felt the blood rush to my ears. The thumping was so loud, my eyes scanning the room constantly to make sure he hadn't sneaked in.

He should be here doing this with me. This was *our* gender reveal, and he wasn't here. I was overwhelmed with sadness suddenly, he said he wanted to be here for it all and yet he hasn't shown.

"You ready?" Connie asked as she held her phone up, my mum was next to her snapping photos.

"As ready as I'll ever be," I nibbled on my bottom lip as I lifted my trembling hand, slowly pulling it back as I lined up the needle.

Chewing on the inside of my cheek, I had to do anything to stop myself from crying over Killian. I was exhausted with it all. Everything had been going so well, it had been going pretty fucking perfect actually.

I could hear the distinct muffle of Connie's voice as she began counting down from ten…

My eyes moved to the door, silently begging he was going to be here.

Nine.

Why wouldn't he show?

Eight.

Maybe something had happened to him, it was unlike him to ghost me and Connie.

Seven.

Adele. I swallowed the sickly feeling that crept up my throat.

Six.

No, now I was being stupid.

Five.

He wouldn't do that.

Four.
Would he?
Three.
Of course, he wouldn't.
Two.
He is going to show up.
One.

I hesitated for just a moment, staring at the door wishing he'd burst through saying 'baby I'm here'.

But he didn't show.

My heart splintered as the realisation began to drip through to me, he wasn't coming. I went into auto-pilot, pinning a fake smile onto my face as I popped the balloon and watched as the pink confetti floated through the air before it fell to the floor.

I heard the odd surprised gasp, the excited screams that echoed and the tears of joy from my parents.

But none of that mattered.

Because all that mattered was me trying my best not to burst into tears of disappointment that he didn't make it.

He made a promise.

And then he broke it.

And the worst thing in all of this, was that in this perfect moment of joy and happiness, all I wanted was to share it with Killian.

CHAPTER 44

Once everyone had gone, me and Connie began cleaning up the hall. My mum and dad had headed back to the apartment for a lay down. They got in early this morning and was crashing in the hotel where Connie worked.

"You don't have to stay," Connie chimed as she swept up the pink confetti that was all over the wooden floor.

"Of course, I'll stay. I'm not going to let you tidy by yourself," I laughed, but all I wanted to do was curl up on my sofa and cry.

I felt like he had broken my heart all over again and I was over it.

I bagged the empty cups and plates into a trash bag, trying to ignore the internal battle with myself. I was arguing at why he didn't turn up, there must have been some hell of a reason, but then again… he was a prick for not showing.

Me and Connie were chatting as we finished up with the hall when we heard banging footsteps from outside. Both our heads snapped towards the door when we saw the double doors of the hall fly open. Killian's eyes finding mine instantly, his breath heaving and ragged as he looked around the now empty room. His hand flew to his hair, tugging at the root. His face fell, his eyes glossy as they burned into mine once more. His lips pressed into a thin line, his hand falling from his hair as both of his arms fell to the side of his body. I heard the choke of a groan leave him when he realised he had fucked up.

I couldn't tear my gaze from him, the burn in my throat was unbearable as I tried to swallow it away but it wouldn't budge. I had never felt disappointment like I did at this moment, and it was soul destroying.

Connie stood next to me, her eyes trying to read my blank expression. I was sure I was drawing blood from the inside of my cheek as I bit hard to stop myself from crumbling into a mess on the floor. I'm sure you could hear my heart cracking as each tense second ticked by.

Her eyes moved from my face once she knew I was ready to stand my own against him. She stormed over to him, flicking her hair over her shoulder in a dramatic way as she stopped in front of him.

"You messed up… big time!" she snapped at him as she knocked her petite frame into him and continued to walk.

Now it was just me and him.

I could see the hollowness in his eyes, he was beating himself up over this.

I dropped the rubbish bag to the floor, crossing my arms across my chest as I stood my ground. If he thought I was going to accept his apology and let him be forgiven easily then he was wrong.

I could hold a grudge. I was as stubborn as a mule. My lips twitched, my eyes glaring at him. I swear if looks could kill he would be six feet under. Neither of us wanted to make the first move. He stood there defeated, I could see it in his eyes. He was racked with guilt, he couldn't even keep eye contact with me for more than a second without looking at the floor.

Enough was enough. I shook my head from side to side,

reaching down and grabbing the rubbish bag as I stormed towards the doors of the hall. I wasn't standing here playing mind games, he was in the wrong.

My heart thudded loudly in my ears as I closed the gap between us, his eyes were steady now and pinned to me. His face didn't falter, his gaze locked on me.

Holding my breath, it took everything in me to ignore the powerful magnetic pull that I felt every time I was near him. As soon as I stepped one foot past him, he spun, grabbing the top of my arm and pulling me back towards him. I dropped my head back as he pushed me against the wall, pinning me there.

"Get off of me," I spat through gritted teeth. My blood was pumping, the rage brewing as he stopped me from getting to where I needed to be.

"No," he whispered, his voice barely audible.

"Killian, I am serious," I growl, my small hands pressing against his chest as I shove him off me.

He stood still, not moving an inch which wound me up even more. I shoved him again.

"Reese," his tone was sharp as he edged closer to me.

"Fuck you," I spat shoving him again. It felt good to let the anger out, the deep rage that had been brewing inside of me since this morning finally surfacing. But it wasn't just the rage of today, it was the anger and hurt that he had put me through from the moment I met him. I continued shoving him, him finally faltering a few steps backwards before lunging himself at me, his hands gripping and clasping my face as he tried to press his forehead against mine. I pulled back, I didn't want him close to me. Lifting my arm, I slapped his face hard. The sound of my palm on his cheek echoed around the small hall. His head turned to the side from the force of the slap. He scoffed a laugh, rubbing his lower lip with his index finger and thumb. I was panting, my eyes wide as I watched his eyes darken, his jaw ticked as his eyes roamed over me. I felt my skin prick and tingle before the shivers skimmed over my skin like pure silk. The butterflies flurried in my stomach, the intense heat spreading over me and that delicious, wanting ache in my pussy was evident.

He rushed towards me, his hands on my face, my arms round his neck as he lifted me up as if I weighed of air. His teeth grazed against my jaw line, my lips parting as a gasp left me when he hit my back against the wall.

"Reese," he groaned as his lips trailed down to my neck, biting and sucking on my skin.

"Yes," I whispered, my teeth sinking into my bottom lip as his hands made quick work of pushing my dress round my waist and slipping my knickers to the side. I clung onto him as he unbuckled his belt from his suit trousers, fisting his thick cock and slamming inside of me.

The delicious burn of him filling me was indescribable. It was so right, but so very wrong. I had been craving him for months. His hips thrust into me fast and hard, his cock slipping in and out of my soaked pussy.

I moaned, my sex tightening around him already.

"Fuck, you feel so good," he groaned, his mouth covering mine as our lips locked and our tongues danced. His hands clung to under my bum, spreading me a little more as he hit me deeper now, the tip of his cock stroked my g-spot, my orgasm building.

"I'm so close," I whispered against his mouth, my teeth sinking into his bottom lip. He was so deep, but I needed him deeper. I rocked my hips forward, meeting his thrusts. My pussy clenched round him before my orgasm shattered through me fast and without warning. I screamed out as it hit me like a freight train. Killian's hand wrapped over my mouth, drowning my moans out as he found his own release, filling me. His head dropped forward, pressing his forehead against mine as we both panted, trying to catch our breaths.

"Reese," his voice was soft, his fingers brushing some hair that had falling into my eyes.

I pulled back, wiggling out of his grip and pulling my dress down.

"Where are you going?" I heard Killian call out, I heard the buckle of his belt hitting as he ran towards me.

"Home," I snarled, grabbing the rubbish bag and storming for the door.

"Reese, don't go!" he bellowed, I heard him fumble over his own feet. I stayed strong, storming for the door and letting it shut on him.

I dumped the bag in the bin and continued out to the streets. Killian was hot on my tail, but I wasn't going to stop. The streets were busy, the spring air beginning to chill as the sun began to set. I rushed through Central Park, I didn't know where I was really heading but I just knew I needed the air in my lungs, I needed to feel the chill on my skin to slap me back to reality before I got clouded by Killian and the lust that he made me feel. I wasn't silly. I knew what I felt for him was so much more than lust, but I didn't want to get myself wrapped up in what I really felt.

I felt a tug on my wrist as Killian spun me round to face him.

"Stop running from me," he panted, his eyes volleying back and forth from mine. My brows pinched slightly, my lips curling into a sarcastic smile as I scoffed a laugh.

"I'm not running." I tugged my arm from his firm grip, "I am going home." I rolled my eyes, shaking my head from side to side as I turn to continue walking.

"What is happening? I thought we had sorted out the animosity between us back at the hall?" his voice was like nails on a chalkboard, it done something to me. I stopped dead in my tracks, smirking as I licked my top lip before I turned to face him.

"Sorry?" I pouted, not quite sure if I had just heard him right.

"Back at the hall… was that not a make-up fuck?" he looked round his surroundings sheepishly as he lowered his voice.

I tipped my head back, a deep laugh leaving me. It wasn't a giggle, it wasn't a chuckle it was full blown hysteria that ripped through me.

"So, you think not turning up to your baby's gender reveal and your baby mama's birthday party is all forgiven because you gave me an orgasm?" I snapped, not giving two hoots how loud my voice was and who was standing in ear shot. "I was that horny, anyone could have got me off," I bit at him.

He stood frozen, his mouth dropping open at my words. Turning quickly, I continued walking through to the park and in the direction of my home.

Hopefully Killian got the message.

I didn't want to speak to him.

Once I was out of the park, I looked over my shoulder to see that he wasn't following. I instantly felt relief sweep over me. I heard my phone beep in my cross-body bag. I unzipped it quickly to see Connie's name flashing on the screen.

"Hey," I breathed as I held my hand up to signal a taxi.

"Did you sort it? Sorry I just left you, but I was so angry," she huffed, I could hear clattering behind her.

"Not really," my voice was low.

"Oh," she fell silent for a moment, I could hear her breathing quicken down the phone, "well, I don't blame you to be honest. He has a lot of grovelling to do." I could hear the smile in her voice.

"He really does. If he thinks that he can waltz into the hall and try and charm me thinking I'll forgive him… then well, he has another thing coming."

Connie laughed, agreeing with me.

"You tell him boo. Anyway, I've got to go. I am cooking dinner for my moms and Tryst."

"No worries love, I'll speak to you tomorrow," I said, wishing her a goodnight and hanging up the phone. Unstrapping my seatbelt as I saw my apartment block approach, I pulled out the notes from my purse and slipped them through the small opening for the driver.

"Have a nice evening," I called out as I climbed out of the taxi, closing the door behind me. Frank wished me good evening, I just nodded sweetly before walking towards the lift. I felt a spike of anxiety course through me at the thought that he would show up while my parents were in my apartment. I really didn't need the drama tonight; I didn't want this to be the first time that my parents met the father of their granddaughter.

Once the lift doors opened on my floor, I held my breath as I walked towards my apartment when I saw Killian standing outside the door of my home.

"Not today, Satan," I shook my head furiously side to side, "this isn't happening." I moved my index finger between me and him as I closed the gap between us.

"Reese, just give me an hour to explain..." he pleaded with me. I could hear the guilt in his voice and it broke my heart but I couldn't do this tonight.

"No," I whispered, slipping past him and standing by my front door. "Today was supposed to be a happy day Killian. A day for us to share with our friends and family, a day to celebrate my birthday and yet it's a day now filled with upset. I will always remember this day as the day you broke your promise to me." My voice cracked, needles pricking behind my eyes as the tears began to pool. Slipping my key into the lock, I heard it unlock. "It's too late, I don't want excuses. I wanted you there with me today, beside me." I dropped my head as I looked at the floor, my stomach coiling, "But you couldn't do that, because we weren't important enough to you." I lifted my head slowly as our eyes connected, I could see the pain and anguish that was flickering through his brown eyes. I could see this was hurting him. "And I'm sorry Killian, but me and your daughter don't deserve to be second best," I sighed, "the only time that us being second best is okay, is if it's because of Connie." My gaze penetrated his.

"You screwed me, I screwed you, we screwed each other." I could hear the exasperation in my voice. I twisted the door handle to let myself into my apartment. "Goodbye, Killian," I whispered through the tears that began to fall, shutting the door on him and slipping the safety chain across. I waited a moment for my heart to stop racing before sliding down the door, bringing my knees to my chest and sobbing.

CHAPTER 45

It had been five days since my birthday. Five days since Killian broke his promise. Five days since I last spoke to him, and no doubt broke his heart as well as my own in the process. I lay on the sofa, looking at the ceiling. I was sleeping on it while my parents were here, they needed the bed more than I did. Plus, I forgot what sleep felt like.

I drum my fingers on top of my knuckles as I rested my hands on top of my bump. Turning my head, I saw my diary sitting on the coffee table. I had written in it every night, it was sort of like a coping mechanism. I wrote in it a hell of a lot once I lost Elijah. I got through two in the last three years, and my mum and dad gave me this one as a belated Christmas present. It was stunningly beautiful, black roses on the hardback leather with a pink heart in the centre. Subtle and understated but pretty.

I leant over, reaching for it and grabbing the pen that sat next to it. Opening the first few pages, I skimmed through them until I found my silk ribbon that indicated where I got to last night.

It was a good anger release, and by the time I had written it all out I burst into tears and let out the pain I was feeling.

I cried silently, I didn't want my parents hearing me and I didn't want to go into what was triggering me. I had lost a great love once, I wasn't going to let myself lose another one. So the best thing for me to do was to put my walls up and focus on being the best mum I could be to our daughter.

Tapping the pen on the paper, I felt my eyes begging to well. I was sick of crying. I was sick of being sad and hurt because people don't think about the consequences of their actions.

Dear Heart,

~~You screwed me.~~
~~Killian Hayes screwed me.~~
I screwed myself.

I question myself every second of the day of how I ended up in this mess. This wasn't the plan I had in mind. This wasn't how I saw my future, but yet, here I am.

I wanted to trust and believe what the tarot card reader said to me, I wanted to believe that Elijah was working the puppet strings above us to make my life perfect but it didn't seem that way. It seemed that I was the only one getting hurt repeatedly. The only other guy I felt I was falling for couldn't even show for my birthday. A small, silly promise that he failed to keep. To some it might not be a big deal, but to me it was a huge deal. I didn't trust easily after losing Elijah, but something about Killian felt like home to me. Like we had known each other so much longer than just under a year. We had a connection, emotionally and physically and I couldn't deny that. He felt familiar, he felt like someone I had met before in another life.

We agreed to be friends because we couldn't be anything more than that. We were toxic. We were going to always end up a disaster. Some people just weren't meant to get their happily ever after and I truly believe that I am one of them.

But, come to think of it... I was going to get my happily ever after. My daughter. My little rainbow. My hand-picked gift from heaven itself, from my guardian angel. She was going to be my happily ever after... maybe this was my new sole purpose in life. To be a mum to this perfect, baby girl that would be coming into my life in about five to six months. She would show me a love like I have never felt before, a connection that runs so much deeper than the surface, a bond that would never be broken. We would always be tied together.

Me and Her.

Her and Me.

She would be the only person I would love most in this world. No one would compare to her.

My darling daughter.

I know she will heal me; she will show me this devastating world in a completely new light like I have never seen it before.

I will become a better person for her. I need to.

"It's me and you baby girl," I whispered as I rubbed my bump gently, her little kicks always reminding me she was right here with me. She would always be here with me.

Dear Heart,

I won't let you screw this up.

This was a test and I have passed with flying colours.

I am not going to shed one more tear over Killian fucking Hayes.

THE NEXT MORNING, MY PARENTS WERE UP AND OUT EARLY. They flew home later this evening and wanted a few bits to take back with them. I pottered around the apartment and tidied up. Not that it needed much, I just wanted to keep my mind busy.

Dumping all my emotions into my diary felt good, but it didn't completely rid me of my guilt or emotions. I knew I was being harsh with Killian, but I couldn't keep forgiving him for him to just tear me down again.

I was too vulnerable and delicate for this.

Chopping the pillows on the sofa, I sprayed some air

freshener round to cover the stuffiness. I slipped the large window up, the sweet, fresh spring air filling my apartment suddenly.

I smiled as I inhaled deeply filling my lungs. Today was going to be a good day.

Padding through my bedroom, I grabbed some clothes before stripping down and having a warm shower. The water felt good on my aching shoulders and back. The sofa was comfortable but not suitable for a bed.

Once dressed, I pulled my honey blonde hair into a high ponytail. I looked behind me at my small suitcase sitting by the radiator. I had booked a flight back home to England, I was supposed to be leaving tonight but I was still undecided what I wanted to do.

I was adamant I wanted the baby here, it would do me good to head home for a couple of weeks before my next appointment to check the baby's heart. Plus, it would do me good to get away for a bit, time to clear my head.

I hadn't gone into much detail about Killian to my parents, but they knew enough. I was devastated as I would have loved for their short visit to have been a little different and for them to have met Killian and spent some time with him. But alas, it wasn't meant to be. They've had a fab time exploring New York and doing all the tourist attractions, but I think they were both ready to land on home turf and slip back into their routine. I heard a light knock on the door, I walked into the lounge and saw my spare keys sitting on the work top that my parents had forgotten. I rolled my eyes in a playful manner, one side of my mouth lifting as I headed to the door.

"Honestly, how can you forget your..." I swung the door open, beaming from ear to ear before my breath was snatched from my lungs at the sight of Killian. My smile quickly faded as I pushed the door with force to shut it on him but his shoe stopped that from happening.

His long fingers wrapped round the edge of the door, his head craning around it .

"Please, I just want ten minutes…" his voice trailed off.

I sighed, stepping back and dropping my head as he walked past me. I gently closed the door behind him and watched as he placed his phone and keys on the countertop next to my spare keys.

"You can have five minutes," my tone vicious as I spat at him.

"Can I be excused from using any of those minutes while I quickly use your rest room?" his eyes glistened slightly, but I was unsure whether it was with playfulness or regret.

I nodded, not wanting to give him any of my breath because he stole it from me without even realising.

His eyes fell, a weak smile attempting to cross his lips, but it was soon back to a grim looking Killian.

Once he was out of sight, I gasped, walking over to the kitchen as I rubbed my lips together. I flicked the kettle on, I needed a cup of tea. I heard Killian's phone buzz, my head snapped round but quickly I was back facing the kettle when it buzzed again. I couldn't ignore the niggle in my gut for me to look. I stepped back, leaning the top half of my body to check the bathroom door. It was still closed, and I was pretty sure I hadn't heard the flush go yet.

Moving quickly to the worktop I picked his phone up to see Adele's name and two unread messages.

I swiped his phone up, unlocking it straight away.

Silly man for not having a passcode on his phone.

The messages opened; my eyes widened.

ADELE

Saturday was a lot; things are still unfinished between us Killian.

Then, underneath it was a message that she had sent straight after.

ADELE

In business and pleasure ;)

Who the fuck sends winking faces like that anymore?

My blood boiled. Saturday was the day of my birthday and my gender reveal. My whole body shook and trembled.

I heard Killian's rushed footsteps before they stopped suddenly.

My head snapped up to look at him, his eyes volleying from his phone to my face. His beautiful but deceitful brown eyes widening as each second passed. I threw his phone at him with force, hoping it would have hit him, but the God of a man has reflexes of a Ninja. His hand shot up as he grabbed the phone. His eyes down casting on the screen of his phone, his head shaking side to side before he looked back up at me.

"Reese..." he gasped, his hand rubbing over his mouth, "it's not what it looks like, I promise," he walked towards me, but I stopped him, holding my hand up towards him.

"Don't you fucking dare," I shouted, my voice trembling but not out of sadness, no. I was fucking infuriated. I was like a bull who was having a red flag waved in front of it. My eyes were wide and bulging, my breaths harsh and ragged as I breathed through my nose.

"I don't want your promises Killian! You obviously can't keep them!" the hoarseness in my voice made my throat burn.

He didn't say anything, just dropped his arm by his side, his face falling as his eyes closed. The room was drowning in silence, neither of us saying a word. I concentrated on my breathing, my hand sitting under my bump as I inhaled deeply and exhaled trying to calm myself down.

"So, you were with Adele?" I finally managed, but this time I didn't shout. There was nothing but disappointment lacing my voice as the realisation kicked in.

He nodded solemnly. His fingers tightening around his phone, his other hand was balled into a tight fist by his side.

"You missed my birthday, and more importantly our gender reveal to be with Adele," the words choked me as I spoke them, barely able to finish my sentence.

He said nothing.

"I can't do this," I whispered, the hot tears threatening to fall but I tried my hardest to blink them away. The burn in my throat becoming unbearable as I fought so hard with my body.

"Reese, please," he begged as I walked past him and towards my bedroom. I sat on the edge of the bed as my brain processed the last fifteen minutes. My eyes were pinned to the wall, my fingers clutching the bed cover underneath me.

Killian was in the doorway, leaning up against it as I felt his burning gaze on me. I didn't give him the satisfaction of looking up. I couldn't even bring myself to look at him.

"Just go," I whispered to the room, praying he heard me.

He didn't say anything. He stayed mute.

"Please," my throat tight as I sniffed, the choked sobs threatening to escape.

"You're leaving?" his voice splintered through me, not able to resist the pull any longer my head slowly turned to face him. His eyes didn't meet mine though, they were narrowed and hooded as they focused on my suitcase.

I felt the rush of air leave me; my lips were parted as I tried to find my voice.

I shrugged, but I knew the truth. The harsh reality finally sinking in.

I was leaving and I wasn't about to let him stop me.

Jumping when I heard the door knock, I sprung from the bed and rushed into the hallway.

Swinging the door open I saw my mum and dad, their smiles fading slightly when they saw my face and Killian standing behind me.

"Everything okay?" my mum asked as she edged past me, dragging my dad along with her.

"Yes, everything is perfect," I nodded; a fake smile plastered onto my face, "Killian was just leaving."

"I was?" he whispered as he closed the gap between us.

"You were," I nodded firmly, my eyes casting up to his and for the first time in a while I felt the connection. I felt his emotions, but most of all I felt his pain.

"Can we talk..." he begged; his voice so low that only I could hear it.

"No," I managed, a tear rolling down my cheek but before I had a chance to swipe it away, his thumb had for me.

"Don't do this."

"I didn't do anything Killian, you only have yourself to blame for that," I choked, as I stepped aside so he could leave.

I didn't turn back to face him, I couldn't bear to look at him because it hurt too much. The pain that was crashing down on me was unbearable, it was hard to breathe without him but I knew this was what I had to do.

He lingered for a moment, as if waiting to see if I would change my mind but that wasn't going to happen.

I heard my father approach from behind me, his arm reaching above my head as his fingers wrapped round the edge of the door.

"My daughter asked you to leave," his voice was firm but not all threatening or demanding. Killian still stood, his eyes glassing over as he watched me. His jaw clenched; I heard his breath slowly leave his lips as he finally gave in. He was waiting for that eye contact; he was waiting for me to bare everything to him again. He was waiting for our souls to connect.

He was waiting for that earth shattering, ground moving moment to spark through both of us like it did on the many occasions at the beginning of our relationship. But I had nothing left to give.

He nodded, edging towards the door and I don't know

why I did it, but I looked up at him and watched a lone tear roll down his cheek as he left.

All I wanted to do was wipe it away, wrap my arms around his neck and tell him I didn't want to leave and I didn't want him to leave me.

Because the truth was, I was obsessively and utterly in love with him.

CHAPTER 46
KILLIAN

I HAD ROYALLY FUCKED UP.

I could have made her listen to why I wasn't there on Saturday but what was the point? She didn't want to listen. My words would have fallen on deaf ears.

I sat in my office in my apartment, drinking whiskey as I stared into the empty room. Sighing heavily when I heard the front door go, I heard the angry stomps get closer.

Three… two… one…

"What the fuck are you doing?" Connie's angry voice ripped through me as her poisonous words fired at me.

"Having a drink, what does it look like?" I scoffed as I took another mouthful of the burning amber.

"You're such a chauvinistic pig," she shouted as something hit me in the side of the head. I turned to face her before looking at the floor next to me to see her sneaker.

"What the fuck?!" I shouted, slamming my glass down, "You threw your fucking sneaker at me!?"

"Because you're being a douche." Connie smirked, leaning up against the door frame.

"Just let it go, Connie." My voice was gruff as my fingers wrapped back round my glass.

"What like you're letting Reese go?" her voice was sharp.

I felt my breath catch, the pain searing through me. My stomach coiled, my eyes burning from the constant prick of tears that were forming.

"She doesn't want me. We're destruction Connie. If we were meant to work, we would be together."

Connie let out a cackle before walking towards me, slamming her hands on my desk.

"She does want you. She wants you more than anything but you're so self-obsessed and focused on everything else around you but her. Fuck, you spent the day and night with Adele instead of being next to her when you promised you would be there for her. Do you not see it? Are you really that fucking naïve?" I could feel the anger Connie was feeling, her words were flying towards me like burning arrows, each one hitting me in the heart and puncturing it, making me bleed.

I finally looked up at her, her raging brown eyes batted back and forth from mine.

"It wasn't like that…" I whispered.

"But it was…" she sighed, "to Reese, it was like that. It was much more than what you are trying to convince us all it wasn't," she stood slowly but she didn't avert her eyes from mine. "All she wanted was for you to be there for her, to put her first once in a while. But you couldn't do that. You were too busy still trying to chase an old hag and for what? Because you have some fucked up ties with her," Connie scoffed, "I don't get it… she has you by the balls and has done for as long as I can remember. Just fire her ass and move the fuck on."

"It's not just some fucked up tie, Connie," I felt the bile rising in my throat, it didn't matter how much I tried I couldn't swallow it back down.

"Do you have a secret love child with her or something?" Connie's playful laugh riddles me with guilt. My eyes begin to fill as I nibble on the inside of my cheek.

Connie's eyes meet mine and the laughter slips, her eyes widen, and her smile disappears.

"Dad…" Connie whispers, her eyes volleying so fast back and forth between mine as she waits for me to answer her.

"It's you, Connie. You're the tie."

CHAPTER 47
REESE

We sat in the taxi in gridlocked traffic. I was grateful that my dad always plans ahead and suggested we leave earlier than we needed to.

I looked out the window at the city that I was leaving for a couple of weeks, or maybe longer. I hadn't decided whether I was coming back or not or whether I should just cut all ties and stay at home.

Selfish? Yes.

But I would never stop Killian seeing his daughter. I would do visits here; he would do visits to England. We could make long distance parenting work.

I reached into my bag and pulled out my diary, my fingers delicately tracing over the silver detailing that surrounded the pink heart. Flipping the pages, I skimmed through the last few months. So much had happened, from the moment I landed on American soil I felt like the rug was pulled from under my feet.

Maybe this was for the best, maybe this is what was supposed to happen. Killian can now pursue a relationship with Adele without being racked with guilt and I can move on with my life. It was cleaner this way.

I nodded to myself as I continued turning the pages, a rush of emotions surging through me.

I had three quarters of the book left before I would need a new diary, it was always a bittersweet moment for me. I had a new diary ready for all new memories, but it also meant closing the diary on my past and that's what I found the hardest. Leaving the past behind and living in the moment.

I began flicking the pages with my thumb when I noticed scribbles on the back pages. My heart raced as I turned the last page to see a diary entry from Killian. How had he got my diary?

I choked as I began to read.

Reese,

I don't even know if you will get this diary entry, but it's the only way I can tell you what has been going on. I have tried but I can't muster the words, or more to the point - you don't let me.

Let's address the burning question that no doubt you have asked yourself. How did I get your diary?

You can thank your mom for that. After I left earlier today, your mom followed me and found me sitting on the sidewalk outside of the apartment block. She sat next to me silently for a while, neither of us speaking because let's face it - I didn't know what to say to her and vice versa. You will always be their priority and that's why she sought me out. You would have never been that sad if you really wanted me to go.

You were angry with me - no, sorry... you were, and no doubt still are, disappointed in me. Heck, I am disappointed in myself.

First of all - I am so fucking sorry, Buttercup. I never meant for things to get this out of control. The thought of you wasting your tears on me breaks my heart. The thought of me hurting you for my own selfishness makes me sick to my stomach. You deserve so much more, you deserve to be truly happy Reese. After everything you have been through, you are still so loving and caring and kind. You will always put others above yourself which I admire, and I hope I can be a little more like you going forward.

Don't for one second doubt my feelings for you - I have and always will be in love with you. You were a wrecking ball in my life all those months ago but fuck, I am glad you came into my life. Everything before you was so dull and monotonous.

You made me see color again. You made me see how beautiful the world really can be, but also how bitterly cruel it can be too. There is no way you should have lost your Elijah, neither of you deserved that kind of loss and suffering at such a young age. You radiate love and light up every single room you walk into. I love watching you smile, I love to be the one who makes you smile but let's be honest, I have made you cry more than I have made you smile for the last few weeks and for that I am truly sorry.

Your birthday party. I broke my promise, and that was a real asshole thing to do. But please believe me when I tell you it wasn't intentional. Yes, I was with Adele. It wasn't out of choice and when I tell you she is nothing to me, I mean it. She is just someone who I have a past with, someone whom I share a tie with. It's complicated and messy but I <u>promise</u> I will explain all.

I never got yours and Connie's messages on the morning of ~~your party~~, our party. It wasn't until I was looking through my phone, the messages from you and Connie had been recently deleted and sat in a separate folder. I was so confused as to why I hadn't heard from either of you. And when I confronted Adele, she sat there with no remorse at what she had done. She is a vile human being and I can't believe I even have her in my life. I know that is no excuse, I should have been watching the clock but things got heated between me and Adele, things were said that needed to be resolved and before I knew it, I was too late.

Fuck, Reese... the look on your face when I burst through that door haunts me. I hated making you sad, I hated the look you gave me. I could see how hard you were trying to be strong, but I could also see the pain in your eyes. Your eyes never lie. They were one of the first things I fell in love with. You showed me every ounce of emotion through your beautiful opal eyes. On one of our first meetings, I swear I saw your soul. It bared everything to me.

I am not expecting forgiveness because what I done is unforgivable. I should have never made you this sad. You don't deserve to be sad.

From the asshole behaviour I showed at the start - to not showing up at the courthouse, but the thought of having to stand there and lie to the judge about not being in love with you was almost insufferable. How could I lie about the way you make me feel? You turn my world on its axis and make me doubt every, single, fucking feeling I had ever felt prior to you. And most importantly - I do not expect forgiveness for not showing at the party.

I suppose the point of this letter is to get

everything out that has been laying heavy on my heart, and this is my opportunity.

I don't want to let you out of my heart. I don't want you to leave my head. I will never get over the taste of your lips and I don't want to.

I hope to God that you read this before you leave for the airport, but if you don't – I hope that one day you find it.

I hope that one day you realise just how much I love you. How much I have always loved you.

Because you Reese Hernández are it for me. My beginning, my middle, my end... My always.

It has always been you.

It will always be you.

I love you.

My heart is yours if you want it.

Always,

Killian x

A tear fell onto the bottom of the page, smudging his name slightly. I couldn't hold back anymore, I let them fall. And each one that fell, felt like a slither of hurt that was wrapped around my heart.

"Reese?" my dad whispered as he leant forward and looked at me.

"She's fine," my mum's voice was soft as she reassured my dad.

He loved me.

I snapped my head up, wiping the tears away and slamming the diary shut. Slipping it in my bag, I looked ahead at the traffic and then behind. We weren't moving.

"I've got to go," I whispered, opening the taxi door and grabbing my bag.

"What about your suitcase?" my mum said, a silly grin on her face.

"Oh, just accept you're going to miss your flight," I choked as more tears began to fall "I'll meet you at home."

Slamming the door shut, I began weaving through the traffic to get onto the pavement. I couldn't be that far from home.

Panting, I rushed down the hall towards the private lift that serviced Killian's penthouse.

I was sweating, I was out of breath, but I didn't care. I looked at myself in the mirrors, swiping my ring fingers under my eyes. My cheeks were flushed, my eyes bright. I ran my fingers through the end of my hair, trying to make it look a little tidier than it currently was.

Screw it.

This is what he is getting.

The lift doors pinged open; my shaky breath escaped me as I looked down the wide hallway to the front door. My heart was racing in my chest, the blood rushing in my ears causing a loud thump. I swallowed, gliding my clammy palms down my dress.

"You got this," I whispered.

My legs started moving and with each step I took that brought me closer to him the nerves crashed over me.

Stopping, I lifted my hand ready to knock but before I did, I inhaled deeply and tried to calm my erratic heart.

Knock, knock, knock.

I waited and with each, long, agonising second, I began to doubt my actions. Not because I didn't love him, but in case it was too late.

I heard the handle click; my eyes dropped as I saw it turn. Everything happening in slow motion as my eyes slowly lifted to see Killian standing there. Eyes wide and red raw, lips parted and his hair a beautiful mess.

"Reese," he breathed, but my lips cut him off as I lunged myself at him, my arms round his neck as I kissed him as if he was my only source of oxygen, as if without him I would surely die.

His hands skimmed down my side, cupping my bum and lifting me up. My legs automatically wrapping round his waist.

"You came back," he managed through breathless kisses.

I nodded, tears of happiness streaming down my face.

"I'm sorry," I whispered against his lips.

"For what?"

"For everything."

"You have no reason to be sorry," he reassured me, breaking away as his eyes burned into mine. "Do you understand me? You have nothing to be sorry for."

I nodded, nibbling my trembling lip to stop myself from becoming a crying mess.

"Forgive me," he whispered as he carried me up the stairs to his bedroom.

"Always."

He dropped me to the bed, his burning eyes raking over me and I blushed under his intense stare.

"Fuck, you're so beautiful. I never told you enough before, but I will spend the rest of my life telling you and showing you just how beautiful you are to me."

He pulled his tee over his head and threw it over the other side of his bedroom, revealing his toned torso. His chest pecs were hard, covered in a dark dusting of chest hair. His pink scar peeking through certain thinner parts of his hair. My heart instantly aching at the thought that he could have lost his life.

"Don't feel sad for me," he whispered as he edges towards me, leaning over me and placing a kiss on my lips, lingering a moment more. The mint mixed with whiskey was a delicious combination.

Falling to his knees, his callous hands grip my thighs as he spreads my legs, his eyes falling to the apex of my thighs.

"I have missed your taste," his voice was low, I heard the growl rumble through him.

His hands glided up to the top of my knickers, hooking his fingers into them and tugging them down and off my legs.

"I want you to come on my tongue, then I want you to come all over my cock…" his eyes flicked up, "do you understand?"

I panted while nodding, already feeling my pussy pulse at the thought. Pushing my dress up over my hips, he dragged it over my head and tossed it on the floor. Next was my bra, kneeling up and pressing his chest against mine he worked the strap before slipping it down my arms.

His eyes marvelled over my naked body, his teeth sinking into his bottom lip as he bit down.

"So, fucking beautiful," he whispered as his fingers trailed down the middle of my breasts and over my swollen tummy.

"Lay back, Buttercup," he ordered gently.

I prop myself on my elbows as I watch him, his eyes filled with desire and want and just that look was enough to make me want to come. My orgasm was already teetering on the cliff and he hadn't even touched me.

"So eager, brat," the use of his old nickname for me made my stomach coil and my pussy clench.

I moaned; his intense stare was overwhelming. His mouth was hot and ready, but he was nowhere near me.

"Please, Killian," I begged, my fingers tightening around the already crumpled bed sheet beneath me.

"Please what?" he teased, his finger trailed up and down the inside of my thigh but not where I needed him most.

"Make me come, I am so horny for you," I blushed at my words, but it was the truth.

"I can see your tight little cunt glistening for me," he groaned as he lowered himself down, his hands gripping the top of my thigh as he dug his fingers into my skin.

I could just see his burning eyes looking at me when his tongue glided through my slick folds, my head tipping back as the pleasure ripped through me.

"So fucking sweet," he moaned as he lapped up my wetness, swirling his tongue over my clit which caused my hips to buck forward.

A delectable moan escaped me as I watched him, my hungry eyes wanting to see what he was doing to me. He slipped his tongue down my folds, teasing at my soaked opening then gliding it back towards my clit.

"Fuck," I whispered as he done it again. My hips began gyrating over his tongue, I needed more. I wanted his tongue deep inside of me, stroking my inner walls and making me come so fucking hard I forgot about everything.

"I need more," I begged, my legs beginning to tremble. His pushed my thighs further apart, my pussy stretched and open for him as his tongue lashed harder over my clit.

Sitting up a little more, my fingers entwined in Killian's hair while my other hand was wrapped in the bedsheet as if I was clinging on for dear life. My eyes watched as his expert tongue brought me closer to my release. Our eyes connected for a moment as Killian buried his tongue deeper inside of me and ate my pussy as if it was his last meal. My toes curled, a shiver crashed over me, and my stomach coiled. My orgasm ripped through me causing me to cry out, my whole body trembling as Killian continued helping me ride through my explosive orgasm and making sure he got every last drop of me.

I fell back on the bed, my skin tingling, a light ringing in my ear as I calmed my breathing. I needed a minute to come back down to earth.

I felt the bed dip, Killian was naked and next to me. Licking my lips at his thick, hard cock I sat up slowly and climbed onto my knees. Smashing my lips into his, our tongues danced as my arousal coated my own tastebuds as well as his. His hand was in my hair, gripping hard as he tugged my head back. I couldn't move, my eyes pinned to the ceiling. I felt his breath on my neck, his teeth grazing along my jaw line. I felt a spark course through me, his fingers began rubbing over my clit, then plunging into my hot, soaking pussy.

I gasped.

He sucked on my nipple, making it pert then biting the skin softly. Slipping another finger inside of me, I felt my legs buckle slightly. His breath was on my ear, his lips hovering.

"I want you on your fucking knees ready to suck my cock like the brat you are. I want you looking up at me while I throat fuck you and when I am ready, I want your mouth open as I watch my cum spurt down your pretty fucking throat," he groaned, "and you're not to waste a single, fucking, drop."

Pulling his fingers out of me abruptly, he let go of my hair and stood from the bed. I moved to the edge on shaky legs and did as he asked. I got on my knees gladly, a sweet smile gracing my face as I licked my lips slowly.

My fingers wrapped around his cock, pumping him slowly as I watched the bead of cum sit on the tip of his dick. His hand moved round the back of my head, pulling me closer towards him. Pushing the tip of him past my lips I moaned at the fullness I felt as I had him in my mouth. A groan left him as his grip tightened. I took him deep, holding him at the back of my throat before drawing him out of my hot and wet mouth slowly. I wanted to tease him, I wanted to give him the best fucking head of his life.

I done it again, in the slow and torturous manner that I did before.

"Oh, baby," he groaned, his hips bucking forward harshly. His large cock hitting the back of my throat and causing a gag.

"Good girl, you can take it," he praised me, his voice low and sultry.

He done it again. But this time, I was prepared. No gagging for me.

Unwrapping my fingers, both of my hands pressed against his hips as I gripped onto him, pulling him out to the tip then taking him deep.

My eyes watered, but I was loving it. I loved watching him come undone under my mouth, I loved that I made him feel this way.

"Buttercup..." he called but his voice was dragging. He tugged at the root of my hair, pulling me away from him and resting the tip of his cock on my lips.

"You look so fucking pretty with my cock in your mouth," he growled.

I tugged away, my fingers wrapping round his cock once more as I glided my flat tongue up the base of his length. Once at the tip I flicked my tongue over his head and took him deep into my mouth.

His head tipped back, his fingers gripping tighter as he met my thrusts with his own. My eyes began to stream at the harshness of his punishing thrusts, but I didn't want him to stop. My free hand skimmed down my body as I circled two fingers on my burning, swollen clit.

"Jesus," he spat through gritted teeth as he watched me,

but I didn't take my eyes off of him. I wanted him to use me how he wanted, I wanted him to come so fucking hard and if it meant him doing this to me, then I was here for it.

"I'm going to come," he spat, pulling his cock from my mouth harshly. He pulled my head back so I was looking up and I opened my mouth like he wanted me to. Sticking my tongue out flat he pressed the tip of his cock on my tongue as I felt it contract before spurting his hot cum into my mouth.

I swallowed every bit of it like he asked, then let my tongue run down the base of his cock, gliding it back up to lick the head of him clean.

He looked down at me and smiled, "Such a good, fucking girl. Now stand up, lay on your back and spread your fucking legs wide for me." His eyes darkened as he licked his lips, his hand still fisting his hard cock.

I shivered with excitement and anticipation.

He rubbed the tip of his cock over my clit, slipping it in between my folds slowly teasing me at my entrance.

I was exhausted but I would never tire of him, we had spent the evening losing ourselves in each other and he promised this would be the last time of the evening.

I was close to coming, every sense and every nerve ending was vibrating and buzzing. Each of them more sensitive than the time before. Grabbing the vibrator from next to him, he switched it on and pressed it against my clit before plunging his cock into my soaked pussy. That's all it took. An earth-shattering orgasm blasting through me, Killian coming with me.

CHAPTER 48

We were sitting in the bath, me between Killian's legs as he wiped a soft sponge over my sensitive and delicate skin.

"I'm so glad you came back," I felt Killian's voice vibrate and rumble through his body as I lay back into him, his arms cocooning me and landing on my bump as our daughter kicked through my skin and into his hands.

"I'm glad I came back," I smiled as I watched the skin on my tummy flick where her little movements were.

"Were you really going to leave?" he asked, I could hear the vulnerability in his voice.

I shook my head from side to side.

"I just needed to get away. Put some distance between us so we could actually see how we felt when we were thousands of miles away," I whispered quietly. "I love you, Killian. More than anything but I just was in such a low place, I wanted to go home."

I felt his lips press on the top of my head as I sunk lower into the warm bath.

"This is your home, with me." His breath was cool on the back of my neck causing my skin to erupt in goosebumps.

"I know," turning my head I placed a kiss on the top of his arm, his muscles flexing under my touch.

The silence fell between us, but it was a welcome silence. It was tranquil and mellow. Just the sound of our shallow breaths filling the void between us.

I felt Killian move behind me, fidgeting almost.

"Baby, I need to tell you something… well… a couple things actually." I heard the worry that was lacing his deep, husky voice.

I span round so I was facing him, my hands clasping the side of his face as I made him look me deep in the eyes, "Then tell me, tell me it all, lay it on me." My voice was calm.

I heard him inhale deeply, the sharp intake of breath making his breath catch. I started to worry, I could see the complete fear in his eyes.

"Baby, what is it?" my eyes volleyed back and forth to his.

He didn't say anything.

"You're scaring me… what's happened?"

I felt his head drop, it was heavy in my hands but I pulled it back up so he had to look at me in the eyes. "Tell me," my voice a little sterner now.

"I'm just trying to muster the words babe…" his eyes closed for a split second before they were back on me. "First off, Lordes PR…" he trailed off, "well… it's yours." He stopped for a moment, my eyes widening at the words that just left his mouth, "but only if you want it."

"But… I mean…" I stammered, "what about Adele?"

"Adele is done, finished, no more…" he rubbed his lips together, "that's what I was sorting out a few weeks back… when I missed our party."

I couldn't speak, words failed me.

"I know that still doesn't make it better, but that's where I was… I had to finalise the paperwork. It was meant to be done a couple of months back, but she was being hostile and making it an absolute ball ache but it's done. The company is in your name… if you want it."

I blinked a couple of times, just trying to register all of this in my head.

"And the reason it was such a ball ache for me to sort out was because…" he stilled, I dropped my hand and placed it on his chest. I could feel how fast his heart was beating, it was jack hammering inside his chest.

This is it.

This is where he was going to tell me that he and Adele used to be a thing and then slept together the day of my party.

I held my breath, puffing out my cheeks ready to receive the blow that was surely going to knock the air out of my lungs.

"Adele is Connie's mom," he rushed the words out so quickly it took me a moment to decipher the absolute craziness that just came from his mouth.

"I'm sorry…" I whispered, I'm sure my ears were playing tricks on me. My brows furrowed as I tried to replay his words. I held my index finger up, my eyes closing for a second. "Can you say that again?" my eyes pinged open, my brows sitting high in my forehead as I readied myself for the words again.

He sighed deeply.

"Adele is Connie's birth mother."

My mouth dropped open, my eyes bulging from my head as I stared at him completely dumbfounded.

Well shit.

TURNS OUT KILLIAN HASN'T HEARD FROM CONNIE SINCE HE TOLD her the news. He asked me to try her but with no avail. She didn't want to be spoken to and I completely got it. All she knew had been a lie. Her mums had assured Killian she was okay but to give her space.

My heart hurt for Connie, but I wanted to respect her wishes. I had left her some voicemails and some text messages telling her that I would be here for her when she was ready. She was not only pissed at her dad, she was pissed at her mums as well. She always believed that they got Killian's sample from a sperm bank, but they didn't. Adele got pregnant by Killian after a drunken night, Adele wanted nothing to do with the baby. Killian's sperm was in a sperm bank and he had spoken to Lara and Katie but they never got round to using his sample. Adele agreed to give Connie up to Lara and Katie under a closed adoption, meaning her and Killian had no parental rights to Connie once the papers were signed.

Obviously, Killian was a big part of Connie's life and would still continue to be if she wanted him there.

I wasn't sure why Killian thought now was a good time to drop the bomb on Connie, but I suppose he had his reasons. Maybe this is why Adele was being such hard work with signing the papers over? Maybe she was holding something over his head to do with Connie and he couldn't risk anything happening to her.

It was a lot to take in over a relaxing, post sex bubble bath.

But I had to trust what Killian said, and when Connie was ready, she can fill in the blanks.

CHAPTER 49

I lay under Killian's arm, my head on his chest. His fingertips tracing shapes on my bare back. My hand splayed on his lower stomach, I felt comfort listening to his steady heartbeat.

"Can I tell you about my heart transplant?" his question shocked me but made me feel happy at the same time.

"Only if you want to tell me about it," I smiled, my head still on his chest.

"I do," he craned his neck down, placing a soft kiss on my temple.

"Then I am all ears."

"So you know the issues I had with my heart. Well, I was over in London on business. I was trying to merge one of my businesses over there. I was on medication and was told to try not to elevate my stress levels but that's easier said than done." I heard the grunt that left him. "I was walking home, the air was crisp the night drawing in – winter was hiding just around the corner. Once I was in my hotel room, I was relaxing on the sofa flicking through the channels. Suddenly, I couldn't breathe. I sat up abruptly, trying to catch my breath.

But the more I tried, the harder it seemed. That's when the panic began to set in. I was all alone in a foreign country and I didn't know what to do." His fingers stopped their trail for the moment, "Come to think of it, I remember being exhausted but I put it down to jetlag." I lifted my head up and looked at him. He was looking ahead as if he was remembering the events of that night.

"I called 999 and was blue lighted to the Royal London," he stopped for a moment, I lay my head back on his chest and listened to his heart that thumped loudly. "As soon as I was in the hospital, I was rushed through and hooked up to all the machines…" his voice cracked, "Reese, I had never been so scared in all my life," he whispered, as if it was too much for him to even speak about.

My heart hurt for him, the thought of him being that far from home.

"They spoke to my doctor about my condition, within a couple of hours I was on the transplant list. I never thought I would get lucky… I honestly thought I would have died in that hospital… all alone."

My throat grew thick, the tears falling. I couldn't wipe them away quick enough as they fell onto his scar. I pushed up, placing soft, butterfly kisses along his scar and my finger following my trail.

"But you didn't… you're here," I beamed; my eyes still glassy as I sniffled.

"I was in that hospital for a month in total," he stilled for a moment, his arm gripping me and holding me tight. "Then, one night my doctor came round to tell me that they had found a donor, a young man who had died that night."

I felt myself stiffen, Killian's grip tighter as he held me where I was.

"Once I received the transplant, I knew I had to thank his family… because if it wasn't for the tragic loss of their son, I would have died." His vice shook, his heat thrashed around in his chest as was mine. I couldn't calm my breaths; they were fast and harsh as I continued listening to him.

"A month ago, after a lot of work I found his family. Donors stay anonymous, but I wanted to reach out and just say thank you."

"What date did you receive your transplant?" I whispered, afraid to speak any louder. My eyes darted around the empty room as I waited for him to answer.

"The twentieth of October," his voice was cool, his grip hadn't loosened.

"The day after Elijah died," I choked silent sobs, my tears drenching Killian's skin.

I pushed up, turning to look at him waiting for confirmation of what I already knew.

He nodded slowly; his eyes pinned to mine before I broke out in an uncontrollable sob.

"Baby," he soothed me, grabbing my face and kissed away my tears. "Listen to me."

My heart felt so full and so broken at the same time. I felt constricted and confused with the emotions that were ripping through me.

"You lost a great love…"

I nodded, sniffling as the burn in my throat caused me to gasp.

"But you found a greater love in me. And I know I will never replace Elijah… I would never want to," he held me, his lips pressing over each of my eyelids before he rested his forehead against mine.

"This heart, it still beats for you my love… it's only ever beat for you," he pulled back, tilting my head up to look at him, "it will always only beat for you."

He covered his mouth with mine as the overwhelming love consumed me, making the hole that I had carried around since Elijah passed, whole again.

"I love you, Buttercup,"

I sniffed, my hands reaching up to touch his scar. My eyes lingered for a moment before my eyes found his. "But not as much as I love you, Killian."

EPILOGUE

I sat at my desk at Lordes PR. I felt at home here. I felt content. It had taken a bit of adjusting from working alongside Killian to now working by myself and heading up a company, but I was enjoying it. I made it work. We were growing as a company in the last six months, and we had just signed two big names alongside Harlen. I decided against maternity leave, I wanted to work right up until the last minute which would be soon as I was due to pop any day now. I had the sign off from my doctor, baby girl was growing nicely and there were no further concerns with her heart which was a big relief for me and Killian.

My eyes moved from my desk as I looked at the picture of me and him that was on my desk. We were both smiling, so carefree and happy. We were in London, standing in Elijah's favourite cove in Cornwall. Killian seemed at home there, and part of me wondered whether it was because he was carrying a piece of Elijah with him.

Since we've been back in New York, I have found him on real estate websites looking for cute little houses right on the cove where we stayed. I think he is a little obsessed. I told him I would think about it, because honestly, as much as I love New York... I love England more.

My phone buzzed, Killian's name flashing up on the screen. Smirking, I unlocked my phone and read his message.

KILLIAN

Outside. X

Slipping my phone into my bag, I locked my computer and headed for the door. Swinging it open, I jumped when I saw Killian standing there, a big 'baby, I'm here' smile on his face as he leant up against the doorframe.

"You said you were outside," I muttered as he leant in, wrapping his arm around my waist and kissing me softly.

"I did, I meant outside your office..." he quipped, smirking, "did you not get that from my very detailed message?" he wiggled his eyebrows up and down before laughing.

"Come on old man, let's get you home."

"Who you calling old man? Brat." He growled, dragging me towards the lift. Pushing the button impatiently, he huffed as he waited.

Once the doors pinged, he pulled me inside as he pushed me up against the wall of the lift, his hand wrapping round the base of my throat as his eyes burned into mine... his lips hovering just above mine.

"I'll show you old man," he threatened, my stomach flipped, my heart rate spiked, and I felt that delicious burn deep inside ignite.

As soon as we were in our house, Killian stripped me from head to toe. Falling to his knees he placed a kiss on my petite bump before spinning me and pushing me towards the bed.

"I want you on all fours baby," he groaned, fisting his hard cock as he pumped himself slowly.

I did as he said. Kneeling on all fours, Killian knelt behind me on the floor, his hands on my hips as he pulled my aching pussy towards his mouth. His expert tongue swirled at my soaked opening, licking and sucking. Gliding between my folds, he teased at my clit as he pumped two fingers deep inside of me. My pussy clenched, my back arched as he stroked my g-spot, my toes curling in anticipation of my impending orgasm.

He stopped suddenly, standing and walking to the drawer of our bedside unit. Pulling out my silver, metal bullet vibrator he stalked back to the bed and glided the cool metal down my spine before he teased it in my pussy. It began vibrating, pulsing at my entrance but he soon moved it, slowly pulling it through my spread cheeks and teasing the tip in my arse.

"Killian," I begged, "fuck me, take all of me. Make me yours in every way," panting, I looked over my shoulder at him. His eyes alight.

"But the baby…" he stopped, removing the vibrator from the place no man had gone before.

"The baby will be fine; I've googled it and called the doctor," I moaned out as the pleasure rippled through me.

"You spoke to Dr Kyra about me taking your peach virginity?" I could hear the shock in his voice.

I snorted

"My what?!"

"Peach…" he chuckled, "she can hear… I don't want to say a-s-s" he spelt it out.

I rolled my eyes, irritation coursing through me now.

"Killian Hayes, either get back here and fuck me into next week or I swear to lucifer I will take my vibrator – that is still named Harlen by the way – and fuck myself," my voice came out a little more possessed than I would have liked but I was horny, frustrated and hormonal… and well, maybe a little bit hungry too. Who was I kidding? I was always fucking hungry.

"You wouldn't dare…" he pinched his brow, holding the vibrator up in the air.

"Try me, old man."

I heard the deep, primal growl that left his throat. I knew how to wind him up and calling him old man or threatening him with Harlen was the red cloth I needed to get him back with me.

The vibrator buzzed as he pressed it against my arse, holding it there before slipping it down my crease and teasing at my pussy.

"Fuck," I whispered, turning my head to the side and I bit my skin on my arm.

Pushing the vibrator through my wet folds, he held it over my clit. He gently pulled me up onto my knees.

"Hold the vibrator there, don't fucking move it."

I panted a moan, my skin tingling from the immense pleasure that rippled through me.

"And don't come."

His fingers dipped inside my soaked pussy, slipping it in and out before swirling my arousal at my bum.

My breath shook, faltering slightly as he done it again. My hips began rocking onto the vibrator that buzzed on my sensitive clit.

"Just getting you ready for me… are you sure about this Buttercup?" he asked.

"Yes," I snapped through gritted teeth as I tried my best to hold off my orgasm.

His hands held my hips, pushing me forward slightly as he pushed his thick tip at my tight opening, nudging slightly.

I stopped breathing as I stilled.

"Keep breathing baby," his voice was tight as he tried to breathe himself, nudging that little bit further in. His fingertip sat at the opening of my pussy when all of a sudden, I felt something deep inside of me snap.

"Oh, fuck!" I cried out.

"Baby, you've just squirted… fuuuuuck," he groaned as he nudged further into me. "You're so wet."

"I didn't squirt!" I screamed, moving forward slightly.

"What?" his voice sounded confused.

"I think my waters have broken." The sheer panic laced my voice. Killian moved quickly, holding me as he checked me over.

"Are you okay?" he asked.

"I'm fine," I whispered, sliding off the bed. Killian helped me stand and as soon as he did, the gush came.

"Yup," I panted, "my waters have gone."

WE PULLED UP AT THE HOSPITAL, DOCTOR KYRA WAS THERE TO greet us as Killian helped me out the car. My contractions were coming quick and frequently. I felt like she was about to fall out.

Doctor Kyra helped me into a wheelchair as she whizzed me through the labour suite.

"I need to push," I cried out, the sweat dripping from my hair line.

"Just try and hold off, I need to examine you."

"Hold off!? Have you ever felt like you've got a watermelon about to shoot out of your vagina?" I howled, my stomach tightening with another contraction.

Kyra helped me onto the bed, Killian was holding my hand as he kissed my forehead.

"I need pain relief, please, anything." I cried out, "I can't take it." I thrashed on the bed, the pain unbearable. No matter how I moved, how I sat, I was uncomfortable.

Kyra examined me, her brows shooting up. "Okay, Reese. You're already at nine centimetres, you ready to meet your daughter?" she smiled.

"No, I'm not." I shook my head, trying to squeeze my legs together.

Kyra pushed my legs open, giving me a scowl as she shook her head from side to side.

"Baby… baby…" Killian distracted me, he turned my face towards him and held it there. "You've got this," he moved closer to me, pressing his forehead against mine. "Now you're going to listen to Kyra, and you're going to deliver our beautiful daughter into this world." He moved away, pressing his lips to mine as I lingered but our moment was soon over when a contraction ripped through me.

"Okay Reese, push."

I pushed my chin to my chest and bared down like I was told to in my birthing classes.

"Excellent, okay, on your next contraction… push a little harder for me okay. She is already crowning."

"She is eager to meet you," Killian whispered as he watched.

"Shit!" I cried as my stomach tightened.

"That's it Reese, push my darling, push." Kyra said as the midwife stood next to her with a towel. I felt the burn as I continued pushing through the contraction that was ripping through me.

"Brilliant Reese, her head is out, take a breather then on the next contraction give me one last push."

It felt uncomfortable, but it didn't take long for the last contraction to appear and as soon as I felt it, I pushed with everything I had when suddenly, I heard her piercing cry.

"Happy Birthday, darling," Kyra said, standing and handing my delicate daughter to me. Kyra pulled down my top, placing her on my bare chest then covered her with a light blanket.

I kissed the top of her head, happy tears streamed down my face. Killian hovered over me, kissing my head, kissing my nose then finally, his lips on mine. My heart skipped a beat.

It was so full.

I had everything I had ever dreamed of.

A man who loved every ounce of me and a beautiful daughter whom I shared her with him.

"Do we have a name?" Kyra asked as she held a pen over a small ankle tag.

I looked at Killian, he nodded before we both turned to the Doctor.

"Celeste Iris Hayes," I smiled, my eyes watering again as I looked down at her.

She was my little miracle, rainbow baby. That's what her name meant. Miracle and Rainbow.

She was the rainbow after the turbulent storm.

She was our happily ever after.

THE END

CONNIE

I sat on the tour bus, a shadow of my former self. How could I have been so stupid and naïve. Everything I thought I knew was a lie.

My moms lied to me.

My dad lied to me.

And worst of all, I had that vile, hag of a woman who was my birth mom.

The hate that coursed through my veins and the thought made me feel sick.

I wasn't going back.

As soon as those words left my father's mouth, I ran until I couldn't run anymore.

I confronted my moms, they didn't have to say anything. Their faces said it all. They were full of guilt and deceit and that's what broke me the most. The fact that they couldn't even find the words to tell me what had happened. How it had happened.

Maybe I could have forgiven them all if they took the time out to tell me the truth, but by the time they were ready to actually sit me down and talk about it. It was too late.

I had already lost any sadness I had. I just wanted out.

I wanted to run away.

Away from New York.

Away from my moms.

Away from my dad and definitely away from the bitch of a dead-beat mom.

So, what do you do when you want to run away and escape reality for a little bit?

You become a groupie and tour with your rockstar boyfriend.

Maybe I will forgive, but I will never forget.

Ever.

The only one who didn't screw me over was Reese, and when I was ready, I would call her. I would meet up with her and explain everything. But now, I wanted to numb out the pain with alcohol, sex, drugs and rock 'n' roll.

Goodbye to innocent Connie.

Hello reckless and scorned Connie.

You haven't seen nothing yet, and I can't wait for you to read my story.

ACKNOWLEDGEMENTS

Dan. My best friend. My husband. My world. Thank you for pushing me to start this crazy journey. I love you to the moon and back.

Thanks firstly to Robyn, for keeping me in check and always being there when I needed you.

My girls, our little group. Thank you for the constant support and love you give me. I am so grateful to have you in my life and being with me on this crazy author journey.

My BETA's and friends, Sophie and Harriet. Thank you for being honest and loving my characters as much as I do.

Leanne, thank you for always being here for me. You're a friend for life.

Lea Joan, thank you once again for squeezing this in last minute. You have always been by my side in my author journey and I am so grateful that I get to work with you.

And lastly, my readers... without you, none of this would have been possible.
    My loyal fans, I owe it all to you.

Printed in Dunstable, United Kingdom